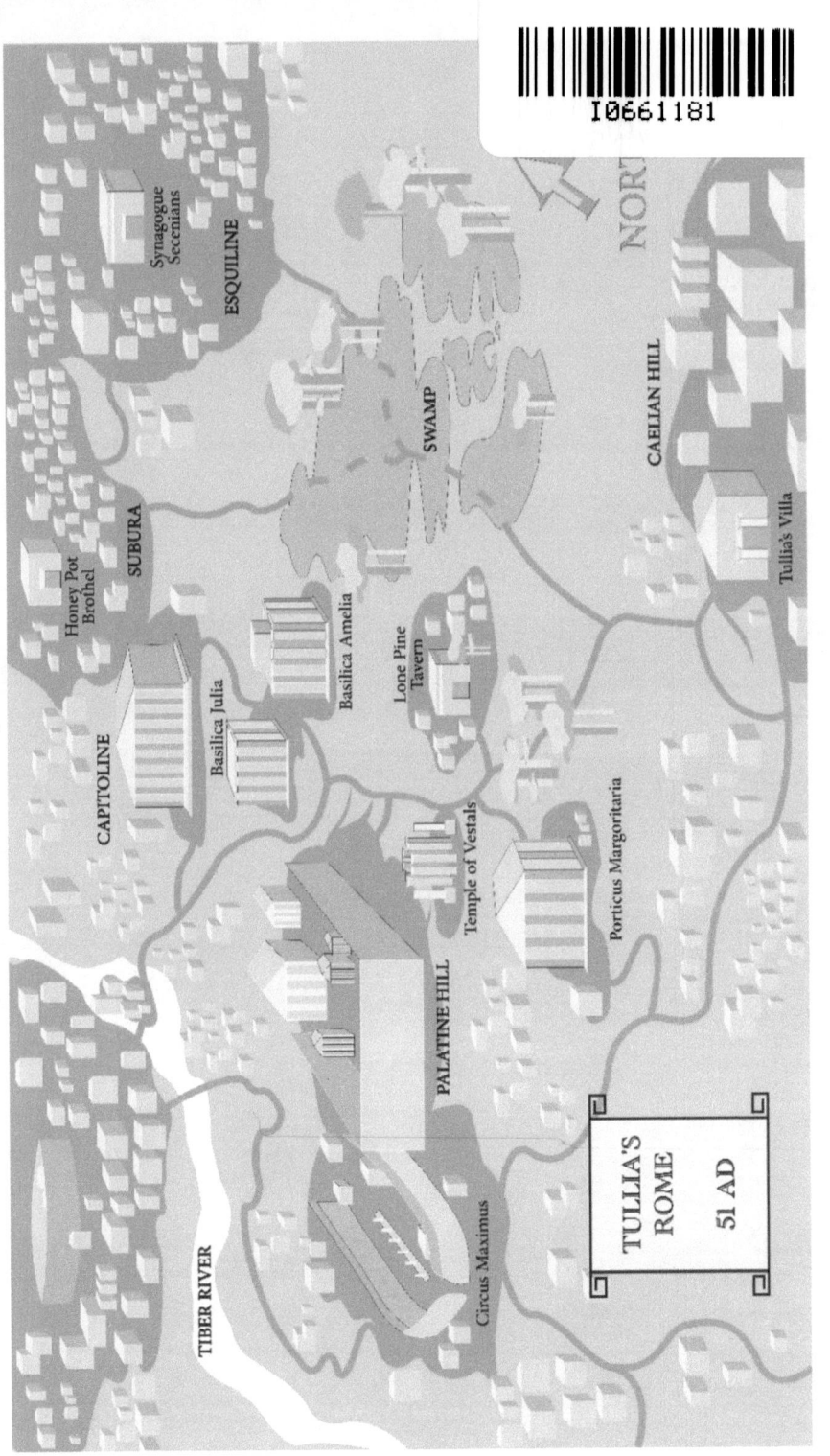

TULLIA'S ROME

51 AD

NORTH

CAPITOLINE

SUBURA

ESQUILINE

Honey Pot Brothel

Synagogue Secenians

Basilica Julia

Basilica Amelia

SWAMP

Lone Pine Tavern

PALATINE HILL

Temple of Vestals

Porticus Margoritaria

CAELIAN HILL

Tullia's Villa

TIBER RIVER

Circus Maximus

The
Domina
& The Slave

The Domina & The Slave

FORBIDDEN LOVE & BETRAYAL IN ANCIENT ROME

Stan Nahman

DEEDS PUBLISHING | ATHENS, GEORGIA

Published by Deeds Publishing in Athens, GA
www.deedspublishing.com

Printed in The United States of America

Interior and cover design by Mark Babcock

ISBN 978-1-961505-55-1

Books are available in quantity for promotional or premium use. For information, email info@deedspublishing.com.

First Edition, 2026

10 9 8 7 6 5 4 3 2 1

Dramatis Personae

OTHER CHARACTERS

Aemilius Ben-Turrina: Jewish priest
Amunus: Popular Pompeii artist
Auntie: Family proprietor of the Pompeii villa
Cresimus: Brothel owner
Maronella: Prostitute
Phoebe: Prostitute, Maronella's niece
Sabina: Prostitute
Sextus: Family lawyer
Siculus: Family accountant
Urbanus: Roman Jew and potter

The Sappho in the Fresco

The speaker adjusted the flexible neck of the podium microphone, its creak and grind overwhelming the din of the audience. The room quieted.

"Good morning. My name is Dr. Addison Sharp, and I'm a professor of archeology."

Clothed in a comfortable white lab coat, scarlet turtleneck, and black culottes, she peered at the one hundred academics sitting in the cozy, state-of-the-art conference room. She smiled; a slender face centered between strands of wispy brown hair. The tips of both ears popped out on each side. Her peers called her the Mouse.

Pushing tortoiseshell glasses higher on her nose, she took a breath. "For five years, we explored several burial chambers from an ancient Jewish catacomb in Central Rome. I'm happy to share those results with you today."

The screen behind her flashed a picture of a faded painting from antiquity. A young woman, clothed in a green tunic draped with a purple shawl, gazed out. Wide-set eyes, a small nose, and high cheekbones conveyed a look of intelligent concentration. An elegant gold fishnet capped a head of black curls. The wavy hairstyle, atypical in the first century, suggested a streak of independence. Gold hoops dangled from each ear while a purple stone set in a golden finger ring matched the shawl. A wax tablet rested in the left hand and the right held a writing stylus, the tip of which appeared to delicately touch scarlet lips.

The speaker swept the image with her laser pointer. "But first, here is one of the most famous frescos recovered from the rubble of Pompeii, buried after the eruption of Vesuvius in 79 A.D. Housed in the Naples Archaeological Museum, historians call her the Sappho girl, a poet from Greek antiquity. Notice she's holding a stylus and wax writing tablet. The paucity of women writers from the first century offered no other plausible name, so it has been assumed she represents the ancient Greek writer. However, we now know the identity of this woman and it is not Sappho."

The room rumbled with surprised whispers and the rustle of papers.

Ignoring the background noise, she advanced the slide, and a sparkling white, three-story villa appeared, its neoclassical pediment supported by eight ionic columns above a wide, sixteen-step apron.

"Villa Torlonia, or Casino Nobile, is the property under which the catacombs are located. We investigated rumors that some tombs remained intact, but were inaccessible due to cave-ins."

An image of a rubble-filled tunnel replaced the villa.

"Behind this debris, we discovered a burial compartment with undisturbed tombs."

The screen changed again, revealing an opening to a hexagonal chamber. Five walls had individual crypts carved deep into the bedrock, allowing the dead to be slipped, feet-first, into each final resting place.

Chiseled into the wall between each set of crypts, brown Corinthian-style columns rose to the twelve-foot ceiling, giving the chamber an open feel. Carved acanthus leaves, still brilliant green, capped each column. Frescos adorned the walls—red seven-branch menorahs, green palm trees, and brown and red colored fish. The chamber floor had a magnificent mosaic showing the great Temple in Jerusalem and the construction of Rome's colosseum, the latter indicated by human figurines engaged in physical activity.

At the top of each wall, six-inch Latin writing depicting distinct family pedigrees appeared to have been cut in the stone yesterday.

The speaker pointed to one name, FLACCVS. "The Flaccus family crypt. The top tomb is sealed but the second crypt below it is open."

The next image showed a stone box within the crypt and COMMENTARIVS T FLACCVS neatly chiseled across the end.

There was no sound but the soft hum of the projector fan.

The Mouse gazed at the audience. "Commentarius T Flaccus or the journal of T Flaccus."

She paused, watching members of the audience lean forward in their seats and enjoying the anticipation. *Here we go.* "In this tightly sealed box, we discovered thirty well-preserved papyrus scrolls—the personal diary of Tullia Cornelius Flaccus, a patrician wife of a first-century Roman senator."

What began as a murmur became pandemonium. People stood and shouted questions of astonishment and confusion. Others gestured and spoke to each other or in small groups.

Sharp raised her hands, to no avail, resorting to loud taps

3

on the microphone. After a long minute, the group quieted. "There will be plenty of time for questions. But first, I ask you to look at the document my assistants are distributing." She gestured to either side of the stage, where two shadows stepped into the aisles and moved toward the audience.

"Before you, and taken from her writings, is the biography of Tullia Flaccus, a literate, thoughtful, and rebellious woman from first-century Rome. And as you will see, we had it all wrong—*she* is The Sappho in the Fresco."

PART I

Yosef's Rule

1

"Yosef, lift your tunic. I want to see your genitals." Fourteen-year-old Tullia Flaccus raised a dark eyebrow and stared at the terrified houseboy. She knew the perfect braids encircling her head, soft brown eyes, and engaging smile made her pretty. She knew also that Yosef would lay with her. He had to, if she so instructed.

A year older and a domestic slave for eight years, Yosef's black hair and dark eyes belayed his Judean roots, and his lankiness foreshadowed his emerging adolescence. He'd begun as her childhood playmate, but through the years the increasing chasm of slavery led to Tullia's domination—and his unquestioned submission.

Now, overcome with desire, Tullia decided to bed Yosef. She loved him, and she owned him. The way she saw it, she could not lose.

Her plan was set in motion a week earlier. This morning Mama, Faustina, and the slave girls were at the market. Tullia normally went with them, but today she feigned a vague illness, concocting the needed excuse to remain at the villa, alone at last with Yosef.

"Yosef. Lift your tunic." Perched on the edge of her bed in the small room, she waited. Having cast off her linen under-

7

tunic, and sitting naked beneath a brilliant blue silk robe, she felt her cheeks warm and her heart thunder.

Frowning, he inched up his coarse woolen shirt, early sexual arousal evident.

She caught her breath. A wrinkled line appeared in the middle of his forehead. Ignoring his confused look, she returned a gentle gaze. It was all she could do to not grab him in her frenzy for desire. Instead, she slipped free of the robe and reclined. Opening her arms, she beckoned him in a soft voice. "Yosef, come lay with me."

Like a trapped animal, the boy cringed, and his eyes darted around the room. He avoided Tullia's gaze and turned to the orange privacy curtain draped across the room's entrance. Stepping away from the bed, he dropped the hem of his tunic and set his jaw. "No, Domina."

The room grew silent with Tullia's shock. She bolted upright and glared. *Slaves can't refuse!* Anger replaced her lust. She pointed at him, curling her finger, and snarled. "Are you refusing me?"

He did not answer.

"Yosef, I can have you killed!" she hissed.

His young face hardened, and she glimpsed the look of the man he would become. "You can, but still I won't," he said in rough Latin.

Turning, he swept aside the privacy curtain and left. The drape swung in his wake, returning to stillness as Tullia's emotions rose.

Yosef, you horrible boy! She leaped from the bed, the robe sliding to the floor in a silky heap. Stepping to the small clothing rack opposite the bed, she snatched a tunic, pulled it over her head, and spun toward the door. Blinded by rage, as well as the crimson tunic still bunched around her head, she tripped on the forgotten robe and tumbled to the floor. Angry tears welled. *Oh Yosef, I will get you for this! I am your Domina, your owner. I will have you whipped to within an inch of your life.*

The last thought gave her pause as she scooted against the bed. She felt the fury ebb as her skin came in contact with the cool floor tiles. Wiping her nose, she wished she could tell on him. *But who can I tell? Mama? Hah! Laying with a slave boy? She might not just beat me; she might kill me.*

Such behavior with a slave, a person of the lowest birth, risked her relationship with her parents, and worse, could bring the ultraconservative and unforgiving wrath of Rome's aristocracy down on the family, ruining the Flaccus name for generations.

But none of it mattered, for she could only think of Yosef with love and desire.

The tightness in her chest eased and her fists relaxed. *There's nobody to tell. We must keep it a secret. I will. He surely will, for to admit anything would bring blame and punishment to him. Slaves are never innocent.*

She shook her head. Images tumbled through her mind, Mama in her favorite beige stola and flashing a loving smile, Poppi, a towering warrior wearing boots and a scratchy woolen tunic but always with a deep laugh and gentle hug for his daughter, and, finally, Yosef. Yosef, always by her side in the patio garden or Forum market. Yosef absently fussing with a shelf of scrolls while she wrote in her diary, and his glance and smile when her tutor came. She sighed. *Oh, Yosef, I love you—your happy face, your little jokes.*

Pulling her knees to her chest, she sat in a tight ball, rocking herself, and wondered how he could not want her. *How did this happen? What did I do wrong?*

She didn't know, but she couldn't wait around either. Jumping up and smoothing her tunic, she ran from her corner room. Crossing into the atrium, she saw him, at the vestibule, reaching for the front door.

"Yosef!"

His hand rested on the large wooden handle.

"Domina?" he said, dropping his head.

"Please don't go."

"What'd you want, Domina?"

Walking toward him, she extended her hand and spoke softly. "I'm very sorry for my words. I'm not angry. Come with me now."

Yosef did not turn around, nor did he press forth. Tullia gently eased her fingers into his and led him back across the stone floor. They passed the kitchen on the right, the red brick oven glowing with a few embers and the braziers sitting cold beneath a small vent hood. A large and spotless wooden worktable dominated the center of the room. The triclinium, for dining, rested between the kitchen and the back of the villa.

Three bedchambers and a fourth open room—a study area with a worktable—occupied the left side of the home. The open area contained a wall with cubbies for scrolls, their wooden handles protruding in a bumpy brown mosaic. Adjacent shelves disclosed neatly stacked wax tablets, and a selection of styluses and writing quills. A couch with a blue linen cover and three wooden chairs surrounded the table. Unlike most women of their day, Tullia and her mother were literate and spent several hours each week at the table. Mama wrote letters and helped Poppi with finances, while Tullia kept a diary.

They crossed the back of the house to a colonnaded court-yard and garden. A private space in one corner contained a covered privy and a small sunken tub. At the center of the garden gurgled a white marble fountain. Ten years earlier, Poppi brought running water to the villa by tapping the near-by Marcia aqueduct, alleviating reliance on rainfall for water and allowing for private bathing.

A sculpted fish, with a stream of water flowing from its mouth, formed the centerpiece of the fountain. Tullia noticed it first. It always looked like it was smiling.

The surrounding trim bushes and colorful flowers resulted from Yosef's meticulous ministering. Together with the smiling fish, it eased her tension. Leading Yosef to a stone bench near the fountain, she sat, gesturing for him to do the same.

She watched him. Rigid with his head down, he perched on the far end of the bench. *He waits, just like a slave should. He seems different. But is he, or am I?* She fidgeted with a raw edginess, as if trapped in an itchy tunic. *What is wrong with me?*

"Yosef, why did you not lay with me? I know you wanted to."

"It was wrong." He directed the answer at his toes.

"Yosef, look up. It's me, Tullia," she said. "Tell me."

He raised his head. His usual smile of small white teeth and dimples was absent and replaced with tight lips and a furrowed brow. Locking his dark eyes with her brown ones, he spoke in a wavering voice.

"We can't lay. It's wrong."

Tullia shifted to face him, crossing her legs. "How so? We both wanted to. I can't see how that made it wrong."

"A rule."

"Rule? What rule?"

"Love your fellow as yourself."

She relaxed her shoulders and sighed. It was not a Roman rule. "Love your fellow? Is this a riddle?"

"Domina, it says to treat others the same as yourself. If I was you, a rich girl, I'd not lay with a slave — it could ruin your life. We lay, it breaks rule. I won't break it."

"Whose rule is this?"

"God's."

She squinted. "Which god?"

"Just God. My God. I have just one."

"More riddles? How is there only one god? Where did you learn *that*?"

"I'm a Jew. We have one God, I think."

Tullia rolled her eyes. "You think? What else do you think Jews think?"

He shifted on the bench and appeared to ponder. His lower lip jutted out. "I came here young. I remember the Rule and ten commands."

"Commands?" She crossed her arms and huffed. "From whom? And what are they?"

"Rules from God. The Rule or a command helps me do right."

Enough of this. She felt her face flush as she pointed at him. "Yosef, what is right is what I say!"

His face twitched as if stung by a bee. "Yes, Domina."

Her stomach knotted. Agitated by a wave of uneasiness, she excused him, and he left without another word, head bowed again. She stood and looked at the happy fish, willing it to help. But despite its gentle gurgle, the tightness at her center remained.

2

Two days after the discussion with Yosef, Tullia sat at the study table picking at a purple fig and staring at the small scroll that was her diary. Her stomach twisted every time she replayed the encounter on the patio, confused about this Rule of his. Feeling short-tempered, she wondered if she *did* make the rules.

Trying to write in the scroll, she was distracted by the sniveling of the eight-year-old house girl who accidentally bumped her as she delivered the food. "What's wrong with you, Atia? Can't you do anything right?" she snapped.

The innocent girl burst into tears and ran from the room. *Stupid slave.*

Faustina entered the study. A former slave since the time of Tiberius forty years earlier, she, like many other freedwomen, chose to remain and live with the family as an employee. Wearing a dull gray tunic with a faded pink headscarf, she padded over to Tullia. Despite a bent posture common for her age, she remained spry and energetic.

"Domina, you've upset Atia."

Tullia reclined and crossed her arms. "She's a child. No, she's a slave. She doesn't even speak our language. Is she stupid?"

Faustina put her gnarled hands on the table and leaned in. "You do not speak her language. Does that make you stupid?"

"No, it doesn't. But in Rome, it makes *her* stupid," Tullia snarled, ignoring the older woman's affronted look. "Get me my writing stylus," she ordered, shifting her thoughts to the next entry in her diary.

Faustina's sharp slap across her face shocked her.

"Listen to me, you snobby little turnip!" snarled the freed-woman, her wrinkled face inches from Tullia, her garlic breath stale. "Whatever's going on is no excuse to mistreat others, including slaves, and especially little girls. Unless you want me to tell your Mama of your inexcusable behavior, you'd better grow up." Faustina rose and pointed a crooked finger. "Go to your room and stay away from me and the girls until dinner!"

With tear-streaked cheeks, an aggressive retort formed on the tip of Tullia's tongue. But one look at Faustina, who glared like an angry cobra, told the girl to keep quiet. Grabbing her diary in one hand, she shoved back her chair and stomped off. Halfway to her bedchamber, she glimpsed Yosef watching from the kitchen and her humiliation worsened. A huff escaped her as she tore at the curtain to her room.

She slammed the scroll on a small table by her clothing rack and plopped down on the bed. Her face felt flushed as she cried. She knew Faustina's slap was deserved. She was angry with herself and taking it out on others. Embarrassment tightened her stomach when she thought about Yosef's refusal to lay with her, churning up her anger. All over some dumb rule? She did not understand and felt foolish. She squeezed her eyes tightly and tried to push away the confusion. Finding no answers, she gave up and lay down. Confusion swirled behind muffled sobs until she dozed off.

It was late afternoon when she awakened, feeling better,

but no less certain of what should be done. Rising, she spotted a wax writing tablet and two candied dates on the small table. Faustina. The woman's honey dates, each stuffed with pine nuts, fried in honey, and salted, ranked as the house-favorite treat. Tullia grabbed one and popped it in her mouth.

That's better, she thought as she chewed. She reached for the tablet. *Faustina's probably sorry for the slap.* A sudden thought froze her. *Faustina can't read or write!* Frowning, she looked at the two Latin words: *MEMENTO REGULA*. "Remember the Rule," she read aloud.

The Rule could only mean one thing. *Yosef? He can write?* She turned the thought over and felt the pull of curiosity. The Rule. She had not spoken to Yosef since the garden, but the Rule lingered. Love your fellow as yourself. Treat others as you would treat yourself. Don't lay with the rich girl because it breaks the Rule. *Humph! What about what the rich girl wants? He broke his own stupid rule.* She didn't suppose there was any rule about that.

She rinsed her hands in a small basin by the bed, dried them, and smoothed her wrinkled tunic. Leaving the second date and the tablet, she hurried to the kitchen and found not Yosef but Faustina and the girls baking bread. Judging by the flour smeared on two little faces, it appeared Faustina was doing all the work.

Tullia paused and was considering backing out without a word when all three looked up. The words came out before she could stop them. "Faustina, I'm sorry."

The older woman dusted off her hands and embraced her. "Domina, growing up is hard. You'll be fine."

Tullia turned to the two girls, Atia and Chloe. Orphans

from one of Poppi's battles, both had been house slaves for a year. Atia, with a button nose and engaging amber eyes, fluttered around like a brown-haired butterfly, chattering in her native tongue. In contrast, Chloe seemed slow and rarely spoke. A bony redhead with tiny green eyes, she clung to Atia like a lost dog.

Gripping the end of the kitchen worktable, Atia squinted, cautious as a cornered cat. Chloe remained motionless.

"Atia, Chloe, I'm sorry for being so cross. It's not your fault, but mine."

Atia relaxed. Chloe did not change. "Yes, Domina," said Atia. The two scampered out.

"That's all you'll get," interjected Faustina with a wry smile.

Tullia heard the chatter of Atia's high-pitched voice as the girls ran into the atrium, where one side was adorned with a vivid Persian rug, its reds, blues, and yellows brightening the area. She knew they would frolic on the room's crimson couch and soft pillows, much like she had done when she was their age. Her toy box still sat beneath the couch, now the purview of the girls.

Drifting from the kitchen to the patio, Tullia pondered Yosef's rule and realized she had applied it by accident. If she were Faustina or the girls, *she* would want the Domina to apologize for her bad behavior. Perhaps there was some truth to it, even if it prevented him from laying with her.

Crossing to the far corner of the garden, she found the empty sunken tub, its smooth, gray-mortar interior studded with a decorative mosaic of red, blue, and black ceramic tiles cascading down to a central drain, sealed with a flat leather-lined wooden plug. A carved white marble bird served as a spigot, with a valve at its base controlling the flow of unheated water from the main line. Too small for underfloor heating, the pool had to rely on hot water carried from the kitchen to warm it.

After visiting the adjacent privy, she found Yosef by the patio bench, the long shadows of the afternoon creeping across the garden. Kneeling, he picked at a stubborn weed with a small spade.

She sat. "Thank you for the honey dates and the note."

He looked up, gave a small head dip, then returned to his work.

"You told me to remember the Rule." She patted the seat next to her. "Please, come sit with me."

He dusted dirt off his knees and joined her on the bench. Without her asking, he turned to face her.

Their eyes met. Tullia's heart flipped as warmth rushed to her cheeks, the social chasm between them forgotten.

"I didn't know you could write. Where did you learn?"

"Your lessons."

"My lessons?" she repeated. "Did you learn Greek, too?"

"Some. I knew Aramaic, but most I forgot."

"How did you learn from my lessons?"

"I listen. When tutor came, I clean the study. Nobody noticed. I learn."

Nobody noticed echoed through her mind. She looked away, absently smoothing her tunic.

"But you can write?" she finally asked.

Blushing, he murmured, "I take tablet and copy."

She put her hand on his. "Don't worry, I won't tell."

They giggled. Tullia lingered on the glow of his cheeks, then leaned in, feeling the same spark of desire from earlier.

"Yosef, will you call me Tullia when we are alone?"

The boy pulled his hand back, fidgeting as the words left her mouth. A moment passed. Her stomach tightened.

He gripped the edge of the bench. White-knuckled, he spoke in a low voice. "Only then. I could be beaten or sold."

She jerked back. "Yosef! That would never happen!"

He gave her a withering look. "No, Domina. You own me. Your Mama can beat or sell me just for the other day."

Her insides twisted. He was right. Being personal with a slave was strictly forbidden, but the concept, which she had known her entire life, was suddenly diminished. Its importance faded before her love for him.

She stood. *No!* she thought and took two deep breaths. "Please wait."

Walking around the edge of the enclosed patio, she trailed her hand across the soft tops of green bushes. She smelled the fresh scents of the flowers and plants. Jumbled thoughts danced around Yosef's rule, but there was no consistency. None that she could find. At the fountain, she splashed cool water on her face, dried with a towel hanging from a built-in hook on the front, and returned to the bench.

"How does the rule apply to slaves?"

He flashed a small smile. "Domina, it doesn't. Slavery breaks it. Who'd ever wanna be a slave?"

Nobody, she thought, and the concept clicked. "Yosef, I know why I've never heard of this rule. When you are rich and powerful, you don't have to care."

The corners of his mouth fell. "Yes, Domina, now you know."

3

Yosef remained on the patio after Tullia departed, listening to the fountain gurgle as the afternoon light faded. Gazing around the lush garden, his heart thundered at the thought of her. *I wish I could be around you all the time*, he mused. Yet he remained troubled by recent events. It was made worse by his newfound thoughts about girls in general. He would see them on shopping trips and wrestle with curiosity. Faustina scolded him once for staring. He was bothered at how often they crowded his thoughts, and then, two days ago, when he saw Tullia's seductive nakedness, his heart nearly leaped out of his chest. But the Rule jumped in. He told her why they could not lay. And now, she had thought about the Rule and brought up the thorny issues of using it for slaves. She was beginning to understand, and he loved her even more for it.

He remembered how the Rule came to him. Even as a little boy in Judea, he was taught to treat all people equally. In his mind, this matched the Rule.

One day a beggar family came to their modest farm and approached his father. "Can you spare some food?" called a skinny, gray-bearded man. A stick-like woman stood behind him, clutching the hand of a hollow-eyed girl about Yosef's age.

"What has happened?" asked his father, crossing a dusty area by their small barn.

The man raised his left arm stump. "I lost my hand in a wagon accident. I could not work. We are on our way to my sister in Ashkelon. We have not eaten in two days."

His parents fed the decrepit family and sent them away with extra food.

"Yosef, remember to always treat others fairly," said his father with knitted brows. "This is what good people do."

Yosef's tense face relaxed as he recalled the rare memory, and realized his parents lived by the Rule.

He returned his thoughts to the day of the failed seduction. Yes, he applied the Rule, but looking back he shuddered at the bigger issue. *What were we thinking? We could both have been killed. A slave laying with the Domina? Dear Lord, that was so dangerous.* Despite the collision of joy and fear, the images burnt into his memory brought a smile to his face.

He whispered aloud, "It was still the best day of my life."

4

The following day, Tullia's tutor, Tibullus, arrived for a morning lesson. Draped in an off-gray tunic with sticks for arms, he clutched a scroll and two tablets with arthritic hands. Beneath his cap sprouted stringy gray hair. The tutor for many of the children of Rome's aristocracy and Tullia's teacher for eight years, the gentle old Greek was an expert at coaxing her cooperation, even on her worst days. She was neither the best nor the worst of the tantrums, insults, and petulance he experienced daily. Still, Mama warned her each time to be on her best behavior when he visited.

On this day, the old tutor shuffled to the study area, sniffling and honking. He blew his nose every few moments and admitted to a headache before they even started.

Tullia wondered why he had bothered to come. He could barely breathe, much less talk.

"Teacher, do you not feel well?" she asked.

He coughed and swallowed, a grotesque sound. "Ah, nod really, Domina."

"Well, let's give it a try."

Halfway through a lesson translating Latin to Greek, Tullia flinched for the last time. One more sniffle or snort and she thought she might scream. Wondering how to get out of it, she remembered Yosef's rule. *Of course!*

"Teacher, it seems you really don't feel well. I think we

22

should cancel the rest of the lesson so you can go home and rest." She hoped with all her heart he would say yes.

He raised his brow, surprising her. "Why, I would appreciate dat, Domina." He blew his nose.

"Then, Teacher, go home. No more lessons today. I'll tell Mama."

After another coughing bout, he gathered his materials and smiled. Before today, she had never noticed his yellow, broken teeth.

"Thank you, Domina, you are very kind."

He patted his eyes with a cloth and shocked her by taking her hand. She returned a small smile and led him to the front door.

"Goodbye," she said. He gave a final wave and left the villa.

Tullia closed the door. Grinning, she walked through the atrium, surprising Atia who was sitting on the rug and untangling a piece of string. Tullia grabbed and tickled her. Atia wriggled away, and dashed into the kitchen, giggling.

Tullia continued to the patio, feeling like a caged bird with newfound freedom. *She used the Rule!* Stepping outside, the fragrant bouquet of rose blooms and oleander bushes lifted her spirits higher.

Mama came through the door. "Where's Tibullus, and why the grin?"

"He was sick, I sent him home. He seemed to appreciate it."

Her mother, sixteen years Tullia's senior, could have been her sister. The same head of thick black hair, smooth skin, and equally penetrating eyes made her an attractive Roman noblewoman.

"In that case, I want you and Yosef to go to the market. Faustina and the girls are busy."

Tullia hid her smile.

"Yes, Mama."

5

An hour later, Tullia emerged with her braided hair twisted into a tight bun and held fast by ivory hairpins. She wore her favorite blue tunic, red leather belt, and delicate gold necklace.

"Domina, you look the role of a prosperous senator's daughter," declared Faustina, as she helped cover Tullia's head with a light blue silk scarf. As an unmarried girl, she did not wear a full-face veil.

Yosef, clad in a simple brown tunic and thin leather sandals, waited by the front door. He carried a burlap bag for their purchases. Two guards from the villa joined them. Balbus, six *pedes* in height—his head level with that of a horse—stood by, his wide-set eyes alert, and heavy brow creased. As Poppi's righthand man from the army, he was the senior house protector. Quintus, his junior officer from the Britannia campaign, stood shorter, more at a horse's withers, but was all muscle and sinew. Tullia thought him handsome with wavy black hair and thin lips always suggesting a smile.

The group followed the cobblestone street of the *Vicus Cyclops* down the hill and eastward. Sunshine glimmered off the white villas of the affluent neighborhood, their brick-red roofs sharp against the blue sky. Grape vines tethering bunches of hard green fruit snaked over and across white privacy walls. Unruly red rose bushes grew in open areas. As they walked at a leisurely pace, the gentle breeze felt like feathers on Tullia's face, and she delighted in the sweet smells of flowers.

Tullia glanced at the cobblestones, free of dirt, leaves, and refuse. She had never seen the nightly sweeper crews but knew they were slaves from several of the most well-to-do households and tasked with keeping the main neighborhood streets clean. Her parents found the efforts frivolous and did not participate.

Tullia wondered if the night slaves slept all day, keeping them away from the children of the house. Most families adhered to a strict separation between slaves and children, anyway, making her relationship with Yosef uncommon. *We are lucky.*

Tullia pushed those thoughts out of her mind, returning her attention to the walk. A spring buoyed her step as she skipped along, Yosef lagging.

"Domina, so fast?"

She eased her pace. "I tried the Rule today. I let Teacher go home early since he was ill. I think it's what he wanted."

He stiffened. "That it? No pay for coming?"

She stopped, a stab of concern threatening her good mood.

"I don't know. Mama pays him. And why does it matter?"

"Long walk from the Subura. Wouldn't you want pay?"

She frowned. "I guess so, but he was sick, and not having to teach seemed more important."

"To you," he countered. "You don't need money."

His words stung like Faustina's slap.

"That's not fair!" she protested. "Despite what you say, I did what was right. You could stand to apply your own stupid rule right now. How do you think your question makes me feel?"

She jutted her jaw like a sparring boxer. Yosef shifted his gaze downward. "Domina, sorry. It was mean."

"Yes, it was. I hope now *you* have learned something."

She strutted ahead, and he dropped behind. Neither spoke.

After a few strides, his footfalls reached her ears. He'd caught up. Tullia said nothing, but he coughed and offered a sheepish grin. "Please use Rule and forgive me, since that's what I want."

She snorted, then giggled. The tension lifted.

On their right, the din of men yelling, pulleys squeaking, and braying donkeys lugging creaky carts drowned conversation. The air grew dusty from the construction of a new building's colonnade, and its surrounding beige travertine wall.

"A new public bath," yelled Tullia.

"By Claudius," replied Yosef.

"How do you know?" she asked, tilting her head in surprise.

"I heard Balbus."

Tullia watched the boy beside her as they walked. *What else does he know?* She realized her understanding of Yosef, until the failed seduction, was limited to banal discussions, with little time for actual conversation. An ache rose within her, a deep longing to get to know him better.

Leaving the construction behind, they followed the road until it became the Via Sacra, the main thoroughfare through the Forum. Scattered umbrella pines bordered their route, with their majestic canopies shading the road. An open field on the right was clogged with carts and wagons, each hitched to snorting horses or honking mules—the parking area for visiting merchants. People bustled around the animals, offering water in buckets or feeding with hay.

"So many carts and animals," noted Tullia, wrinkling her nose at the smell of manure.

"They come at night and stay. No carts during the day—Caesar's rule," offered Yosef.

Tullia's eyes widened in astonishment, but before she could respond, he added with a wink, "I heard Teacher tell you."

"You are full of surprises," she said with a good-hearted huff.

As the Via swept to the left, a red-brick building, nestled beneath a tall pine, sat on the right. Boisterous noises came from an open door beneath a wooden porch.

"Stay to this side," said Tullia, pushing Yosef to the left. "That's the Lone Pine Tavern and not for ladies."

As they moved away, Tullia pointed. "I suppose you know the name of this building?" she asked, jerking her chin toward a single-story, colonnaded, gray granite structure across the street from the tavern. The bustle of shoppers and merchants, and the din of commerce rose as they approached. Now well clear of the animals, Tullia appreciated the fragrant aromas from the sweet scents of the perfumiers' wares.

"Porticus Margaritaria."

More astonishment. "And up there?" She pointed at the next building, its white marble walls far more elegant than the Porticus and reaching two stories to a brilliant red-orange terra-cotta roof.

"Pontifex Maximus and Vestal virgins, each house separated by patio," he said with a wry grin.

He was right. She gave a soft slap to his arm. "Yosef!"

He shrugged, cheeks glowing red.

Looking at the Palatine hill looming above the home of

the Vestals, Tullia admired the palace of Emperor Claudius. A row of bright green pointed cypress trees flanked a wide apron of porphyry stone steps, their imperial purple hue gleaming in the midday sun. At the top of the stairway was an enormous portico, the entrance protected by barred iron gates at least two stories in height. Above, four levels of terraced colonnades ascended the hill, the top floor capped with three white marble pediments, their triangular faces decorated with detailed carvings of gods, men, and battles depicting the history of the city.

She pointed. "What do you think?"

"Big," said Yosef.

They continued to walk, passing the Temple of Castor and Pollux, its glimmering marble stairway rising to meet eight brilliant white columns supporting a crimson tile roof. The single door was open to the public.

Tullia steered them rightward, toward the colonnaded, two-story Basilica Aemilia. The marble building housed vendor booths on its stone patios, and for a fee, beneath the covered columns. To attract customers, merchants hung colorful flags or banners, all flapping in the warm breeze. They never failed to bring the crowds in, Tullia among them.

The girl scoured the vendors, easing between booths, fingering several items, and hefting others in between her hands as she made purchases. Yosef carried the bulging burlap sack with their acquisitions: two sponges and a fired, blue ceramic plate for Faustina, a brown wool blanket for Mama, a yellow silk scarf for Tullia, and a thick leather belt for Poppi.

At each booth, Tullia ground down the prices with aristocratic haughtiness, leaving vendors shaking their heads and Tullia relishing in small victories.

"I never fight you for money," said Yosef.

Tullia saw the teasing glint in his eyes and suppressed a sharp retort. "They ask too much and always raise the price if they think you look rich." She gestured for him to open the sack to add her latest purchase. "There's no room for your rule in business dealings, or you'd soon be out of money."

The sweet aromas of boiled honey and cinnamon drifted through the air. Tullia took in a deep breath and looked at Yosef, who dipped his head and swung his hand out, palm up.

Weaving between shoppers, they followed the fragrant bouquet to a small booth beneath a tall umbrella pine adjacent to the Temple of Castor. Upon their arrival, the elderly proprietor fished a dozen pinenut-stuffed dates out of a pot of honey bubbling on a small brazier. Dropping them on a cooling rack, he deftly added a pinch of salt and turned to her, raising his wrinkled brow.

"Five for ten."

He meant five dates for ten sesterces, but Tullia shook her head. "It should be ten for five."

He flashed a toothless grin. "Five for five then."

That was acceptable. Tullia handed over the coins, which the elderly man took with an appreciative cackle, dropping them in a shabby box. "Thank you, Domina."

They carried their treasures to the center of the Forum and sat on a stone bench adjacent to the Lacus Curtius, a small lake contained in a twelve-sided granite basin, thirty feet across.

As they listened to the gurgle of a white marble fountain across from the lake, Tullia ate two candies. Yosef had three.

After drinking from the fountain spigot, its water flowing

out of a carved lion's mouth and into a shallow pool below, they washed their sticky fingers and ventured to a grassy knoll behind the Basilica Aemilia.

The ground rolled down a gentle slope to a swamp. Tullia pointed across the marshy area to a disorganized horizon of brown wooden structures — stubby one-story buildings interspersed between taller two-and-three-story insulae. "That's the Subura, where Teacher lives."

"About a mile," said Yosef.

She raised her brow. "You know this, too?"

"He told your mama."

They spread the new blanket, joining the other groups lounging on the ground. Tullia relaxed in the peace of the meadow and the warm afternoon sun. Her belly was full, fingers no longer sticky, and Yosef was by her side. Balbus and Quintus too — although appearing to loiter, she knew they watched for trouble. The comforting thought allowed her eyelids to flutter, then close as Yosef dozed off beside her.

Tullia awakened to a sharp nudge. Someone said her name, drawing out the syllables in a lilting tone. A shadow blocked the sun as she squinted at a blurry figure above her.

"Sleeping with the slave boys now?" smirked the voice.

Tullia sat up and recognized her former friend, Valeria Buteo. Before she could speak, Balbus arrived from nowhere, his hand resting on the grip of a large knife.

"It's fine, Balbus," she said, standing and dusting off her tunic. The big man retreated. Only then did Tullia realize Yosef stood off to the side, looking down, as if ashamed. The sight of his hunched figure spurred unpleasant memories from over two years ago, the last time she had spoken with the rude girl.

At twelve, Tullia had received an invitation to Valeria's thirteenth birthday celebration. Thrilled to attend her first party, Tullia and Mama spent a day shopping for the perfect gift. In the Forum they scoured the artisan booths, deciding on a small ring—nothing more than a girl's trinket.

Her mother quibbled over the price with a fat vendor.

"But Domina, it is from Alexandria and came from a Pharaoh's tomb! Eight sesterces is a steal!"

"Indeed, it would be, were it not from Latium," Mama said. A polished chip of crimson granite fixed to a thin copper loop; the piece was common.

Clutching his chest, the dramatic merchant raised his bushy eyebrows. "Ah, the Domina compares my wares to local junk."

"I'll give you two or I'll go find local junk elsewhere."

They paid two.

Tullia clapped as they walked away. "Oh, Mama! It's so pretty. Valeria will love it!"

At the party, aristocratic mothers watched from couches arranged on the gray-black marble floor while their girls sat on brilliant Persian throw rugs scattered with red and blue silk pillows. Tullia learned later the source of the family money—Valeria's father reigned over one of Rome's largest slave markets.

Throughout the afternoon, Valeria opened gifts in order of oldest to youngest attendees. As the youngest, Tullia was last, but she held no fear of being scrutinized. Valeria's gifts were mostly similar to hers—cheap knick-knacks purchased at the Forum, but one girl stole the show as her mother carried in a squirming puppy. Valeria cuddled the friendly ball of energy, and it licked her face.

Once the dog settled in her lap, Valeria held out her hand for the last present. Tullia passed it over with pride.

The birthday girl opened the small parcel and wrinkled her nose. "I don't wear red," she scoffed. "Just keep it." She tossed the bundle back.

Stunned, Tullia fought tears amidst soft snickering from the other girls. But before she could cry, Valeria called out. "Mother, can we eat? I'm hungry."

The group's attention shifted to food. Tullia sat among them and pulled into herself, yearning for the miserable afternoon to end. She didn't eat a single bite.

Once home, she cried all night, and despite Mama's reassurances, worried she had made a fool of herself. It took weeks and everyone—Mama, Poppi, Faustina, Yosef—to make her realize she did nothing wrong. Valeria was spiteful and ungrateful. Their friendship ended and Atia eventually got the ring.

Now, Tullia appraised the girl with renewed vision. *Time has not been good to you*, she thought with thinly suppressed glee.

Valeria, now a gangly three inches taller than her, flashed a cold smile of crooked teeth. "Is that slave the best you can do?"

Framed by frizzy black curls, and a complexion puckered by clusters of ruby-red acne, Valeria's cheeks and chin offered a rugged, inflamed landscape. Light black sideburn fuzz, too sparse to shave or pluck, wove between eruptions, giving her horsey face a scorched appearance.

"Why, Valeria, it's been years," gushed Tullia, taking her former friend's hands. "How nice to see you. And it looks like you were right about that old birthday ring, red is certainly not your color." She put a hand to her own cheek. "Does the sun irritate your pimples?"

"W-wha?" stuttered Valeria, her high-pitched voice resembling a whinny. She began to cry and wobble, jerking her hands out of Tullia's. A slave hurried forward, catching her and leading her away underneath the watchful eye and sardonic smile of Balbus.

Tullia's heart burst with delight at the sight of Valeria's receding back, and even more so when Yosef came sidling up.

"Happy?" He knew the story of the ring.

She turned to him, grinning. "Thrilled. I think we're now even."

"So much for the Rule."

She felt her cheeks flush. "That's right, Yosef, so much for the Rule." Tullia shook a menacing finger his way. "Sometimes you need action, and she got some. You don't know everything about when to use the Rule."

He dropped his head. "Sorry." After a beat, he gestured toward the blanket.

Tullia sat. "I was right about her face, though. The gods, or your God, have not been kind to her."

"Yes, but so mean?" Despite the question, his eyes glimmered.

She stuck out her tongue. "She deserved it." Together they snickered.

After several moments, Tullia reclined and propped herself on one elbow. "Yosef, tell me about when you were little."

6

Yosef told her of his earliest memories — the swish of his mama's long skirts, her sandals, the cool stone floor. He would play among her legs and hems when she walked. Grabbing on, then tumbling off with a giggle. She would pick him up and laugh, "Oh, Yosef."

"My parents were Sarah and Yosef. Our house was brown. We had red curtains." Still sitting, he closed his eyes, searching for memories. "We lived by a river, where David beat Goliath."

Another moment passed before a new memory unfurled, this one of the sweet smell of the olive trees and the crispness of the dry air. "We picked olives." He gave a satisfied sigh. "It was home."

"Sounds lovely," she said.

"There was a wooden box of grain." Yosef raised a hand, imagining his fingers running through the seeds. "I couldn't lift the top. We had goats and chickens." The birds tickled his memory — always scratching away and clucking in an endless search for tidbits. "The chickens ran from me, but they were the only ones."

"But you were so little!"

His lids opened at the warmth in her voice. He looked down at her. Her flushed cheeks and bright eyes made his heart stutter. *Dearest Tullia. I am yours forever.*

Beaming, she met his gaze. "What?"

"Nothing." Seized by a wave of desire, he reached for her hand. His voice cracked. "You're so pretty." He pulled his hand back, embarrassed. "Sorry."

Raising her eyebrows, she mouthed, "Don't be."

In the short silence, he felt her mutual love wash over him. He tried to tell her. "Tullia—" but she cut him off.

She sat up. "Now who's this David and Go-lion?"

"Goliath," he corrected. "A story. A little Jew killed a giant named Goliath."

"Who told the story? The same priest who taught you the Rule?"

"Yes. Skinny man, like stick. He smelled. We went every week, me and Mama. The men chanted. After, we repeat the Rule and commandments. I was glad when it ended."

She continued to look at him.

He felt another rush of love, cherishing these private moments with her. *I wish it could always be like this.*

The caw of a crow, boys playing, and a baby bawling surrounded the serene moment as he savored the pure delight of Tullia's proximity. But a dark feeling emerged. *We should stop now, while it's nice.* The flow of happy memories was ending, met by a gloom he did not wish to share.

He turned toward her. "Can we go?"

"But Yosef, is that all? How did Poppi find you?"

He shook his head, dreading the question. "It's bad."

"Yosef, go on."

He felt his heart sink.

"Go. On."

He knew the tone—he had no choice but to continue. "Soldiers came."

He told her of the hot day, the quiet farm sounds interrupted by harsh voices and the bray of a mule. Playing under a familiar tree near the house, he looked up to see men walking toward him, calling out in a foreign language. The flash of body armor and swords made him curious. He watched his father approach with a raised hand in greeting, only for him to fall after a single, clean strike from the soldier's sword.

"Mama yelled for me to run."

Tullia leaned in. "Yosef, I had no idea. What happened?"

He shrugged. "I guess they're dead."

"Who would do this?"

"Romans," he answered. His eyes wandered around their grassy spot in the meadow. "Like soldiers here."

She stiffened. "Romans? But why?"

"Faustina says Rome's at war with Jews."

"Poppi fights wars. I never heard about wars with Jews."

"Still war." He hesitated. She had broken eye contact and was staring down at the blanket.

"Domina?"

She blinked and returned his gaze, her voice softer. "Sorry, go ahead."

"You sure?"

"It's fine."

This will ruin the day, he thought. Still, the need to share the terrible experience made him go on, despite the uncomfortable topic. "I woke up in a wagon with others. It had a roof and bars. It creaked. I was hot and thirsty." His stomach tightened with the memory.

Tullia froze with a wide-eyed stare. "And?"

"We rode day and night. Terrible smells. Water and bread

once or twice a day. I threw up." An unpleasant fullness filled his throat. Swallowing, he pushed it away. "A little girl was there. Her family had begged for food from us. We sat together, and I held her hand. Her head was bloody. She never spoke. She died in the wagon."

"Oh, Yosef." Her expression changed to concern.

"It got worse."

Her lips pressed together. "You must tell me."

He hesitated, knowing he would hurt her. The thought of watering down his words flitted through his mind, but he dismissed it. She should know. She had everything and he... *no*, he reprimanded himself. *No! It's not that way. She just needs to hear how hard it was.* For a guilty moment, he wondered if it would deepen her love for him.

"After days we stopped. They put us in an open area, like Forum. Wagons full of people all around."

Tullia gasped.

"It was hot. The stones burned my feet."

"It was a slave market!"

"Yes, in Antioch."

He described the shoppers, Romans in battle garb, and the civilians, all in long, ankle-length brown or white robes. Bedouins with dusty keffiyehs on their heads and the ebony Numidians wearing kufi caps with brightly patterned weaves of yellow, orange, and black.

"We waited. Your Poppi and Balbus waved me over. I wet myself."

He paused for breath. "A soldier pulled the little girl out by her arm. She made a brown streak on the stones as he dragged her away." Yosef swallowed.

Tullia's lower lip quivered, and tears streamed down her cheeks. "That poor girl." Her eyes grew wide with understanding, and she sobbed. He wanted to pull her close, but it was impossible. Even holding her hand felt like too much.

Tullia rocked forward and vomited. Balbus and Quintus rushed to her side as Yosef draped his arm across her back. Together, they helped the stricken girl stumble home.

Oh Tullia, I am so sorry.

Guilt and misery tugged at him on the walk, but he hoped her knowing would somehow bring them closer.

7

Tullia struggled with nightmares for two days, losing sleep, and growing irritable. Except for a rare trip to the kitchen for a crust of bread, and necessary forays to the privy, she stayed in her cubicle, gnawing on feelings of guilt, sadness, and frustration. Questions about where slaves came from, and the terrors of their captivity haunted her.

On the third day, she sat on her bed staring at her dirty feet and sighed. Her reflection in the small wall mirror showed swollen eyes, tangled oily hair, and a stained, filthy tunic.

Faustina entered the room. "Domina, is it cramps? We have willow bark for you to chew."

The girl hugged herself. "It's not that."

"Well, what then?"

Tullia looked up, fidgeting. "You were a slave, but now you aren't. What does it feel like, the difference?"

The old woman's face relaxed. She sat on the bed. Extending a chicken claw of a hand, she stroked Tullia's shoulder. "Why do you ask?"

Tullia gathered her thoughts. "You are the same person, but were a slave one moment, and free the next. How did that happen?"

"Good masters can free slaves."

"So, Mama and Poppi freed you, but you're still here. What changed?"

Faustina moved her hand to Tullia's. "A slave has no choice. If she refuses, she can be sold or killed. A freedwoman can refuse, and will only lose her job, not her life. I follow orders and live here because I choose to. I have a choice."

"Then Yosef doesn't have a choice."

"It's true, he does not, but he has a home, food, and kind masters. It's better than nothing."

Tullia looked at her hands. "I guess so."

"Domina, he's a slave boy, rightfully owned by your family," Faustina reiterated, her tone gentle. "Your Poppi bought and paid for him. He would have probably died in the war was it not for your Poppi. He owes his life to your family."

"But a slave is not really a person since he's owned by somebody and has no choice but to do what they say," she argued, tears pricking at her eyes once more. "Then one day, like with you, he's free and is now a person. It's not fair. Who would ever choose to be a slave?"

"It's not about choice. Be practical. Who'd do the work? You? Your Mama?"

"Slaves could be freed, then. Paid, like Teacher, or like you." *Maybe we can do that for Yosef.*

"Then your family would not be rich. It costs too much to pay everybody, plus some people will want to be paid, but won't do the work. A slave will do the work and costs less."

Tullia folded her arms. It still didn't seem right.

Faustina stood. "Don't worry about Yosef. He's a good houseboy and loved by everybody. Now, let's get you cleaned up."

* * *

In the morning, Mama and Tullia sat on the patio bench. "What's all this about Yosef being a slave?" the older woman asked.

Tullia hugged herself, rocking back and forth on the bench, mulling over her words. "It's not about Yosef as much as what happens to people who become slaves," she started.

Her mother frowned. "What do you mean?"

"Yosef told me about the slave market where Poppi got him. It was horrible. A little girl died on the way." Through a stream of tears, Tullia covered her face. "She must have been so scared."

Taking her daughter in her arms, Mama nuzzled her neck and murmured. "There, there, Daughter. You mustn't worry about such things. Slaves depend on us, or they would die. We give them life. There is much sadness in the world you cannot change. You must do your best for your family and friends and try to avoid the ugliness."

Tullia sniffled. "The Jews have a rule that says to treat others the way you would want to be treated. When I use it, I feel better. But how can I follow the Rule with slaves? I'd never want to be one."

"Why Daughter, you're not a Jew, but a Roman. You don't need to follow this rule." Her mother's voice carried an edge. "Where did you hear of this?"

Tullia's mouth went dry. She could not tell the truth for fear of what could happen to Yosef. He might be sold, beaten, even killed. All for a sliver of knowledge.

"Ah, well, I read it." She warmed to a hasty fabrication. "Teacher left a scroll, and I read it in there. It was talking about what Jews believe." She silently prayed to Yosef's God, and any other that would listen, that such information existed and that it would not get Tibullus in trouble.

"That is hardly suitable reading for a girl. I should like to speak—"

"He didn't mean for me to see it," Tullia hurried to add. She swallowed. "It was an accident, Mama, and besides, I think you're right. It doesn't mean anything to us. I see, too, what you mean about sadness. We can't change some things. I'll remember that."

At the end of her ramble, she offered a weak smile and hugged her mother, receiving a reassuring squeeze in return.

Breaking the embrace, Mama took Tullia's hands, turning them over once as if inspecting them. "Don't worry about Yosef. He does a good job."

Tullia felt a glimmer of hope then, for the boy as well as for the fate of her lie.

8

The next morning, Tullia sat at the table enveloped in dread. Her heart thundered at the memory of the terse order issued by her mother earlier. "Get in the study," she said, her mouth a thin line. She turned on her heel without waiting for a response.

Now, Mama sat at the head of the table with Faustina and Yosef to her right. Tullia sat alone, opposite them. Her heart pounded. She failed to relax her tightly curled toes. *Calm down. Just wait.*

Her mother turned her tense face to her daughter, those normally gentle eyes now burning with fury. "You lied to me."

Tullia squeezed her fingers, her mouth dry. She looked down at the table as Mama's voice thundered above her.

"I spoke to Tibullus. He has no such scroll about what the Jews believe, nor did he leave one here."

Crying now, Tullia croaked. "I'm sorry, Ma—"

Her mother's hand shot out, smacking her in the face, followed by a second, harder blow. Tullia's head snapped back, her cheek burning.

"Do not speak!" her mother ordered. "Yosef, get over here."

The boy hurried to Mama's side, fell to his knees, and dropped his head to the floor.

The angry woman eyed his trembling body, then turned to her wide-eyed daughter. "Do you know how the imperial courts deal with slaves suspected of deviousness?"

Sniveling, Tullia shook her head. Yosef remained frozen in submission.

"The Royal House and the Senate have long agreed—the word of a slave is never accepted to be true until he has been tortured."

Jumping up, Tullia shrieked, "Mama, no!"

Her mother's raised hand stopped mid-strike. "Sit down!" she hissed. "Control yourself!"

Mouth agape at the terrifying chill of her mother's voice, Tullia obeyed. Feeling her heart plummet, she tried to quell her shaking hands. Visions of Yosef being whipped or beaten were so terrifying she nearly vomited. Her mind raced. Could she save him? Run away with him? *Won't you punish me, Mama? It's all my fault.* But the thoughts went nowhere, she could only wait.

After an eternity, Mama shifted in her chair. "Look at me."

Tullia complied, wiping her nose with the back of a trembling hand.

"Unlike you, Yosef told the truth when questioned. He admitted to speaking about the Jews and their rules. From what Faustina tells me, and from what I know of Yosef, I don't believe he was trying to influence you for underhanded reasons. This spared him a lashing."

The fullness in Tullia's throat eased with a glimmer of hope.

Unblinking and with eyes locked on her daughter, Mama continued. "Yosef, go squat next to Faustina."

Yosef scurried behind Mama's chair and sat on his heels next to the old servant, head downcast.

"You see, Daughter?" Mama jerked her chin at the boy. "We own Yosef. He does what we say when we say. If he does not, he'll be punished, or more likely, sold."

Panic squeezed Tullia's insides. "Mama, no!" she cried. "It's all my fault; I'll do anything you ask. Please, Mama!" She gulped as tears streamed down her face.

Her mother, palms on the table, leaned in. "Daughter," came her icy voice. "For now, we'll keep the boy, but I will hear no more disruptive talk about slaves, or *any* other rules of this house." She sat up and stabbed a finger at Tullia. "You will end this dangerous friendship. Break even one more rule and Yosef will be shipped to the slave market, and you will be confined to the villa until your marriage."

Lightheaded and sobbing, Tullia felt a flicker of relief. *I'll do anything*, she vowed.

Her mother looked down at Yosef. "Boy." His head jerked up. "You'd do well to remember that we are Romans, not Jews, and *we* make the rules."

She flicked her head at Faustina who barked a sharp command. Yosef sprung up and followed her out of the room.

Mama waited for them to disappear before directing her glacial eyes at her daughter. Tullia stole a glance but could not look up — shame and fear weighed heavily on her chest as the last words were uttered with crushing finality.

"You have violated my trust," her mother intoned, every word slow and drawn out. "It will be a long time before it comes back, if ever. Cross the line again, Tullia, and your little friend will be gone."

9

Tullia walked around the perimeter of the patio, anger rising to the surface of her simmering emotions. *Well, Yosef, this is all because of your stupid rule. Mama is mad at us both. There'll be no more trips to the market, that's for sure.* She scowled and continued the aimless stroll. *It was a stupid lie. It was even stupid to ask Faustina.* In her heart, she knew it would get back to Mama. She rubbed her eyes and fought the confusion. After a few more steps, she heard the reassuring gurgle of the fountain. She plopped down on the marble bench as her stomach churned and tears flowed.

Faustina emerged from the house. She sat and patted Tullia's thigh. "What's wrong?"

"It's Yosef," she wailed, digging her heels into the ground. "It's Mama, it's me."

"Everything will be fine. You lied to your Mama, a terrible mistake, but you did it out of love for Yosef."

Tullia caught her breath through sniffles.

The older woman grew serious. "But your love for him has no future if you want to stay in this family."

Tullia froze. The roil of her stomach twisted to nausea as she pushed down a rising panic. She stuttered at the weight of the insight. "Ah, I ... I guess I always knew."

"You are neither the lover nor the friend, you are the Domina," Faustina reminded her. "Be more than that, and your

Mama will sell Yosef. He knows this and understands, so you must as well. Be the Domina and you can both share the house. It's better than nothing."

Patting Tullia's leg once more, the older woman stood. With a reassuring nod, she returned to the villa.

Tullia calmed herself. Standing, she looked at the smiling fountain fish and groped for something to make sense. Mama won't sell Yosef if I do what she says. She recalled Faustina's words, "It's better than nothing." *Well, it* is *better than nothing.* She addressed the fish. "She's right. I'll follow the rules. It keeps Yosef close. Half of him is better than none." She wiped her eyes. She did not feel good, but she did feel better.

* * *

Tullia avoided Yosef that day. And the next. She did not know if she had the strength, so she remained in her room, pacing between the bed and the wall. Using her wax tablet, she tried every combination of words and phrases she could think of to explain, but each time she failed, using her thumb to smudge the words away.

Four agonizing days passed until she could no longer bear it. Yosef was in the garden. Stepping lightly, she went to find him squatting over bushes, examining their bulbs.

Tullia cleared her throat. He looked up, and she beckoned him to join her on the bench.

He sat stiff-backed, head down.

She took a breath and steeled herself against her emotions, hoping she could tune out her own words. "Yosef, slavery may be wrong, but it's unavoidable. It won't change, but we must."

"Yes, Domina."

Her heart raced. "I want to be your friend and more, but it's impossible," she said, reciting the words she had practiced for hours last night. "Close personal contact is too dangerous for us both. It's simple, I own you and you are below me." She felt her heart rip at the terrible lie. *Please forgive me.* "I hope you understand."

"I do," he said. A pause. "May I go? I have work."

Their eyes met, and his gaze softened, but he did not speak again. Tullia imagined the two halves of her heart breaking into pieces and then dissolving into dust.

She looked away. "Go, then," she whispered, awash in dread.

He left her on the bench as a tear splashed on her tunic.

10

Over the next several weeks, Tullia made good on her word and stayed away from Yosef. *He's just a slave,* she reminded herself whenever she saw him in passing. To her parents, she apologized and swore allegiance to their proud family traditions. If the latter included slavery, then so be it. The Flacci were good masters; she was a good daughter. That was all there was to it. But it was not that easy.

Yosef seemed to spend more time tending the garden. She wanted to visit, to say something, but resisted. She did not trust herself or her mother. Was Faustina expected to report?

The house was too small for them to never see each other. To each of her occasional requests, he immediately complied, issuing a respectful, "Yes, Domina," followed by a quiet retreat. He never looked at her.

* * *

A week passed and Mama summoned her to the study. "You need to spend more time with other girls your age. The group includes Valeria Buteo, so try to get along. Tibullus has another student nearby and will accompany you this afternoon."

Tullia remained silent, pushing down a flicker of annoyance. Even if she voiced her displeasure, it would make no difference. *It's better than nothing.*

Teacher arrived, slumped and barefoot, wearing his usual gray tunic. He carried a battered brown leather shoulder purse.

"Good afternoon, Teacher," greeted Tullia, attired in a blue tunic with matching headscarf and sandals on her feet.

"Domina," he said with a small nod.

They made the short walk to the grassy rise of the Caelian Hill, its slopes studded with wealthy estates, scattered leafy trees, and a cobblestone road weaving through the neighborhood.

"What's this, Teacher?" asked Tullia, pointing at the smooth, dark gray bark of a tall tree.

"A mana ash," he replied. "These slopes used to be covered with them, as well as maples, and hornbeams, but they were long ago cleared for city use."

Her irritation at the prospect of being with Valeria receded a little as Teacher pointed. "Over there's a hornbeam. They have the hardest wood and are used for making ax handles and wagon wheels."

I never thought I'd care so much about trees.

As she walked, an image of Valeria's horsey face flitted through her mind. With a closed-lip smile, she realized there was nothing to fear from the clumsy girl, and she lightened her step.

She returned her attention to the scene before her—a neighborhood checkered by familiar orange-red terra-cotta roofs. The grounds of each estate, demarcated by pointed green cypress trees and beige travertine walls, were accented by stone porticos, columns, or statues of gods, all shimmering in the afternoon sunlight.

She inhaled. "Teacher, I smell the pines, but do not see them."

"It's from the cypresses. They have planted so many, you could have called this cypress hill," he replied, with a small smile.

Continuing in silence, Tullia relaxed, a rising confidence replacing her earlier misgivings. *I can do this. It's a small price to pay to keep Yosef close.*

They arrived at the Buteo address. The sweeping cobblestone drive encircled an oval granite fountain. Four sculpted lions surrounded a throned Jupiter and spewed streams of water splashing loudly into the large pool, every exposed surface darkened by the steady spray.

Trudging up to the front of the mansion, they came to an eight-column portico, reached by ascending stone steps ending on a black marble porch.

Teacher banged on a heavy wooden door and turned to her. "Don't worry, Domina. I have taught them all. You are by far the smartest girl and the only one who can read — including my imaginary scroll about Jewish law." His eyes twinkled and she could not help but smile at the joke about her lie.

"Thank you, Teacher," she said, feeling warm toward him.

"You'll be fine." He winked and descended the steps as a slave opened the door.

Tullia heard the laughter and chatter of girls as she arrived at the same room as Valeria's birthday party three years earlier. The colorful Persian throw rugs over the gray-black marble floor and an open double door to the patio remained. Tullia did not recall the two large windows flanking the back door, their translucent glass surfaces, an expensive rarity in Rome, supplying bright ambient light. *Those are new.*

She saw four girls, all about her age lounging on a large,

orange-colored semicircular sofa accented with red and blue silk pillows.

The room quieted and lanky Valeria approached her. "I forgive you for the insult in the Forum," she said, taking Tullia's hands.

The condescending statement rankled Tullia. Her tongue longed to lash out again. *Imprisonment at home in the villa might be better than this.* But being around the nasty girl and her friends might help take her mind off Yosef. "And I apologize, but red is still not your color."

Valeria squinted, abruptly releasing her hands. "Come on, meet the girls."

Tullia greeted older versions of the same attendees from the birthday party. She settled on the edge of the group and the chatter returned.

"... and they caught Galla and Caelia kissing!" blurted a chubby redhead in a too-tight off-yellow tunic. The other girls hooted and tittered, joining in with Valeria's yuck-yuck laughter.

Tullia pushed down a yawn, fearing an early death.

After a jittery first day, the visits became easier. They shopped at the Forum or lounged in the villa.

Tullia punctuated the vapid gossip with acerbic wit. "Did Caelia ever reach under Galla's tunic?" she asked one day. "You know, every boy has a serpent there that's always trying to get out."

The girls froze. Tullia felt a rising joy at the two with red faces and the two with open-mouthed confusion, the latter included Valeria.

"Oh, never mind," she interjected, having had her fun.

Tullia made no effort to get close to the other girls but discovered a bright spot. Valeria, while she remained caustic, was also surprisingly naïve, bringing delight to Tullia's worst tendencies.

Two months into her new life, Tullia and Valeria lounged alone in the big room at the Buteo villa. The two were casually dressed, keeping in line with a tradition of lightweight loose tunics and calf-skin sandals.

As they lazed on the circular couch, Valeria rattled away. "... and then Julia said, 'Your tunic is ripped!' Can you believe it? In front of everybody!"

At that moment, stultifying boredom made Tullia question, yet again, the decision to leave Yosef.

A change in Valeria's squeaky monotone grabbed her attention. "What did you say?" she asked, half-propping herself up on an elbow.

"*Did* you outgrow your little slave boy?" The insipid girl flashed a malicious grin of cobblestone teeth.

Resisting the urge to insult her, Tullia turned her thoughts inward. *Yes, I no longer show my love for Yosef, yet it remains, and neither you nor anybody will ever know.* She sat up and crossed her legs, formulating a plan to counter Valeria's annoying demeanor. "Don't be stupid. Of course, he's gone." Tullia offered a conspiratorial grin. "Haven't you ever wanted to have a slave boy?" *As if one would want you.*

Still propped on an elbow, Valeria drew back. "Ah, I never really thought about it."

Warming to the moment, Tullia leaned in. "There's nothing like ordering a pretty boy around." Valeria's jaw dropped and her brow furrowed.

Empowered, Tullia spotted one of the Buteo house slaves. She punched the air with a hand and beckoned with a wave, grinning at Valeria as he waddled over.

A sixteen-year-old with red hair, tiny head, and porky body, Memphis resembled a point-up carrot. Tullia knew the Buteos cut all their male slaves, presumably as a precaution against unwanted sexual advances toward their two equally unattractive daughters.

The boy stopped a polite distance away, straight-backed and head down. Tullia rolled her shoulders and pushed her breasts forward. She spoke in a suggestive near whisper. "Memphis?"

His soprano voice peeped. "Domina?"

"Do you like girls?"

Blinking, he stole a glance at her. A deep blush rose from neck to crown before he caught himself and dropped his eyes. Tullia felt her malicious energy spike.

"Do you like this?" She grabbed the hem of Valeria's tunic and flipped, offering a glimpse of dark, pubic fluff.

Valeria leaped up and screamed, "Tullia!" She clutched a handful of tunic and yanked.

Memphis's pink face darkened to purple, mouth agape. He didn't look away.

Valeria's gangly arms flailed toward him. "Memphis! Get out of here!"

The boy jerked out of a trance and scuttled from the room, a plump goose in a rush.

"Why did you do that?" cried Valeria, still standing.

Tullia looked up at her. "Oh, so what? It's not like there was much to see. Besides, he's a fat eunuch, and barely even counts as a boy." *Unlike Yosef, who is strong and smart, and nothing like other slaves.* A flicker of guilt crossed her mind. She knew using Memphis was mean and violated the Rule. Her disgust with Valeria had overcome her self-control. It was too late to apologize but wait—maybe *he* also had some fun at Valeria's expense. She suppressed a grin.

Valeria sat slack jawed, touching a large eruption of acne on her forehead. After a moment she managed a weak laugh.

Tullia sighed to herself. *Oh, you are such a silly cow.* "Never mind, Valeria." She stood. "C'mon, let's change and go to the Forum for some candy dates."

Valeria's mother entered the room. "What's going on in here?"

11

Tullia emerged in the morning with a scowl, trying not to imagine another day at the Buteo's.

Mama came around the corner. "Meet me in the study."

Dread pulled at her. She knew the prank with Valeria would come back to haunt her. But the annoying girl's shock was worth it, as she cracked a half-smile.

Mama arrived. Resigned to her fate, Tullia expected to see her mother strut to the table with a clenched jaw and squinting eyes. Instead, she glided over, took her seat, and touched her daughter's hand. Her face was flushed but relaxed.

"Mama, what is it?" asked Tullia, Valeria forgotten for the moment.

"Your engagement," she said with soft eyes.

Tullia felt a small lump in her throat. *My engagement.* She *had* been thinking about it and knew the time would come. Better than a scolding over Valeria.

"Yes, to Vitalio Silanus. The ceremony will be next year, when he returns from Britannia."

A year was a long time to associate with Valeria, but then again, preparations for the wedding would be needed.

"Who is he?" She felt a spark of interest.

"He's thirty-one years old and works with Poppi in the army. He is the last of the patrician Silanus line and will join the Senate after his marriage."

Tullia's mind roiled. A distinguished soldier and an aristocrat. Her husband.

"What's he like?" she asked, brows raised.

"I met him just before he left for Britannia. He's tall with gray eyes and brown curly hair. He has a longer-than-average nose and two dimples when he smiles."

"Mama, he sounds wonderful. When can we meet?" Her heart pattered as she imagined a dignified senator in a brilliant white toga with a stripe of imperial purple.

"Probably not before the wedding. He is posted far away. He will leave the army and come home to marry."

Tullia ignored a blip of disappointment but knew couples commonly met on their wedding day. It could not be avoided when Rome was at war, which seemed to be always. She squeezed her mother's hands. "Mama, thank you. We will have a good marriage—happy and prosperous."

Her mother's eyes welled. "I know, Daughter." A wry smile emerged. "And I look forward to being a grandmother."

PART II

A Roman Marriage

12

Tullia sat on the patio bench etching words on a wax tablet. The late Roman autumn brought cool crisp days and the musty scents of dried leaves as they rustled and fell in the breeze. And like the season, she knew she was changing. Grinning, she thought of her wedding, now less than a year away. *I will love him and make him happy.* And I will have a baby. She felt a rush of warmth and desire as she contemplated all it involved. *We will make love.*

Faustina came to the door. "Teacher is here."

Tullia hurried in and met Tibullus for the walk to Valeria's. He escorted her on one of her three trips each week. She enjoyed their discussions—far more interesting than Valeria's endless prattle. But the girl had her uses, helping Tullia understand Roman social mores as seen through the eyes of arrogant aristocrats. She hoped it would help her anticipate her future husband's needs.

Tibullus waited in the vestibule in a long-sleeved, gray woolen tunic and a pair of dark-leather boots. She worried about him in the cold and, applying Yosef's Rule, persuaded Mama to buy the shoes. Tullia wore a soft wool, forest-green tunic, draped with a hooded off-white palla. Linen socks in sturdy closed sandals helped keep her feet warm and dry.

"Good morning, Teacher," she said, placing her tablet and stylus in a small shoulder purse.

"Greetings, Domina," he said with a small nod.

Once on their way, she turned to him. "Tell me again about the royal family and the Senate. I thought the Senate made all the decisions," thinking of Vitalio's plan to be a senator.

"Not nowadays, Domina." He ran a hand across his grizzled face. "When Rome was a republic, the Senate and the consuls ran the government. Now, we have the royal family, led by the emperor. The Senate mostly advises."

"How are the senators picked," she probed.

"By the emperor. It's preferred they be rich and of the patrician class."

The information validated what she knew about her future husband. At least his patrician lineage. She naturally assumed he was rich.

"Is Claudius a good emperor?"

He tilted his head. "He's not too bad and has done some good things for Rome."

"Is there a queen?"

"No, an empress—Claudius's wife Agrippina. He also adopted her son, Lucius, changing his name to Nero. He'll probably be the next emperor."

They arrived at the Buteo's, and he continued down the street to his next student.

Valeria, and her tall male escort, met Tullia at the door. The girls were similarly attired, except Valeria wore an awful red palla. Tullia bit back a comment.

"Let's walk today," said the horsey-faced girl. "You need decent shoes for your wedding, and I have the perfect gift for your husband."

* * *

Six months later, the Roman summer arrived, muggy weather pushing the light and fragrant spring aside. Tullia spent the early mornings writing by lamplight, taking advantage of the cool night air always captured by the travertine villa. She wrote about her experiences, as well as what she learned from Teacher, but she was troubled by his recent answer to her question about women writers.

"Since men make all the decisions, it is said there is no need for women to read or write."

"That's ridiculous," she said, her face growing hot.

The old Greek pointed at her. "Yes, Domina, it is. Don't let them stop you."

Clenching her jaw, she vowed to keep writing.

In the late morning, Mama entered the study. "You need a necklace for your wedding and today Rome's best jeweler is taking orders. Come join me on a quick shopping trip."

The air grew thicker as they entered the Forum.

"Great Juno, I'm sticky," growled Mama.

The shade of the colonnaded Basilica Aemelia housing the jeweler's covered hutch offered a mild respite from the heat, but did little to temper Mama's attitude. Following several curt exchanges with the merchant, she eventually agreed on a price.

"Let's go back home," huffed her mother, fanning herself.

"I am tired of Valeria," said Tullia, also happy to leave the market. "I prefer my time with Teacher." She dabbed at the perspiration gathered at her headscarf.

"That's understandable, but I'm glad you spent some time with her and the other girls."

Tullia admitted she did learn a few things.

Her mother continued. "This heat makes me tired. When we get home, we'll have a cool bath."

"Do we have a date for my wedding?" asked Tullia, her heart quickening.

"Three months, in November." Mama's voice carried an edge.

"Mama?" asked Tullia, feeling a jitter of concern.

"I'm sorry, Daughter, it's just this heat."

"Summer is always hot. Is there a problem with the wedding?"

"Well, not really. Let's get to the bath first."

Tullia's insides stayed tight for the rest of the walk.

* * *

Soaking in lilac-scented water, Mama rested her head on the edge of the tub. "Ah, that's better."

Across from her, Tullia submerged completely. She rubbed her face and scalp, letting the cool water refresh. Surfacing, she flipped her wet hair back and wiped her eyes. "Mama, what's the problem with the wedding?"

"It's nothing," she said, bringing her head forward. "The date is set in November, and we'll announce it the month before."

"What's nothing?" ventured Tullia, her stomach knotting.

Mama hesitated. "Well, it's just that Vitalio may not have as much money as we thought."

"How does that matter? We have plenty and my dowry should help him."

Mama gave an unconvincing half-smile. "You're right, it really doesn't."

Tullia suspected it was more than money, but knew the subject was closed.

* * *

The wedding day arrived as a November dusk settled over the villa.

"Mama, is it a bad omen that I am to marry now?" asked Tullia, dressing by the flicker if several lamps in her bedroom.

Her mother straightened the bride's white wool tunic. "No, Daughter. June is not the only month for weddings. Your father and Vitalio are home now from the Britannia campaign, so this is the perfect time."

Reassured, Tullia centered the customary orange veil covering her tightly braided hair, then secured a white wool belt at her waist. By tradition, Vitalio would remove it as they entered the wedding bed. Her heart thundered with nervousness. *I will soon lay with a man.* Curiosity—not love—drove her wonder. She tried not to think of love. Today, of all days, she could not wish for Yosef.

She gathered her courage, and with Mama, left her bedroom, the privacy curtain swishing behind them. The room opened directly into the atrium, the far side of which was arranged for the wedding. Tullia gaped at the scene. Expensive beeswax candles, flickering in waist-high bronze stands, lit their way down a golden path accented by the subtle aroma of honey.

"Oh, Mama," she whispered. "It's beautiful."

As if she had never been in the room, Tullia suddenly appreciated the natural beauty of the fresco on the wall ahead of her—a scene of colorful birds fluttering in leafy branches and warmed by a soft yellow sun. The welcoming murmur of the small crowd, also clad in ritual white tunics, fit perfectly with the bucolic images. She saw Poppi and, for the first time, Vitalio, both smiling as they welcomed her to a small, candlelit altar.

Gazing at her future husband, Tullia caught her breath. She warmed at the gentle look from his soft eyes and a welcoming smile punctuated by two small dimples. She recognized the prominent nose and head of soft brown curls Mama mentioned. "A handsome man," she had said. And it was true. The narrow face fit with his slender fingers. A smile touched her lips as her anxiety eased.

Poppi, his muscular girth now cloaked in a white senatorial toga, gently curled his massive hand around hers. With surprising delicacy, he escorted her to her future husband as Mama joined the other women in the gallery.

At the altar, Tullia signed the marriage contract. Flanked by Poppi and her husband, she turned to the audience, failing to suppress a grin.

"I introduce Vitalio Silanus and his wife, Tullia Flaccus Silanus," boomed her father.

Tullia's eyes welled and her smile widened at the sounds of approval and applause. From across the room, she caught Yosef's eye, and a momentary pang of regret tightened her throat. *Good-bye, Yosef.* Before she had time for other thoughts, Faustina ushered him and the slave girls to the kitchen.

Waiting for the meal call, the men stood talking and the women sat—Tullia and her mother on one couch and three older women on another.

"He is a nice-looking man, if a little thin," came the nasal voice of one of the bitties. Tullia knew Mama cared little for her, but as the wife of a deceased senator, Poppi insisted she be invited.

"There will be challenges, but we all learned to adjust," continued a younger woman from the couch, staring at Tullia with pursed lips and tiny, porcine eyes.

Tullia's chest tightened as she listened to the three know-it-alls offer a litany of unwanted or useless marital advice.

Faustina finally announced the feast, and Tullia eased out a breath.

Mama seemed to read her mind. She looked at her three guests. "Would you give me a moment with my daughter?" The ladies left the room, each trying to outdo the other with another story of the horrors of men or marriage. Mama patted Tullia's thigh. "Don't worry, your union will take some getting used to. And remember, you can always talk to me."

Tullia relaxed her clenched jaw and reached for a hug. "Thank you, Mama."

At the meal, Tullia felt her face flush with every glance from Vitalio. She tried to calm her breathing as the interminable festivities wound down.

"It's time for the kidnapping," announced Poppi.

Historically, the groom was expected to "take" his bride and carry her off to the wedding bed.

The small crowd stood, watching as Vitalio mimed a rough grab of Tullia and led her away. Reaching out with her free arm, she raised her brow in a silent plea for help. None came, but the audience clapped as Vitalio swept aside her bedroom drape. The curtain dropped into place, and she faced him, her back to the fleece-covered bed.

"My sweet Tullia," whispered Vitalio, removing her veil and cupping her face in his warm hands.

Shuddering as his soft lips brushed hers, she thought her heart might burst. He pulled her in, and they kissed. She opened her mouth at the gentle tickle of his tongue. After more kisses, he slowly untied the soft wool sash and pulled the tunic over her head. Trembling, she took his proffered hand as he helped her lay on the warm bed.

In the next moment, he came to her, naked and lean. Her body responded to his delicate caresses, and she felt her muscles relax. He took his time with her and, ever so slowly, she surrendered her virginity. The expected discomfort eased under his tender touches and kisses. As he coaxed her to sleep, she wondered if it just might work after all.

* * *

For two days they kept to themselves, the nights filled with growing familiarity, the days with conversation.

On the third day, Vitalio excused himself to meet with a senator.

Tullia and Mama shared a couch in the atrium. "Mama, he is so gentle and considerate." A warm feeling touched her insides.

Her mother took her hand. "I am so glad to hear it."

"We talk about everything. He likes that I read and keep a journal. And he compliments me on my appearance and—," she hesitated, her face on fire, "my body."

The corners of Mama's lips turned up. "Don't be embarrassed. It's good he sees just how lovely you are."

Tullia's face cooled as her discomfort faded. "Mama, I just feel so comfortable around him."

"I'm happy for you, Daughter," she replied with a warm look.

Late on the second day, the newlyweds strolled around the patio, Tullia's heavy blue stola warding off the late autumn chill. "Tomorrow, we will give you my dowry," she said, hugging his arm.

Vitalio, clad in a brown wool cape over a thick tunic, pulled her in. "A profitable farm is a generous offering. I will then join the Senate."

My husband will be a senator. She swelled with pride.

Vitalio's senatorial appointment was confirmed, and he spent his days away. He returned for late meals and lovemaking with Tullia. Her comfort levels improved under his gentle ministering.

She also undertook additional responsibilities as a wife, including visiting other senators' wives, attending specific social events, and cooking, although Faustina and the house slaves did most of it.

Tullia and her mother also shopped. On these trips, she took the opportunity to share what she had learned from Valeria.

"Not those shoes, Mama," she said, putting the beige pair of leather sandals back on the table. "Valeria says these are the best." She picked up a pair of red, closed-toe leather boots.

"That may be," replied her mother. "But they're too flashy." She raised a brow. "Besides, I thought you said red was not her color." They snickered and settled for the sandals.

Tullia also found more time to write in her journal. Late one week, she stood before the wall of cubbies housing their small library of scrolls. She needed one from the top row.

"May I help, Domina?" asked Yosef, his resonant voice no longer cracking with adolescence and the rustic Latin all but gone.

Her heart skipped a beat. What a difference the year had made. Taller now and muscled, he moved with alluring grace, like a friendly panther, if there was such a thing. "The one with the black handle." She pointed, annoyed at the small tremor of her finger.

He easily extracted the scroll and placed it on the table. "Anything else?"

"No, Yosef. Thank you."

He turned to go.

"Um, Yosef?" she asked, her mouth dry as dust. "I am married now." *That came out wrong.*

He dipped his chin. "You are."

Her mind swirled as she tried to undo the damage. "You are a good slave."

"Thank you, Domina." He bowed and left the room.

She threw her hands over her face. *Great Juno! You are a good slave?* She felt like a blithering idiot. So much for some form of closure. She didn't bother with the scroll but retired to the safety of her bedroom.

* * *

Tullia curled against Vitalio, enjoying the bliss following their morning lovemaking. In those early weeks of the marriage, his kindness and consideration seemed to tame her, and she wondered if she was falling in love.

She opened her eyes as he stirred. "My workload has increased, and I may need to stay away for a night or two."

"Oh, Husband, must you?" she asked, turning to him.

"My responsibilities are extensive," he replied, rising from the bed. "I will know more after today."

"But our nights together…," she whined, feeling like a child.

"Will continue to be nice, but if I am to be successful in the Senate, I have to work very hard." Leaning over, he kissed her forehead.

She sat up, nervous fingers twisting the hem of her gauzy tunic. "I understand but try to come home."

"Don't worry." He finished dressing and left the room.

She rose, placing her bare feet on the stone floor. It felt as cold as her insides.

Clad in a blue silk robe, she joined her mother at the study table. "Mama, Vitalio may need to spend some nights away."

"Is it work?" she asked, without emotion.

"Yes," said Tullia, feeling no better.

Her mother patted her hand. "Try not to worry, some husbands have to work late. He'll probably stay at his apartment in the Subura."

"But why can't he just come home?"

"He may need to meet other senators or work with documents that can't leave his office. There may be many reasons," she offered.

The tightness in Tullia's chest worsened at her mother's wooden responses, especially the suggestion she should not worry. Worry about what?

His absence a night or two each week soon became most nights. Their lovemaking and easy intimacy all but stopped, replaced by a quick rut without tender conversation.

Tullia felt her happiness slipping away. "Vitalio, you are never home anymore," she stated, anger creeping into her voice.

"Do not nag me. I must work. I'll be here on most weekends."

13

Tullia sat on the patio bench with her mother discussing the marriage. A heavy wool blanket covered their legs against the cold of a cloudy January day.

"He's never home but for a night now and then," said Tullia, fighting a tear.

Mama took her hand. "I know, Daughter. It's not unusual for husbands to be away."

"I did not want a loveless marriage," sniffed Tullia. "But I think I have one. I wanted it to be like you and Poppi," she said, giving into a quiet sob.

Her mother pulled her in. "Your father and I are the exception. We found love before marriage. We did not have to look for it after."

Tullia wiped her eyes. "What do you mean?"

"Your marriage was arranged, ours was not."

Tullia drew back in surprise. "It wasn't? Why not?"

Her mother blushed. "My family did not approve of my behavior. I always found trouble by asking questions or reading things not suitable for a woman. They said they regretted letting me learn to read. I refused marriage to several suitors. One day a young man from the army came by. He was at the wrong address. A big man but gentle. I walked him to the right house. From there we found ways to be together. By this time, my parents wanted me out. Your Poppi and I fell in love and my father happily endorsed his request for marriage. I signed the contract, and your father and I left that house forever." There was a hint of a smile and a far-off look. "We spent our wedding night in a private room in the barracks."

Despite the tears, Tullia chuckled. "You *were* lucky—in more than one way. The barracks?"

"Yes," she whispered, her brows raised, her mouth hinting at a mischievous grin.

They sat in comfortable silence for a few moments before Tullia spoke. "Why was I paired with Vitalio?"

"Politics," huffed Mama. "A union between the Silanus and Flaccus families was wanted. Neither Poppi nor I were happy with the arrangement, but pressure on your father forced our hand."

"Pressure from who?" Tullia's insides knotted.

"I don't really know—the emperor, army generals, other senators? Your father did the best he could to satisfy them to secure his government position. Tullia, it happens all the time and is not worth dwelling on. A bigger question is what will you do about trying to make it work with Vitalio?"

The cold grip of reality held Tullia. "There's nothing to make work. He asks little except in the bedroom. Maybe he'll change if I give him a child."

* * *

Tullia redoubled her efforts to be a good wife, always cooperative and never questioning Vitalio. He came and went as he pleased, refrained from discussing his work, and rarely asked about her life. She knew he did not love her, and she no longer blinked away tears at the thought.

During the day, Tullia wrote her feelings in her journal, finding it helped lighten her heart. She also enjoyed the energy and sweet innocence of little Atia.

"Don't be sad, Dormina," she had said, mispronouncing Domina as she wrapped her small fingers around Tullia's hand. "Come, we can bake some bread."

Tullia chortled, allowing the little slave girl to lead her to the kitchen.

Each day she fought the urge to think about Yosef. But the harder she tried, the more often she saw him. When they spoke, his warm eyes seemed to dwell on her longer than usual, stirring pleasant feelings and warmth at her center. She knew she could not go back to him but felt comfort in his presence. *It was better than nothing.*

Three months after the marriage, Emperor Claudius announced a banquet to celebrate the completion of the Claudia aqueduct. Vitalio received an invitation.

14

Tullia examined the petite square bundle. White papyrus secured by fine silk thread of the imperial purple, and a wax stamp embossed with the emperor's ring, it bore Vitalio's name. She knew it was for the emperor's ball, having seen Poppi's identical invitation.

"It came here since Vitalio does not yet have a proper villa," said Mama in response to Tullia's question.

"I guess they don't send royal invitations to the Subura," remarked Tullia dryly. She sighed. "But he'll come by tomorrow to pick it up and I'll suggest we do something together." Repeated attempts to engage him beyond the bedroom had, so far, been unsuccessful.

"Do that, Daughter. You can only try."

In the morning, Tullia met him at the atrium. "Husband, here is the royal invitation. After you read it, maybe we can walk to the Forum for a meal. Just us."

They stood in the area of their wedding, the colorful wall fresco lost on Tullia.

"I don't have time for a frivolous meal," he said, taking the small bundle and popping the seal with a finger. After a glance, he tossed it back to her. "We'll join your parents at the imperial palace on the Palatine." He turned to go, throwing the next words over his shoulder. "Work with your mother to find something suitable to wear. I don't want to be embarrassed."

Tullia fought an angry retort, instead reaching out with one hand. "Husband, are you content? Is there a problem? Don't worry, Mama and I will find just the right ensemble."

Vitalio was already walking away. "I have work to do."

Tullia closed the door on his retreating back and glared. Yosef's rule came to mind. *Well, my husband never heard of the Rule. How inconsiderate.* She simmered with annoyance and retreated to the patio.

Pulling her blue wool palla tighter against the chill, she listened to the gurgle of water from the patio fountain. She addressed the fountain's decorative fish. "What's wrong with my husband?"

Water splashed in reply.

Mama joined her for a walk around the patio. "I heard him."

Tullia shrugged. "He's always like that."

"Try to remember that husbands can be lambs or wolves, and a wife has to be ready for either at any time. Lucky is the wife with a wolf outside and a lamb at home. Poppi is a kind of lamb, more like a gentle giant with all of us, and a ferocious warrior with all the rest. Vitalio may come around."

"Mama, he is neither giant nor gentle, just rude."

* * *

Later, mother, daughter, and Faustina stood in the study and considered three bolts of cloth strewn across the large table.

Mama acknowledged the merchant, a dwarf with a nervous smile.

"Domina, we have three silks to choose from." He spread

his arms before the fabrics. "This lovely yellow-orange from the saffron flower, its color long associated with purity." He dropped his head in an apparent gesture of piety. Recovering, he spread his short arms at the remaining samples. "And we have this light purple, beautifully dyed from shells, and a vibrant scarlet from the madder root."

In a language Tullia assumed was from Germania, the vendor barked an order at his slave. The frizzy-haired woman hurried to straighten and smooth the large sheets of cloth.

"Now, which color do you favor?" asked Mama.

"Yellow," said Tullia without hesitation. She'd made up her mind the moment the merchant appeared. "The purple is too near the imperial shade, and the red is somehow less virtuous."

Mama agreed. They ordered a yellow stola and matching veil for the imperial party.

15

Three days later, warm sunshine replaced the gloom of a cold drizzle. The villa, now fresh from the rain, sparkled and hummed with activity. It was the perfect day for a visit to the palace.

Faustina tried to finish Tullia's hair. "Sit still, Domina."

"This is my first banquet."

"If I poke you with a hairpin, it will be your last." Faustina placed a heavy hand on her shoulder. "Stop squirming."

"Mama says all the important people will be there," Tullia said, twisting underneath the grip. She turned to the small wall mirror to see the progress.

Faustina grunted. "Important means neither kind nor trustworthy. Be careful."

Tullia studied herself. "My hair's fine. Faustina, you worry too much."

The old woman grunted again as she directed Tullia toward the bed. Wearing a white undertunic, the girl slowed long enough to allow Faustina to fold the flowing yellow stola around her body, fasten it at the shoulders, and add a high-waisted belt. Tullia pirouetted and curtsied.

Faustina shook her head but grinned. "You look lovely, Domina."

The transports stood at the entrance to the villa. Tullia hoped they had not been waiting long; she would surely hear it from Vitalio. But as she descended the steps to the two litters, her husband said nothing. His critical eye swept her head to toe, then, finding nothing to complain about, he entered the lead litter with Poppi. The women rode in the second. Each box, borne by eight slaves, and owned by a local transport company, offered sumptuous comfort among pillows, blankets, and throws. Tullia could have laid down if she wanted to, but the gentle rocking motion would have put her straight to sleep, so she half-reclined and tried to relax.

"Mama, what will this be like?"

Before answering, her mother adjusted her daughter's yellow headscarf and matching semi-transparent veil. "There, much better." She offered a curt nod.

Tullia wondered about the odd gesture, but her mother continued before she could ask.

"Once we arrive, we enter through imperial gates and follow the men to where guards check the guest list. After we are in, Poppi and your husband will leave us to tend to their business, and we'll mingle with the women."

The litter stopped. From her reclined position, Tullia wriggled toward the drape-covered exit.

"Wait," said her mother.

Tullia paused and peeked through a gap in the curtain. She craned her neck toward the front. A handful of litters stood ahead of them. "There's a line," she exclaimed.

"There always is for these banquets. Sit back, it will be a few moments." The litter inched forward.

They stopped and started three more times before she felt a lowering to the ground. An attendant opened her mother's curbside door, and they disembarked. Mama helped her out, her mouth a straight line and brow furrowed.

"Mama? What's wrong?" Asked Tullia, as her skin prickled.

"It's nothing. Just stay close," came the clipped reply.

Following the men across a small plaza, they ascended the white marble steps leading to the palace's iron gates. As she mounted the stairway, Tullia looked over her shoulder at the Forum below. She recognized the back of the temple of the Vestals and to the left, the bench where she had eaten honey dates with Yosef a year earlier. Her throat twisted. *Oh, Yosef.* She wished he was here—walking ahead, behind, side by side, she didn't care. She just wanted him with her.

It cannot be. Our fates are what they are. I hope your God will watch over you.

Ahead of her lagging daughter, Mama turned and gave a sharp wave. "Tullia! Come on!"

The memory broke, images of Yosef crumbling before her eyes. Blinking, Tullia scurried up and whispered. "Sorry."

"Pay attention," Mama scolded. "There are rules and protocols. Stay with me."

The gates opened, swinging slowly inward. They followed the men toward two thirty-foot high doors, open for guests and painted the Tyrian purple of the emperor. The vestibule led to a white marble atrium rimmed by a forty-foot colonnade of porphyry granite. Vast draperies of every hue hung from the arches and flapped gently in the breeze. The late afternoon sun captured the colorful opulence, mesmerizing Tullia.

Mama turned to her. "Close your mouth and come on."

"It's like a dream," Tullia croaked before she obeyed.

"Hurry up, or it'll become a nightmare." She leaned in. "Tullia, follow my lead. These are dangerous people."

"Wha…?" She whispered, as the tingle of fear returned.

"They have all the power. They take what they want. Be polite and do not stare." She turned, and they moved across the atrium toward a receiving line.

Ahead of them, Poppi and Vitalio conversed with an elegantly dressed woman. Wearing a lavender silk stola, she stood no taller than Tullia. Drawn to the woman's elaborate hairstyle, Tullia recognized a typical *vitta* of imperial purple. As thick as her little finger, strands of hair were woven into a thick cord and provided the front border of the coiffure. Eight evenly sewn small pearls adorned the front of the *vitta*. Behind it, tight pin curls cascaded across the top of her head and nestled against the front of a white, turban-like *infula*. The ends of the violet *vittae* streamed down her neck and across each shoulder.

So engrossed was she in the detail of the woman's hairstyle that Tullia failed to register that the men had moved on. A hard pinch to her arm surprised her, then Mama's quick tug made her step forward—right before the empress, Julia Agrippina, the most powerful woman in Rome. All that she knew of the empress was from Tibullus: Agrippina had married Emperor Claudius four years earlier, when she was thirty-nine, and now played a major role—though the specifics he did not reveal, or perhaps he did not know—in running the empire.

Unlike Tullia and her mother, Agrippina wore no veil, and her head and neck were visible. Emerald earrings, each with a white pearl on a short gold chain, dangled from her lobes, and a braided gold necklace, studded with small rubies and sapphires with a central gold medallion depicting the Emperor Claudius, encircled her neck. Both arms were wrapped in long spirals of gold bracelets, and gold rings with rubies or amethysts adorned the fingers of each hand. Tullia noticed the gold-rimmed cameo pinned to the shoulder of Agrippina's stola, recognizing the profile of Antonia Minor, grandmother of the empress.

Piercing amber eyes engaged them as Agrippina took Mama's hand. "Ah, Fulvia, you are well I trust?" Before her mother could answer, Agrippina turned to Tullia. "And who is this little apple blossom?"

Mama dropped her head and curtsied. "Thank you for your consideration, Highness, you are too kind. This is my daughter Tullia."

Tullia copied her mother. "Your Highness."

The empress waved a hand to her side, then again. On the second gesture, a young man appeared, dressed in a white wool tunic bearing the purple stripe of the Imperial House. "This is my son, and heir to the throne, Prince Nero."

The boy had none of his mother's elegance. A bored expression sat on his face as he thrust his hand toward Mama, who curtsied and kissed an oversized gold ring. As she rose, he flipped his hand at Tullia's waist. She also bent down and kissed the ring. He jerked his arm back as if her lips burned.

Ignoring both guests, Nero addressed his mother. "May I walk this Tullia around the room? She's pretty enough."

Unblinking, Agrippina looked at Mama and answered. "Of course you may."

Mama shooed Tullia toward Nero. "Please."

The boy grabbed Tullia's hand. "Come on."

He strutted away. Tullia stumbled after him, toward the din of the crowd, her mouth watering at the savory aroma of roasting pork as it mingled with the smoky scent of wood fires burning beneath an open corner of the room. She watched a line of slaves delivering food to the patrons as Nero pulled her into the large banquet room.

At least two hundred feet across, the open space included a sunken central area with three sides occupied by colorful couches, tables, and chairs, all bustling with people. Gray marble walls rose at least two stories, and on the fourth wall at the far end of the room and before eight columns supporting a white marble pediment sat Claudius. On a throne and surrounded by guards, he greeted people escorted to him by palace officials.

Out of earshot of his mother, Nero stopped. He slipped a coin into her hand and raised his chin. "Look at it."

Tullia turned it over. The shiny aureus showed profiles of Julia Agrippina on one side and Nero on the other. She glanced at it, then, unsure of how long the appropriate admiring should be, held it toward him.

"Keep it," he said. "It just came out and proclaims that I'll be the next emperor."

Tullia mumbled a thank you and slipped it into a concealed pocket at her waist.

Nero's lips lifted into an arrogant smile. "You'll be proud to have known me." Again, he grabbed her hand and moved off.

Tullia considered yanking her hand away, but that would only bring disaster. She had to maintain grace for her Poppi's sake, and her husband's. Her feet carried her after the prince, her yellow-orange stola billowing behind her as they weaved through the crowd. Where was he going?

Near the third wall, Nero slowed, his demeanor shifting to that of a normal fifteen-year-old. Slender and pale, his tunic looked too big for him. He offered her a shy grin as he engaged her with soft brown eyes. She relaxed and returned a small smile.

"When were you married?" he asked.

"Three months ago, it's still new."

A commotion in the center of the room distracted the prince. Tullia turned to see that a slave had dropped a plate of food. Bits of meat and vegetables lay scattered on the ground, several attendants scurrying in haste to clean up the mess.

Nero sneered at the noisy scene and his eyes lost their warmth. "Fools. No wonder they are slaves."

Tullia did not know how to respond, but it hardly mattered. Nero guided her away from the scene, still scoffing.

"So, who'd you marry? That skinny senator with your fat Papa?"

Before she could answer, they arrived at a couch several feet behind the emperor's table. Nero pushed her down and pressed an arm and leg against her. She tried to edge away, but his hand came down on her thigh. Tullia froze.

Suddenly, two boys burst from behind the couch, laughing. Nero's hand vanished, and both he and Tullia jumped up.

A few years younger than Nero, both lads were clad in elegant white tunics. They danced and taunted, pointing hysterically at the pair. "Nero's got a girlfriend; Nero's got a girlfriend!"

Nero lunged at one of them and gave a two-step pursuit. The lads darted out of reach.

His stocky partner wagged a finger. "Now, now, you are to be married, be a good boy! Hah!"

The other boy returned, and the two invaders resumed their boisterous giggling as they faked kissing each other. Tullia bit the inside of her lip to keep from smiling.

Clenching his fists, Nero again dashed after the smaller of the two, this time giving chase around the edge of the room.

The stout lad remained, laughing. He looked at a puzzled Tullia. "Hi. I'm Titus." He pointed at the running boys. "Nero's after Britannicus, his step-brother. He'll never catch him." Before Tullia could ask why, his expression shifted into friendliness. "My father's Vespasian and is friends with emperor Claudius. I live here while he's away." He raised his eyebrows. "Who're you?"

His openness did more to relax her in seconds than in the time she'd spent with Nero's boastfulness. She offered a warm smile. "My name is Tullia Flaccus, my father is General Flaccus."

The boy's eyes widened. "A general! I'll be one too, someday, I hope."

At that moment, Britannicus raced to Titus's side, breathing easily and unfazed by the chase. "Let's go."

Titus waved. "Bye, Tullia." The boys loped into the crowd, their laughter fading.

A winded, red-cheeked Nero stomped up. "They're two little guttersnipes. When I'm emperor, they'll see who's boss."

Tullia remained standing, but the prince pulled her back down onto the couch. "Well, was that him?"

The momentary excitement left her confused by the question. "Who?"

"The scrawny man with your father. Is he your husband?"

Annoyance bit at her. She looked away and gave a curt nod.

The prince appeared unbothered by her rudeness. Instead, he surveyed the crowd. "I'm to be married in June. She's not pretty like you, but my mother says it's a necessary alliance."

Startled by the compliment, Tullia's irritation eased, only to return when he cut off her thanks.

"I've already had several virgins, so I don't expect any surprises from her. She's lucky to have me. I assume you were a virgin?"

The question jolted her like a slap. Anger erupted and her mind raced. *Lucky to have you? And was I a virgin? You are indeed a bully! May the gods strike you dead!* With effort, she succeeded in keeping these thoughts hidden and simply sat, hoping the question would go away.

Nero watched her. "So, were-you-a-virgin?" he asked in an icy voice.

Tullia recoiled wondering what to say.

Before she could stammer out a response, he flashed a cruel smile. "No matter." His eyes then glittered with an emotion that made her tremble. "Virgin or not, let's have some fun."

He clapped his hands and called to an obese blond-haired slave, at least ten years his senior. The man scurried to serve his master. Kneeling, he held a tray of sweets above his head.

Nero looked at Tullia with a vicious smile.

"Do you find joy in the rule of others?"

Fear rippled through her chest.

The future emperor leaned toward her and spoke in a soft, conspiratorial tone. "He's a eunuch; no balls. It makes his pike shrink." He cackled a scratchy laugh. "It's so funny!"

Turning to the slave, he spoke in a voice devoid of humor. "Put the tray down and stand." The big man complied.

"Show the mistress your tiny pike."

Without hesitation, the eunuch began to raise his tunic.

"Nero! What's this?" Agrippina marched toward her son, her lavender stola dancing along the ground in her haste. Heads turned, following her. Coming to a halt before the couch, she placed a hand on her hip and surveyed the scene with a tight-lipped expression. Without looking at the slave, she dismissed him with an irritated wave. Then her head whipped to the right, landing on Tullia.

"Return to your mother."

Trembling, Tullia stood and bowed to Agrippina. "Your Highness." She turned to Nero, "Your Grace."

Neither party acknowledged her gesture. As Tullia hurried away, voices rose behind her and more heads turned, gawking at the scene unfolding before them. Tullia rushed past them, scanning the crowd for a sign of Mama, Poppi, even Vitalio.

Mama was the first face she saw. She stood toward the entrance to the banquet room, and upon seeing her daughter's harried face, opened her arms. Tullia fell into them, sobbing.

"Oh, Mama! What a horrible boy. I don't know what would've happened if his mother hadn't come."

"Not so loud," Mama whispered. Her firm grip guided Tullia to a corner couch. Once they were out of eyeshot of the main crowd, she gave her daughter a hug, but her words were firm. "These are very dangerous people, Daughter. Never make disparaging remarks about the royal family. Now smile and act relaxed. We'll discuss this at home. But first, we must slip away. Whatever he said or did, we cannot afford to be remembered."

Tullia tried to suppress her jitters. After a reasonable pause, Mama stood, and Tullia took her arm. They traversed the room to Poppi. Mama whispered in his ear. His bushy eyebrows lifted as he cast a wary look at the royal tables, then with a neutral expression, he strode to a mid-level imperial clerk. Tullia and Mama trailed after him, the girl only hearing snippets of his conversation — *unwell wife, early departure.* The clerk gave a dismissive wave of his hand. Tullia thought they could go then, but Poppi redirected them toward Vitalio, who stood closer to the center of the room.

The senator's face registered no interest, nor did he look at Tullia. "I have ongoing business," he declared, speaking before Poppi was done. "I must stay."

He turned back to a bronze-skinned buxom slave, thinly clad in a revealing Greek-style white toga. Her face showed a sultry expression as she held an empty silver food tray.

Tullia watched with dull interest. The question of what sort of business lurked on the tip of her tongue, but before she knew it, her parents were corralling her along, past the huge imperial doors and wrought iron gates, and down the steps to the street where Balbus and the bodyguards waited.

16

No one spoke as they walked along the Via Sacra. Torches mounted on posts lit their way across the darkened Forum. Tullia, still rattled by Nero's behavior, turned the events over in her mind. Clenching her fists, she felt her face flush. *Was I a virgin? Who would ask that?* She released an exasperated breath and continued to mull over events. Sadness replaced her anger at the memory of that poor slave having to answer to Nero. She felt her shoulders sag. *His life must be terrible.* The pop of a pine torch stopped a rising sense of guilt, and she checked her surroundings.

On the left loomed the Lone Pine Tavern, named for the enormous stone pine growing between the Via and the red brick building. Weak light and noisy voices came from the open door.

As they passed by, Tullia fingered the coin in her pocket. She pulled it out and threw it at the tree. It made no sound as it landed in the pine straw. *Keep your filthy coin!*

Her mother glanced over. "What was that?"

Tullia feigned nonchalance. "Nothing, just a pebble."

Her mind snapped back to the slave, thoughts roiling faster. A deep, unpleasant feeling seized her, rooting her to a spot just beyond the pine. She raised her hand to her mouth and let out a strident moan of realization. *I treated Yosef just like Nero treated that slave.* She shuddered, tears welling.

Her parents stopped, and Mama reached for her. "Tullia, don't worry. It's over."

Poppi looked on with concern.

Tullia wept and shook her head, pushing Mama's hands away. "It's not that." She gasped for breath as the tears increased.

Poppi took a step closer. "Daughter?"

Enveloped in a blanket of guilt, she stumbled forward, knees like jelly. Her parents fell back, but she could feel their worried looks trained on her back. The heavy weight of remorse tugged at her, and she realized the only way to unburden herself was to confess to her parents and hope they might help.

Faustina greeted them at the door, and in a silent display of understanding that came from the longevity of her work, hurried to light the lamps in the study. Tullia ushered her puzzled parents to the lighted room as the older servant finished, heading sharply for the kitchen.

Mama pursed her lips, watching Faustina disappear. "Tullia, what's going on?"

Ignoring the question, Tullia gestured for them to sit. She could feel the dried tears on her cheeks and chin. Faustina reappeared, carrying cups of watered wine, which she set down on the table before them. Nobody drank.

Mama tapped a finger on the table. "Well, what is it?"

Through puffy eyes, Tullia regarded her parents. She sat, folding her hands on the table. "There's more with Nero," she began. "First, he asked if I was a virgin when I married. I was too shocked or scared to answer, so he asked if I enjoyed ordering others around. He commanded a slave to pull up his tunic and show me his … his genitals. That's — that's when the empress stopped him."

The additional information froze her parents. Shadows danced to the flicker of the lamps, and the room had the weak scent of burning oil.

Her mother's face turned to sympathy. "Tullia, I'm so sorry."

As she reached for her daughter, Poppi, red-faced and snorting like a bull, jumped from his chair and roared, "A virgin? Despicable!"

Before he could continue, his wife raised her hand. "Gaius! Sit down. You'll only make things worse."

He sat, gripping the table edge, his knuckles white.

Tullia flinched. If he reacted like that to Nero's transgression, he would not look kindly upon hers. "There's more," she said. "I'm no different than Nero."

The room quieted. Poppi looked confused but Mama squinted. "What are you talking about?"

She folded her hands in her lap. "Two summers ago, you and the girls went to the market and left me here with Yosef. I did the same thing to him."

"The same …?" The question died on Poppi's lips.

Tullia looked down at the table. "I am no better than that horrible prince."

He remained silent.

Mama looked hard at her. "Did what, exactly?"

Tullia met her gaze, and speaking low but steady, offered an unvarnished description of the failed seduction, of Yosef's response, and of the Rule's role in his refusal to lay with her.

Her mother's glare deepened. But it was Poppi's reaction

that cut. When she was done, he pushed himself away from the table and stood up, ignoring his wife's raised hand.

"I command men at war, not the squabbles of women, children, and slaves," he said roughly. He would not look at his daughter. "Work it out."

Tullia lowered her head as he left. Shame burned her cheeks, more so than her mother's steely expression.

"Once again, it appears that Yosef is the more virtuous of the two of you," she said. "At least *he* could resist temptation."

The vicious barb would have reduced the old Tullia to tears, but not tonight. After three months of marriage and the day's indignities, the remark triggered her ire. She glowered at her mother. "What a terrible thing to say! I would remind you that I'm no longer a child and you *cannot* scold me like that. I have endured the abuses of the future emperor, likely insulted him, and have shared with you my deepest secret: an act of a child and born of love. Yosef's virtuous response has *nothing* to do with it."

"Very well. Your behavior with Yosef was childish and mean, but you have lied yet again—this time a lie of omission."

Tullia had the clear conviction that her mother was wrong, and now knew she would never understand. Her anger receded.

"Mama, I have not lied again. I have told you the truth, but like before, your focus on a lie misses the point. Don't you see? I ordered Yosef to embarrass himself because I could." An angry sob escaped her. "No matter what you think about slaves, it was wrong, and it was cruel."

"Enough, Daughter." Mama's voice rose. "He had no

choice but to do what you order. In the eyes of Rome, *and this house*, you did nothing wrong. Despite this, I still disapprove of your behavior and can forgive Yosef for ignoring your ridiculous order."

Tullia softened her tone further, as if she was talking to a child. "Mama, Nero made me feel like he owned me. I felt like a slave and didn't like it. Yosef must have felt the same way. Is that any way to treat somebody you love?"

Mama stood up. "Tullia, I will not have the slave discussion with you again. Yosef does what he's told because he has to. Your behavior toward him was not virtuous, but was dangerous. As you say, the foolish act of a child." She stepped around the table and grasped her daughter's chin in her hand. "Yosef's low birth is far beneath you. You'd better grow up and accept it. You can't feel sorry for the chicken that is killed for dinner; what would we eat? And you can't feel sorry for the slave that follows orders; who would do the work? Both must be treated with virtue and not be abused. We are obliged since we own both the chicken and the slave."

She released her daughter and arched a brow as if waiting for a rebellious comment, but there was none. Tullia recognized the futility of the discussion. Her mother would never understand. As she slumped in her chair, shadows dancing across her body, she felt the nagging question return.

But what if you love the chicken?

17

The kalends of April arrived, and with it, a patio garden bursting with new flowers. Tullia sensed the wispy fragrance of blooming violets and the spicy aroma of the geraniums bordering the patio walls. Buttercups surrounded the gurgling fountain. She sat on the bench and stroked her stomach. They weren't the only ones nurturing new life. Tullia's gradually swelling belly, now at three months, had become the dominating focus between her and Mama.

"I wonder if the baby will soften Vitalio," said Tullia.

"Perhaps," replied Mama. "But…"

Tullia shrugged. "I know. He's really not been around." The thought tightened her chest. "When he does come by, he has seemed kinder."

"Just watch him and take care of my grandbaby," she patted her daughter's hand, but Tullia felt no reassurance.

Three weeks later, Vitalio visited. "Get me some wine," he demanded, storming through the front door.

A surprised Tullia flicked her head at Faustina who hurried to the kitchen.

Her heart thundering, Tullia followed him to the study. "Husband, is something wrong?"

He glared at her. "Nothing you can help with. Where's that wine?"

Faustina placed a full cup and a pitcher before him. He

took a sloppy gulp. "Your foolish pregnancy is making you fat and is embarrassing."

Tullia froze as her cheeks grew hot. "Vit—."

He cut her off. "Why do women always grow sloppy when they are with child? Where's that old woman? I want some bread."

Faustina was ready and arrived with the food.

Tullia stood at his side, wondering where the old Vitalio went. A mixture of fear and anger bit at her. She put a hand across her belly and waited for the next insult, hoping he was all talk tonight and nothing else.

He rose. "Find something to wear that fits you better. You look like a sow."

Without another word, he strutted to the door and left.

Mama came out of her bedroom. "Try to ignore him."

Tullia gave a sad smile. "You said husbands could be either lambs or wolves, but nothing about them being billy goats." Her mother's embrace eased Tullia's tension, but not a small kernel of fear.

The warm summer arrived, with minimal contact from Vitalio until late July, Tullia's sixth month. Wet from an afternoon rainstorm, he pushed through the front door. "Tullia?" he snapped. "Get me a dry toga."

She looked at Faustina. "Bring it in."

Tullia followed him into her bedroom. Gray light filtered through the shutter slats of the window as she watched him unpin the wet garment and remove it. After he tossed it on the floor, he sat on the bed in a light undertunic.

"Husband, it is good to see you," she lied, fighting a tremor in her voice.

He ignored the greeting but returned an oily smile. "Come here."

She sidled forward her heart pounding. He grabbed and turned her, one hand on her belly, the other roughly caressing her bottom. "You may be fat, but you are nice and soft. It's been too long, wife."

He pushed her onto the bed and raised the hem of her tunic. She released a silent breath and tried to think of the hot bath she would take afterward. He grunted and it was over. She felt her face relax as he rose and left the bed.

He donned the dry toga folded on a table outside the bedroom curtain.

"Not bad," he chuckled, and left the villa.

Tullia lay on the bed, eyes dry, her face flushed with anger. What kind of marriage is this? She shook her head in resignation as she rose. It was tolerable, but she had the sinking feeling it would be worse.

Faustina met her in the atrium. "Domina, your bath is ready."

* * *

One evening, in the eighth month of the pregnancy, Vitalio arrived unannounced and entered her bedroom as she adjusted a belted robe before the wall mirror.

Dressed in a senatorial toga with its stripe of purple, and wearing expensive leather sandals, he gave the casual observer an impression of success. Up close, bloodshot eyes, blackened teeth, and soiled clothing bespoke of his debauched life.

Tullia pushed down a thread of bile as she tried to ig-

96

nore his filthy appearance and the foul odor of stagnant wine. Forcing a smile, she stroked her belly. "You are almost a father."

Vitalio coughed, cleared the phlegm, and swallowed. "When can we have relations? I'm your husband."

She could not hide an expression of astonishment.

He seemed not to notice. "So when?" he repeated. One hand brushed his loins as he licked his lips.

Fighting a rising panic, she held up her hands. "Please Vitalio, I am too far along."

Snorting, he pointed at her. "My wishes come before yours, and certainly before that child."

She heard a strain in her voice. "I only ask you to wait until our baby is born, then I can be all you need."

"Need?" He glared. "I do not *need* you. You are fat and dis-respectful—a terrible wife."

She recoiled at the insult. "Then why are you here?" she growled, unable to keep the bitterness from her voice. She knew she needed to leave.

Several curls of dark hair fell over her face as she turned her back to him, but just as suddenly, he was on her—one hand wrenched her shoulder, sending a sharp sting down her arm. Tullia bit back a scream as Vitalio shoved her forward onto the bed. Propped on her elbows, she fought to keep the weight off her belly. Sweat, grime, and musk filled her nose as heavy weight descended on her back, fingers scrabbling at the edges of her robe. She heard the swish as he opened his toga. A familiar pushing sensation lapped at her hips, and she feared for her baby.

"N-no," she gasped before his hand pushed down on the back of her head. "I'm too far along," she yelled facedown.

"Shut — *up*," he muttered, grinding as he tried to move into position.

Tullia wriggled underneath him. Slapping his hands and edging her knees together, she finally heard him grunt in exasperation. The weight released. Gingerly, she rose to her knees and half-turned. He was off the bed, standing and silhouetted against the dim light of two flickering lamps. She worked her way to the side of the bed and sat, hoping he would leave.

A slap ricocheted off the side of her face. Tullia's hand flew to her cheek, eyes watering, as she faced him again. "I'm your husband!" he snarled, jabbing her in the chest once, then again. "This is my *right*, do you hear?"

She gasped and rubbed her cheek. "Vitalio, please try to understand, it's too dangerous."

"You are a self-centered whore!"

He surprised her with a vicious blow to the head, knocking her back onto the bed. Darkness blinded her vision, but her ears caught the stream of insults he screamed as he left.

Pulling into the fetal position, Tullia closed her eyes and sobbed. More than anger, she felt the dread of loneliness and the futility of a hopeless marriage. *I am trapped with a cruel pig.* She shook with a heavy sob.

After a few moments, she sensed movement in the room and heard a soft voice. "Domina?"

Yosef? Her crying slowed.

Kneeling at the bedside, he whispered, "Are you alright?"

Too stunned to speak, she lifted her head. She recognized him with her good right eye, the left already swollen shut.

He grimaced at her appearance and sat on the bed, cradling her head in his lap. "Oh, Domina."

With a wave of relief, her sobbing returned. "No, Yosef, I'm not alright. Say my name. Call me Tullia."

He bent down to her ear. "Oh, Tullia."

She pulled him to her. Their lips touched and she moaned, deepening the kiss. With rising desire, she shifted the massive bulk of her belly and tightened her embrace. Liberated from two years of suppressed grief, deep gulping sobs racked her frame as she clung to him, her hold unrelenting.

Pulling away, he whispered. "Tullia, relax your grip. I don't want you to have the baby tonight."

Soft laughter replaced the sobs.

"Oh Yosef, what have I done? To me, to you?"

"Only what was required."

She gave him a final hug. "You should go; Mama won't approve." He hesitated, but after a moment let go. Tullia grabbed his hand just before he rose, tracing his palm lines with a slender finger. "Thank you," she whispered.

* * *

The next morning Tullia stood alone, watching water streaming from the patio fountain. Mama joined her, looking more tight-lipped than usual. "Please find Yosef and come to the study." Tullia's purple eye drew no comment from her mother.

Mama sat at the head of the table, Tullia on her left. Yosef stood a respectful distance behind Tullia. The sun streamed from two kitchen windows, precluding a need for lamps. The scent of the morning's baked bread lingered.

Mama gestured to her right. "Yosef, sit."

He slipped in across from her daughter, head bowed.

Tullia watched her mother with her good eye. Neither nervous nor impatient, she waited, unsure of the direction of the meeting, but certain that something needed to change with her husband. The purple grape pushing her left eyelid closed gave solid testimony to this fact. Despite it all, she knew her mother would not have approved of Yosef's visit — something she surely knew about. Why else would she have them both here? With no compunction, she thought, *Mama, if you want to fight, I will fight, but something must change.*

Mama sighed and pointed at Tullia's eye. "I'm aware of everything that happened last night, including Yosef's visit."

"Ma—"

Her mother shook her head. "Wait and listen." She pushed a lock of hair behind Tullia's ear. "Your husband was a poor choice. Except for a seed—" She nudged her chin at her daughter's abdomen "—he offers nothing. Unless we take action, you will not survive this marriage."

Tullia clasped her hands together and directed her eyes to the table underneath them.

"It is not enough that he spends weeks at a time away from here," Mama continued. Her head tilted as if she were weighing her next words, but Tullia could not wait for them to come.

"I think I know how my husband spends his nights."

"Of course you do, Daughter. You are no fool." Her mother's lips twisted. "But you have no proof."

Tullia fell silent. Was her mother suggesting there was nothing she could do?

"You may not have proof," said Mama, "but I do." Her lips became a thin line. "Daughter, listen to me and try to understand."

What's going on? A feeling of dread descended.

"On my instruction, Balbus watched your husband. After his first visit to a brothel, we feared he would spread disease to you, so we made an arrangement."

"What sort of arrangement?" Tullia asked, heart in her throat.

"We found a young whore—new to the business and with only a single suitor. We gave her an apartment in the Subura and arranged for her to seduce and hold Vitalio. In his shallowness, he fell for it. He only sees you and Cicada—and she is sworn to see only him and knows if she breaks the bargain, all will be lost for her."

Tullia took a moment to gather her thoughts. It made his behaviors more logical but was nonetheless sordid. She pursed her lips and flattened one palm against the surface of the table. "Is she the only one?"

"As far as we know, Daughter."

"And it continues?"

Her mother dropped her head in acknowledgment.

Across the table, Yosef's eyes lifted, and Tullia felt them on her, but she could not look at him. She knew he was angry—not at her, but for her.

Mama leaned forward and Yosef's gaze broke. "Your husband was never going to remain faithful, but with Cicada's help, we are trying to limit your exposure."

Despite the shock, the information eased the tension in her chest. She knew he would see others but putting a name to it made it more real. Well, she hoped Cicada kept to the arrangement. "I guess it makes us sisters of sorts," she said with a mirthless smile. "And if he tires of her?"

"He is shallow, and she knows the stakes. Given the current circumstances," another nod at Tullia's broken face, "we will do all we can to limit your nights with him."

They were quiet for several moments.

Mama broke the silence. "But back to your marriage. It's clear the kindness Vitalio once showed you will never return. Which means things must change."

Tullia held her breath and pushed down the onrushing hope gathering in her chest. Yosef remained immobile.

Approaching footfalls made their heads turn. Faustina, dusting her hands on her apron, stood behind Yosef's chair.

Mama looked at her. "Faustina and I have discussed the situation. You will continue to be civil with Vitalio and act the role of a good wife, but we must minimize your time alone with him. We'll claim illnesses on your part or find other excuses. You'll sleep with me or the slave girls, if necessary."

Nodding, Tullia felt both relief and anxiety, but a loose end dangled. Thankfully, her mother did not make her wait. Shifting her eyes, the older woman looked to her right.

"Yosef." His head snapped up. No longer the lanky adolescent, he now towered over Tullia. Her insides twitched with joy as her love for him swept away Vitalio.

"Domina?" came the respectful low rumble.

"You are now charged with Tullia's safety. Don't let him harm her again."

His eyes glimmered with dark ferocity. "I will protect her with my life," he vowed.

"I know what I ask is dangerous," Mama said. "But—"

"Should it come to death with the senator, I will not die alone," he interjected.

The declaration resonated through the room. As much as Tullia's heart warmed at the ardor of Yosef's promise, fear led her to an oath of her own. *It must never come to that.*

She faced her mother. "I would rather run away than let Vitalio kill Yosef. We can go back to his home in Judea."

"Well, hopefully, that will not be necessary." Her mother's wry smile made Tullia realize the naivety of the suggestion. "We'll just need to keep an eye on you and Vitalio."

Faustina winked at Tullia, patting the small knife she kept concealed beneath her tunic.

"For now," Mama continued, "you both have my permission to rekindle your friendship, but it must be deeply hidden. And Tullia, friendship *only*. No foolishness."

Tullia caught her breath at the groundswell of joy washing away the misery of the last two years. She blinked, paralyzed by bliss.

Mama pointed at her. "Tullia, if Vitalio suspects you're carrying on with a slave, he'll kill you both, and there'll be nothing me or your father can do about it. Remember, for women, adultery is a capital crime, and with a slave, unthinkable." She addressed them both. "You must conduct yourselves no different today than you did before last night. But balanced against your husband's behaviors," she pointed at Tullia's purple eye slit. "It's the best choice for now."

Yosef leaned slightly forward.

"Yes, Yosef?"

"He'll never know."

"Yes, I'm sure, but you must be very careful."

Tullia suppressed a grin as she regained her senses. *I know we can do it.*

Serious now, she turned to her mother and gestured at Yosef and Faustina. "We'll make this work. The four of us are the real family. Our love will triumph over his cruelty, and it will start with a new baby."

Tullia grinned at Yosef.

Mama sighed. "You have a few moments, but then you must separate."

Meeting over, Mama and Faustina left, leaving the two lovers standing in the room.

Tullia's eyes twinkled. He returned her gaze with a sheepish grin. "Domina?"

She giggled. "Slave?"

They embraced.

PART III

The Sappho in the Fresco

18

In the morning warmth of what would soon be another muggy summer day, Tullia sat on the patio bench. Amidst the lush greenery of the garden and the fragrant scent of red rose blooms, she watched Dracus. *Is he really almost four years old?*

The house slave Atia, now twelve, held the child's hand as he tottered under the colonnade in a tiny blue tunic and white nappy. The little boy giggled and ran his hand along the soft green boxwoods bordering the garden. His brother Marcus, less than a year old, remained indoors under the watchful eye of Faustina.

Tullia stepped to the patio fountain and addressed the gurgling stone fish. "Well, here we are. Dracus is growing, and Marcus, thank Juno, is healthy. I will never lay with Vitalio again." The last part she hoped would soon be true.

A voice interrupted her thoughts. "Domina?"

She turned. *Yosef. Beautiful Yosef.* Her heart thumped as she appraised him. Jet black hair and rosy cheeks remained from his childhood, but now eight inches taller and one hundred *libras* heavier, his imposing figure towered. She imagined the elite Celtic warrior from the writings of Polybius. *Please let our lives together continue.*

"Dracus, wait!" chirped Atia. Tullia chuckled as the third

lap around the patio began. She followed the race for a moment before turning back to the man before her.

"Yosef, good morning."

Even in the safety of her own garden, she had to be formal. Only a handful of the household knew them to be the equals they were at night and in their private moments: Faustina, Atia and Chloe, Balbus, and Quintus. Balbus kept the secret from Poppi, putting Tullia's safety above military loyalty. At least Tullia suspected as much. Quintus followed Balbus. Her mother never acknowledged she knew, but she had to—it had been over three years, and it was a small villa. The fateful decision to allow Tullia to rekindle her friendship with Yosef made Mama complacent in the ruse. Both women exhibited discretion, and the topic was never discussed.

"Are we on schedule?" asked Tullia.

"Yes. I'll ride to the Nomentana farm today." The largest of the three Flaccus farms, it occupied twenty-five hundred acres east of Rome on the Via Nomentana. "I'll supervise the final packing of the wagons and return with them tomorrow. It's only twelve miles."

"The line will be long at dusk."

He raised his brow.

"Sorry, I know you know," she said. But still she worried about the crowds entering at night.

Rome's municipal rules prohibited all carts and wagons during the day, making night the time for animal-drawn traffic to enter the city and conduct business. The law stipulated a dawn departure, or fines would be levied.

He bowed and retreated into the villa.

Tullia returned to the fish. "We will go to Pompeii, away

from Rome and Vitalio. I can't wait." The fish bubbled, but she heard, "Enjoy." She leaned in. "I will."

"You will what?" Her mother stepped beside her.

They exchanged a chaste kiss. "I'll go to Pompeii and get away from this heat. You, too. We should be ready the day after Yosef gets back."

"That's what I wanted to discuss." They moved to the bench. "I can't go this time. With your father and Balbus away at Nero's war in Parthia, I must stay and watch the businesses."

Tullia frowned. "Mama, no. You never get to go."

Her mother had missed the trip last year. A sore on her foot swelled and grew so tender she couldn't walk. She had refused to see a doctor, much less abide by their bloodletting techniques, so it was only after weeks of pain that Faustina's salves and saltwater soaks allowed a huge thorn, as long as the width of a coin, to emerge.

"It can't be helped. You, Yosef, and the girls can go, Faustina will stay here with me. I need to spend more time with Siculus anyway." Siculus, the family accountant, had a second-floor office in an insula on the Aventine, less than a mile from the villa.

Tullia pouted. "Well, alright, but we'll miss you—the boys especially."

Mama touched her daughter's cheek. "Maybe next year. But please give Auntie my regrets."

They entered the house as Dracus and Atia completed their fifth lap. The young slave and her ward stopped in front of Tullia and Mama, the little boy all giggles and wiggles. Pointing a chubby finger, Dracus flashed white baby teeth. "Nonna," he gurgled happily.

* * *

They left for Pompeii two days later, Tullia and the boys in the second of a three-wagon caravan. The custom-made horse-drawn carriage, driven by a single guard, boasted open windows adorned with russet-colored privacy curtains and padded walls, upholstered in dark blue silk. A vivid, color-co-ordinated Persian carpet covered the floor and muted the sound. A thick feather mattress over the rug softened the ride. Strewn with blankets and pillows, the interior resembled a large bed.

The lead wagon, also horse-drawn, and built for utility with solid wooden wheels, carried supplies, several caged ca-pons, and the slave girls. An oversized third cart, pulled by a mule team, transported materials necessary for construct-ing a temporary camp befitting the wealthy family. Yosef and Quintus would lead six mounted men, and another half-doz-en foot soldiers covered the flanks and rear of the group.

The small convoy assembled in early morning darkness. Yosef opened the rear door of Tullia's cabin. A small lamp mounted on the wall flickered in the dim space. "Comfort-able?"

She pushed her chin toward her left, where Marcus dozed in a cradle, then right at Dracus sleeping in a soft nest of blan-kets. Propped against the front wall by several thick pillows and wrapped in a soft cotton blanket, she wriggled deeper into the cozy cocoon. "We are quite comfortable, thank you."

He spread his hands. "Looks that way. It'll be slow and bumpy until we reach milestone two outside the *Porta*."

"I remember. We'll be fine."

He closed the door.

Tullia lifted the linen shade. Darkness covered them, but yellow light from torches borne by the first two riders illuminated the dark street.

The drape fell back as the carriage lurched forward. Thumping along the cobblestone *Vicus Cyclopis*, and crossing under the gigantic Claudia aqueduct, they headed for the Circus Maximus and the intersection with the Via Appia. Tullia closed her eyes and sat back. Even without looking, she knew every step they took. Within moments they reached the shadow of the horse stables tucked into the curve of the Circus and joined the noisy din of vehicles departing the city. Tullia eyed her mental roadmap. They would turn south on the Via, and the road would be flanked by the partially cleared slopes of the Caelian hill. It was always bumpy. Thankfully, it was a short ride to the lights of the *Porta Capena*, a southern gate in the Servian Wall.

The wagon creaked to a stop. Men shouted, mules brayed, and horses snorted. The carriage filled with the aroma of manure and the woody scent of burning torches. They had reached the gate.

Pulling a window curtain to the side again, she saw a wide, well-lit road with imperial guards shooing away vagrants. Jewish beggars in particular frequented the site, an easy place to seek money or food from the line of exiting wagons.

One of Yosef's guards came to the window. "No fear, Domina, we'll keep them away."

She thanked him and dropped the drape. Next to her, Dracus and Marcus had not moved; the stop-and-go traffic was of no burden to them.

As they approached the checkpoint, Tullia heard a guard.

His voice was rough, and the single word issued from his mouth was not a question.

"Papers."

There was a pause, followed by Yosef's voice. "We're a senatorial party traveling to Pompeii. The family of Senator Gaius Flaccus."

After a few beats, she heard the reply. "Safe journeys."

The caravan resumed its bumpy trek behind other wagons, many turning off on roads or paths intersecting the Via. Traffic thinned by the second milestone and they moved onto a well-traveled earthen path adjacent to the cobblestone road. The ride became smooth and quiet.

* * *

As dawn broke, Tullia opened the drapes to a fresh country breeze carrying the scent of pine and a fruity aroma. Rows of mulberry trees lined the path, the ground bearing their hapless fruit, which lay squashed on the road before them by countless passing carts or picked at by hungry birds.

At milestone three, she recognized the famous tomb of Caecilia Metella, its pointed gray travertine rotunda stretching into the summer sky of the new day. From her studies, she knew Caecilia was the wife of Marcus—the son of Crassus, a rich Roman general and political ally of both Pompey and Julius Caesar. From previous family trips, Tullia knew many tombs dotted the Via Appia for the first several miles of the journey, but Caecilia Metella's stood as the most majestic.

Leaving the necropolis, Tullia watched leafy hardwoods and conifers replace the stones of the tombs. She heard the long song of a nightingale and the staccato chirp of a lark sparrow. A cool breeze carried the scent of fresh-cut grasses from an open pasture dotted with chattering workers bent over their scythes and forks. An empty hay wagon, hitched to a braying mule, awaited its next load. Out the right-side window ran the cobblestone via. They passed a mother, a crying baby in her arms, sitting on the bench of a two-wheeled cart. Behind her, the orange necks of two terra cotta wine amphorae jutted above a jumble of boxes and duffles. Pulled by a single ox and led by a bearded man in a soiled tunic, they trundled the other way, back toward Rome.

With the gentle rock of the carriage, Tullia released a slow breath and soon surrendered to heavy eyelids.

* * *

The wagon gave a small jolt and she awakened. Happily, the boys slept on. She opened a drape. Ahead loomed milestone eleven, the waist-high, gray granite post standing between the dirt path and the cobblestone road. A bright sun sparkled as the earthy aroma of the forest filled the air. A few birds called. *It must be nearing midday.*

Yosef rode up to her open window. "We'll break at Lake Albano, about four more miles. Can you make it until then?"

She yawned. "We'll be fine. Will we reach Tres Tabernae today?"

"We should. It's another ten miles past the lake, but we're making great time. This will be our longest day, over thirty miles."

"And the Christians?"

"They should be gone."

A few weeks earlier, a group from the Christian cult had ridden from Rome to Tres Tabernae, a tiny post station boasting three businesses and an intersection of three roads. The Christians escorted one of their leaders, Paul of Tarsus, back to Rome. His arrival had created a stir among anti-Christian factions. Aware of the unrest and hearing unflattering rumors about the cult, Tullia, and Yosef worried their presence in Tres Tabernae would ignite anti-Roman sentiments. Tullia made a mental note to include this in her diary.

"We should stop at least a mile short of the settlement," suggested Yosef.

Tullia agreed.

By late afternoon, Yosef found a site for their camp two miles from Tres Tabernae. Following a gap through the woods, they crested a small knoll and to a broad field—plenty of room and out of sight from the road.

"Easily defendable, if it comes to that," said Yosef, sweeping his hand across the area.

Tullia disembarked. Atia and Chloe gathered the children. "I should hope not," she replied, having never given it a thought.

"It won't, but I like to be careful."

The guards erected a large tent for the family. Furnished with a table, two small chairs, and a narrow bed, it offered comfort, protection from the elements, and, most importantly, privacy. One draped corner included a sleeping area for both slave girls and her boys. Tullia would occupy the bed.

Yosef checked with her after the accommodations were complete. "Satisfactory, I hope."

"Yes. And the men?"

"They'll sleep under the stars, beneath wagons, or in tents, and rotate guard duty." His eyes twinkled. "And don't worry, each man would rather die in service of the family rather than face the wrath of Balbus should any harm befall you or the children."

Tullia allowed herself a small laugh as she followed him out to where dinner was being prepared. How good it was to have Balbus with her, even when he wasn't physically present.

In the evening, following an outdoor meal of roasted capon, Faustina's bread, carrots from the farm, and watered wine, she and her family returned to the tent. Several lamps lit the interior and gave a weak scent of burning oil. Chloe and Atia retired behind the curtain and put the children and themselves to bed.

Tullia settled at the make-shift desk, well-lit by a table lamp with four flickering wicks. As she removed a wax tablet from her writing box, Yosef entered.

"Domina."

She looked up and failed to suppress a grin. "Slave."

He offered a phony bow.

She went to his open arms and breathed in his warm, familiar scent. Contentment stroked her heart as they exchanged a slow kiss. She squeezed, molding her body against his, and felt a rising desire.

He pushed away and winked. "I see you still follow the Rule."

"Oh, no." Her lower lip jutted out in a mock pout. "I thought you were applying the Rule to me, but I guess we should wait for Pompeii."

Laughing, they sat, and she poured wine.

He gestured at the tablet. "Progress?"

She completed a small edit with her stylus. "Oh, yes, and soon to be reviewed."

"At your service."

Tullia's equal in written Latin, Yosef occasionally commented on drafts of her journal. His opinion often contrasted with her aristocratic perspective, sparking debates, and airing their differences.

She recalled their earlier exchange in the villa over the problems of the rich and those of the poor:

"Not every day is perfect for the rich," argued Tullia, quill in hand and a sheet of papyrus before her. Yosef could be so stubborn.

A half-smile crossed his face, and she knew he had goaded her into another debate.

Sitting opposite her at the table, he used the fine grit of a sand solution to polish three small table lamps. "I am not saying they don't, but your bad day is deciding which silk scarf to add to your collection. Every day is a bad day for hungry people."

"I will not feel guilty about our money," she snapped, pointing her quill at him. "It's not like *you* don't benefit." She felt warmth creep into her cheeks.

"I know," he said, not reacting to her hint of wrath. He dried the last shiny lamp and rested his hands on the table. "I just feel sorry for them."

"You are a gentle lamb and friend of the people," she said, annoyance replaced by a heart brimming with love.

He waved away the comment and stood to go. "That may be, but I need to fill these lamps, or I will have no friends in this house."

"Try to have a good day," she quipped. He did not reply as he left the room.

She enjoyed their sparring; the discussions always brought them closer. Maybe she *should* do more for the poor. She had promised herself to think about it.

Now, in the tent, she closed the cover to her tablet. Yosef did not review every entry—some were for her alone—but often she found his thoughts useful. The final drafts from the tablets were later transcribed onto papyrus, twenty sheets to the scroll.

After a sip of wine, he lifted his chin at the tablet. "How many scrolls so far?"

"Two, and they're stored at the villa in Rome."

"Do they really go back eight years?"

She crossed her arms. "They do. I began two years before you foolishly refused my attempt at seduction."

He offered a wry grin. "That's right, back when you started talking to the patio fish."

"I had things to say!" Her smile took the sting out of her small reprimand. "And my diary allowed me to practice writing." As she acquired mastery of written Latin, a compulsion to document events and her feelings, emerged—especially when dealing with Vitalio early in her marriage. As an adult, she found the writing uplifting, and the inclusion of Yosef, stimulating. "It makes me happy to think my children, and their children, will be able to know me when I'm gone." She gestured at the tablet. "You can read this in Pompeii."

"I look forward to it," he whispered, kissing her once more on the lips before departing.

Tullia prepared for bed, smoothing an indigo silk nightshirt over her body. In the eight months since the birth of her last child, she had regained a trim figure. Glancing in a small hand mirror, she saw dark curly hair and soft brown eyes with a hint of crow's feet. *Well, I'm a bit older than that silly girl who tried to seduce Yosef, but much smarter.*

Laying down, she failed at sleep. Recurring thoughts of Vitalio made her grimace. In her mind, she had a one-sided discussion. "You are cruel and arrogant. You do what you please. You embarrass my family." If she lived by Yosef's Rule, she should use it with her husband. *How do I ever extend the rule to a hateful man?* Her stomach churned, but she knew it was more than Vitalio.

Much more.

She blew a puff of air from her lips and turned on her side. *Oh Yosef, I think I am pregnant with your baby.*

19

At sunrise the next day, their journey resumed, now eighteen miles to another post station, Tratturo Canlo. For a change of pace, Tullia rode next to the carriage driver, leaving the boys with Atia and Chloe. Chirping birds announced the morning, a perfect serenade to a fresh new day. Enjoying the view from the front of the wagon, she stole a glance at the driver. He sat rigidly and as far away as possible.

"It's a nice morning," she said politely.

"Yes," he mumbled.

She looked at his white knuckles as he squeezed the reigns. "Relax and tell me your name."

"Catus, Domina."

"Well, Catus, I wanted to see the countryside. I hope you don't mind."

His posture remained stiff. "No, Domina."

The sounds of clattering hooves gave both of them relief, Tullia especially, upon seeing Yosef ride up. "Catus, I see you have a partner," he chortled.

The driver glanced at him and stiffened further.

Yosef frowned in mock sympathy. "Don't worry, she'll be fine up there with you."

Catus did not look reassured.

Tullia turned her attention to the road. To the left sat a brick building with a closed wooden door. She assumed this was the tavern. The road from Atium, on her right, intersected and ended at the Via Appia. At the corner of the two roads sat a travertine building embedded with a concrete sign proclaiming it as a post station. A few stone huts bordered the road, but she saw no people.

Leaving the small hamlet, she enjoyed a gentle breeze on her face and the rhythmic creaks of the wagon. Compared to the rugged terrain coming from Lake Albano, the day's journey would be easy, crossing the rolling hills and pastures east of the Lepini mountains.

The gentle ride on the dirt path adjacent to the cobblestones helped ease her angst over the pregnancy. The baby might be Vitalio's, as she recalled her single encounter with him in the last few months. But in her heart, she felt it was Yosef's. Whether that was a good thing or not was another issue. She touched her belly. *Yosef's baby.* Her body jittered with fear. If Vitalio concluded it was Yosef's, he would kill them all.

I must leave him.

The thought made her heart jump and then relax as her mind flowed freely. Divorce was a simple matter, but the process was not. Her family had enough money and political influence to extract her from the marriage, but it would take time. She would start when she got home. The tightness in her chest eased, but not completely.

She took in the scenery as the wagon squeaked along. Struck by nature's exhilarating freshness, she took a deep breath and tried to let her worries fade. A crow cawed; a horse snorted. The grassy fragrance of the rolling landscape mingled with the leathery scent of the laboring animals lending comfort and tranquility to the moment. She half-dozed, leaning back against the wooden paneling of the carriage cabin.

The sudden halt of the wagon roused her. A strange rustling reached her ears. Beside her, Catus sat straight-backed, eyes alert. Seeing her awake, he raised a finger to his lips and slowly pushed his chin at the five mounted men emerging from a host of trees ahead.

Quintus, leading with one other guard, reined in his horse. "Stop! We are a senatorial party from Rome."

In response, the riders increased their pace, pulling up thirty feet short of the battle-tested soldier. The strangers fanned out, staying to the left of the dirt path and avoiding the cobblestones on the right. Their clothes were grungy and stained, their expressions hungry and unafraid.

Tullia watched with a dry mouth and pounding heart.

A thick, muscular man with black hair streaming beneath a dented battle helmet urged his mount one step closer. "We'll let ya go, but'll take the wagons," he said in unpolished Latin.

Quintus replied by leveling his long metal spear at the man's chest. "Your last warning or you will die."

The bandit, wearing a stained tunic and threadbare scarlet centurion's jacket, sneered and uttered a profanity. With a nod, he kicked his horse forward. His men followed, swords drawn, incomprehensible battle screams rising from the depths of their throats.

Tullia jumped as someone touched her arm. She glanced down and saw one of the guards crouching at her side. His five colleagues lined up behind him, all concealed by the wagon. "Don't worry, Domina. They're outnumbered. Come this way," he whispered.

Catus gave her a reassuring nod. Tullia shot a nervous look at Quintus before letting the man help her to the ground. At his direction, she slipped through the partially open door at the back of the wagon.

"Domina?" Atia was quickly at her side. "Who—who are they?"

Tullia looked over her head, confirming her boys still slept. Eyes closed and hands tucked away, they were undisturbed. Next to them lay Chloe, wide-eyed with a blanket pulled to her chin.

"Bandits," Tullia whispered, turning back to Atia. "Sit with Chloe, keep her quiet."

The young slave moved to the trembling redhead, whispering in her ear to quell the tears. She also cuddled Dracus, now awake and beginning to whimper. Marcus slept on.

Tullia crept to a window and peeked around the drape. Her heart thundered as she watched the intruders close in on Quintus and his partner. *Yosef, where are you?*

In answer to her prayers, Yosef and six horsemen exploded from the trees behind the brigands. Thundering at full gallop, they engaged the robbers out of her view. She dropped the drape and moved over to the girls, putting an arm around Chloe. Despite her anxiety, Tullia sat still and listened as she tried to control her breathing. Battle cries and the clangs of metal mixed into a violent slurry. Horses snorted and the dull thump of objects falling on the ground accompanied the gradual decrescendo of combat noise. An eerie silence followed.

Tullia extended her arm to Atia and pulled her in. The three remained frozen, listening. Even Dracus had quieted. Insects buzzed and a horse nickered. After several tense moments, relieved laughter and victory yelps filled the cabin. Tullia blew out a breath at the comforting mêlée and let her muscles relax.

Yosef opened the carriage door. "Domina?"

She faced him, her voice shaking. "I'm fine. Anybody hurt? Who were they?"

Before he could answer, Dracus fully awakened. Crying, he filled the cabin with a scream, rousing his brother who joined the ruckus. Together the din overwhelmed the outdoor sounds.

Yosef offered a sympathetic smile and raised his voice. "We're all fine. I'll come back."

Tullia wanted fresh air. "Can you keep it open?"

After securing the door, Yosef loped away.

Tullia tried to relax. Still trembling inside, she offered a shaky, unconvincing smile to the girls. *Thank Juno for the men!* The family had never encountered thieves in years past. Atia and Chloe emerged from shock and soon quieted the boys.

Quintus peeked into the carriage. "Domina, no harm done. Local outlaws, all dead. We'll pull forward a few hundred paces for a short break."

The wagon lurched before she could agree.

After a few moments, they stopped, and Yosef returned. Dracus waited at the door and Yosef set him on the ground. Feeling stronger, Tullia disembarked with Marcus in her arms. Atia took the baby, and, with Chloe, led the children away.

Yosef took Tullia's hand. "Are you alright?"

"Yes, but I'll be better in a moment." She puffed her cheeks.

"Ah," he said, gesturing to the left.

Following his gaze, she slipped into the cover of thick bushes and wandered in several feet.

Returning, she smiled at her broad-shouldered hero. "That's better. Yosef, what happened?"

"Road bandits. The men are putting the bodies back in the woods. We've also acquired five horses."

"Who knew encountering thieves could be so profitable," she said, half-joking to settle her nerves. Yosef looked at her with sympathetic eyes.

After a two-hour lunch of bread, cheese, and wine, they resumed. The new horses, tethered to the last wagon, seemed content with the arrangement.

The following day, they crossed through the Pontine Marshes. The acrid smell of mud and dead vegetation accompanied the muggy heat. Sea birds squawked and clouds of mosquitos buzzed. Closing the window drapes and the constant use of hand fans helped with the bugs, but at the cost of a sticky interior and irritable children. Canals kept the road from flooding, but adjacent mud and water eliminated the soft dirt path, forcing the caravan onto rugged cobblestones that prevented any rest.

As Tullia considered leaving her noisy children on the road, she felt the wagon begin to ascend. *Thank Juno*, she thought.

She turned to Atia and Chloe. "We're leaving that wretched swamp. We'll cross a mountain and drop into Tarracina."

Atia blinked and swiped at a mosquito. "Yes, Domina."

Chloe said nothing, but one hand rubbed an angry red welt on the inside of her arm. Tullia opened the drapes. A cool breeze washed away the oppressive air and the bugs. Humming to herself, she relaxed, lying back on the damp bedding and attempting to rest.

* * *

The Villa Tulleus, a two-story, travertine building, glowed golden yellow in the late afternoon sun. The estate, constructed in the rolling hills west of the mountain, overlooked the northern outskirts of Tarracina, with the shimmering blue Tyrrhenian Sea beyond. Tullia recognized the stables and corral adjacent to the building and knew the horses and the men would have a restful night.

The exhausted caravan clattered up to the modest villa. A spry yet skinny man of fifty emerged from the open front door and hurried over to Tullia's coach.

Uncle Tucca stood with open arms. "Dear Tullia. So good to have you visit. Come in."

Tullia and the family followed him into the villa and Yosef took the wagons and remaining entourage to the outbuildings. He would stay with the men that night.

Tucca called for a slave as they came through the entrance. "You and your family will have a bath before dinner."

"Thank you, Uncle, that would be very nice."

"The marshes will wear you out," he responded, ushering them to the back of the villa. Larger than Tullia's bath in Rome, Tucca's allowed them all to bathe together in comfort, with warm water from the kitchen replenished by house slaves. Rose hips lent a sweet fragrance to the pool, but it went unnoticed by the boys as they splashed and giggled with Chloe. Tullia inhaled the scented steam and relaxed as Atia scrubbed her back. When she was done, Tullia turned and did the same for the girl.

Atia giggled, moving her finger in circles on the water's surface. "It tickles."

After bathing, they joined Tucca at his table for a hot meal of stewed fish with oysters, bread, olives, and wine. "Your men have a table with the same offerings," he said as they ate. "Everybody should sleep well tonight."

"Thank you, Uncle," said Tullia. "You are too kind."

He waved his hand. "It's nothing. Now tell me of my brother and your Mama."

"Poppi is on campaign in the East. Mama stayed behind for business, nothing else is really new." *Except Yosef is my man now.* She omitted this detail and returned her attention to her host. "But Uncle, how is your shipping company?"

He opened his hands at the grandeur of the room. "We are obviously doing well. Rome has stayed out of our business. As long as the grain flows northward, Rome is happy. And speaking of which, how is the new emperor?"

Tullia pushed down her distaste for Nero. "It's his second year and I understand he is well-liked. Since he is barely eighteen, it's rumored his mother makes most of the decisions." The gossip did not surprise her, considering what she knew of both people.

Tucca exhaled. "Let's hope it continues."

Tullia agreed, but had her doubts.

The meal and discussions complete, the travelers retired to a single large bedroom and all quickly found sleep.

20

Two days later and twenty miles from Capua, the caravan encountered a large military force camped on the north side of the road.

Yosef approached Tullia's carriage. "An imperial delegation returning to Rome from Pompeii. They know your father and have offered hospitality."

Tullia paused. They would be safe with Poppi's allies. After the tedium of the long trip, the prospect of new faces and discussions also lifted her spirits. "It sounds wonderful. Please accept on my behalf."

The party stopped at a site adjacent to the imperial camp. The slave girls walked the children around the area while Yosef and the men erected the family shelter.

Emerging from the wagon, Tullia saw open country with meadows and a few small farms. The green panorama stretched westward into the late afternoon sun. The rich fragrance from a recent spelt harvest sweetened the air. A few gulls cawed, far from the sea fifteen miles away. As she turned to admire the view, the tension of the trip drained away.

Yosef came to her. "Peaceful, isn't it?"

"It's lovely. Much nicer than the swamp, and quite relaxing."

"We'll have some time to admire it together." From the corner of her eye, she saw his hand reach for her back, only to withdraw. "But for now, your travel home is ready."

She took another deep breath, stretched, and allowed him to escort her back to the tent. Once inside, she removed her traveling wrap, and away from the company of others, allowed herself to glean a good look at him. With just the two of them now, her eyes lingered. He had donned his finest dark brown tunic, gathered at the waist with an elegant black leather belt and iron buckle — her Saturnalia gift to him the previous December. On his feet he wore formal leather sandals, their straps extending up and around his muscular calves.

Her lips brushed his. "Mars never looked better."

He returned a soft kiss. "And He thanks you, Domina, although as a Jew, I do not recognize your pagan gods," he said with a teasing look.

She snorted. "As an intelligent Roman, neither do I. Now, who's this royal party?"

"A young nobleman named Titus Vespasianus."

"Titus? Blond, stocky, a nice smile?" She could not hide her enthusiasm.

Yosef tilted his head. "You know him?"

"Oh, yes." She sat down and absently rubbed one foot as she recalled the night they met. "Remember when I attended that imperial ball, right after I married? It was there I met Nero and this Titus. He was the only good thing about that party. He must be seventeen or eighteen now."

"That sounds right. He's done well for himself," mused Yosef. "He appears to be in charge."

As Tullia relayed her experience, he helped her remove layers down to her light undertunic. She gave herself a sponge bath as she chattered. "Nero was vicious and cruel. Titus and another boy, Britannicus, teased him. They were so much fun. I always wondered what happened to them."

"He has apparently remained with the Imperial House."

"It must be terrible if he's around Nero. He's probably happy to get away." She hesitated at her next thought. "Yosef, there's something you should know about that night of the banquet."

"The business with the big slave? Of course, I know. I heard everything you told your parents that night."

Her shoulders sagged in relief as the burden of guilt lessened. "Yosef, I have felt terrible about asking you to lift your tunic back then. It made me no better than Nero." She fought tears.

He pulled her into his arms. "There is a big difference between love and malice." He stroked her hair. "You were young and in love."

"I still am—at least in love," she croaked, pushing down a sob and squeezing him.

"Easy, you don't want red eyes for Titus."

The tightness in her chest continued to ease. "I'll be fine, and thank you for being so understanding."

He shrugged. "Let's get you dressed."

After slipping into a powder blue stola and soft calf-skin slippers, she collected her hair into a stylish bun. Two gold hoop earrings and a delicate gold necklace completed the look.

"It's all I have in the wagon. There's more in Pompeii, but this will have to do."

Yosef winked. "Domina, you will definitely do."

"You are not objective but thank you." She gave him a peck on the cheek as he helped her into a lightweight, sapphire wrap. The loose hood covered her head.

They made the short walk to Titus's camp, a smaller version of a standard square campaign installation: enclosed by a defensive ditch, a central command tent, and flanking neat rows of soldier tents.

Two men guarded the entry point, snapping to attention on their arrival. "Domina," said one, dipping his head. "This way."

He led them to the command post. Cookfires burned at cross aisles, their smokey pine scent mixing with the pungent aroma of leeks in a pork stew—common fare for the legions. Soldiers, free of battle garb, milled about in tunics eating and drinking. Their boisterous laughter died when they spotted the guests, as they jumped up and murmured "Domina."

Tullia wanted to tell Yosef it was what respect looked like, but he trailed behind her.

Their escort passed them to a slave at the entrance to the temporary imperial residence. Larger than her own, the interior boasted matching orange, black, and gray Persian rugs, a scarlet couch strewn with black pillows, and a large table and chairs. Mouthwatering aromas from roasted lamb filled the space as slaves scurried to prepare the table.

A well-developed young man in a simple white tunic and sandals greeted them as they entered. Intense but warm blue eyes scrutinized them, and a confident smile creased his round face. Puffy cheeks spoke to his still young age as he bowed.

"Ah, Lady Tullia," rumbled Titus. His voice had deepened. He took her hands. "I remember you from years ago. You have only grown more beautiful."

Tullia beamed and removed her hood. "Master Titus, you grew up." She felt no compulsion for further formalities; after all, they were both patricians. His warm manner, like the boy she knew before, further encouraged familiarity.

Nodding in agreement, he gestured toward Yosef, standing a respectful distance behind Tullia. "You were with the soldier earlier."

Yosef bowed his head. "Yes, Lord Titus."

"Yosef is my personal attendant," said Tullia. "And has been with my family since I was a child. Where I go, he goes. Would you allow him to join us for dinner?"

Her tone left no room for questions, something Titus seemed to understand.

"Sure. Welcome, Yosef." He shook Yosef's hand, then led them to the table. The servants added a third setting as they fussed with plates of food and poured wine. Once done, they bowed and retreated, leaving the three to dine in privacy.

The host turned to his guests. "So, Lady Tullia, what brings you to the country?"

"Yosef, my two boys, and I are going to our cottage in Pompeii to escape the miserable Roman summer."

"Indeed. The seashore is much nicer, plus the town is intimate and safe." Titus chewed in a thoughtful, patient manner.

"We've gone every year since I was a girl. And you? Why are you and your men here?"

"Two months ago, and just north of the marshes, brigands roughed up a magistrate. We're to rid the Via Appia of the scoundrels."

"Well, we may know something about that," she replied, gesturing for Yosef to explain.

Matter-of-factly, Yosef told the story of the road bandits. "They were dangerous, but outnumbered," he concluded.

"I was terrified," admitted Tullia, swallowing a bite of lamb. "But when I saw how quickly Yosef and his men dispatched them, I realized we were never in any real peril." She hoped her words did not betray the angst she still felt.

Titus cocked a brow and looked at Yosef with new respect. "You lead the men?"

"I do, Lord," he replied, holding the young nobleman's gaze.

Titus did not react to such familiarity from a slave, but rather pointed his fork. "Yosef, I think together we could win some battles."

"Gentleman, can we return to our dinner?" asked Tullia, proud of Yosef, but ready to move on.

Titus waved a careless hand. "Of course, you're right. Enough about battles and bandits. Tell me, Lady Tullia, what of your father, General Flaccus?"

A frown tugged at her lips. "He's in Parthia with two legions."

"A pointless war," Titus said solemnly, echoing her expression with a frown of his own. "But our emperor is fat on power and thin on sense."

Tullia exchanged a surprised look with Yosef. Their host chuckled.

"Do you not remember the banquet well, Lady Tullia?"

"I do," she answered, heat rising to her cheeks, "but I thought, perhaps with time —"

"Nero and I might have mended our differences?" Titus asked. A dimple grew in his left cheek, then vanished. "Unfortunately, not. What has grown for him is his ego and self-importance, mitigated only by his idiocy."

Tullia felt Yosef's interest rise alongside her own.

Titus looked up and blew out an unapologetic breath. "Yes, it's blasphemy, but I know more than most in this case." His tone was not smug but rather desolate. "I grew up with Nero," he said. "He is unfit to rule and does not scare me." His eyes locked onto Tullia's. "I assume I can count on your discretion about this conversation."

She could not help leaning forward. "Of course. Rest assured we are your allies."

Titus's grin returned. "I never had a doubt." He rubbed his hands together. "Fortunately, Nero is easily annoyed. I enjoy picking at him every chance I get. Emperor or not, there's not much he can do about it—my father commands five legions and Nero needs him. Neither Nero nor his mother is so stupid as to try to cross us."

Tullia's thoughts cut in. *Why, Titus, it seems you are a fearless schemer. They're no match for you.*

"… especially after what he did to Britannicus."

She snapped back to the conversation. "Excuse me, what happened to Britannicus?" An image of Titus's small, vivacious companion flitted through her mind. She remembered how easily he had avoided Nero's lumbering chase.

"Nero killed him with poison," Titus said. "And nearly got me as well if I had taken one more sip of his drink." His eyes hardened, seeing something neither Tullia nor Yosef could. "I'll never forgive Nero for killing one I considered my brother."

The room grew silent as Titus's tense aura touched his guests. With his scarlet cheeks and clenched jaw, Tullia read his hatred of Nero and the emergence of Titus the warrior. She felt the tingle of a shared loathing as memories of Nero's reprehensible behavior rushed back.

She put a hand on his. "I am so sorry."

Titus's hand twitched under hers, but then he removed it and tapped her lightly on the fingers. "I thank you, Lady Tullia. Life is tricky in the palace, but I know the game."

"If ever we can be of service, please let us know," said Yosef in a clear voice. He looked directly at their host.

Fearing Titus's reaction to such a blunt manner, Tullia took Yosef's hand. "Yes, please do."

Titus boomed a deep laugh and tilted his head. "As I suspected. More than an attendant? A slave, but not really? Lady Tullia, you play a dangerous game yourself."

Relieved, Tullia raised her hands in mock surrender. "Yes, I do. Yosef and I have been together for three years." *And I might be carrying his baby.* "If you know my husband, you'll understand my choice."

"I do." He made a rude sound, and they laughed. "You can trust me."

"I surely hope so," Yosef added.

Titus wagged a finger. "You can. The *honorable* Vitalio Silanus is well known for all the wrong reasons. He is corrupt and unpopular in the Senate." He leaned back and pointed at Yosef. "Slave or not, I have no doubt you are the better man." His attention shifted back to Tullia, his face wearing a grimace. "But be careful. Adulterous wives can end up exiled to an island or worse, but adultery with a slave is almost too vile to contemplate. Society will not see it your way. This path could prove fatal to you both."

Tullia's meal suddenly felt heavy. "We know the risks and the rules. That's why I'll begin divorce proceedings upon our return to Rome."

Titus pounded his fist on the table. "By Juno, that's the spirit!" He took a gulp from his cup and smacked his lips. "Let me help if I can. I'll be your eyes and ears in the Senate and imperial court."

The warmth of his response, and the intimacy of the discussion, gave Tullia confidence she could weather a stormy divorce, never mind the pregnancy.

"Dear Titus, thank you for your candor and support. We'll get this done, you'll see," she said.

Over a dessert of honey cakes and wine, they relaxed, discussing the weather, Pompeii in the summer, and the five days remaining in Tullia's journey.

After finishing the final course, Titus stood. "Thank you both for a wonderful evening. Enjoy Pompeii and good luck with the future. If you need me, send a message anytime."

Tullia hugged her host. "Thank you, dear Titus."

Yosef shook his hand again, then he followed Tullia out of the tent. Side-by-side, but not touching, they crossed the imperial camp.

Once they were out of earshot and just footsteps from their own settlement, Yosef chuckled. "Divorce?"

She offered a sheepish look. "I meant to bring it up with you earlier, but there hasn't been time. I need to be free of him. Then we can be together openly."

"There's the little problem that you own me."

"I'm working on that." She bit her lip. "Part of the divorce decree will be that I get the slaves. As soon as I'm free of Vitalio, you'll have your freedom." A tense laugh escaped her. "I hope you'll choose to stay with me."

He put his arm around her. "It shouldn't be an issue unless another girl asks to see my genitals."

* * *

The next day, as the sun crept over the green mountains to the east, the caravan departed for Capua. The soft dirt path had returned, allowing for easy, well-rested travel. On the west bank of the Volterno River, they crossed a stone bridge and continued into the town.

Tullia again sat on the front bench with the nervous Catus, admiring the view and enjoying the warm afternoon, despite the slow traffic. At an intersection, the Via Appia turned northeast toward Caudine Forks, running past the enormous Amphitheater of Augustus. From her seat in the wagon, she counted six, two-story arched travertine supports flanking a larger, arching entry gate. A second set of arches loomed above the first and reached into the blue sky.

"You only see six of the eighty first-floor arches, Domina," said Catus. "They say it seats forty-thousand."

It was the most he had said to her on the entire trip. "Why Catus, how do you know that?" She tried to keep the shock from her voice.

"My grandfather was one of Augustus's soldiers sent to build it. He told me the story when I was a boy."

Unsure whether the building or Catus talking gave her the most amazement, she remained quiet and confined her attention to the massive structure.

Yosef arrived. "It's an impressive arena, isn't it?"

"Very," agreed Tullia. She gave a false frown. "But I'll miss the Via."

"Me too, but it's out of our way now."

They took the right fork, staying east.

After two days, they reached Nola, and turning south, followed the aqueduct road to Pompeii.

On the morning of the last day, Tullia stood in a meadow gazing at Vesuvius's summit as the men broke camp and the slave girls and children frolicked nearby. The rising sun illuminated the mountain, its green slopes and pointed gray peak in sharp contrast to the brilliant blue sky. A fluffy plume of white smoke floated from the summit. The cool morning breeze carried a weak aroma of pine. She touched her belly and wondered if she could just hide here with Yosef and their baby, away from Rome and away from Vitalio. But a sense of responsibility crept in. She raised her chin to the mountain. "I know it's impossible, but I also know once we get past all this, we'll have the life we want." The tops of the pines rustled in the wind as if to reassure her.

"We should make Pompeii by midday," came Yosef's soft voice behind her.

Tullia sighed, relieved he did not hear her musings. "It's so beautiful out here, but I'll be glad to get to the cottage and settle down."

He came to her shoulder and leaned over. "Me too. I'm tired of sleeping with men."

"Enough of that," she giggled, heat rising from her blushing cheeks. "Let's go."

Their entourage joined a noisy queue of walkers and wagons entering Pompeii under the Nola gate's stone archway. Tullia inhaled the salty air of a sea breeze and heard the caw of gulls. The port city was also cooler. Awash in pleasant childhood memories, she tried to relax. Hand on her belly, she reassured herself again. *We'll get through everything, one step at a time.*

Heavy midmorning traffic inched along the narrow one-way street—unlike Rome, there were no rules prohibiting daytime cart traffic in Pompeii. Despite being anxious to get to the house, Tullia appreciated the sluggish pace as it minimized the jolts and shakes of uneven cobblestones. Foot traffic bustled on narrow sidewalks tightly bordered by shops—potters, jewelers, bakeries, and taverns, to name a few. Most businesses had residences above and some had yellow, orange, or blue canopies over open doors. The gray-green color of the limestone tufa sidewalks contrasted with the red brick of the buildings.

The sweet aroma of fresh-baked bread floated into the carriage, softening the edge of the brackish air. Tullia's stomach growled. The boys awakened. Dracus looked out a window and garbled away in gibberish. Marcus, not quite crying, appeared to be processing the sounds and smells from Atia's lap. Chubby hands grasped thin air as he squirmed and squealed.

Squeezing between the slow-moving wagon and the elevated curb, Yosef walked his mount to their window. "Busy today. Shall I get some bread?"

She sighed in relief. "Oh, could you? At this rate, we may never get there."

He nodded, moving away as traffic ground to another halt. Tullia let one arm hang out of the window and closed her eyes.

"Domina." Yosef reappeared, hands full. "An ox cart lost a wheel," he reported. "They've just fixed it."

Her heart winced. "It only takes one." Reaching through the open window, she accepted two small round loaves, golden brown and still warm, and a purple fig. "Thank you. This helps."

"No wine right now," he said. "Sorry."

"We have water."

"I'll ride ahead to the cottage."

"Good fortune for you," she replied.

He turned his horse and left. Sitting back, Tullia handed Dracus a small piece from the round roll. Marcus had calmed and slept, so she, Atia, and Chloe split the rest.

Chewing a warm wedge, she pictured the vacation home. On a bluff immediately above the sea, she longed for the calming churn of the surf. Boasting a panoramic view of the bay, she remembered showing Poppi she could count. Not more than six years old, she pointed and called out each fishing vessel bobbing home to the busy Pompeii marina. With a happy frown, she missed those days, but knew the memories would also help her children enjoy their stay. The cottage, with its prestigious address on the Via Consolare sat five blocks west of the *Porta Marina* and the city's flourishing seafaring businesses.

Hours later, the entourage crossed the Via Vesuvio and the cottage soon came into view. A gabled portico of travertine shielded the front door and narrow porch from the weather. Covered with orange terra-cotta tiles, the roof contrasted with the beige stone of the building. Trim cypress trees, shooting high above the roof, grew at each end of the porch.

Bypassing the front door, her carriage continued left to the open access to the cottage's adjacent plaza. Enclosed by an iron gate and brick wall, the space served as a delivery and storage area. The wagon pulled in and Yosef helped Tullia and the sleeping Marcus disembark. Dracus scurried down the steps, crab-like, and spun around until Atia and Chloe, who took Marcus from Yosef, corralled him.

Beneath a scarlet sunshade on a raised wooden porch stood Auntie, a huge, gray-haired woman. The widow of a Roman magistrate and a close family friend, she lived in and cared for the cottage. Wearing a flowing purple tunic, custom-made to encompass her girth, the sixty-year-old tottered forward like an enormous eggplant and opened her arms.

"Auntie." Her hug buried Tullia in her bosom. Wriggling free, Tullia looked at Auntie's smiling face. "It's so good to be here. We've missed you."

"As have I, child. But where's your Mama?"

"She couldn't come."

"Again?" Gray eyebrows disappeared into the elderly woman's hair. "Oh, Tullia, I'm so sorry. Business?"

"Yes, always business. Poppi got called up, so she had to stay back."

"That damn emperor and his stupid wars." She turned to Yosef. "My, my, who's this? Is that Yosef, the giant?"

Grinning, he reached for her. "It's good to see you too, Auntie."

"Well, thank you, Yosef. I see you're keeping pace with me and still growing." Before he could answer, Atia and Chloe arrived with the children and received hugs from the elderly widow.

"You know where the honey dates are, so go ahead," she said to Atia, who herded Chloe and the children into the kitchen for a feast. Turning back to the couple, she raised a brow at Tullia. "It's now almost three years and I trust Yosef continues to be the answer to your disgusting husband? And when shall we never have to hear from him again?"

Age and marrying for love granted Auntie a sharp tongue

and an even sharper wit. The older woman had no patience for politically driven marriages such as Tullia's.

"As soon as I return to Rome," Tullia answered. "I'll start divorce proceedings."

Auntie gave her an approving nod. "Remember, even though I now live at the beach, I still know many magistrates who will gladly assist. If need be, I can contact them."

"Oh, Auntie, that would be wonderful."

Yosef smiled and hugged the plump woman. "Thank you, Auntie. We'll need all the help we can get." He excused himself to assist with unpacking.

The two women entered the cottage through a side door, Auntie chattering like a squirrel. Passing through the kitchen, they entered a hall, its stone tiles covered with a vivid scarlet and gold Persian rug. The atrium to the left shimmered in the bright light from the open shutters of three large windows overlooking the bay, as well as sunbeams through the roof's opening centered over a small impluvium. Collecting rainwater, it fed a subterranean water tank. Adjacent to the shallow pool stood a waist-high marble puteal, its cylindrical sides carved with fish and dolphins, giving access to the water in the cistern.

Before them hung three privacy curtains: orange, blue, and gray, each in the doorway of a bedchamber. Two couches, their wooden frames covered by matching green and purple-striped throws and topped with green cushions, nestled in the corner. A three-legged wooden table rested between them.

As Auntie pulled Tullia toward the patio on the right, Atia, Chloe, and Dracus scurried by and jumped into the large pool of the fountain. Like the house in Rome, the cottage had piped-in water feeding the fountain as well as a small privy and bath.

A smiling Yosef arrived, carrying baby Marcus. "Sorry." He stepped through to the garden and the sounds of splashing and giggling intensified.

Auntie stopped short of the patio door and pointed to the left. "Tullia, look at that wall. What do you see?"

"A blank wall."

"Exactly!" Auntie tapped her lips. "It needs something, and that something is you."

"What do you mean?"

"Your portrait, right there." She pointed, then framed the space with her hands. "An artist is coming tomorrow to paint your picture on that wall."

"What?"

"Yes, your picture. Actually, a fresco. You're so beautiful, your likeness should be preserved for future generations." Auntie's eyes sparkled. "It's my present for your twentieth birthday. Do it now, for if you wait..." Her voice drifted off and she gestured to her rotund figure.

"Oh Auntie, I don't know." *Her portrait?* Tullia felt her face flush as she touched the smooth white plaster. It seemed absurd to display her face for everyone to see.

"You don't know?" repeated Auntie with a laugh. "That's fine, child, because I *do* know. I know that wall needs you."

Bemused, Tullia observed the wall again, trying to imagine her face looking back at her. Frivolous or not, it captured her imagination. Her children and grandchildren could see who she was. She warmed at the thought, then turned. Gazing at Auntie's earnest face she realized she could also apply Yosef's rule and give her hostess what she wanted.

She raised her hands. "Alright. When?"

Auntie clapped and hugged her again. "In the morning. He insisted on the fourth hour—when the light is best."

The nervousness crept back in. "Who's this artist?"

"Amunus, Pompeii's most popular. He does frescos and mosaics. Remember the Saturninus villa? You passed right by it on the Via Nola when you came in. He did the huge floor mosaic of Alexander the Great."

"I know the villa, but not the mosaic," Tullia said, scrunching her face in an effort to recall.

"No matter." Auntie waved her hand, then gripped Tullia's arms again, nearly shaking with excitement. "He's a very good artist, but a bit eccentric. You'll have to be patient with him."

Tullia, becoming comfortable with the idea, waved away the comment. "I'm sure it will be fine. But now that I know what's coming, I need to get out of these clothes and into a proper bath."

21

The artist arrived on time, impressing Tullia—she had been watching the patio sundial.

Bassa, the cottage's old and cranky freedwoman, escorted a rail-thin man to Tullia and Auntie. "The artist."

Resembling a dandelion gone to seed, forty-year-old Amunus sported an explosion of gray-streaked, frizzy red hair. He wore a baggy gray tunic and shabby leather sandals housing bony feet. With energetic blue eyes flitting around the room and random body tics, he fluttered like an unkempt moth.

"Amunus," Auntie said, guiding Tullia forward by the elbow. "This is the Domina and your subject."

His head twitched in what Tullia assumed was a nod. "Where's it going?" he demanded.

The man offered neither greeting nor any sign of respect appropriate for an aristocrat of Tullia's standing. She squinted. "Where's what going?"

He gave an exasperated sigh and looked at Auntie.

Tullia's back stiffened. "Where does what go?" she repeated. Still, the artist would not look at her.

Auntie cut in. "It goes on this wall here, Amunus."

Still ignoring Tullia, the artist pulled a chair aside and went to inspect the wall. In the early morning light, bright sunshine had transformed the blank space into a brilliant white canvas, not that the artist seemed to care. He bobbed up and down on the balls of his feet as he hugged himself, each hand creeping out from under a skinny arm. One step forward, two steps back. Tullia said his name, but she was ignored yet again. Her fists clenched. The artist shuffled, to the left, then to the right. He mumbled, gyrated, and caressed the surface. He put his face to the wall, sniffed, and licked.

Tullia flinched at the sight. "What are you doing? Hey, Artist?"

Amunus continued to study the wall. Without turning around, he flung a hand back in dismissal.

Wide-eyed at his insolence, and her face burning, Tullia lunged for him. He was saved by Auntie as she gripped Tullia's arm and yanked her back. "Tullia! Be patient."

At her words, the artist jerked his head around and looked at both of them, his face impassive. He didn't seem to notice that Auntie's arms were now wrapped around the younger woman, nor that he'd come within an inch of being dragged out by his hair and unceremoniously tossed onto the street.

Tullia slowed her breathing, incredulous at his detachment. Flecks of dust swirled around his fluffy hair as she waited for him to speak. He remained silent, his eyes jumping between the two women.

"The wall will do," he finally said to Auntie. His mouth turned into a frown, one hand sweeping the air. "But not those clothes." It took a moment for the women to realize he was now speaking to Tullia. "Formal attire will be required. You'll sit in that chair and face me while I sketch your image. I fill in the colors when I do the fresco."

Tullia recoiled at his continued impertinence, but just as

quickly wondered if he had a point. She looked down. No, he certainly did not. She was clothed in an expensive blue tunic and matching belt, favorites of hers and good enough to signal her standing. Clearing her throat, she recaptured her aristocratic poise and ventured in a calm voice.

"Mister artist, I would like to wear what I choose," she said, with no intention of saying his name.

Amunus flicked a hand. "Absolutely not. A shapeless tunic is not appropriate for this fresco. You must be more, ah, regal. Not like a house girl."

Tullia's grace evaporated, and she raised a hand to deliver a much-deserved slap. Auntie caught her arm again. "Stop!"

"Domina?" A quiet voice came from behind them; it was Yosef. "Is there a problem?"

Tullia froze, embarrassed. Auntie's grip slackened, and she stepped away as Tullia answered. "Ah, no, we're fine."

Yosef's eyes bounced from her to Amunus to Auntie. "Very well, call if you need me." He slipped away.

Tullia glowered at the artist, who receded a step and finally looked in her direction with renewed focus. "I apologize if I have offended you in some way."

Auntie gestured at him. "Give us a moment." As the artist turned back to the wall, she pulled Tullia away and whispered. "Will you relax."

"Relax?" hissed Tullia, feeling herself swell with indignation. "He is an impertinent little rat. Licking the walls? Calling me a house girl? He is lucky I do not have him killed!"

"Tullia," coaxed Auntie, "he is an artist who understands nothing but art. He does not live in your world, but in a world of his own."

"Well, he's not long for either."

"Calm down and think. He's right about the clothes. You need something that makes you look more like the prosperous and intelligent woman that you are. Now, come on."

She took Tullia's hand and escorted her back to Amunus, who turned as they approached. From a side table, Auntie handed Tullia a stylus and wax tablet.

"You can pose with these and make it look like you are going to write."

The artist heard the suggestion. "No, no!" he blurted. "Just a portrait."

Tullia broke from Auntie and turned to Amunus. "I will wear formal attire. I *will* have the writing materials, and you *will* paint my picture." Her voice hardened. "Before you had a choice; now you don't. I am a senator's wife, and your impertinence may cost you your useless life. If I don't like what you paint, it'll be your last fresco." She paused. "What now, *artist?*" The last word shot from her mouth like spittle.

Amunus cringed, his voice cracking. "Y-yes, D-Domina. Name the time tomorrow and I will be here."

Tullia turned her back on him, pleasure rippling down her spine. "Auntie, please set it up and get this urchin out of my house."

As Auntie hustled the artist away, Tullia turned and bumped into Yosef coming from the kitchen. She made eye contact and realized he heard the exchanges. "Not a word," she scowled.

He grinned as she escaped to the patio.

That night, they argued about the day. "Tullia, he's harmless and lives outside the world of your rules."

"Then what's he doing even coming around here?"

"According to Auntie, he's a great artist, and people tolerate him."

"Well, that remains to be seen. And don't think for one moment that I'll apply your rule to that grubby little dormouse. He's done nothing to deserve it."

Yosef sighed and hugged her. "Let it go. He is not worth losing sleep over. Tomorrow will show if he's any good."

She snarled but agreed to forgo judgment.

22

Amunus returned the following day with an easel, canvas, and a wooden box of charcoals. He arranged his tools on a table in front of the chair and bobbled once more on the balls of his feet. His eyes paid close attention to his subject as he bowed.

"You look quite lovely today, Domina."

His now pious behavior rankled her. "What, no house girl?" she demanded.

He blinked and dropped his head further. "My apologies, Domina, I meant no disrespect."

"Then begin."

He gestured at the chair. Sitting, she watched him like a tiger ready to pounce. He paused for a moment over the tablet and stylus, then took both, positioning the former in her left hand. The stylus he proffered to her right.

"Domina, if you would, please touch the tip of your lips, as if you are thinking of what to write."

Auntie looked on, beaming. "Tullia, you are absolutely beautiful."

Despite herself, Tullia felt proud. For the painting, she chose a green tunic and a purple shawl. She capped her black curls with a fine gold fishnet, and with matching earrings, felt regal. Rounding out the elegance was a gold ring mounted with a purple stone on her left hand.

The artist's cool blue eyes appraised her as they flitted up, down, left, right. He sighed, touched his chin, and started the process again. Tullia tried not to fidget. What was he waiting for? Before she could speak, he spun to the box of charcoals, grabbed a piece, and jumped to the easel. She heard frenetic scratching. Dark dust filled the air, and she fought a sneeze. His black fingers flew into the box for another chunk, then flashed back to the canvas. He dusted, mumbled, blew, sketched, and stared. Tullia's arm holding the stylus grew fatigued. How much longer? She needed to rest and scratch her nose. But before she broke her pose, the artist stopped.

Looking at the picture and back to his subject, he made two quick revisions and receded a step. A hand swept the air, his abrupt demeanor from the previous day returning. "It's done; you can go."

"Done? Why, you just started."

"I'm done," he insisted. He walked back to the table and hastily began packing his materials. "I'll work from the sketch to do the final fresco and fill in the colors then."

Tullia opened her mouth to object—he had gone too fast. Something must be wrong. Auntie's reverent gasp distracted her, followed by the sound of clapping.

"Oh, Tullia!" exclaimed the older woman. She turned, her eyes dancing. "You must see this."

Tullia rose from the chair. She stepped around the easel and stopped, speechless. The lines and shading revealed her in perfect black and white. Despite her annoyance during the sketch, he had captured large warm eyes and a soft face. The stylus just touched her thin lips, hinting at some writing to come. Her arched brows conveyed a thoughtfulness she had not felt as he worked. Stunned, she realized he had captured all the things she wanted to be. How did that come from such a man? Even her irritation receded.

The artist, again oblivious to his surroundings, fussed with his materials, turning over each piece of charcoal before tucking them away.

Before she could speak, he picked up his box and turned to go. "I'll leave the sketch and begin preparations for the fresco in the morning. Assuming I have met your approval, Domina." A hint of a wry smile crossed his narrow face.

Looking at the sketch, she understood his acceptance by society and suspected he did, too. But she did not have to like it, still smarting from his earlier insolence. Whether hubris or the ignorance of a truly creative mind, it was no excuse for his behavior. Maybe in Pompeii, people were more tolerant. She knew he would not last long in Rome, considering all power rested on social status. In her circle, acceptable punishment for rudeness by the lower classes, including artists, could be anything from a beating, jail, or death. And no matter how good they painted, artists were barely above slaves.

She lifted her chin. "It does. Plan to proceed in the morning." She waved in dismissal.

"Domina," he said with a bow as Bassa escorted him from the room.

"I told you he was a good artist," said Auntie.

Tullia grunted. "It's his only asset."

"But it's enough," she chided.

* * *

In the morning, Amunus arrived to prepare for the fresco. He dropped a box of materials on the table and offered a respectful bow. "Domina."

She dipped her chin, resisting the urge to squint.

The artist pointed a skinny finger at the wall. "Today I'll apply a base."

"Good," said Tullia, waiting for more information. None came. Her emerging irritation was balanced by curiosity, so she sat in the chair as he dumped a sack of white powder into a bucket.

"I need water," he said, shocking her by speaking.

She pointed to the puteal, a few steps away. "Over there."

On his return, he added water to the powder until he was satisfied with its consistency.

As she watched his slender hands spread the wet plaster on the wall, she raised her brows in surprise. There was a flowing grace to his movements—the perfect arc of every sweep of the trowel, the delicate touch-ups of bumps and pits she could barely see. *Maybe he's not so bad.*

He completed the work and gathered his materials. "I will return in three days and do the final painting on wet plaster."

"This is wet," she said.

"It's too rough. Three days." And he departed.

Remaining in the chair and unbothered by his abruptness, she wondered if she was getting used to him. As she tried to picture the final painting, ideas came to her about how it might look, and what she wanted later generations to see.

"He would ignore any suggestions I might make," she said, chuckling.

"What suggestions?" asked Auntie, coming into the room.

"Oh, nothing," Tullia replied, realizing the charcoal sketch captured all she could want, all it needed was color.

23

As promised, the artist returned in three days to complete the fresco. Tullia and Yosef left for a walk on the beach when he arrived.

"I'll handle everything. Have a good time," said Auntie.

Tullia wanted to watch him paint.

"He will drive you mad if you stay. You will constantly ask questions he will never answer. We should go to the beach," insisted Yosef.

She pursed her lips but agreed.

Cloaked in a gauzy pale-blue stola over a long-sleeved undertunic, Tullia adjusted a floppy straw hat and took Yosef's arm. Unlike Tullia, Yosef had no concerns about tanning, wearing a simple off-white tunic. But in a nod to her insistence, he wore a similar sun hat.

Deserted in the early hour, the gentle trail wound through green shrubs and grasses, ending at the black-sand beach.

Tullia pulled Yosef to the right. "Let's go away from the marina."

For easier barefoot walking, they ventured onto sand packed hard by the surf. A small fishing boat bobbed in the distance. They passed a wooden shed housing two overturned hulls, sitting up by the scruffy beach vegetation, beyond high tide.

Tullia slowed her steps, digging her bare toes into the

sand. Suddenly, Yosef stopped. He turned his back to the sea and faced her. "What's bothering you, besides the artist?"

Her hands landed on her belly. *The fact that I am carrying your baby*, she thought, but pushed it away. It was not the right time.

"I'm worried about Titus's words. Vitalio *will* kill us both if he finds out what's going on."

His forehead scrunched. "Three years we've been together, and now you worry?"

"Ah, well, yes." He had a point but now, she carried his baby. "I feel it's just too risky to stay married to him. Maybe it's because we are together so freely in Pompeii. Nobody knows us here."

"That is true, but we can't stay forever. The sooner you are free of him, the better." He picked up a piece of gray driftwood and threw it into the water. Tullia watched it float and bob with the waves.

She sighed. "I wish getting rid of Vitalio was as easy as throwing away that stick."

Yosef draped his arm around her and pointed her in the direction of the villa. "Come on, let's go back. Auntie will know the procedures for divorce. And maybe the artist is gone, and your portrait is ready."

She laid her head on his shoulder as they walked, tasting the salt air and embracing the tranquil moment. The mention of the picture also helped take her mind off the divorce and the pregnancy, but it was all so complicated.

Leaving the beach, they trudged up the hill to the front of the house, hoping to see the final painting from the atrium.

Auntie met them at the door and seized Tullia's arm the moment she saw her. "Oh, come see! Quick!"

"Auntie—wait, our feet," Tullia said, using her free hand to hastily dust the sand from her soles. Yosef did the same, but Auntie, mumbling something incoherent, pulled them along into the house. Waddling like a pudgy mallard, she urged them through the atrium.

"Come on, come on."

The chalky odors of plaster and wet paint reached their noses. Auntie pushed them forward and clapped her hands.

"Oh, Auntie," Tullia breathed, unable to say more.

Vivid purples, greens, and golds charmed the room as her image looked out. Using the delicate touch of the stylus to her lips, the artist had captured the fleeting moment of a far-away thought. Her eyes, not fixed ahead, but focused down and away from the viewer conveyed a sense of innocent vulnerability. The relaxed sweep of the shawl across her shoulders further contributed to a creative nonchalance, despite her expensive jewelry. She also liked her hair and how the artist had conveyed her sense of order, giving perfect symmetry to the hairnet.

Tullia felt her face flush at the wave of pride she felt looking at the beautiful image. *Could that be me?* She hoped so with her every fiber. Relaxing her shoulders, she exhaled, satisfied her descendants would know her.

The excited voices of others interrupted her musings.

"Domina, it looks just like you!" exclaimed Atia, clapping alongside Auntie.

Chloe grunted and pointed. Even Dracus, gurgling and grinning, seemed to recognize his mama.

Yosef's arm found its way around her waist. "You're very beautiful."

"I… I think he did do a good job," said Tullia, struggling for words.

Auntie snorted. "He did more than that, it's a masterpiece."

Unsure of what to say, Tullia held her hands up to the fresco and wiggled her fingers. "I never realized they were so long."

"As long as they don't grow," Auntie quipped. "Then we'd have to get him to paint a new one each year." The light faded from her eyes as she looked about the room, nodding to Atia and Chloe to leave, then turning to Tullia. "When you're ready, join me for an early dinner. We need to discuss your divorce."

Tullia wanted to stay and admire the fresco, but there was no point delaying the inevitable. Taking Yosef's hand, she joined Auntie on the cool patio where Bassa had laid out bread, olives, and a main course of steamed clams with carrots. Auntie sighed as she plopped onto a small couch and Yosef poured watered wine. At first, no one brought up the topic. Plates were filled and cleaned off as they ate, discussing the fresco and its talented but eccentric artist.

Pushing her plate away after three helpings, Auntie straightened. "I'm sure you know that in a marriage, either party can seek a divorce. The emperor and magistrates are usually not involved. A simple letter and it's done." She flicked her hand in dismissal.

Tullia fiddled with a bread crust. "And if Vitalio refuses?"

"He cannot. If he tries, he will fail. The courts will rule in your favor. The law clearly stipulates that divorce must be granted if requested. Vitalio can get a lawyer, but it will be a difficult fight."

"It can't be that simple," she said.

Auntie wrinkled her nose. "It's not. First, your father will need to support the request, which is uncertain. More importantly, Vitalio also has grounds for divorce; he can accuse you of adultery, a crime of which you are guilty. He can take your children and leave you to your parents. And since your Poppi knows nothing of the affair, he may be angry enough to disown you." She smacked her lips together and put her hands on the table. "Remember what happened to Julia."

Tullia knew the classic story of a father's fury. Over fifty years earlier, the promiscuous behavior of Emperor Augustus's only daughter, Julia, led him to renounce and exile her to an island. He never forgave her. Tullia was unsure if having a string of married lovers was worse than carrying on with a slave, but she nonetheless understood how wayward daughters could be treated by angry fathers.

Her mouth dry, Tullia dreaded the thought of Poppi being angry. Marrying Mama bucked Rome's traditions, but his rebelliousness ended there. Now, he adhered to the rules. He chose Vitalio because he had to. As much as he loved his daughter, she feared he would blame her for the failed marriage. That might change had he known of the abuse. *We should have told him earlier.* It was too late now. Her only hope was to gamble that his love for her would ease his wrath. But with deepening dread, she knew surviving his anger over the marriage paled next to the problematic affair with Yosef. Turning to the other two, she knew what was coming.

Auntie, stone-faced, pointed at her. "Worse yet, you have committed not just adultery, but adultery with a slave—a capital offense."

Her words were an echo of Titus's, but the bluntness still stung. Tullia sat, her mind numb. *A capital offense.* Vaguely aware of the statute, she had hidden behind her heart, ignoring the risks. An absent husband and a passive, if not supportive mother contributed to an illusion of security. *No more. There will be no life with Yosef.*

She rubbed her temples and raised her voice. "But what could I have done? My husband is a vicious animal and an adulterer; I loathe his very presence. And I love Yosef, whom I —" She softened her tone and looked at the table. "I'm pregnant with his baby."

Auntie froze.

Yosef flinched. "You're pregnant," he repeated.

Tullia looked up with a small grimace. "Yes."

"Great Juno!" exclaimed Auntie. One hand nervously pulled the fingers of the other. "What's next? Maybe you should move to Egypt and change your name. Do you have any *other* surprises?"

Tullia ignored the sarcasm. "That's it. Vitalio and I had relations at about the right time, but I think the baby is Yosef's. What can I do?"

The older woman stiffened. "Not much. Besides killing you both, we can add your baby to the list — unless he thinks it's his. It might buy you some time, but it doesn't help Yosef."

Tullia slumped. It had always been simple. Take the risk with Yosef or ignore her feelings and be miserable with a pig of a man. A feeling of dread clawed at her. She pushed her chair back, knocking it over and standing. "I need some time."

Her steps took her through the patio to the gate and

the beach. Descending the dozen stone steps leading to the earthen path, she grappled with regret, anger, and sadness.

The afternoon sun had slipped behind clouds and a cool breeze greeted her at the beach. The soft shush of the surf, and the warm sand between her toes, helped ease her tightness. With a few deep breaths, she looked out to sea. *My course with Yosef leads to certain death, but a life with Vitalio would be far worse.*

Cold water splashed her feet. *Worse than death.* There had to be a way to leave her husband. Even the idea of Egypt seemed a viable, albeit extreme option.

She addressed the horizon. "Without Poppi, I can never leave Vitalio. How do I convince him to help me?"

Gnawing on the problem, she wandered the beach. With dusk closing in, she sat on an old driftwood log, listening and watching the surf. She wondered if Balbus could help. He loved her like a daughter and Poppi trusted him with his life. It was a possibility since the old soldier knew about the affair.

She inhaled the salty air as she watched the fins of two dolphins cut through the water. *Maybe a mother dolphin and her daughter*, she thought. A mother and a daughter. Her mother. *Of course, her mother!*

With newfound energy, she returned to the cottage.

At the patio, Yosef and Auntie remained at the table, now clear except for three glasses of wine.

"You're back," said Yosef.

Tullia sat and reached for a glass.

"Are you better?" asked Auntie.

"Yes, and I think I have an answer." She sipped. "We need Poppi. With him on our side, Vitalio can be defeated, and

Yosef can be freed. But the only person who can convince him is Mama."

"We came to the same conclusion while you were gone," said Auntie. "Since she probably knows about the affair, I think she'll be fine with a divorce. The trick will be to convince your father."

Spirits on the rise, Tullia sat taller. "Well, we still have another month in Pompeii. It's plenty of time to figure out a plan for Mama."

"Not to mention Yosef's baby," added Auntie.

24

The click of a gull's beak on a window slat startled Tullia. "Sorry, you can't come in," she said, looking up from her tablet and squinting against a low afternoon sun. The bird cawed and flew away, leaving her sitting at the small table before her portrait. Her back popped as she stretched. In the two hours since Auntie and the household had gone to the market, she had puzzled over a plan for Mama. Writing the events of the previous days helped her think. She decided she would start with the pregnancy, hoping a third grandchild would soften her for what Tullia would be asking next.

A commotion at the front door signaled the end of the writing session. The family burst in, chattering and laughing.

Tullia crossed the atrium, hugging the children before the slave girls swept them out to the garden for a bath. "How did it go?" she asked Yosef, giving him a squeeze.

"It was fine. We visited a small petting zoo and saw a smelly two-humped camel. Dracus sloshed into a wet pile of dung and proceeded to play with it." He lifted his chin toward the patio. "Hence the bath." She swept her hand through the air. "That explains it. Where's Auntie?"

"Not far. She stopped at the post for a letter."

A few moments later, Auntie huffed through the open front door, her hair wet from exertion. She clutched a papyrus sheet. "A letter from your mama," she stuttered. "Your Poppi's been killed in the war." She waved the paper at Yosef as the tears began. "You read it, I can't."

Tullia's hands went to her mouth as her stomach twisted into a tight knot.

Yosef took the letter and read out loud:

Auntie,

Poppi was killed in a battle in southern Parthia, and Balbus was wounded. This occurred sometime in June, about when Tullia left for Pompeii. He has been buried in Antioch and Balbus is on his way home.

Please give my love to Tullia and help her through this difficult time. I will have more in the next letter. Until then, keep her in Pompeii.

Fulvia

Tullia trembled and took his arm. "Killed?" She looked at nothing, darkness converging on her vision, and tightened her hold on Yosef as a dark wave of grief gripped her soul. Her raspy breath, bubbling through a torrent of tears, choked her. She gulped air and cried—slowly at first, then the dam broke loose and with it all her composure.

Yosef pulled her to him. Her face in his chest, she sobbed, vaguely aware that they were moving—something soft supported her, then another pair of arms encased. Auntie, weeping, laid her head on Tullia's shoulder, offering murmurs of comfort.

As Tullia cried, memories surfaced. The gentle bear. His booming laugh. Strong arms encircling and protecting her.

The soft look of love in his eyes when he heard she was pregnant with Dracus. She suddenly longed for the soft purr of his voice as she curled next to him in a summer thunderstorm. She would never know such safety again. Never again. Never. She moaned and said his name. Her legs limp, gentle hands helped her lie on the couch. She swirled in grief, seeing nothing and too weak to help.

* * *

She opened her crusty eyes to late afternoon shadows, realizing she had slept since the morning. Alone on the couch, she sniveled and rubbed the sleep from her face. Poppi was gone. She took a deep breath and ventured with shaky steps out to the patio fountain. Splashing cool water on her face, she felt the awful void of the loss reemerge, and with it came the fear for those left behind. *Mama and me. And Yosef.* Where it left Vitalio, she could not say, but she knew he would be more dangerous than ever. The reality of Poppi's death would see that happen.

Dracus scuttled out to the patio. "Mama! Mama!"

In a single motion, she wiped away her tears and forced a gentle smile. "Why, Dracus, what have we here?"

A tiny green tree frog wriggled in his small fist, its front legs paddling in a fruitless attempt at escape.

Atia rushed from the cottage, sweeping the patio before her eyes landed on the mother and her child. "Domina, I'm so sorry. I turned around, and he was gone."

"It's fine," said Tullia, pulling Dracus to her. "Let me take him now. Go back in." As Atia turned to go, Tullia gently removed the wriggling creature from his hand. "Now, where shall we put him?"

Her son pulled her over to the gurgling fountain, he pointed at the base. "Ba-gaba."

"Down here?" she asked, squatting. Dracus flicked a hand at the site. She released the tiny animal who, in two jumps, leaped to the safety of a small mulberry tree. The boy squealed with joy.

"There, he's happy now." She picked up her son, carrying him into the cottage, his soft cheek against her face.

"Let me help," offered Atia, eyes full. "He needs his nap."

"No," replied Tullia, wanting to be with her son. "I'll take him. See if they need help with the meal."

Atia wiped her nose. "I'm so sorry, Domina," she said, leaving.

Tullia put a quiet Dracus on the bed—he seemed ready to sleep. After she covered him and checked on Marcus dozing in his crib, she took a moment to think. Where does this leave Mama and my family, never mind Yosef? If Vitalio inherited everything, as was the custom, she knew all of their lives would be ruined. She prayed Poppi had made a strong will that gave the family fortune to Mama. Her husband would be angry, no, furious, but there would be nothing he could do. Sitting on the edge of the bed, she shook at her next thought. Careful not to wake Dracus, she left the room, needing to talk with Yosef and Auntie.

She found them at the table picking at a cold meal. After sending Atia to watch the boys, she sat. "Thank you for your comfort earlier."

Auntie reached for her hand. "These are hard times, child."

Yosef gave a sad smile but remained silent.

Tullia narrowed her eyes. "If Mama inherited everything, she is in grave danger. All Vitalio has to do is kill her, and he gets it all."

Yosef and Auntie exchanged a knowing look.

"If *we* can think of it, your mother has," said Yosef. "She'll be way ahead of us."

"I agree," said Auntie. "She'll have made plans to protect herself and the family fortune."

Tullia put her face in her hands and moaned. The urgency she felt for her mother outweighed her grief. She looked at them. "We *must* get back to Rome."

"Not before the next letter," said Auntie. "There'll be something in there."

"I think that's why she told you to stay in Pompeii," said Yosef.

Looking at their faces, Tullia knew they were right. "So, we wait."

* * *

After three agonizing days, a terse note arrived. The writing was scrawled, far untidier than the last one, as if written in a great rush.

> *Tullia,*
> *Go to cousin Varus's villa in Ostia. Leave the day after you get this. I will meet you there.*
> *Mama*

25

Yosef shouldered a small duffle with their travel belongings and made his goodbyes to Auntie and the family. "To the marina, then," he said to Quintus.

Giving Tullia his arm, they followed the soldier through the humid fog of the early morning. The cool air helped clear his head while the sad cry of a shearwater matched his mood. Holding Tullia for much of the night, Yosef had listened to her renewed grief over Poppi and fear for her mother. He had wiped her tears and helped coax her to sleep. The expression of her feelings over her father's death brought forth his own, mostly sadness and emptiness tempered by the reality of professional soldiers. Like slaves, they could be killed at any time.

The moment he read the first note about Poppi's death, his chest tightened with concern, in part for his situation, but more for the survival of Tullia's family, including his baby. Vitalio would stop at nothing to acquire the family fortune. The second note started their journey down an uncertain road, but one sure to lead to Vitalio. But that was days ahead in Ostia. He refocused his attention this morning on crossing the bay from Pompeii to Putoli.

Reaching the wooden dock, Yosef felt Tullia shiver in the cold. He pulled her closer, happy she had agreed to the hooded cape over a heavy linen tunic, and eventually, the practical leather *calcei* on her feet. Yosef, protected from the chill by a wool cloak over a belted tunic, had opted for less clumsy sandals.

Through the gray dawn, he saw the bobbing fishing fleet. Deckhands and crew scurried by, shouting or swearing as they tossed ropes, baskets, or boxes into their boats.

Tullia sunk deeper against Yosef. "I am the only woman," she whispered.

He tightened his hold. "Don't worry, they are busy trying to put to sea." He watched the workers move through their routines, squinting at any man whose eyes lingered on Tullia and glad for the knife on his belt.

At that moment, Quintus stopped. "Here we are."

A boat captain, his deeply tanned face the color of cowhide, waved them to the pointed stern of a vessel moored midway down the line of at least twenty boats. He bowed deeply. "Welcome, Domina Flaccus and Master Yosef. I'm Marius and honored to assist you in your journey." His raspy voice sounded like the scrape of a knife on a wheel. "And this is my crew," he offered, pointing into the boat.

Four muscular men in loincloths dipped their heads, mumbling "Domina" in low voices.

Before they boarded, Yosef turned to Quintus. "Thank you. We'll send word as soon as we can." They shook hands and the soldier departed.

Marius extended a thick hand. "Come aboard, we have cleared a place for you." He led them to a wide chair shaded by a blue canopy. "You should be most comfortable here."

The boat tipped slightly as they edged past the horizontal wooden tiller, then between the rowers and toward the padded seat of the chair.

"It's more like a little couch," commented Tullia, pulling a folded blanket over her legs.

Impressed at the accommodations, Yosef pointed to a haphazard pile of nets, traps, and harpoons sitting on the dock. "That's what he cleared out for us. Remember, he's a commercial fisherman by trade."

She offered a sidewise glance. "And how can he afford to lose a day to us?" she whispered.

Yosef chuckled. "Easy, we have covered twice his expenses for the day, plus he can brag about transporting a senator's wife."

As they talked, the captain moved to the tiller and issued orders. "Man the oars."

After a dockhand released the mooring line, Yosef felt the jolt of the first strokes as the oarsmen cut through the water. As a boy, he once crossed the Tiber with Balbus to pick up flour from the Janiculum water mill, sparking his interest in swimming. For two years thereafter, Balbus took him to a public bath in Ostia used by the army to teach swimming to military recruits. As Yosef grew older, the lessons stopped but he remained an accomplished swimmer.

"The water in the bay today looks pretty smooth. I doubt you will be seasick," called Marius.

Yosef raised his chin in acknowledgment. "Let me know if you get queasy," he said to Tullia, speaking in a soft voice.

"I think I'm alright but feel tight with nerves."

Yosef, also on edge, tried to relax his shoulders. "We should make Putoli by afternoon, spend the night, and catch one of the family's grain ships to Ostia in the morning." Repeating the plan allowed him to consider flaws as well as look past his angst.

Facing the stern, Yosef watched the rippling backs of the rowers as they drew their oars to their chests, glad to be a passenger. He saw the early morning sunlight illuminate the gray dome and green skirts of Vesuvius, as the brick and wooden warehouses of the Pompeii marina grew smaller. Gulls cawed and followed the vessel, and a fresh sea breeze replaced the musty smells of the fishing boat.

"There's the cottage," he said, pointing.

"And here we are, on our way to Ostia," she said, taking his hand and squeezing.

On our way to Ostia. The crude plan came together quickly with the sea journey easily outlined, their fate in Ostia less clear. It all hinged on Mama—if she made it, and what she knew. They were fighting a ruthless senator. His muscles tightened again.

"Yosef?" asked Tullia, concern in her eyes.

He didn't realize she sensed his change. "It's nothing, just trying to stretch."

"You are a bad liar."

Not wanting to discuss the unknowns with her, he lied again. "I hope we find that grain ship."

"I'm sure we will."

He was also sure but continued the ruse. "I know, but I worry."

"Well, don't. But I'm concerned about Auntie and the children. What will happen to them?"

He was glad for the change of topic. Their fate was on more solid footing. "Quintus and I discussed it last night. He'll guide them back to Rome. Probably overland unless we arrange for them to come by sea. We'll have a better idea after we meet with your mother."

"That sounds fine," and she curled closer to him.

After releasing a slow breath, he willed himself to be calm and listened to the captain call "pull" in a regular, slow beat. The crew settled into a steady rhythm, skimming across the smooth water. Yosef's lids grew heavy in the warm sun, and he dozed, lulled by the melodic thrum.

By midday, they passed the island of Nisidia, turning north into the bustling Putoli harbor. Dwarfed by at least a dozen grain ships, Marius guided the craft to the northwest edge of the docks, where other fishing vessels bobbed with the waves.

At a crude berth, a sailor tied their boat parallel to the concrete dock. After he stepped ashore, Marius helped Tullia disembark, Yosef behind her. Standing on the dock, Yosef turned to the captain. "Thank you, Marius, for safe passage."

He bowed. "It was my pleasure, Master Yosef." He pointed. "The ship we discussed earlier is the fourth one over, the *Ceres*." He paused. "Named for the goddess of grain, you know."

Yosef feigned surprise. "Oh, yes. Very well and thank you again."

As they crossed the wharf, Tullia snickered. "Didn't you know the meaning of Ceres?"

He snorted. "Of course, but why ruin his joy by telling him?"

"This is why I love you."

Walking along the busy pier, its shoreline bordered by open warehouses, rigging repair shops, and taverns, they encountered men wheeling carts loaded with crates of merchandise or others lugging sacks of grain. In their path, a bag had ruptured, spilling grain onto the concrete wharf. The sweet aroma of fresh durum wheat dominated the sea smells. Emboldened gulls landed in the pile in a fearless quest for food. Laughing boys chased the birds as men swept and shoveled, trying to repackage the valuable load.

Yosef steered them around the chaos. "Messy business. There will be more than grain in that bag."

"Thank Juno the good bakeries sift before they mill," she offered, making a face. "I prefer my bread without pebbles."

Yosef smacked his lips, recalling the unpleasant grit of bad bread. "Me, too."

At the *Ceres*, Yosef found the captain, a ruddy-faced skinny whip of a man named Cotta. "This is the Domina Flaccus. Her family owns your vessel."

Cotta stepped back, recognition stirring in his eyes. "Why, yes, Domina. I met you once in Ostia when you were very young." He bowed. "How may I help you?"

Tullia dipped her chin. "Thank you, Captain Cotta. My man Yosef and I are in urgent need of transport to Ostia, our cousin Varus awaits us."

Cotta extended his hand. "Welcome, Yosef. It looks like the Domina has an able-bodied companion."

"Where I go, he goes," offered Tullia without further explanation.

Yosef saw comprehension in Cotta's face. "Very well. Ostia it is. I can offer a small guest quarter for you. Yosef, can you bunk with the crew?"

"That would be fine," replied Yosef, wanting them to remain as unmemorable as possible.

"Very well. We leave in the morning and should make Ostia in three or four days, weather permitting."

"Dear captain, that would be most appreciated," said Tullia.

"You will need decent accommodations for tonight. Come with me."

They followed him across the wharf to a cobblestone road leading up a small hill. After two blocks, they came to a large, whitewashed cottage. The sea captain stopped before steps leading to the entrance.

"The harbormaster and his wife live here. When a senator or magistrate needs a meal or a room, they can usually help." He gave a wry smile. "Much nicer and safer than the taverns on the docks."

As good as his word, Cotta made the introductions. They were welcomed to the home and given dinner and lodging. Yosef bid Tullia a good night as an older slave named Gellia accompanied him to the slaves' quarters at the back of the cottage. Lit by flickering wall lamps, the room housed several sleeping pallets.

"That's yours," snarled Gellia, pointing to a pallet in the corner. "We save that for the slaves of muckety-mucks who pass through."

Several of the house slaves lounged on other pallets watching.

Twenty years younger and a head taller, Yosef raised his brows and gave a false frown. He looked down at the petulant slave. "Gellia, it's been a long day." He cracked his knuckles and continued in a cold voice. "And unless you want this slave of a muckety-muck to break your nose, I'd suggest you reconsider your attitude." Using his thumb and forefinger, he thumped the shocked man in the middle of the forehead. "Where do you sleep?"

The wide-eyed Gellia stepped back and pointed to a tidy bed in the opposite corner.

"Excellent. I'll take it. You can have the muckety-muck pallet for the night. Also, I'm a light sleeper with a big knife, so do be a good boy."

Yosef heard the unmistakable snicker of the other slaves and knew Gellia would not be a problem.

As he stretched out on the well-padded pallet, Yosef reflected on their good fortune—the uneventful bay crossing, securing a berth on the *Ceres*, and decent accommodations for the night. But not feeling as confident as he sounded earlier, he fidgeted all night, on alert for Gellia.

At first light, they returned to the *Ceres* for the voyage to Ostia.

26

Tullia and Yosef enjoyed good weather, making Ostia in three days.

"It's impressive. Many more ships than Putoli," said Yosef. "All of Rome's grain passes through this harbor." He applied a cool cloth to Tullia's forehead. "You'll feel better once you get off the boat."

Tullia remained silent, caring nothing about the harbor. With closed eyes, she willed Yosef's ministrations to ease her headache. Unlike the bay, the sea was not smooth, rocking the boat day and night. Unrelenting nausea marred the trip — she ate little and spent most of her time in bed.

Yosef, obviously impressed by Ostia, continued his chatter. "The grain goes up the Tiber to Rome on barges, but the river's too small for the ships, so we dock here, and the cargo is moved by wagon to warehouses over on the river."

"Yosef, I don't care," she snapped. "I just want off this boat."

She pushed down bile as Yosef helped her up to the deck.

"Take a little time at the rail before you get off. It's about an hour round trip to Varus's. I need to go and find a ride," he said, apparently unbothered by her crankiness.

She squeezed out a half-smile, and he left. Hearing the din beyond the ship, she lifted her throbbing head to a busy wharf humming with men lugging bags of grain to waiting wagons. Mule's brayed, gulls cawed, and sails snapped in the breeze, none of which helped her headache. Squinting against her discomfort, she saw the concrete wharf snake off to her left and into the city. Across from her rested several wooden warehouses, doors open for business. At the edge of the row of buildings sat a two-story, red brick structure she recognized as the marina bathhouse where Yosef learned to swim. She blew out a raspy breath. Never mind swimming, but a hot bath would feel nice right now.

Cotta arrived, helped her disembark, and led her to a bench on the dock. "You will feel better soon, Domina. Take care."

As he departed, she thanked him and enjoyed the feeling of the wooden slats beneath her. She curled her fingers on the edge, hanging on as the swaying in her head regressed. *That will be my last boat ride.*

Yosef appeared with a driver and an open carriage. "He knows the address."

Tullia swallowed and stood, glad for his strong hands as they helped her into the coach. Nausea receding, she forced a weak smile. "I feel better. My headache is almost gone."

Yosef reached into the carriage and patted her leg. "In another day you'll be fine."

He hopped aboard and they lurched forward, clip-clopping along the concrete wharf, dodging men and wagons, finally making it to the cobblestone road into the city.

"I thought the ride would be bumpier," said Tullia, fearing the return of her headache.

"I noticed that also. The stones in the streets are packed much tighter than the country roads," replied Yosef.

At the city center, they turned at the Temple of Jupiter, its sixteen-step apron leading through the eight-column portico into the gray granite building and joined the eastbound traffic to exit the city.

"It does not seem as busy as Pompeii," commented Tullia, feeling her stomach continue to relax.

"It's hard to know. This street is wider, and it seems most of those buildings are warehouses or for storage," replied Yosef.

"He's right," came the tenor voice of the young carriage driver. "Except for the city baths," he gestured at a white granite building on the right, "and the theater up ahead."

Flanked by two umbrella pines, the curved wall of the brick amphitheater rose several stories above the road. "It seats about four thousand," offered their impromptu tour guide.

At the arched Roman Gate, they passed into the lush countryside, the road shaded by pines and tall trees, their green leaves rustling in the breeze. The salt air gave way to pine scents and the weak must of the forest.

"I prefer the smells of the land over the sea," said Tullia, taking a deep breath, pleased the nausea was nearly gone.

"You're just a city girl at heart," whispered Yosef.

In short order, the carriage turned onto a crushed shell drive.

"Here we are," announced the driver.

Varus's modest country villa, with its vine-covered brick walls, and a trellised outdoor eating nook, sat on the left side of the road. Once they stopped at the front door, two house slaves hurried to help them disembark. Yosef paid the driver.

Mama stood on the porch. Tullia rushed to her, falling into her arms as she had done years ago at the imperial banquet. "Oh, Mama," she moaned, her legs weak but her insides awash in comfort that they had both made it. The feeling was tempered by grief for Poppi. Further, in the back of her mind lurked fear over Vitalio and what he might do. Her stomach reknotted. Holding on tight to her mother, she tried to push it all down and regain some composure.

Her mother eventually pulled away. "I'm so thankful you made it. How was the trip?" she asked, touching her daughter's tear-streaked cheek.

Ignoring her inner turmoil, Tullia made a face. "I was sick on the boat."

To her surprise, the corner of her mother's lip lifted for a fleeting second before her eyes misted over. "Just like your Poppi."

They both cried at the mention of his name.

"Remember the time he tried to bake bread?" sniffled Tullia through a sad smile.

Mama raised her brows. "Faustina was so mad she chased him out of the kitchen. It took the rest of the day for her to clean up his mess."

Tullia recalled how Poppi shrunk under Faustina's verbal assault, a deep warmth creeping into her chest. The feeling layered over sadness as she stuttered. "And he burned them. Two loaves, like black rocks from Pompeii."

Mother and daughter both chuckled through tears.

The shared memory made Tullia swell with love for her parents. Now it was only Mama. *Poppi is gone.* It was time to face the uncertain future together, and, happily, with Yosef. Her heart fluttered. She knew he was strong.

Mama straightened; her face serious. "Varus and Siculus

will return soon. There'll be plenty of time to grieve, but for now, we must get down to business." Stepping to Yosef, who had waited patiently with the slaves, she offered a sad smile. "Welcome back. Thank you for your protection."

Before he could speak, she hugged him. Tullia joined in, wrapping her arms around them both.

Breaking the embrace, Mama led them across a modest atrium furnished with a single orange couch and wooden table sitting beneath a striking wall fresco. Depicting a marine scene, a fishing boat floated in choppy white-capped waters beneath an azure sky. Two gray dolphins dove next to the vessel as men pulled up a net full of red, brown, and shiny silver fish. Tullia remembered the painting from family visits. It triggered more memories of Poppi, and she pushed them away.

"After the two of you clean up, come back here," said Mama, gesturing to a dining table.

Yosef and Tullia walked out to a colonnaded patio, its center flush with vegetation. The area included a fountain and an enclosed privy. Like the Flaccus villa in Rome, cousin Varus's home tapped a local aqueduct and enjoyed the luxury of running water.

A house girl followed them with tunics and towels, intent on helping them bathe at the fountain, but Yosef took the fresh laundry and sent her away. Confusion flitted across the girl's face, but she only curtsied and left.

Turning back to Tullia, Yosef helped her clean up from a large bowl of steaming water and the bubbling pool from the fountain. As she donned a clean, pale-yellow tunic of soft Egyptian cotton—a gift from her father—she imagined Poppi's earnest face as he must have deliberated over the choice. *A general and a warrior selecting a dress for his daughter.* Warm sadness punctuated the memory.

As she mused, Yosef washed and slipped into a fresh tunic. Too short and oversized at the waist, it required a belt to bunch the excess material.

Tullia giggled. "You look like a tiny turtle in a giant gray shell. It must be Cousin Varus's."

"Better than nothing." He held out his arms and did a mock spin.

Leaving the soiled clothing on an adjacent bench, they returned to the villa, Yosef trailing her at a respectful distance. Tullia did not want to presume that her cousin knew anything out of the ordinary. She was sure Mama had long guessed of their relationship but wanted to remain discreet. She touched her tummy. The time for full disclosure was coming.

Mama and two men stood over the table, which was now littered with glasses of wine, and plates of olives, cheese, and prawn patties. The smell of freshly baked bread lingered in the air. "Tullia, you will remember Varus, your father's cousin," said Mama, gesturing at the bigger of the two.

Nearly Poppi's age, portly, and bearing a friendly face that reminded her of Titus, Varus had gray curly hair and spoke with a soft lisp. "The thervants have been sent to Ostia to shop. The villa is empty." He raised his brow at Yosef. "Thorry about the tunic."

Yosef bowed his head. "It's fine. Thank you."

Mama gestured at the other man, who edged forward. "You both know Siculus."

The family accountant resembled a nervous chicken with

his red, skinny neck, and bulging, jumpy eyes. He bobbed his head at the newcomers and chirped, twisting his fingers over and over as he spoke. "We're glad you made it."

"Please," Varus said, spreading a hand out wide. "Let's thit and eat."

Nobody questioned Yosef's presence at the table.

Mama cleared the air. "Varus and Siculus know Yosef is more to you than a servant. Continued discretion is advised, but your secret is safe." Both men's faces conveyed their agreement.

After they finished eating, Mama looked at Tullia. "Your father's death is far more than a tragedy. It's raised serious dangers for all of us. Your Poppi's power kept Vitalio's vicious ambitions in check. Given a chance, he would steal the family fortune and have us all killed. We must discuss our finances in the event I'm murdered."

Tullia felt a chill. "Mama? Have there been threats?" she asked with a shaky voice.

"Nothing yet. But you two must be made aware of our situation, in case of the worst. Vitalio will use all methods of chicanery to steal everything. That would certainly include violence."

"We know that all too well," said Tullia, tightening her lips at brutal memories. How many times had he called her a whore? Who could count anymore?

The hitting started barely five months into the marriage—a week after he called her a sow. She and Mama had returned late from a visit to the Lucullus pleasure gardens, the blooms and aromas of spring in abundance.

Faustina opened the door with a taught look. "Domina, the senator awaits you in your bedroom. He appears drunk."

She entered the room. "Husband?" she asked, her insides twisting. The odor of sour wine filled the space.

Vitalio sat on the bed gripping a cup. "Where have you been?" he growled, squinting. Before she could answer he threw the cup, jumped forward, and slapped her.

Her head snapped back, and he hit her again. Grabbing her shoulders, he threw her on the bed and straddled her. "I've been here for hours," he hissed, his fetid breath on her face. She struggled but stopped after a third blow. Knowing what was coming, dark dread covered her fear.

After he finished, he left the room without a sound. The heat on her cheeks and the burn between her legs held her on the bed for several moments until she slowly sat up, jaw clenched, eyes dry — too enraged for tears.

Mama arrived, patting Tullia's forehead with a damp cloth. "We will have to be more careful."

Tullia pushed her hand away. "Yes. I'll need to avoid my pig of a husband," she snapped. She looked at her mother and blew out an angry breath. "I wish I could kill him," she said, spitting out the words in a staccato burst.

Vitalio surprised her two more times — always in Poppi's absence — with insults and violence, one time wrenching her shoulder so badly she wore a sling for a week. Each visit ended with her rape.

The physical abuse culminated in his vicious backhand during the eighth month of her first pregnancy. At least it reopened the door to Yosef.

* * *

Reliving the misery of those early days, Tullia fully recognized Mama's fears. They had to outsmart Vitalio and needed to start now.

The memories melted as Mama grasped her hand. Tullia swallowed thickly. "And Poppi's will?"

"It's legal; everything has come to me," her mother affirmed. "The document is being held by a trusted magistrate in Rome. As long as I'm alive, I have control. I've also made a will of my own, giving all to you if I die, but in practical terms, your husband would control everything. Which means—"

"The first step is to divorce Vitalio," said Tullia, finishing the statement.

"Yes, and we'll initiate proceedings when we return."

"It may not be easy," said Tullia, recalling Auntie's words.

Her mother sighed. "That's true. By law, easy. You request it, and it's done. But in practical terms, it will take time. He'll contest the petition, arguing he's the surviving male heir, and therefore should be in charge of both the family and the fortune. But the argument will not outweigh your right to divorce, nor the power of the will. A good lawyer will claim a woman such as myself would be incapable of managing such a large estate. It's nonsense, but there'll be judges sympathetic to the view. We'll fight it, of course."

"How long with the court?" she asked.

"At least a year," said Siculus. A hand twirled in the air as he spoke.

Yosef leaned in.

"Yes, Yosef?" asked her mother.

"A year is a long time. What of your personal protection?"

"Taken care of now that Balbus is back and healed. He's

assembled a loyal group of men now protecting the villa and the family. I traveled here in secrecy with six of his guards."

Tullia crossed her arms. "So, we're trapped."

"We are and will be until we are rid of Vitalio," confirmed Mama.

"We need to destroy him in the courts or kill him," snarled Tullia. The words rushed out before she knew what she was saying, only that it felt good saying them.

Siculus squeaked and drew trembling circles on the table, his foot tapping loudly on the stone floor. Varus coughed, quickly scanning the room for intruders. Yosef studied the floor.

Her mother ignored the statement. "Let's focus on the legal route for now." A finger flicked to her left. "Siculus is here to review the Flaccus estate. You both need to understand the business side of the family." She turned to the tense little man.

His Adam's apple bobbing, Siculus consulted a paper and offered a clipped synopsis. "You have three farms totaling two thousand acres with two hundred workers, including slaves and freedmen. The main crops are wheat, olives, and wine. Each farm also has livestock. The annual income from the farms is about two hundred and forty thousand sesterces. You're also invested in other agricultural businesses and grain shipping, for another one point five million in annual revenue." He paused. "The *Ceres* is one of our ships."

"Auntie told us," noted Tullia.

The jumpy man continued, eyes widening and closing in equal measure. "There are no debts. Less household expenses and other overhead, the net annual income for the family is one point six million." He chirped and clucked through his words. "With all properties, investments, and other assets, you're worth around ten million sesterces, above the average for a senatorial family."

Tullia listened with an occasional nod. "I wondered about that."

"Your Poppi was very thmart about business," said Varus.

"Cousin Varus assists me in the marine investments," added Siculus. He glanced at Mama, his face scarlet. She flicked her chin toward him. "There is one more thing. Your father approved a monthly stipend for your husband. He never misses his payday."

"I'm not surprised," huffed Tullia, with a grim smile. She suspected it all along—after all, Cicada had needs and wine was not cheap.

Mama stood, signaling the end of the meeting. "There's much to learn. Tomorrow we'll go through the details. But first, I need a little time with Tullia and Yosef."

The group adjourned. Mama beckoned the two of them to the patio. The dim light of dusk, bolstered by the yellow flicker of three oil lamps, lit the area.

Tullia and Yosef took the patio bench as Mama sat in a chair opposite.

Her mother crossed her arms.

The fountain murmured.

Tullia fidgeted under her gaze.

Mama tilted her head. "Did you really think I had no knowledge of what you two have been up to for three years?"

Tullia froze. "Uhm," she mumbled, face on fire.

Even Yosef, staring at the ground, blushed.

"Ah—" stammered Tullia, her stomach in a knot, yet she was somehow relieved. "How?"

"Tullia. Are you really so naïve? After all, you live in my house. I am neither deaf nor blind—but I appreciated your attempts at discretion."

The gray fog of deceit lifted and with it, Tullia's spirits. She reached for her mother. "Oh, Mama, it has not been easy. We both feared for you, as well as the family reputation. But in the end, being together was all that mattered."

"And you?" asked Mama, looking at Yosef with brows raised.

He opened his hands. "I love your daughter more than life itself." He leaned forward and Tullia saw him grow larger, stronger, emerging now as a man, not a slave. Her heart nearly burst with love. "Domina, Tullia and I have the same rare gift shared by you and Poppi—we are together for love."

Tullia took his hand. Such perfect words. Mama had to now realize she was no longer a child, but a woman with an abiding love for a strong and very capable man. Call him a slave—but he was a man.

"Yosef is my true love. I will live with him or die with him," she said, and stood.

Yosef joined her.

Mama came to them, eyes glimmering. "I know all that." She pulled them in for a hug. "I love you both, but fear for you. There are hard times ahead." Stepping back, she looked at Yosef, her face relaxed, warm. "Tullia could not have picked a better man."

Yosef, taller than both women, looked down at Mama. "Thank you, Domina. We are a family." He flashed a mischievous smile of white teeth. "With your permission, I will wait to call you Mama until after the divorce."

Soft laughter followed and Tullia felt the air grow lighter.

"Can we move on?" said Mama, waving them back to the bench. "So, how far along are you?" She failed to suppress a twitch of a smile.

Tullia sighed, knowing it had to come up. "About four months." She paused. "But how did you know?"

"I'm your mother, you have a glow. I assume it's Yosef's."

"Yes, or so we hope," said Tullia.

"I would think so," replied Mama. "Although Vitalio was around once in the past few months," she swept her hand toward them. "Once cannot compare to many."

Tullia shrugged, unbothered. The whole discussion was leaving her tired. "Ma—," she began.

Her mother cut her off. "There's no need for explanations. This outcome was inevitable." Her face relaxed into a smile. "I could use a granddaughter."

Tullia stalled for time and rubbed her eyes—there was nothing further to say. She would divorce Vitalio, have her baby, and marry Yosef. It would all be easier with Mama's help.

Her mother furrowed her brow. "Back to the divorce. As you probably know, your affair with Yosef, at the very least, gives Vitalio solid grounds for divorce and at worst, Yosef's execution." She pointed at Tullia's belly. "As long as he thinks it's his child, you would probably be spared the sword, but after the baby comes, you'd be at his mercy. We must succeed with *your* divorce petition. And, obviously, until then, it's vital for you two to remain extremely discrete. He must never be able to prove the affair."

Tullia straightened. "We have hid it for three years, we will continue."

"Good," said Mama. "All of our lives depend on it." She turned to Yosef. "Once the divorce is complete, you'll be given your freedom. You will become a Flaccus through marriage to Tullia, assuming you can handle her."

Yosef stroked his chin. "Oh, I think I can do it. I have been practicing."

They all chortled.

PART IV

Enslavement

27

After one day in Ostia, Tullia, her mother, and Yosef returned to Rome. Tullia missed her children, and despite her problems, looked forward to seeing them. They were expected to return from Pompeii within a week.

On arrival, Faustina greeted them, pointing to her black eye. "Your husband just left, demanding to know where Siculus had gone. I didn't know and would not have told if I did."

Tullia rushed forward. "Oh, Faustina, I'm so sorry." She embraced the older woman and began to seethe with anger.

"Bastard," hissed Mama. "Did he say anything else?"

"Nothing I can repeat. We're still cleaning up." She spread her hand across the room.

Tullia saw torn privacy curtains and overturned furniture as Balbus joined them.

"It's my fault," he said. "The men and I were fixing a wagon wheel in the corral and missed the ruckus."

Faustina shrugged, raising her chin at Balbus. "If he had been in here, the senator might have shown some restraint, but it's also his home. He would have done as he pleased."

Balbus looked down. "My apologies, Domina. I should have been inside."

"What's done is done," said Mama, with a wave of her hand. "We will just need to be more careful."

Balbus dropped his head further, his face crimson. "You may be sure, Domina."

Yosef, sparing Balbus further embarrassment pointed at a broken window shutter. "Let me help with that," he said, nudging him from the room.

Faustina followed Tullia and Mama into the kitchen.

"What's that?" asked Mama, pointing at a bucket and a crimson stain on the floor.

"The remains of wine. I was cleaning it up. He came in here yelling for the accountant and threw a wine flask."

"He needs money," said Mama. "His allowance from Siculus is due."

Faustina looked at her. "With respect, Domina, he is dangerous."

Mama's lips tightened. "We'll increase the guard. You may be sure Balbus will never let this happen again."

Tullia scowled. "Mama, when's the lawyer coming?"

"I sent ahead. He'll be here tomorrow."

"Well, he can't get here soon enough."

Tullia and her mother joined in the clean-up, Tullia working hard to suppress her fury.

* * *

That night, Tullia sat with Yosef on the patio bench. She fidgeted. "The vacation is over," she said. "We're back in Rome. Vitalio's out there and I'm pregnant with what surely is your child. I'm angry and scared."

He sighed. "There's a plan, starting with the divorce. No matter what, we'll always find a way to welcome the baby."

She looked at him and squeezed his warm hand. "Oh, I know."

They stood. "Go to bed, try to sleep."

"And you?"

"I'll stay with the men tonight." He held her for a long moment before leaving.

Retiring to her cubicle she prepared for bed with growing frustration, but knew she needed to try to be patient.

A nightmare interrupted her restless sleep. She stood alone on the road to Pompeii, heart pumping. A bandit loped over, and bile shot up her throat. She gulped humid air and realized it was Vitalio. Sweat burned her eyes, and she screamed into a lifeless landscape. Turning to run, her legs wouldn't move. With nowhere to go, she ducked, and then Yosef, thank goodness, came to her side. He gently swept her hair off her forehead, his gentle fingers dancing. She eased out a breath, calmer now. But as he opened his mouth to speak, Vitalio appeared. Her heart twisted in agony as he wielded his sword. He made a vicious hack, and Tullia caught the metallic smell of blood as Yosef's head became a scarlet cloud. Yosef! Through the dream, she heard herself gurgle his name. Vitalio turned, and, with a smile of rotten teeth, pointed the weapon at her belly. "Now, whore, for the bastard."

She snapped awake, bedclothes stuck to her clammy body. Wiping her brow, she shifted to the edge of the bed and shivered. *He will come, and he will kill us all, and there is nothing we can do.* She lay awake until dawn.

The morning came, and Tullia, nervous and tired, joined

Mama, Yosef, Balbus, and a stranger at the table in the study. Knowing she must not look her best, Tullia tried to muster a smile but felt a lump in her throat instead. She swallowed it down. She could not cry before the talk even started.

Mama introduced her. "Sextus is the trusted jurist who made Poppi's will ironclad. Vitalio cannot contest it."

The wiry man acknowledged her. "You are correct, Domina. I have heard from his lawyer and do not think they will contest." He shuffled papers and shifted his attention to Tullia. "Now, regarding the divorce."

His articulate diction and direct manner impressed Tullia, but she sensed hesitation in his voice. Her hand rubbed her belly, trying to mitigate the growing unease.

"Here is the letter to your husband, declaring your desire to divorce." He passed it to her. "Please read and sign."

Tullia skimmed the short note and saw nothing alarming. She relaxed her tight shoulders. "It looks fine to me." She dipped a reed in thick black ink and signed. "What's next?"

"I'll deliver it to the senator." He looked at Mama who dipped her chin. "I'm also aware of your relationship with Yosef."

Tullia flinched, understanding his earlier hesitation. Her cheeks burned as she engaged Sextus, who returned her look with a steady expression. There was no judgment in it.

The lawyer's eyes didn't waver from hers. "Domina, you have committed adultery, and with a slave no less. This will surely complicate the divorce."

Tullia knew all this, yet it did not stop her rising turmoil within. A deep breath quelled it momentarily. "How?"

"If your husband is aware, and I have reason to believe he

is, the divorce will be null and void," Sextus recited. "You'll remain in the marriage, and, in the eyes of the law, subject to your husband's discipline."

Tullia felt faint. She opened her mouth to ask how Vitalio could know, then closed it. Knowing the answer to her next question, she croaked, "What discipline?"

Sextus set his jaw. "Your husband has the legal right to kill you, exile you to an island, or do just about anything else. You're at his mercy."

Even though she knew this, dread still washed over her. Around the table, Yosef sat as if carved out of ice, and Balbus was reduced to nothing more than a silent shadow. Mama's lips were a thin line. There was nothing to say. His mercy would be no mercy.

* * *

After another restless night, Tullia joined her mother for breakfast, the room bright as morning sunlight streamed through the villa. "Mama, have a bite," said Tullia, passing her a small wedge of honey-dipped bread.

She held up her hand. "Not right now. I'll wait and have something before I go see Siculus."

Tullia frowned. "You should eat."

A loud banging from the front door interrupted the morning calm. Tullia heard Balbus rumble a greeting.

"Move aside," barked Vitalio.

Tullia's insides twisted. She jumped up as her husband and four armed men entered the room. Mama remained seated, squinting at Vitalio. Balbus and Yosef trailed the intruders.

Having not seen Vitalio in six months, Tullia gripped the table edge with rising concern. Dressed in a sparkling white senatorial toga, new leather sandals, and apparently fresh from the barber, his forked locks, in the Augustan style, marched across his forehead in a confident line. His erect posture exuded a new self-assurance, as her throat tightened.

"Fulvia, Tullia. You've returned from your summer vacation. Welcome home."

The senator's gaze settled on Tullia. His eyes tracked down her body, pausing at her pelvis. He looked up, smirking. "And so, it's true, you are with child?"

Tullia tried to steady herself. *He knows about Yosef.* She opened her mouth, but a wave of nausea hit her, and she could say nothing.

"Wife? Are you there?"

She looked into his reptilian eyes, and summoning every scrap of courage, offered a weak smile. "Yes, Vitalio. I'm pregnant with our third child. Due in five months." Her heart slammed against her chest.

Before he could reply, Mama stood. "You should be ashamed of yourself. Wrecking the house and striking Faustina."

His demeanor did not change. "Did she say that? She must be confused — the silly woman lost her balance and fell. These older slaves, you know how their faculties fade with time."

"Faustina's *not* a—" Tulia began.

Mama flicked her hands in dismissal. "In any case, Siculus is back and has your money. Your allowance will continue as before."

"Oh, I have it." He patted his waist. The jangle of coins cut through the tense air, and his smile disappeared. "I won't contest the will, but rest assured, this ridiculous divorce will not stand."

Tullia's rising anger overcame her fear. She pointed at him. "It's legal, you'll see."

He cackled. "Oh, wife, yes, we shall *see*. You have no leverage. I'm very much aware of your antics." He shifted his gaze to her belly. "And take care of *our* child. Maybe your slave boy can help." A vicious sneer morphed into a scowl, but after a moment he turned on his heel and departed, trailed by his men as Balbus ushered them to the door. Yosef remained at the table.

"He-he knows," Tullia gasped, wobbling as she sat down, Mama across the table with Yosef standing behind her.

Her mouth was dusty dry. "He knows about us," she repeated.

A muscle jumped in Yosef's jaw. "So it seems."

Mama opened a hand. "That cannot be helped anymore. We must think, and first about the baby—"

My baby. Yosef's baby. The dark haze of her nightmare returned, Vitalio's vicious face inches from hers, his sword poised to cut the child from her belly. Her heart thundered, she grew lost in a buzzing sound, and the room went dark.

Later, Tullia awoke to the dim flicker of an oil lamp, Faustina at the bedside. She felt the old housekeeper's warm, wrinkled hand on her forehead. "You fainted."

Tullia sat up gingerly, feeling nausea recede. "H-how long have I been out?"

"Since the third hour. It's now the sixth."

The memories roared back, and she squeezed her eyes against tears of anguish.

"W-where is everyone? Mama? Yosef…"

"They're meeting with Sextus. Domina called him to return after Vitalio left."

"I should be there."

Faustina offered her arm and led her out of the bedroom toward the atrium. Tullia walked slowly, breathing in and out to calm her unsteady heart. In the study, three figures sat around the table, bathed in flickering light from the lamps and two large torches. Black smoke from the latter rose and exited through the opening in the atrium roof.

Yosef saw her first; rising, he relieved Faustina and helped her to a chair.

"Feeling better?" asked Mama.

Tullia rubbed her face and leaned back. "Not really, but we have to figure out a plan."

"We agree," she said. "Sextus was kind enough to return and discuss Vitalio's visit."

The jurist furrowed his brow. "If he has proof of the affair, and we assume he does, it's enough to quash the divorce request. When it comes to an adulterous wife, a husband has the legal right to kill her. When a slave is involved in such an affair, it's mandatory execution for him."

The nausea returned, but Yosef's reaction distracted Tullia. His remorseful glance pricked her. "For three years he could have done something," he said. "Why now?"

"Yes, why now?" asked Tullia.

Mama took her hand. "Your father. I don't know if he knew about Yosef, but I'm sure he would do anything to protect you and this house from scandal. Vitalio knew it would have been very risky to confront Poppi with any suspicions." She held up three fingers, ticking them off with her next words. "After all, he had his allowance, a whore, and freedom. There was neither reason nor opportunity to upset the cart."

Her hands opened. "But with Poppi's death, Vitalio's now free to act. We assume he had to wait until you got back from Pompeii to take action. The baby has become the unexpected twist and probably prevented mayhem."

Tullia wondered if she heard her correctly. "What do you mean?" she asked, but it was Sextus who answered.

"Not even your husband wants to be seen slaughtering a pregnant woman, nor her lover—slave or not. For fifty years the standard Augustan rules on senatorial behavior have been clear—both the imperial house and the Senate frown on such blatant exhibitions of malice. Butchering a pregnant wife, regardless of her crimes, could lead to Vitalio's expulsion from the Senate, a risk he is likely unwilling to take."

She shuddered. *Butchering!* "So, until I have this baby, we live. After that..."

"You must hope for the best," he replied in that direct way of his. "Or leave."

The room grew silent, save for the soft pop of the torches.

Tullia jumped up. "No. *No!*" She jerked her head around the room as if searching for ghosts and glared at the wide-eyed group. "We need to get out of here!" She pointed at her mother. "Before Poppi died, we talked with Auntie about going to Egypt. We should go! Can't we do that?"

Mama stood, reaching for her. "Running away won't help. We'd be found and our execution would be assured."

Tullia collapsed in her arms, sobbing and sniveling. "W-we just can't stay here. What about Judea?"

"Domina, that would be worse than Egypt," Sextus advised. "The Romans hold Judea, you could never hide there."

Mama held her, rubbing her hands in soothing circles on her back. "Daughter, settle down. For now, we need to work with Sextus on plans for what to do after the baby is born."

Tullia shook loose. "All this talk! Let's just kill the bastard!" She paused a beat, clenched her fists, and stomped out to the garden.

Numb with fury, she marched to the bench and sat. Her hands fiddled with the hem of her tunic as her stomach churned like the waves of the ocean. Her toes scrunched, scraping against stone, not sand from a beach. *We should have stayed in Pompeii*, she thought. *How did it come to this?*

Her inner voice spoke, and Tullia felt her heart flinch. *You started this mess*, it reminded her, then morphing into her mother's voice. *You did.* Her back slumped, elbows falling to her knees. Tears ran down her cheeks and onto her chin, but she didn't wipe them away. The burden of her marriage rested on her shoulders like an immovable weight crushing her into submission. Into hopelessness. *We can't run and we can't kill him. We're trapped. He owns me like … like a slave.*

Yosef's patient, loving face appeared before her closed eyes. Tullia's lip trembled. She wanted to go to him, to take away his slave's pain, but she didn't know just how far it reached. She would never know. But she knew now that what she was feeling was but a taste of what he had felt the moment those soldiers cut down his father and threw him in the wagon. She knew that a slave's life was always at the mercy of another.

28

A week after Vitalio's visit, the children and house girls arrived from Pompeii. Dracus ran through the house yelling and Marcus cried, as Atia and Faustina tried unsuccessfully to calm the chaos. Tullia's spirits rose with their safe arrival.

She addressed Quintus over the din. "They all seem fine."

"Yes, Domina. But they have been cooped up for ten days."

"We'll need to keep them busy then," she said, as joy filled her chest.

A day after the family settled into the villa, Tullia went to Mama. "Let's go to the forum," she said. "We need to shop, and Dracus is still wound up from the trip."

"I was thinking the same thing," replied Mama. "Vitalio or not, we must get on with our lives."

Leaving the house, Tullia inhaled the crisp autumn air and felt the warm sun on her face. The tension after Vitalio's visit was eased by the simple plans for the day. Dracus, prancing along, gripped her finger with his hand. He gurgled and pointed. The knot in her stomach lessened.

"Yes, that's a tree," she confirmed for him. He giggled, the innocent joy warming her heart.

Next to them walked Mama and Faustina, with Yosef and Balbus close behind.

The tree-lined Via Sacra thickened with people as it

wormed around the Lone Pine Tavern and the huge market of the Porticus Margaritaria.

Jostled by the flow of people, Tullia picked Dracus up. "This makes me nervous," she confided to Yosef. Her heart had jumped, the earlier calm replaced by caution and a tight vigilance.

"We're fine," he reassured. "Over there." He led them to a cluster of merchant stalls adjacent to a splashing fountain, its rectangular granite borders offering a perfect seat.

"That's better," she said, putting Dracus on the ground and releasing a breath. "I don't know what's gotten into me."

"Remember, when you carry Dracus, you are actually carrying three," offered Yosef.

"That is not helpful. Walk him around the fountain, I'll wait here." Yosef's head disappeared into the crowd. As she watched Mama and Faustina shop at a millinery booth a few steps away, she wondered if she was overreacting. It was unlikely Vitalio would follow them here—he could more easily do his dirty work in the privacy of the villa. She scooped some cool water and dabbed her face, feeling better.

Balbus hurried by, breaking the serene moment. "What?" she called, jumping up.

"Yosef," he said, looking into the throng of people ahead.

She followed his gaze, catching the top of Yosef's head bobbing as if running. Fear rippled down her spine as she raced after him. *Dracus!* Her worst nightmare was coming true.

Just as quickly, Balbus stopped, Yosef and Dracus before him.

Tullia heard the end of Yosef's explanation. "... he ran after a man leading a baby goat. It was nothing." Both men guffawed.

"It's not funny," snapped Tullia gasping for breath. "I thought you had lost him," she gulped. "I was terrified." Tears burned as she used her shaking arms to pull in her son.

Faustina and Mama came over as the men quieted.

Yosef reached for her. "Tull—"

She twisted away. "No. I just want to go home."

"Daughter?" Mama's soft voice offered little comfort.

"I want to go," she rasped, failing to suppress her trembling voice.

In the comfort of the villa, Tullia retired to her bedroom, failing at sleep. Mama sat on the edge of the bed. "Try to relax. Everything is fine," she coaxed.

Head on the pillow, Tullia moaned. "I am having trouble with this divorce. I see Vitalio around every corner." She turned and pulled herself closer to her mother. "I have bad feelings about the coming weeks."

Mama stroked Tullia's head. "We are doing what we can. I have asked Balbus to increase the guard. It might be wise for you and the children to remain in the villa until it's over."

The idea of confinement irked her, but Tullia could offer nothing better.

* * *

Over the weeks, and despite the increased vigilance, despair dogged Tullia. Futile thoughts of how to escape her husband's grasp abolished the joys of the pregnancy and the happy family reunion. Moving through each day felt like she was underwater.

Yosef took her by the elbow one evening, guiding her out to the patio.

"You can't keep sulking," he said.

"And why not? Once the baby is out, Vitalio will kill us all."

He stepped to face her, putting his hands on her shoulders. She felt the strength of his grip.

"Listen to me. These years with you have been the best of my life. I refuse to worry about what I don't know. And neither should you. Of course I'm nervous, but we don't know what Vitalio may do after the child is born. You heard Sextus, murder is frowned upon these days by the Senate. Use this time to think about things we might do to survive."

"I feel like a lamb waiting for slaughter."

He shook his head. "Tullia, you're acting like it. Put your thoughts toward the child and the household. Help Faustina and Atia. Talk to your mother. If you get more involved, you'll feel better."

She wrinkled her nose, but knew he was right. *I need to do something.* Her spirits nudged up a notch and she offered a weak smile. "That's pretty brazen talk for a slave."

"So sell me. C'mon, you can do *better* than this." He pulled her to him and whispered. "Would it help if I lifted my tunic?"

"Yosef!" she said, pushing him away, but snickering.

"Sorry, Domina." He gave a half-grin. "Now, can you please try a little harder?"

They returned to the villa. With her spirits improved, she vowed to do better.

* * *

The increased presence of Balbus and his men gave Tullia the needed comfort to relax with the boys. She even felt a secret joy at the pregnancy. Certainly, it was Yosef's. The divorce might be over before the winter, when the baby was due. They would be free then—at least she could allow herself to hope so.

The house confinement also afforded time to update her journal. As she recorded events, thoughts of escape if the divorce failed began to germinate. *What* about *Egypt? Why not?* She was sure cousin Varus had connections in Alexandria. They could travel in secret on a ship like the *Ceres*—not that she ever wanted another sea journey. There was plenty of money, money to buy them time. It would not be permanent, just temporary until—until what? In a flash, she knew. Until Balbus or his allies could eliminate Vitalio. His death was the only way to ensure safety.

As if it had already happened, the rising warmth of contentment surged through her body. Her face relaxed with an unconscious smile. She also saw where to draw the line with Yosef's Rule. Evil men were not privy to its consideration. She was sure this was true, even if Yosef never said it.

Trying to formulate a plan raised several questions.

Leaving the journal page on the small table in her bedroom, she found her mother in the study. "Mama? I want to talk about Egypt," said Tullia, sitting and tapping eager fingers on the table.

Her mother looked up from a papyrus list. "Egypt? Most of our grain shipments come from there," she said, gesturing at the sheet with her reed. Tullia recognized a tally of income and expenses from one of the Ostia shipping businesses, and decided it might be a good time to share her idea.

"If the divorce fails, we need a plan. I want to talk seriously about going to Egypt."

A hint of a smile flitted across Mama's face. "We already covered this."

"Not seriously," replied Tullia, leaning forward. "I have thought about it. We can secretly arrange passage to Alexandria on a boat like the *Ceres*. We have the money and I'm sure can find a way to blend in. And it would be temporary. Only—" She hesitated. "Until the threat of Vitalio passes."

Mama stiffened. "Tullia—"

Her daughter cut her off. "Years ago, you said I would not survive the marriage if something didn't change. Yosef helped then, but there's nothing he can do now. It's up to us. We *have* to consider this."

Mama's face changed to a hard stare, and she dropped her voice. "Do you know what you are suggesting?"

Tullia squinted. "Do you want to live the rest of your life in constant fear of a vicious man? I don't. If he quashes the divorce, he will squeeze the life out of us, unless we kill him first. I am certain Balbus knows people who, for the right price, will help."

Both women sat for several minutes, not speaking.

Mama gathered her papers. "I will ask Siculus and Sextus to come later today to discuss the logistics of relocation *without* the other matter. The less they know, the better."

"I understand," said Tullia, hiding her joy with a solemn nod.

The two men arrived, and Mama took the lead. "Should the divorce fail, we need to reconsider our options."

"Domina?" inquired the lawyer.

"Yes. Specifically, Egypt."

The jurist's face remained impassive, but Siculus squirmed.

Tullia tapped her hand on the table. "Yes, Egypt. We can catch a boat in Ostia and travel to Alexandria in secret. I am sure Varus can arrange passage," she said, shifting her gaze to Siculus. "I assume we have money if we choose to relocate."

"Yes, whatever you need," he said, mopping his forehead. "We can liquidate assets, and you can travel with plenty of money. Sextus and I can hide the rest and channel it to you as needed. Vitalio knows only a small part of the financial picture."

Sextus seemed to consider the plan. "And what would you do in Alexandria?"

"Disappear and remain anonymous," said Tullia with more confidence than she felt. But it had to be said. The plan was not perfect yet.

Sextus pulled his beard, staring hard at Tullia. She knew instinctively the old soldier understood the temporary nature of the move. "Very well. It might work. I have family living in the Greek quarter that could help. I'll give you a letter of introduction."

After the meeting, Tullia explained the plan to Yosef.

"It might work," he said, touching his chin thoughtfully. "The reason for the temporary nature of the stay is a bit tricky."

"But necessary," she insisted.

"I understand and agree there *is* no other option."

* * *

The cool days of November gave way to a colder December.

Siculus reported that Vitalio did nothing except pick up his allowance.

Tullia huddled with Yosef and her mother on the patio bench. "It's already the Ides and there is still no word on the divorce," said Tullia, trying to relax by fruitlessly massaging her belly.

"I don't think it will come in time," said Mama with a grim face. "Your baby will be born, and you will still be married. I will let Sextus know we need to leave within a week of the baby's birth. There is simply no choice."

"I'll begin to prepare the household for a discrete departure," offered Yosef.

The final two weeks of the pregnancy went smoothly — the plan was polished, the loose ends tied up. As expected, six days before the planned departure, Aurelia Flaccus Silanus was born, her arrival tempered by a harsh reality. She was a miniature version of Yosef. There could be no question about her paternity.

Three days after the birth, Mama came to Tullia's room. Propped by pillows, Tullia rested, and Aurelia slept next to her in a cocoon of blankets. "I feel fine. I am stronger every day. I'll be ready to travel by the end of the week. I pray to Juno that Vitalio stays away until then."

Her mother worked a corner of a blanket between her fingers. "We should be able to get out on time. We'll travel overnight to Ostia. Nobody in Rome knows we're leaving except the household and Balbus. If anyone should ask, we'll leave word that our destination is north, to Valentia in Hispania."

Tullia set her jaw. "I'll be ready."

29

In the morning, as Tullia sat for her breakfast, there was a bang and a crash at the front door. She jumped up to see at least twenty men pouring into the house. Yosef staggered along, roughly constrained by two men.

Screaming as the invaders filled the house, she knew immediately they were doomed. Hopelessly outnumbered, the ten home guards thundered in from the patio.

"Stop!" shouted Tullia. "Don't fight them." Her men pulled back.

Vitalio strutted forward, crossing to the study like a conquering king. "A wise decision." He gestured to a space adjacent to the front door with one hand while examining his nails on the other. "Bind the guards and have them face that wall." His men complied, herding the home force to the area.

Vitalio faced Tullia, his lips pulled back in a grim smile. He pointed to the corner of the room. "Get over there."

"Vitalio, I-I just had our baby." Tullia placed one hand on her still-tender stomach. "I can't stand too long."

"Do it."

Her nerves jangled as she edged over to the corner, but the sound of feet slapping on stone made her pause. Mama and the remaining household entered the study area, halting when they saw Vitalio.

"Fulvia, you and the rest of them, over there." He pointed.

"Join my wife." He spit out the last word as if it was a bitter walnut.

"What do you think you're doing?" demanded Mama.

Vitalio jerked his chin at two of the guards, who grasped her by each arm and hauled her to the corner. Tullia followed, along with Faustina, the house girls, and the boys. She wrapped an arm over Dracus and Marcus, then looked around, a sudden swell of panic rising. Where was—?

A loud wail answered her question. Tullia's eyes shot to her husband, and when he made no sign that he'd heard anything, she gestured at Atia, who scurried away. The two men with Yosef shoved him over to the group, his wrists now bound behind him, as Atia returned with Aurelia.

A bolt of fear shot down Tullia's spine as she looked at Vitalio. His hands were steady without the tremor of recent drink. Worse yet, beneath his raised brows she saw the familiar evil twinkle in his eyes. She sensed a terrible turning point for the family.

They waited.

The children cried.

Vitalio gestured to a nervous-looking young guard. "Milo, take the slave girls and the noisy brood out to the patio and guard them." He complied; the room quieted.

Vitalio crossed his arms and smirked as he regarded Mama, Tullia, Faustina, and Yosef. "We caught Balbus returning from the accountant, he cannot help you."

Mama stepped forward. "Vit—"

His punch caught her full in the face. She tumbled down, striking her head on the edge of the heavy wooden table before collapsing. Groggy but awake, she sprawled on the floor, blood oozing from her nose. Faustina knelt to minister to her.

"No," growled Vitalio. With a heavy boot common to the legions, he kicked the older woman aside. "Put her there," he ordered. Two men pulled Mama up, dropping her in a chair as her head lolled back. Tullia's stomach lurched. Despite the kick, Faustina hobbled back to Mama's side, placing her hand on her shoulder.

"I'll do the talking," Vitalio continued, pacing back and forth. He jabbed a finger at his chest. "I'm the man of the Flaccus family, the Flaccus fortune, *and* the Flaccus future. I'm also not the father of that baby." His steps stopped; eyes boring into Yosef. "Looks like it belongs to slave boy."

No one spoke. A thunderous silence reigned, broken only by Tullia's shallow breathing.

Vitalio whipped around and stalked to the corner, his face inches from her own. "Deny it!" he seethed. "I dare you."

"I will not," she whispered.

A backhand slammed her cheek. Dazed, she managed to stay on her feet. The room spun.

"Hah!" he crowed. "I knew it! You are no better than the lowest whore, a *lupae*! An affair with a slave?" He hit her again. She tottered into Yosef, grabbing his arm, fighting to stay up. Yosef remained immobile, an anchor in the storm. Blood flooded her mouth. Dizziness threatened to take over, but she squeezed her eyes to clear her head.

Her grip on Yosef slackened. Alarmed, Tullia opened her eyes. Two more guards had grabbed Yosef by either arm and with another wrench, pulled him free of her—and straight toward her waiting husband. *No, no.*

Tullia found her balance with the wall. Her lip throbbed. "What're you doing?"

Vitalio made no answer. She started to step forward, but a guard grabbed the back of her tunic.

Her husband gestured at the men flanking Yosef. "Do it."

A knife flashed and split Yosef's tunic down the middle, exposing his naked midsection and thin loincloth. Like a tiny crimson worm, a rivulet of blood tracked down his chest from a small nick. He did not react to the superficial cut. Several passes with the blade removed the remaining garment and the rest of his tunic, leaving him naked and exposed, tattered linens at his feet.

Vitalio sniggered. "The aristocratic lady and her little slave boy. I should kill you both—as is my right." His eyes glowered into hers. "Do you understand *lupae*? It is my right!"

He wheezed through several breaths and grimaced like a gargoyle, thrusting a shaking hand toward her throat. Clawed fingernails brushed her skin. Her impending death washed away the fear; she was as helpless as an injured warrior bleeding out on a lonely corner of the battlefield, yet she would not cower. She pursed her lips and glared, waiting for the end.

It never came. Vitalio's eyes cut into her, holding them both in a breathless stalemate, but after several moments the tempest abated, and the madness left his eyes.

Tullia exhaled. She could almost sense the relief arising from her now awake mother and Faustina.

Vitalio cracked his knuckles and twisted around, regarding the group. He opened his arms in a show of false piety. "Ah, but I am a compassionate man."

He barred his teeth without mirth, abolishing Tullia's relief. Her tender belly tightened.

After walking back and forth before Tullia and Yosef, Vitalio halted and pointed at her. "I'll give you a choice, *lupae*. You can keep your little slave boy, but he'll be a eunuch." He flicked a finger at the guard with the knife. The man knelt and grabbed Yosef's scrotum, wielding the blade to make the fatal slice.

"No!" screamed Tullia. She lunged at her husband, but a sharp yank pulled her back.

Vitalio snorted. "If not that, then let's sell him, balls intact. I've had a nice offer from a brothel owner seeking fresh male stock for his establishment on *Clivus Suburanus*. Do you know the place?" He tapped his chin. "Ah, probably not."

Tullia struggled against the guard, her chest heaving with the effort. Her husband offered an indulgent smile and again spread his arms.

"Your choice, *lupae*. Balls or brothel?"

Seized with terror, Tullia froze as she tried to think. Was there a way to keep Yosef here and unharmed? But she had nothing to offer. Sending Yosef to a brothel physically uninjured was a poor second choice, and the idea ripped her apart. She looked to Yosef for guidance. With a tiny head bob, he gestured at the front door. She knew he agreed. The brothel.

She swallowed what felt like gravel and looked at her husband. "Sell him," she croaked.

He clapped his hands. "A fine decision! This way we both profit. I'll even split the proceeds with you! After all, *lupae*, we *are* married."

His bark of a laugh cut through the room and sliced into Tullia's heart. Swinging around, he swept a hand in the air. The guards turned on their heels, pushing Yosef in front of them.

Vitalio gestured at his remaining men. "Take the house force into the street and release them. Remind them that if they come back, they will be killed." He gave a short, sharp whistle, and Milo returned with Atia, Chloe, and the children. He joined the rest of the invaders, filing out the front door.

The villa empty except for Vitalio and the household, he addressed his wife. "Don't even think about going anywhere," he warned, baring his teeth. A stiff finger shot in her direction. "Two guards will remain outside."

Tullia said nothing.

Vitalio walked backward, eyes on her, every word springing from his lips with glee. "This is only the beginning, *wife*."

Then he was gone, slamming the door behind him.

30

Tullia turned to Faustina. "Hurry and lock the door." She faced a weepy Atia. "He's gone, dry your eyes. Take Chloe and the children into the bedroom while Faustina and I help Mama." Wiping her runny nose, the girl left.

Faustina, favoring her leg, returned.

"Are you all right?" Tullia felt a jolt of guilt at making the older worker go to the door. "He gave you a pretty good kick."

"I'll be fine." Faustina pulled a rag from her tunic and pressed it against Mama's face to staunch the bleeding. Tullia knelt beside them, afraid to look at her mother until she heard her regular breathing.

She half-rose on her knees. "Mama?"

After a few moments, her mother whispered, voice strained. "We're in grave danger." She took a ragged breath. "If they have Balbus, we must get word to Sextus. His connections with the judiciary and the senate can investigate Vitalio's behavior. He's our last hope. Without help, Vitalio can hold us indefinitely and do what he will."

Panic squeezed Tullia's insides. She couldn't go, scaling the patio wall would be too rough on her still-recovering body. "Maybe—maybe Atia can?" she ventured. "She can get over the patio wall and find him in the Aventine—it's less than a mile."

Tullia found Atia on the bedroom floor with Dracus as

he played with a small ball. Marcus dozed on the bed next to Chloe and Aurelia slept in her crib.

"Atia, I need to ask you to do something," said Tullia, waving her forward.

The petite house slave nodded to Chloe, who went to Dracus.

"Yes, Domina. What can I do?" She asked, her eyes twinkling with interest.

"We need you to climb the patio wall and go tell Sextus what's happened and that we are in trouble. You know where he is."

The girl straightened her tunic. "I can do it."

"It's risky and you'll have to run fast."

"I can do it."

Emerging from the bedroom, they met Faustina at the patio door, who hugged Atia. "Be careful, dear girl, and come back safe."

Atia flashed a lopsided smile. "I know where to go over the wall and how to sneak away. I can do it."

Tullia felt her eyes well as Atia scurried out the door and into the garden. She watched her climb a mulberry tree in the corner and slip over the wall. Tullia felt a rush of love for the fearless thirteen-year-old.

"I hope she makes it," said Faustina with a grim smile.

"Me, too," said Tullia, her heart in her throat.

Faustina joined Chloe and the children.

Tullia returned to Mama, feeling her energy drain and along with it, hope. Yosef was gone, Balbus was gone, and trapped like animals, they waited to be killed. She had nobody to blame but herself—the affair with Yosef and now

Aurelia's birth had put her Mother, and the household, in grave danger. She had even sent an innocent slave girl on a life-threatening mission.

Fighting a black miasma of guilt and grief, she turned to her mother. "Mama, I'm so sorry for all I have done."

Her mother formed a sad smile. "Daughter, we have all had a hand in it. I never wanted this marriage and should have fought harder to prevent it. But the real culprit is Vitalio. Right now, we must be strong and resist him at every turn. I will die at his hands before giving in."

Icy tentacles of fear clutched Tullia's core. Mama was right, they had to resist. She tried to remember Yosef's words about not giving up. It further stirred her courage. *I must not quit. Even in a brothel, Yosef won't quit.*

Tullia took a breath. "We've seen what my husband will do. If Atia fails, I'll kill him. I'd rather suffer the consequences than gamble on his goodwill." She would fetch and hide a knife in her tunic and kill him when he returned. The thought gave her new strength.

Mama shed a few tears. "Oh Tullia, I fear you may be right. Better death at the hands of the authorities than Vitalio." She squeezed her daughter's arm. "I'm sorry it's come to this."

Before Tullia could answer, there was a pounding at the front door. "Open up!"

Tullia crossed the atrium with a sense of foreboding. Atia? She unlocked the door. It flew open. A big guard stood holding Atia by one arm, the girl's nose bloody and left eye swollen.

"You were told to stay here. You broke the rules." He tossed the semiconscious girl at Tullia like she was a wet rag. "Now stay put. And leave this unlocked." His closed fist crashed into Tullia's chest and he pulled the door shut. She staggered back, winded but unhurt.

Tullia moved Atia to a couch in the study.

Faustina came. "Chloe has the children. Let me see."

She performed a cursory examination. "Just a couple of bumps." They wiped the blood from the girl's nose. "I don't think it's broken. She'll soon have a black eye."

Atia blinked her good eye and sniffled. "I went over the back wall and almost made the street. I couldn't outrun a big guard. I'm sorry." They helped her into a bedroom to rest.

That night, as Aurelia nursed, Tullia sat in bed, alone with her thoughts. Yosef was gone. She knew he would find a way to survive, but thinking of the brothel made her wince. *I pray for you, Yosef. I hope your God will watch over you.* Eyes closed; her mind spun back to her husband. His cruelty now well established; she reaffirmed her pledge to try and kill him. She shook her head. *How can I even be thinking this?* But the answer never changed—there was no choice. One way or the other, they were condemned. Killing Vitalio stood as the lesser of two bad evils.

The finality of the thought lent unexpected comfort to the moment. At least it was something. She stroked her baby's soft hair. "Enjoy tonight little one. It may all end tomorrow, on only your fifth day of life." She lay back, baby in her arms, and tried to sleep.

31

Vitalio returned in the morning with eight rough men. He again assembled the household in the corner. Mama had regained sufficient strength to stand tall with Faustina and Tullia.

Tullia's hand idly brushed her tunic, feeling the knife hidden in its folds. Her mind raced to picture an opportunity to use it.

Vitalio addressed a guard, older and rougher than Milo. "Take the children and house girls back to the patio. Check them all for weapons."

Tullia's heart leaped, knowing she would be searched. She grasped her center and fell forward. "I'm bleeding," she croaked, as she hit the floor, willing Vitalio to come forward. Her right hand had snaked beneath her hem and clutched the handle of the knife. *Come on Vitalio.*

Ignoring the ruse, her husband simply gestured to a huge blond-haired man. "Say hello to Rupinus. He'll be in charge in my absence." The thug gave a surly grin of rotten teeth and leered at Mama.

Vitalio looked at Rupinus and pointed at the three women. "Search them."

Tullia saw her moment slipping away. Leaping up, she pulled the knife and lurched at Vitalio. Rupinus caught her in the midst of a harmless thrust, squeezing her wrist so hard she dropped the knife.

"Oh, *lupae*. Such a predictable tactic," snorted Vitalio. "Finish searching her."

More of a molestation, Rupinus found no other weapons, shoving her into the corner. After roughly searching Mama and Faustina, he slammed two more knives on the table.

At that moment, the patio guard returned. "Found one, on the short girl. The redhead had nothing." He added Atia's small knife to the pile.

Tullia secretly cheered at the cache—at least they were all thinking the same thing. Vitalio interrupted her joy with a vicious slap, aggravating her swollen lip from the day before. She stood her ground as anger pushed past her fear.

"If we find any more knives, they'll be used to cut the holder," said Vitalio, slicing a flat hand in the air. She met his eyes and glared.

Rupinus stepped to Vitalio's side. The big thug stood close enough for Tullia to hear his rapid breathing and smell fetid breath. *Is he excited?* She glanced at him. She saw evil desire in his tiny eyes as he licked his lips. He reminded her of a feral pig. Heart racing, she grabbed her mother's hand.

The senator hawked and spit on the floor. "Rupinus will have the money. You'll need his permission to spend. There'll be no more visitors or outings. You'll be allowed to shop for food under guard but otherwise imprisoned here until I have secured the Flaccus fortune. As the head of the Flaccus family, this is my legal right." He looked at Mama. "Understand?"

She folded her arms and said nothing.

Vitalio's gaze sharpened; he eyed Rupinus and then returned to Mama. "Do—you—understand?"

"You can't—"

Mama's arm pulled back to strike, but just as quick Rupinus snatched it out of the air. At the same moment, Vitalio shot a fist into her already swollen face. He repeated the blow, smashing her nose. Blood ran in a scarlet torrent around her feet, her knees buckling, but Rupinus—laughing loudly—held her upright. When the punches stopped, he dropped her at Vitalio's feet. Her arms flailed as she tried to right herself, sputtering blood. Vitalio kicked her head. She slumped face down, barely moving as he pummeled her with more vicious kicks. Each blow of his heavy boots sounded like the whump of a broom beating dust from a rug. After what seemed an eternity, the outburst ended; Mama's semi-conscious moans mercifully ebbing into a silent coma.

Vitalio snorted like a bull as the sweat dripped off his chin. He glowered at her motionless figure. Wiping his face, he turned to Rupinus. "Take her."

With an evil grin, the goon grabbed Mama by the back of her tunic and dragged her bloody mass into a bedroom, leaving a rust streak in his wake. Tullia flinched at the sound of clothes ripping, then pressed her lips tightly at the guttural sounds of her mother's rape.

Vitalio moved to the couch on one side of the table. He reclined, crossing one leg over the other, and looked at Faustina.

"Get me some bread and wine."

She hobbled out.

Tullia stood alone, catatonic, and steeped in terror. *Oh, Mama.* It was the only thought she could summon.

"Sit," he commanded.

Numb, she eased down to the floor and put her arms

around her knees. Her heart pounded. Faustina returned and placed food and drink before the tyrant. Joining Tullia, she dropped to her knees. One arm draped over the younger woman's shoulder.

Vitalio drank and chewed to the malevolent rhythm of thudding and rasping from the other room. He smacked his lips, his gaze never leaving Tullia. "I never wanted you," he belched. "It was only about your money, but your father stood in the way. Then your mother. Soon they'll both be out of the picture and it will just be you."

He squinted through glacial eyes. "As I see it, though, you're lucky. Your bastard daughter delayed things and were it not for the Senate and its silly rules about wife killing, I'd slice you into little chunks right now." He barked out a laugh and took another noisy sip. "But nothing says I can't keep you here for starvation, torture, or whatever I choose. You won't have to worry about dying—not yet." A hungry gleam lit his eyes. "We'll string it out for a while."

She heard him, but his words carried no meaning, bouncing off appalling mental images of her mother's violation. She felt nauseous with fear, wanting to rip down the curtain and rush in to save her mother, but remained frozen, astounded by the depth of his malice and the helpless grief pulling at her chest.

Eventually, Rupinus emerged, wiping his mouth with the back of his hand and licking his lips. Vitalio stood. He summoned his man with the children and had him usher them into the corner, where Faustina pulled them close.

"There now," grinned Vitalio. "Such a lovely sight." His face changed into a look of unbidden fury, directed at his wife.

"Do as you are told and there'll be no trouble. It won't be long until I find the fortune. Then we'll decide what to do with you."

He left, leaving Rupinus and four of the men.

"Get back to work and stay out of my way," commanded Rupinus, picking up Vitalio's unfinished cup of wine.

Tullia exchanged a nervous look with Faustina, who jerked her chin in the direction of Mama's bedroom. *Mama*, thought the young woman, her heart leaping into her throat.

Naked on the bed, with tattered clothes strewn about, her mother resembled a battlefield casualty. Studded with grape-purple welts, her bloated belly had borne the brunt of the trauma. Both eyes were unseen beneath swollen puckers of crimson tissue. Bite marks on her breasts and soiled linens between her legs spoke to the final violations.

Grazing her broken mother's face with her fingertips, Tullia whispered. "Oh, Mama." Her tears fell, mingling with her mother's blood.

Faustina's arms encircled Tullia. "Let me look," she said in a quiet voice. Tullia eased back. Faustina checked Mama. "It's very bad; we must try to keep her comfortable. She is dying."

Tullia froze, numb to the gruesome scene. Her mangled mother lay motionless; breath sputtering. As her chest fell for the last time, pink-tinged foam bubbled at the corner of her mouth. Then nothing.

Tullia sensed what had happened. *No!* roared her inner voice. She turned to Faustina, eyes burning with tears. "She needs a doctor. We must take her there now. There's no time to lose," she jabbered, the words rushing out in a torrent. She shook her mother's shoulders. "Wake up, wake up!" she whimpered. Letting out a long moan, she fell across Mama's chest, her face cheek to cheek. *Oh, Mama.*

She felt Faustina's warm hands pull her up. "She is gone, Domina."

Tullia sagged into the older servant's arms, sobbing.

After a few moments, Faustina's whisper broke through the fog. "Domina, you must pull yourself together, there is much we must do. We *have* to go on before the men come."

With effort, Tullia tore herself away and tried to focus.

"We will clean her as best we can, then we must go back out. You cannot fight them. You could suffer the same fate, only worse since they have to keep you alive. Domina, *you* are now a slave. We are *both* now slaves with a terrible master."

The statement broke through Tullia's anguish. She would grieve later. Now, she had to go on. Hugging Faustina with all her strength, she found comfort in the feel of the old servant's ribs and bony spine.

Tullia stepped back. "I am so sorry for everything I have caused." A new wave of sobs rushed forth.

Faustina grabbed her shoulders and shook. The old woman's dark brown eyes blazed. "Stop! Never cry. Slaves cannot cry. Never show what you feel—it can be used for punishment. You must pull into yourself and become invisible." Her grip loosened but still squeezed. "Think of Yosef, find your strength."

Yosef. Tullia's heart twisted from fear. *It may be worse for him. He will find strength in our love and so will I.*

She wiped her eyes and took a breath. "I understand."

Tullia fought to maintain her composure as she helped bathe her mother's broken body, tears flowing freely. Memories washed over her, but through the torment, she continued to clean the wounds.

Finishing their task, Tullia stood over her mother and released a breath. "Let's put her arms here," she said, crossing them over the bruised chest. "So she's at peace."

They covered the body with a clean blanket and crept from the room.

Emerging into the atrium, Tullia squinted against the late afternoon sunlight slanting across the joyless villa. She felt the pull of depression in every step but resisted, knowing she had to get through this moment, the next, and all the coming moments.

Eyes on the floor, Tullia gazed at crusty pools of Mama's blood. "Sir, my mother is dead. May we arrange a burial at her family site?"

Reclined on the couch, Rupinus belched. "Call me master. Old woman, get me more wine." Faustina hurried out.

Tullia took a slow breath, loosening her fists until they lay flat against her thighs. "Master, may we arrange a burial for my mother?"

"No," he spat. "We're to toss her body in the Tiber for the whore that she was. Get your people from the patio and clean up the floor."

As she went to the garden, she heard him order two men to dispose of Mama's body. Her knees buckled and she fell, one palm hitting the ground. Tears splashed. A sob escaped her. *Slaves don't cry*, Faustina's sharp words echoed. Seized with terror, Tullia hastily wiped her face and stood, ignoring the bruises and scrapes on her knees. As the panicking servants and children rushed forward, she prayed they could survive another day.

32

The gray gloom of winter following Mama's death matched Tullia's attitude. They killed Mama as easily as you swat a fly. Any of them could be next. She especially worried about Dracus, and his natural tendency to talk to anyone. One guard roughly pushed him away and he cried.

Tullia hurried to his side. "Here, here," she whispered, leading him into a bedroom.

"Mama?" he whined. Tullia's heart crumbled at his innocent plea.

She soothed her confused little boy. "You did nothing wrong. The men do not like to talk. Talk to me, Faustina, Atia, or Chloe, but don't bother the men."

He blinked back tears. "Yes, Mama."

Atia came in and led him away. Tullia wondered how the terror of this nightmare would affect him. Would he even live? If he did, but she dies, will it be the street for him? The misery of worry made her knees weak.

In a matter of days, anger replaced Tullia's gloom. More bread; more wine; clean this floor—each rude order from Rupinus threw another log on Tullia's burning anger.

She cornered Faustina. "What a pig," she seethed, fury bubbling forth.

"Domina! Stop this," admonished Faustina. "He is not deaf,

and your anger is a reason for a beating—you, me, even the children. Do not let him see your rage. Do not let him win."

Tullia relaxed her fists and blew out a breath. Faustina was right. They could use the servants or the children to control her if they sensed resistance.

"I will do better," she said, wrath reduced to a searing ember she knew she would always carry. *It will give me the energy to defeat them.*

Soon Tullia matched Faustina and Atia's demeanors—eyes downcast, a little slump to the walk, and silent, always silent when padding through the villa or whispering to the children.

Despite projecting the façade of a subservient slave, the ember flared five days after Mama died and earned Tullia her first beating.

It started with an altercation in a bedchamber.

"What are you doing?" came Atia's nervous voice.

"Taking what I want, you little whore."

Tullia heard a slap as she rushed into the room. Atia stood on the bed, kicking out as a guard, known as Linus, grabbed her leg. Striking his head, her bare foot had no effect. The man pulled her in. A vicious backhand knocked her down and he tore at her tunic.

Tullia grabbed an empty terra-cotta chamber pot and smashed it across the man's head. He fell forward, unmoving. A whimpering Atia wriggled out from under her assailant and jumped to Tullia.

Rupinus entered the room. "What's going on in here?"

Tullia glowered at him. "That man tried to violate this little girl. I stopped him."

Rupinus backhanded Tullia, her arm still around Atia's shoulders. He shoved them out the door. "Get out of here. I'll deal with you later."

Tullia staggered to a waiting Faustina. The older woman took Atia, whose nose bled and left eye swelled.

"Linus tried to rape Atia," gasped Tullia. "Help her to bed."

Rupinus emerged, grabbing Tullia's arm, and landing another backhand to her face. Dazed, she stumbled. He dragged her to the atrium and groped her still-tender genitals. He spun her and landed a solid kick to her buttocks. She sprawled face down on the cool tiles. He dropped and straddled her, grinding. Leaning close, he bit her ear and snarled. "First the mother, then the daughter?" he smirked. "Oh, maybe not today. But argue with me again and it will be worse for you and the slave girl."

He pushed with his pelvis and stood, leaving her on the floor.

Rising, she straightened her clothes and thought of Atia, careful to keep her face impassive. *If I can get even I will, but can I? The risks to the children!* Her anguished thoughts swirled, offering no answers.

* * *

The next day Tullia saw Linus try again to corner Atia. The young woman evaded his grab and raced to the patio. Linus swore and went to the kitchen.

Seated at the table, Rupinus watched and appeared entertained.

"Master, please," pleaded Tullia.

"What did you say?" he asked, rising.

Not caring she would pay a price, she shouted. "This must stop. My husband would not approve of this savagery."

Coming around the table, Rupinus slapped her twice and kicked her to the floor. Grabbing her by the tunic, he dragged her to the couch and groped. Despite the pain from his probing fingers, she tried to remain limp.

"Ah, now that's better," he said. She endured the degradation in silence until he lost interest. He pushed her onto the floor.

"Get back to work."

The pain dimmed to a dark ache. Without a word, she rose, intent on seeing Atia. She flexed her fingers. *And I will gouge your eyes out if you try to stop me, you filthy animal.*

But Rupinus ignored her.

On the patio, she found Atia and Faustina. "Are you all right?"

Wiping her nose, Atia shrugged. "Yes, Domina. He couldn't catch me." She sighed and locked her good eye with Tullia. "I dream of the day I cut his filthy throat."

Jolted by Atia's determination, Tullia froze. As if seeing the young slave for the first time, she realized Atia was no longer a little girl. Taller now, but still a hand shorter than Tullia, she blossomed with the features of early womanhood—a waist, hints of fullness to her chest, and a sharper jawline. Despite the age difference, Tullia felt a kinship with the young woman, vowing if Atia could do it, she could too.

* * *

Over the coming days, Linus ignored Atia, and Tullia's molestations by Rupinus grew less frequent. She asked Faustina why.

"You brought up your husband to him. He may realize he can't afford to do too much damage, or he'll have to answer for it. Until Vitalio finds the money, he needs you alive." It didn't make her feel any better, but Tullia remained thankful for the respite. To her great relief, the captors showed no interest in Faustina, Chloe, or her three children.

An uneasy household routine developed. On market days, Atia, Chloe, and Faustina shopped. At times, Tullia joined them. When not at the market, she walked the baby and the boys in the open field between the Forum and the Subura where she lounged with Yosef years earlier. All trips were conducted under the watchful eyes of guards—usually Milo and another.

Tullia savored the walks—the cool crisp air, the sunshine, her children. One day, gazing across the field at the Subura, she wondered about Yosef in a brothel. *Dear Yosef, I think of you. Be safe, be strong.*

Rupinus remained drunk most days, and the men seemed bored. Tullia watched the guards and kept her mind sharp. She hungered for information, determination replacing depression. Unsure of an exact plan for revenge or escape, she fretted that time was growing short. How much longer before Vitalio secured the money and came to finish them off?

33

One month into captivity, Atia and Tullia knelt scrubbing the stone floor in the kitchen. A disinterested guard lingered, picking at a sore on his arm. When they were under the kitchen worktable, Atia whispered. "At the market today, a man gave me this." She passed Tullia a rumpled piece of sheepskin.

Tullia shoved it under her tunic. The guard ignored them. She winked at the girl and mouthed, "Thank you."

The floor clean, Tullia approached the lazy guard. "Master, may I go to the privy?"

He said nothing, waving her off.

Looking at the floor, Tullia walked to the patio. Once outside, she hurried to the privy, marveling that Rupinus and the guards were too stupid to remove the door. Next to walks with the boys, she most prized the private moments in the small enclosure.

Open from above but protected from the elements by the higher roof of the colonnaded patio, the room offered ample light. Tullia opened the sheepskin and read the fine script:

Kal Feb N III. No names. Sc has taken the money to Ostia, slowing things. B is free but watched and warned that executions will occur if he interferes. He waits every day at the LPT for contact. Try to meet. Nothing on Y. Sx

Heart thundering, she committed the words to memory

and dropped the sheepskin in the privy, assured the steady rush of water would carry it away.

Returning to the house, her mind swirled. Balbus was not dead, probably because of his connection to the army. Vitalio simply could not murder him without raising suspicion. And Sextus, dear Sextus. His spies were out there watching and keeping him informed. Was it possible to get out of this? The note said yes, and her heart skipped a beat. She returned to the villa, her steps too rapid, her head held too high, and she nearly gave herself away. Catching the mistakes, she assumed a slave's demeanor, slumping and moving slowly.

Rupinus sat at the study table and leered at her.

"Master, may I feed the baby?"

He grunted.

She retired to her bedchamber. Without a privacy curtain, Rupinus could look directly into the corner room. He watched her bare a breast but returned to sharpening his knife and swigging wine once Aurelia latched on.

The rhythm of Aurelia's gentle suckling calmed Tullia as she translated the cryptic message. It was written today, the first day of February, the third year of Nero's reign, and had to be from the lawyer Sextus. Siculus had moved the money to Cousin Varus's in Ostia. *Poor, nervous Siculus*, she thought. He was no doubt also hiding there, shaking alone in a dark room. But that meant Vitalio could find neither the accountant nor the money. She bit her lip, humming softly as she worked to the next line in her mind. Balbus stayed away because of threats. She knew LPT referred to the Lone Pine Tavern on the Forum, the same place she threw away the coin that Nero gave her six years earlier. *Balbus is waiting to hear from us.*

We'll have to try something. Siculus cannot hold out forever. Her thoughts flitted to Yosef. Nothing. Not even a glimpse of him.

Tullia readjusted her position and continued humming as Aurelia suckled. No news was still better than bad news. And with Balbus at least free of confinement, that was their chance. All they needed was a plan.

* * *

That night Faustina left a jug of powerful, undiluted Falernian wine in a corner of the kitchen, certain to be found and consumed by the night guard.

Hours after the household slept, Tullia crept into Faustina's room. Rupinus's man sprawled on the couch, snoring like a braying donkey.

"Faustina!" whispered Tullia. "It worked. He's sleeping."

"I know. I've waited all night. We must be quick."

"How can I meet with Balbus?" asked Tullia.

"I'll have Atia find him tomorrow. The guards don't watch so closely when we shop in the Forum. He'll know what to do."

"Have Atia tell him I'll come to the market and meet him at the Lone Pine. He needs to arrange a distraction for the guards."

"Tomorrow then. We start by finding Balbus; there's nothing to lose."

Tullia tiptoed back to her room, too nervous to sleep. Could the plan work? Can she convince Rupinus to let her go? She pushed away the anxiety and thought of the fountain fish. Even with all the atrocities that had befallen them, she knew it continued to smile. A rush of warmth seized her. But just as quickly, it melted into guilt. Against a backdrop of despair, she replayed dozens of content memories, all with Yosef at the center. *How happy we were out there, the birds chirping and the fountain gurgling. I pray you are well. I cannot imagine the misery I may have brought upon you.* The thought tempered her joy. She closed her eyes and laid back on the bed, mind and body restless. *Forgive me, if you can.*

34

ONE MONTH EARLIER

Yosef left the villa and walked with his captors through the humid morning chill, wetness coating his body from the thick fog. Naked, with wrists bound and barefoot, he watched the wet cobblestones, careful to dodge puddles and debris. The steady pace kept him from shivering outwardly, but inside his gut churned with every step he took away from Tullia.

We could not expect to go on forever, he knew, but the thought did not help. Fear choked him. How long, he wondered, would they last under Vitalio's thumb?

Long ago he resigned his fate to that of a non-person without rights or power. For a slave, death could spring from the shadows at any time. The relationship with Tullia buried the thought in a mental vault. But now, at the mercy of cruel men, he felt a crack in the crypt, recognizing the emergence of the familiar "letting go" of his life. But not today. He pushed it away. It was not only Tullia, but his daughter, Aurelia, who would always need him. Clenching his jaw, he swore he would find a way to get back to them. *I love you both, but I cannot help right now. Be strong, be clever. I am coming.*

"Move it, slave boy." A guard shoved him. "You're soon to be a *scortator*."

Sodomite. Anger grew from Yosef's determination to survive. *I'm not dead yet.*

The guard sneered. "How was it with the Senator's wife, anyway? She good on her knees?"

Yosef turned his head and mockingly raised his brow. "When I get to the brothel, I'll be sure to see how she compares to your mother."

The guard lunged, swinging a wild fist. Yosef ducked and swept the man's legs out from under him. The guard fell into a puddle with a splash.

The party stopped at the commotion. Vitalio looked back. "What's going on?"

Yosef tensed, but the men only guffawed at the sputtering guard.

"Linus slipped and fell," called somebody.

His tunic soaked, Linus stood and wiped muddy water off his bare legs. He glowered at Yosef, but said nothing as Vitalio ordered them to keep moving.

Yosef looked at the sopping man and flung an insult of his own. "*Cunnus.*"

Linus tensed to charge but another guard spun and hit Yosef in the stomach. "Shut up."

Yosef, expecting the blow, gasped and lurched forward for show. The guard pointed at Linus. "Let it go."

Yosef kept walking. Pushing away his longing for Tullia, he considered the situation. They were dangerous but untrained ruffians. Thinking of the Pompeii bandits, he remembered the ease with which he had dispatched two men. Could he do it again? He knew he could slip and fake a fall, bringing his bound hands under his feet. But even with his hands forward, he might kill one or two, but it left too many. He could not win. He could go down fighting but would surely die. No, he would bide his time. His family needed him.

Leaving the road for an earthen path, they crossed a field and entered the Subura. After two blocks on the cobblestone *Clivus Suburanus*, they stopped at the wooden door of a three-story brick building. Latin script chiseled into the adjacent wall, identified The Honey Pot. Beneath the writing, crude figurines featuring the coupling of a man and woman offered clarity about the business. The brothel constituted one of several shops on the ground floor of a modest insula.

Yosef's despair deepened as reality dawned. But he pursed his lips. *You will not give up. Look ahead, find a way. For Tullia, if not for yourself.* He refocused his attention, glancing at the building. *Better brick than wood. Too many fires in the Subura.*

A guard knocked. The lock clicked and the door opened. Vitalio, pushing Yosef forward, followed him in while the rest of his men waited outside.

The moment they entered the brothel, Yosef's mind sprang to life, as he assimilated information, looking for any advantage. He sniffed the foul air and took in the scene. Smoky oil lamps lit a tiny atrium. On the left and behind a crude wine bar, stood a fierce-looking man wearing a dirty blue head rag.

In front of Yosef, the atrium gave way to a hall cloaked by a stained privacy curtain, unmoving in the stale air. He read a large wooden sign, mounted high on a wall, advertising services and prices. Activities for both sexes included intercourse, cunnilingus, and fellatio, each written in Latin followed by rough drawings as a guide for the illiterate clientele. Prices ranged from four to twenty sesterces.

Two women lounged on a bench under the menu, their harsh lives reflected in crudely painted faces, shabby clothing, and an exposed floppy breast from the older woman. Their eyes scanned the men with dull, apathetic gazes.

Behind him, the keyholder closed the door and addressed Vitalio. "Senator, welcome back to The Honey Pot."

The words did not surprise Yosef. He looked at the man with the keys. Heavyset and short, with acne-scarred skin and close-set eyes, he resembled a knobby, myopic pear. A violaceous well-healed scar, running from ear to chin, gave testimony to his violent profession.

"Cresimus," Vitalio gave him a short nod. "This is Yosef, your next young stud."

The brothel owner looked at the prostitutes on the bench and jerked his thumb. Grunting, they slinked around the curtain.

Cresimus, smiling with stunning white teeth, turned to Yosef. "Let's take a look." He wielded a knife beneath Yosef's throat. "Don't do something foolish." He slipped around and cut the ropes binding Yosef's hands. After moving back to face him, he pointed the knife in silent warning, sheathing it on his belt. Taking Yosef's arms, he squeezed, tracking up to the muscular shoulders. He smacked Yosef's wet chest, back, and buttocks. During the examination, Yosef subtly stretched his tight arms but was otherwise immobile. Looking forward, he watched and absorbed every event, every detail.

The chunky man's dark eyes danced with cautious intelligence, his movements precise and effeminate. Smelling of burnt wood, he spoke a guttural, unpolished Latin. A dark brown tunic flowed in waves and bumps and could have concealed a money bag, knife, or figurines of his favorite gods, not that he appeared to be the religious type. Yosef saw soiled but expensive sandals on his feet as the owner circled him again and again. He wondered if Cresimus was more prosperous than the shabby brothel suggested.

"Aye, good stock," the little man crowed, finally stepping back. "Thank you, Senator. I hope you enjoy your next ten free visits."

Vitalio licked his lips, then offered his hand, which the owner took. Sneering, the senator looked back at Yosef. "Good luck, slave boy."

Cresimus closed the door as he left and pointed at Yosef. "You stay."

Yosef obeyed.

The brothel owner shifted his gaze to the wine bar as the man with the head rag dashed toward Yosef. Before Cresimus could reach him, Yosef drove a hard left into his face. The man staggered as Cresimus arrived. Yosef stepped out of the way as the stout brothel owner dragged the man and slammed him into the front wall, the bricks a solid backstop. He followed with a vicious kick to the groin. The man doubled over, immobilized. Cresimus pulled him up and thrust the knife at his throat.

Yosef watched with interest, impressed by the portly owner's agility.

"Not so fast," hissed Cresimus, flicking the blade. A shallow slice oozed the purple of venous blood. "Where's my money?"

"H- here," said the man, no longer looking fierce with blood running out of his nose and neck. He pulled a small bag of coins from his tunic.

Cresimus grabbed it and pointed with the knife. "If I see you again, I will finish the job."

Released, the man pulled the door open and staggered out into the morning gloom.

Yosef maintained his position and waited. He concluded Cresimus was good at his job but wondered why the thief did not escape in the night.

The brothel owner placed the pouch on the bar.

As if reading Yosef's mind, Cresimus said, "He sleeps here and was waiting for a chance to run away with that money. I knew what he was up to, so I locked him in." He brandished a bronze key in front of Yosef. "I planned to deal with him after your arrival."

His voice grew more business-like. "Nice shot with the fist, thank you. Now, you're a fit-looking lad and should be able to command twenty sesterces. So, slave boy, is it girls, boys, or both?"

"None."

The owner looked at him, his close-set eyes blinking. He boomed a deep laugh and punched Yosef's arm. "Well, we shall see, won't we? I'll get a couple of the good whores to show you the ropes while you decide."

"And who will pour your wine and drag out the drunks?" asked Yosef.

Cresimus tilted his head and squinted. "Why? Are you interested?"

"I speak Latin and Greek, and can read, write, and do numbers. I am as good with a knife as I am with my fists. I may be more useful to you out front."

The owner's eyes bored into him for a long moment, and

he flashed a bright smile. "Well now, what have we here? Let's get you a tunic and out of this morning chill. Yosef, is it? I'm Cresimus."

35

The day had finally arrived. Tullia awoke with renewed vigor, eager to see Balbus after so long and determined to set an escape plan in motion. But that morning Rupinus refused her request to leave for the market.

"Please, Master," she begged, sitting on her heels in the atrium. "The others are out with the children, and we need more wine."

Leering, he smirked. "What's in it for me?"

She sighed. "What do you want?" *You filthy pig*, she added in her mind.

He pointed at her breasts. "I want to see them."

She pushed away her anger and disgust. Nothing must keep her from Balbus. "Then I must go."

Nodding, he grinned and sipped some wine.

Careful to keep the table between them, she pulled up her tunic. Due to the one-piece nature of the garment, he got more than he bargained for as she was forced to expose everything from her knees to her neck. Her heart thundered in fear. *What if it's not enough?*

His eyes bounced between her breasts and pubic mound. Tullia let him stare, counting in her head, then began to lower the cloth. Grinning like a hungry animal he stood. "Not so fast," he growled, rounding the table as he panted.

Heart racing, she dropped the hems and stepped back just as a guard entered.

"Rupinus, a message."

The large man snorted but ceased his advance. "What is it?" he asked with an impatient edge.

The guard whispered in his ear. Rupinus raised his eyebrows.

"Master, may I *please* go now?"

He waved his hand. "Just get back here by the fourth hour."

Tullia hurried out. *Thank Juno for that distraction*, she thought. Two guards accosted her, one leading and the other staying behind to watch her every movement.

At the entrance to the Forum stood the Lone Pine Tavern. Ahead, an older couple trundled along, leading a mule cart of firewood and slowing Tullia's progress. With growing exasperation, she watched the overloaded cart edge forward when suddenly, a wheel bobbled and popped off. The cart tipped, dumping firewood across the narrow road. The mule brayed and turned, clogging the street.

The old couple loitered around the mess, confused and unsure as if they didn't quite know what happened. The white-haired woman turned to Tullia and the guards. "Sirs, can you help us?"

"Get out of the way, we'll go around," said the lead guard, pushing her.

"But I have money!" she protested, hitting her waist. An audible jangle could be heard. "I'll give you each twenty sesterces!"

This has to be Balbus's doing, Tullia thought, praying the man could be bought. She turned to the guard. "We're not in that big a hurry and it's easy money for the work. I can wait."

The leader shrugged. "Let's see the money."

A warm smile lit the old woman's face, and she produced a worn cloth bag from her tunic. The guard took the proffered coins, examined them, then jerked his chin toward the tavern without looking at Tullia. "Stay over there 'til we're done."

"May I go in and sit?" she asked, trying to keep the joy out of her voice.

The guard rolled his eyes and pocketed the money. Tullia took that as a yes, hurrying off without a backward glance. If this was the plan, it was working perfectly.

She entered the red-brick building, the room lit by the open door and several five-wicked oil lamps hanging from the low ceiling. To the left sat a waist-high, stone counter with a white marble top punctuated by large sunken jars filled with steaming soups or stews, the pungent aroma of garlic mixing with the earthy smells of barley broth. One end of the counter housed eating utensils—stacks of clean dishes, rows of cups, and a small basket of spoons—at the other, a platter sat heaped with round loaves of bread.

A worker ladling wine from one of the jars froze as Tullia entered the room. She knew it was not unusual for an un-accompanied woman to enter such an establishment—after all, women had to eat also—but his glance was unwelcoming. She looked past him into the room. At least twenty other men huddled around tables laughing, eating, or drinking, none of whom took notice of her.

She spotted Balbus sitting at a corner table as she approached the server. "I'm meeting him," she said, lifting her chin to the back.

The man squinted but resumed his work.

Balbus stood on her arrival, and they hugged.

"Balbus," she cried, "we're trapped. Mama is dead, they killed her in front of me. You must help us." Despite the urgency, a rush of relief washed over her. It was so good to see a friendly face.

The old soldier gestured for her to take a seat, his brow creased with concern and anger. "I know, Domina. They have threatened to kill you all if I make a move."

"We'll die anyway," she retorted, fidgeting in her chair. "Once he has the money, we are no use to him alive. He *must* be stopped." Her eyes bored with a fevered intensity into the soldier's. "Can you arrange what has to be done?"

He looked pained. "I can, but at what cost to you and your family? His death will be investigated, and you may be held responsible."

"Anything is better than Vitalio." She and Faustina had long ago dismissed the dangers. At least with the authorities, she could argue her case. "His cruelty is well known. Daily, the guards molest me and poor Atia. What cost can be worse? With him gone, at least there's hope."

Balbus cringed. His eyes grew cold. "My men are scattered around Rome. I'll work out a plan to finish this. These vicious animals will be stopped."

Tullia's spirits soared. "Oh, Balbus, thank you." She grabbed his huge hand. "You've given me hope."

"Go now. I'll get word to you."

Trying not to cry, she left him in the corner. *Thank Juno. Just a little longer.*

She hurried out the door and her heart sank in horror. Vitalio, Rupinus, and their men stood on the porch. Before she could think, let alone move to warn Balbus, six of the guards thundered into the tavern and the sounds of violent scuffling arose. Bystanders poured out of the entrance behind her, and for a moment she thought she could flee with them, certain Vitalio would lose her among the horde. But her feet remained stuck to the ground. Once the last of the patrons had fled, Rupinus grabbed her tunic and yanked her forward.

Vitalio spun a dagger between his fingers, circling her like a hunter. "Oh *lupae*, how stupid do you think I am? Did you really believe you could escape?" He slapped her so hard Rupinus lost his grip. She staggered back and wiped her bleeding nose.

Her husband snorted. "I suppose I should thank you," he said, closing in. "You have helped me. Sending your slave girl out yesterday to find Balbus gave me the needed excuse to finish him and foil your plot." His head tilted, studying her with contempt. "The proprietor filled me in. When the stupid girl showed up, he tried to enforce the "no children" rule, but Balbus put a knife to his throat and threatened him. He also had bad memories of the man from his army days, so he informed me of the meeting."

He hit her in the stomach, dropping her to her knees. Fighting nausea, she saw an unconscious Balbus, bound and bleeding from a head wound, dragged out.

"Vital—" she managed to sputter.

"Shut up, whore!" He kicked her in the ribs, and she sprawled on the floor of the shallow porch, gasping. Another kick landed in the middle of her back, then he stepped away.

"Pick her up," she heard. "Return her to the villa. If she resists, beat her, but do not kill her. And do not violate her. That pleasure is for me later."

STAN NAHMAN

Rupinus grabbed her arm and hauled her up, shoving her in the direction of home. She stumbled onto the cobblestone road, trying to stem her bleeding nose, and through swollen eyes stole a glance back for Balbus. There was no sign of him. Despair clutched her stomach. He was probably already dead.

At the villa, Rupinus pushed Tullia onto her knees in front of Faustina. "Clean her up and get back to work," he barked, turning on his heel without waiting for an answer.

Faustina knelt. Her warm hand pressed against Tullia's back. "Domina, can you stand?"

Groaning, Tullia rose. Leaning heavily on the older woman's shoulder, she limped to her bedchamber and sat gingerly on the edge of the bed. Elbows on her knees, she stretched her sore back and looked at the floor, exhausted and defeated. Her rib cage ached with every breath.

Faustina returned with a damp cloth. Sitting next to her, she wiped the blood-encrusted spots on Tullia's face. "Domina, what happened?" she asked, softening the cloth's touch around the nose.

Wincing with every word, Tullia gave an abbreviated version of the events. A tear escaped and dribbled down her lip.

Faustina sighed and straightened her back. "Domina, it will only get worse from here."

"Worse?" Tullia echoed, then grimaced at the pain in her ribcage. "How could it get worse? Balbus was our last hope, and he may be dead now. Vitalio will come back. We will die, my children taken, the family shamed and erased from all memory. What could be worse?"

A pitying look entered the servant's eye as she rose to dab

the swollen spots once more. "Until you die, it can always get worse."

Tullia felt her spirit drain away. The harshness of Faustina's words carried a terrifying ring of truth that she had never before contemplated—she never had to. But for Faustina at one point, for Atia and Chloe now, and for Yosef wherever he was, the words were always there. Always haunting them. *There's no limit to the torture that can be inflicted before a slave's death.*

36

The next day, a stiff and groaning Tullia placed Aurelia in her cradle. Her back and chest muscles screamed with every movement. As she wiped her forehead from the exertion, Rupinus approached. "We are cutting rations for the house so there will be more for the men. The senator feels too much money is being squandered on food."

She glared at him. "That's ridiculous and you know it!" His arm shot out, but she turned her head. The backhand glanced off her cheek, but she could not escape the follow-up death grip to her throat.

He squeezed. Hard. She choked, unable to breathe. His grip tightened. Panicking, she struggled but failed to break the hold. Her pulse thudded behind her eyes. Vision blurred. Her arms weakened.

He pulled her up by the throat and dropped her on the bed. "You can fast the rest of the day."

She coughed, recovering her breath. But her thoughts came back sharp and angry. *Vitalio! Dear Juno, please grant me the joy of revenge. Vicious animals!* Panting, she closed her eyes and tried to think. Her anger cooled as clarity dawned. *The first step of torture—starvation!* Anger returned and, with it, a stubborn hatred for Vitalio and the men. *If we are to die, I will resist to the end. I'll protect the children as long as I can.*

* * *

True to his word, Rupinus cut the morning rations.

Tullia, still hungry from the previous day's fast could not control her irritation. "This is all?" she demanded of Rupinus.

He seemed to enjoy her discomfort. "Yes. And there will be no trips to the market this week. There is food for the men, but you and your people will have to live on the scraps."

"And his sons? Are we starving them, too?"

"Everybody. They are *your* children, he does not care."

Her heart sunk at the cruel news. How could a father be so callous?

She took her place at the table, broke a meager crust of bread into pieces, and gave one each to the boys. She took two bites of a shriveled half-fig, split the rest in two, and passed it along to them also. *I will not let them starve.*

Tullia tried to maintain her work routines, but required extra rest. The privy became her sanctuary. She could at least cry and try to think in private.

On her next trip, the door was gone.

She confronted Rupinus.

"You spend too much time hiding in there." He paused. "Oh, now, don't cry. It won't be much longer."

She felt her face flush with embarrassment at the tears that came from nowhere.

But he was not done. "At least your figure is growing trim." He squeezed her buttocks as she turned away.

She found Faustina in the kitchen and rushed into her open arms. "You were right, it's getting worse. And I cried in front of him. I couldn't help it."

Pulling away, Faustina cupped Tullia's face in her hands. "Domina, they are trying to break us. Do not give up. Focus on work, the children, and Yosef. He would want you to go on."

Tullia wiped her eyes, and she felt her face relax at the words. The angry ember she had harbored for so long began to glow. The children—yes, the children.

She took a breath. "As I die, I will protect my children."

Faustina gave a sad smile. "You are a good mother. Stay strong."

After a week of austerity, the adults and slave girls grew haggard and weak. Despite Tullia's efforts, the three children became scrawny and fussy.

Listless, Tullia showed no reaction to Rupinus's groping. "What, no spirit? You are like a limp rag. It's no wonder the senator prefers his whores."

"I'm hungry and weak. Do what you will."

"Get out of my sight."

Happy to, you pig, but I will not give in. You'll have to kill me. She still harbored fading dreams of revenge and the hope that her children might survive—maybe Yosef could find them after she was gone. *If he's alive.*

37

"Master Yosef, wake up," whispered Sabina, a young prostitute from Ostia. She stood at his bedside, her dark silhouette hiding a pock-marked face.

Yosef rolled over, propping himself up on an elbow. "I'm awake. What is it?"

"A drunken man from last night. He's very sick. Can you help me?"

Rising, he pulled a tunic over his *subligaculum*, the shorts he used for sleepwear. He slipped into sandals, not surprised by the visit. In the month since his arrival, Yosef had become the favorite of the working girls. A patient listener with a sympathetic ear and sound advice, he mediated their quibbles. The Rule, his commandments, and common sense guided his thinking. He also protected them from unruly customers. The women trusted him and called on him when needed.

The brothel owner also appreciated his contributions. Just the day before, Cresimus sat on a barstool as Yosef cleaned a few plates. He jabbed a stubby finger at a page in an open scroll. "Well, Yosef, it looks like you were right. Your suggestion to use smaller wine cups for the same price improved profits."

"It's not like they come here to drink," said Yosef.

The proprietor's eyes bounced. "You've made a difference. Even the whores like you. We're like Cicero and Tiro, eh?" He chuckled at the analogy. "Except for the fact that I am not a famous lawyer, Cicero and I are the same—screwing people for money and owning clever slaves."

Yosef knew the reference to the hero and his slave from the Republic. He listened to Tullia's tutor give her lessons in Roman history. He also knew that Cicero's daughter was a bright girl named Tullia. *I pray* my *Tullia is as smart.*

He followed Sabina to her cubicle. *What now?* he wondered. He brought his knife, knowing that often drunks with women lost all judgment. He had spent many nights breaking up fights and throwing out unruly clients, but one incident in particular stood out. Perhaps it was because it was the only one from which he had to sever a body part. Cresimus loved it. More than once, the younger man had caught his owner retelling the story to frequent patrons.

That night Yosef had rushed into the room adjacent to his, having heard a high-pitched scream. He found a naked drunk on top of a nude and face-down prostitute, yelling obscenities. This one was in a particularly violent mood—pulling the young woman's head up by her hair with an arm locked around her throat.

"Enough!" Yosef yelled, pointing with his knife. He grabbed the man's arm. "Get off, you're done here."

The bleary-eyed punter roared, released the girl's hair, and swung a fist at Yosef. The blow went nowhere, and in a fast move, Yosef grabbed the drunk's ear and sliced it off. With a screech, the man tumbled to the floor, clutching his bleeding scalp. The howls of pain brought Cresimus. He sighed, picked up the ear, and helped Yosef drag the inebriated fool out the front door as if it was nothing he hadn't seen a hundred times before.

Cresimus also tossed out the bloody appendage. "Here. You might need this," he said before closing the heavy door on the man's writhing body. He turned to Yosef, who stood wiping his blade clean. "An ear?"

Yosef shrugged. "Easy target. Besides, now we'll know if he returns."

Cresimus guffawed and retired to his study.

Now, in Sabina's tiny cubicle, Yosef found the half-conscious young man face down on the floor. He suppressed a gag at the overpowering stench of vomit.

Sabina wrinkled her nose. "We never did anything. He passed out, then woke up for a moment and tossed it all." On tiptoe, she negotiated the edge of a vile puddle. "I will never get the stink out of here."

Yosef took shallow breaths. As disagreeable as the odors in the brothel could be, this was worse. *How was that possible? Poor Sabina.*

"I'll help you clean up later," he said. "First, let me get him out of here."

He crouched, held his breath, and rolled the man onto his shoulder so he could see his face. Brushing away a grimy felt hat, he found a head of blond hair. Yosef's breath caught. *It couldn't be.* He flopped the man onto his back. By the dim flicker of two oil lamps, he recognized Titus, the young nobleman from Pompeii. *What is he doing here?* Yosef was afraid of the answer.

"Come on," he said, shaking Titus's shoulder. No reply. He shook again, harder.

"Ugh," came a useless groan.

Yosef took a deep breath, then regretted it. Pushing down nausea, he squatted, hooked his arms underneath Titus's shoulders, and heaved him upright. They stood as Titus's head lolled against Yosef's neck.

"Master Titus," Yosef panted, poking him once in the ribs. "Master Titus, I am Yosef. We met on the road to Pompeii last summer. Do you remember?"

The man's eyes opened, then his head rolled to the right.

"Master *Titus*." Another poke, this one sharper and with hard knuckles.

"Ughhh." His head pushed back. "I-I remember," Titus croaked, releasing a foul belch.

Yosef turned his head, fighting back another gag. "Whew. You need a bath and something for a hangover," he said, tightening his grip around the unsteady man. "Let's go."

Leaving Sabina to wash the room, Yosef led the inebriated young man out into the early morning haze.

Ascending the slight incline of the *Clivus*, they entered a small public bath Yosef used to rejuvenate over-cooked customers from the brothel. Limited to a small tepidarium and hot and cold baths, the modest facility lacked the rooms and fancy artwork of better establishments such as the *thermae* of Agrippa—one Yosef was sure a man of Titus's standing was more accustomed to—but it would have to do.

Wall lamps lit the compact lobby, the air heavy with humidity. A short changing bench occupied one side and a draped doorway in the far wall led to the baths. To the right sat a waist-high counter stacked with clean towels and tunics, and staffed by a slender, swarthy man.

"Yosef, good morning. You are the first today. I see you have one. Can he pay?" asked the owner, an Armenian, his eyes glimmering like the earring dangling from his left ear.

Titus looked up with hooded eyes. "How much?"

The proprietor looked him over, wrinkling his nose. "Ten for the bath and judging by the smell of that tunic, ten more for a fresh one."

Grunting, Titus reached a wobbly hand underneath his tunic and returned with a money pouch. The owner extended his hand, but Titus did not move — his eyes were once again glazed over. Yosef nudged him with his shoulder, then took the pouch, extracted the necessary coins, and plopped them into the Armenian's waiting palm. Titus made no complaint.

The owner pocketed the coins, then whistled sharply. Two slaves emerged, relieving Yosef and propelling Titus to the back. Yosef sat on the bench to wait.

In short order, a scrubbed Titus returned, sporting a clean tunic and looking much more like the man he had met in Pompeii. His eyes, now alert, scanned the small lobby and landed on Yosef.

"Thank you."

Yosef inclined his head. "Happy to help." He paused, observing how the young man still swayed somewhat uneasily on his feet.

Glancing at the Armenian, Yosef dipped his chin in thanks.

"Good luck," called the owner, as they left.

"I can offer you something to eat and drink back at The Honey Pot before you depart."

The suggestion was graciously received. Once Titus was seated at the wine bar, Yosef prepared willow bark tea from a kettle on a small brazier. In another cup, he mixed peppermint water to help settle the young man's stomach. Titus accepted it with a nod of thanks and downed it all in one gulp.

"My head hurts," he moaned, one hand raised to massage his temples.

Yosef gave him the tea. "Try this."

The hungover nobleman took a few sips and sighed. "I leave for Germania in the morning. The send-off last night got a little wild." His cheeks flushed red.

"You should be fine by tomorrow," Yosef replied. He didn't want to sound like he was judging him, so he busied himself with slicing a loaf of bread and setting it on top of the bar. "It'll be the kalends of February—new month, fresh start."

Titus took a crust and munched. "Let's hope so."

Yosef tidied the bar. As his hangover eased, Yosef recognized the steely determination of Titus's gaze from the Pompeii trip. You could sense the aura of an intelligent leader, if not a warrior. Yosef knew it was more than just the security of the nobility. *Titus, you'll go far.*

The meager breakfast complete, Titus raised both hands above his head and arched his back. His jaw opened in an enormous yawn. "Ah, that's better. Thank you, Yosef, for your help."

"Glad I could."

Titus watched him a moment, his gaze sliding past to take in the dank interior of the brothel. A wrinkle appeared on his forehead. "You've done me the courtesy of not asking how I came to be here," he began, "but I am afraid I cannot do the same. Whatever are you doing *here*?" He spread an arm wide, then lowered his voice. "And where is Lady Tullia?"

With a sigh, Yosef recounted events landing him in the brothel. His heart fluttered with worry for Tullia. Titus responded to the concern on his face.

"Cheer up, you're lucky to be alive,"Titus said, a small smile on his lips. "The Senate rules limiting frank murder probably got you here rather than dead in the Tiber."

"Most likely," Yosef acknowledged. "I escaped death, but Tullia's trapped by the senator. I fear she'll not be so lucky."

The young nobleman pursed his lips. "There's not enough time for me to help spring her from his grip. But I can send word from the Royal House to the Senate that the situation bears watching. Who's her lawyer?"

Incredulous at the offer, Yosef struggled to speak. "Ah, Antonio Sextus."

"I'll see what I can do."

Yosef's heart thundered with hope; more hope than he'd felt since forced to leave the villa. He wanted to say more, but Titus had left his stool and was digging in his money pouch. He flipped several coins onto the counter, then stopped.

"Are you alright?"

"Oh-oh, yes, Milord," Yosef stuttered. "My deepest thanks for your consideration." He came around the bar and bowed. "And do be careful in Germania."

Titus flashed a cocky smile. "Don't worry. I'll make it a point to return to Rome and see how things turn out for you and Lady Tullia." He raised an eyebrow. "Oh, and keep that old tunic."

They laughed. Yosef escorted him to the door and offered his hand, which Titus shook in a firm but not crushing embrace.

"Take care, Yosef."

"Thank you, sir, and good luck." *And may God watch over you.*

After Titus left, Yosef went straight to Sabina's room, barely holding back a tearful smile. By his God, he would do everything he could to restore that room to its original smell if it meant Titus could help them.

38

Tullia moaned and reached for Yosef. Her arm flopped across her chest as she awakened. Her smile from the pleasant dream quickly melted. Seeing the light threading between the shutters, she recognized another day of misery. Bony Aurelia slept in her cradle. *My poor baby, starvation draining her life away.*

Rising, Tullia splashed water on her face and struggled to remember the day. Two weeks since the Kalends? Or was it three? Her stomach no longer ground with hunger, but water still refreshed. She left Aurelia and dragged herself out to the privy. Atia would see to her.

In the kitchen, she bumped into Faustina, whose gaunt face resembled a skull. "Sorry," mumbled Tullia. A bored guard watched them gather one fig and a single loaf for the household breakfast.

Faustina took her arm and in a low voice said, "Oh, Domina. I too am getting tired, but we must endure." She cracked a tiny smile. "Siculus must have done a great job hiding the money since we are still alive."

Tullia took in her earnest look. "You are so strong," she whispered, awash in gratitude for the steady encouragement.

"I am so old," came the meaningless reply. "But I will not die on my own. They will have to do it. The same for you."

Tullia saw the glimmer of determination in her old face and sighed. "Let's keep going." She twitched the corners of her mouth. "How about some breakfast?" she asked, trying to lighten the mood.

Gathering the single fig and small loaf allocated to the household, they walked to the table where Chloe and the boys sat. Quieter these days, three pairs of sunken eyes followed them in. Atia arrived, trading Aurelia to Tullia for a plate. "You should go nurse her now," said the girl.

"I will. Save me a crust, you all can have the rest."

Retiring to the bedroom, Tullia let Aurelia pull what she could from her shriveled breasts. How much longer? she lamented. *Yosef, Balbus, anybody?*

39

"Master Yosef, I have news."

The younger of the two prostitutes present the day he arrived, approached him in the wine bar. Aunt and niece were both members of the Christian cult, shrugging off Rome's pagan gods. Yosef learned this one day in a conversation with the niece, Phoebe.

"Master Yosef, where are your gods?" she had asked, referring to the small figurines most Romans carried in a pocket or pouch.

"I have none. I worship only a single God," he said, impressed by the question.

"Us, too. We are Christians and have only one God."

"Phoebe, we both worship the same God, but just go about it differently," he offered, familiar with the traditions of the emerging cult.

"Well then, may God watch over you."

"And you."

From that point forward, they shared a small bond, a little extra familiarity.

"Master Yosef? Are you all right?" asked Phoebe.

The memory faded. "Yes, I'm fine, and please Phoebe, just Yosef."

She offered a weak smile, marred by two absent front teeth, the result of an altercation with a violent client. Greasy hair stuck to her skull like a helmet. Her unpainted face showed wear and tear far beyond her fourteen years.

Like the rest of the workers, she ignored his request. "Master, I have news of your household."

His heart stopped. Only a week had passed since Titus's visit. He smoothed both palms against his thighs, failing to dry the sweat that had sprung from them. He tried to calm himself and speak casually.

"Go on."

"The Domina was caught trying to contact her man. He's a prisoner somewhere away from the villa. She and her family are being starved."

His mouth turned to dust. "Phoebe, how do you know this?"

To his surprise, the girl blushed a deep crimson. Looking around the empty bar, she whispered. "One of the guards, Milo, is my man. When he visits me, he talks afterward. He told me last night he doesn't like what he sees, but the money is too good to turn down. He's going to buy me." She flashed a gaped grin and shrugged apologetically.

He patted her hand. "Thank you for telling me this. If you hear anymore, would you please let me know?"

"Yes, Master Yosef." She straightened up and bowed her head. "I am sorry for you. May God watch over your house."

After she left, Yosef paced around the room, tingling with excitement. Time was short. Tullia was still alive, but who knew for how long? And who was Tullia's man? He reasoned it was probably Balbus. Yosef doubted Vitalio had the courage to murder him but would probably hold him as a prisoner. Maybe for a ransom if he could not persuade Tullia or Siculus to give up the money. Too many questions. *I need to do something now.*

Yosef hurried to find Cresimus. From their discussions, he knew his boss neither liked nor trusted the senator, so he was comfortable with an inquiry.

The brothel owner looked up as Yosef entered the cluttered study. "Yosef? Problem?"

"I need your help."

Cresimus raised his brow. "Oh?" He gestured to a chair.

"It is about my household. I've come to know that the senator has imprisoned my family within their villa and is holding the house protector, a man called Balbus, hostage."

The proprietor leaned back with his hands on his belly, not looking overly concerned. "And how do you know this?"

"Phoebe told me. One of her suitors works for the senator."

Cresimus's face creased with a wry smile. "Yosef, when it comes to whores, customers, and information, you will understand my skepticism. Phoebe—"

"—is too young to lie and her story makes sense."

"They are never too young," the stout owner retorted, reminding Yosef of the gritty nature of his profession. "But what of it?"

"I need your help. To free Balbus."

Yosef knew Cresimus's position exposed him to all classes of Roman society—from high-ranking government officials to the criminal element. Finding strongmen to locate and free Balbus was well within his scope, assuming the price was right.

"Why should I?"

"He can rescue my Domina. For your role, you could name your price."

Cresimus jiggled with laughter, leaning forward to slap the table with both hands. "Hah! Yosef, you are talented, but not that talented." He counted on pudgy fingers. "First, this is a risky conversation which I will deny ever happened, second, you do not know he will succeed, and third, you do not have enough money."

Yosef barely heard him. "Listen to me," he urged, trying to keep his desperation in check. "We have never discussed my situation. Balbus has connections all through the city. He can easily marshal a force of fighting men that can take the villa—there's no doubt they would prevail—but if he is imprisoned, nothing can happen. As for the money, the Flaccus family is beyond rich. *I* am the father of the Domina's daughter. She planned to leave the senator and buy my freedom. When her father, both a general and a senator, died in the Parthian war, it all fell apart, and here I am."

To his disappointment, the brothel owner cackled on, tears welling from his crinkled eyes. "Oh, you mean you had a child with the senator's wife, and she planned to give it all up for you?"

The story sounded absurd as Cresimus told it, but no less than its reality, Yosef realized. "Ah, well, yes. I know it sounds ridiculous, but it's true. If you help me and we're successful, I swear that you'll be amply rewarded."

"You *are* full of surprises." Pausing for what seemed an eternity, Cresimus squinted and waggled a finger. "Not a sesterce less than a thousand."

Yosef smiled inside. He knew money was the language of Cresimus. "Accepted."

"There will also be expenses."

"Of course, of course. They'll be covered."

His owner pursed his lips, which Yosef hoped meant he had no more stalls. "All right, deal. If you succeed in reclaiming the fortune, you'd best remember who helped you." He tapped the desk. "If you fail and are caught, you'd better forget."

"You have my word," said Yosef, fighting tears of joy.

"You're grinning like an idiot. Now, tell me what you know."

* * *

Two days later, Balbus strode into The Honey Pot.

"Yosef," he said.

Yosef raced around the bar. "You made it!" he said, too happy for words. They embraced.

"Yes. Three men made quick business of the sloppy guards holding me. I was chained to a wall at the senator's dilapidated family farm. On my release, I went straight to the lawyer, Sextus, for information and funds."

Relief flooded Yosef's chest. Sextus must have been watching the situation at the villa. Was it now possible to plan a rescue? "But how did you know to come here?"

"Sextus. Word came from an official in the Senate as to where you were."

Titus, thought Yosef. His senatorial contact found the lawyer. He swelled with hope.

"We also suspected you were in some way behind my rescue and would need to pay somebody." He patted his pocket. "We'll need to—"

He stopped as Cresimus joined them. "What's all this?"

Yosef cut in. "This is the man you rescued. Meet Balbus."

The brothel owner flinched and looked around. "Wait. I know nothing of this man nor any so-called rescue."

The liberated soldier shook Cresimus's hand. "Thanks for not helping. It will save us from any financial obligations."

The proprietor's face fell.

Balbus grinned. "Don't worry. Once this is over, you'll be fully compensated. Is two hundred today a fair down payment?"

Cresimus flashed his brilliant smile. "Oh, yes. But it will just barely cover my expenses to date." Balbus handed over the coins, chuckling.

Yosef served watered wine.

Balbus turned back to Yosef. "Tell me what you know."

Cresimus listened as they compared notes.

"We need to retake the household before they kill the family," concluded Balbus.

Looking uncomfortable, the brothel owner rose. "This is not for me. I'll leave you to your plans, and don't forget my thousand." He held up the small money pouch Balbus gave him. "Remember, this was only for expenses."

He left. "What's next?" asked Yosef.

"Sextus is working on a way we can lawfully retake the villa and defeat Vitalio. I know Vitalio's gang. They're drunks, thieves, and a few naïve youngsters. My force can sweep them away like the lint they are, but it must be legal."

* * *

A week later, Phoebe reported that the senator would return

to Rome in two days and planned to go directly to the villa to "finish the business."

Yosef sent word to Balbus.

40

For Tullia, the day began innocently enough. With Atia and Chloe's help, the boys were awakened and led to the patio to wash. Tullia followed with Aurelia and sat on the bench nursing. It felt good to sit.

"Domina?" asked Atia, touching her shoulder.

"W-what?" mumbled Tullia. She had fallen asleep. "Oh, sorry." She forced a weak smile. "I'm just so tired."

"You do everything plus feed the baby," reassured Atia, whose young sparkle had faded. She helped Tullia stand.

"You're a very good person," said Tullia, trying not to cry.

Atia squeezed her arm and Tullia wondered if the slave had become the Domina.

Once in the house, she passed Aurelia over to the girl. Moving through mental fog, she joined Faustina in the kitchen.

An unfriendly but attentive guard watched as they prepared a robust breakfast of bread, figs, cheese, and wine for the men. Tullia savored the woody aroma of the baked bread and the sweet smell of the ripe figs. She had long since stopped wishing for either — the guard saw to that. But she did lick juice from her fingers when she could. She and Faustina worked in silence, what was there to say?

The family breakfast — a plate with two figs and a small

loaf—accompanied the meal and would remain after the men finished eating. They always ate everything or took the scraps, leaving nothing but the meager family plate.

The boys shared a fig and half the loaf. The four women split the remaining food.

Speaking was prohibited, but Tullia did not care. What else could they do to them? She addressed Faustina, Atia, and Chloe. "I appreciate how hard you have all worked under these inhuman conditions. I'm hopeful my husband will come to his senses or something will change soon."

"No talking," snapped Rupinus, walking into the room.

Tullia looked up at him. "So what?" she snarled.

Before he could strike her, she cut him off. "Go ahead, there's nothing left."

He turned on his heel and left as Tullia found unexpected energy in her anger. She faced the household. "So, we must keep going."

After breakfast and feeling good about telling off Rupinus, she rounded up the children for a morning walk. *Oh, my poor boys, they look like sticks*, she cried to herself. Despite emaciation, the energy of youth won out and both lads chattered away.

"Hurry, Mama," said Dracus, now four and tugging on her baggy tunic. His brother Marcus toddled and held Chloe's hand, jabbering in baby talk and giggling at Dracus. Tullia carried baby Aurelia in a chest sling as they headed to the open field across from the Subura.

Leaving the villa, her feelings of despair eased at the bright cloudless day. But her stomach gnawed, and despite her earlier confidence, she wondered how much longer they could last. In the nine days since the failed meeting with Balbus, the adults had withered, and three-month-old Aurelia sucked away her own dwindling reserves.

After moving off the road and onto the path through the field, Tullia felt dizzy and stumbled.

"Domina?" asked the guard, catching her by the elbow.

She regained her balance. "Oh, thank you."

"Can you finish the walk?"

Winded, she paused. "I'm fine. Let's sit over there."

He spread a blanket for her and moved to the side, watching Chloe and the boys. Tullia nursed the baby.

With the focus on Aurelia, she missed the approaching guard. He held out a piece of bread. "Left from breakfast."

She took the soft wedge. "Thank you."

Chewing the wonderful morsel, she thought bread had never tasted better.

What a nice boy. Flinching, she thought, *What am I doing? Making friends with my captors?* She vaguely wondered if her depleted condition blurred the lines, but it just didn't seem to matter. *Well, one friend was better than none, right?*

"What's your name?"

He turned, eyebrows raised in sympathy above his young face. "It's Milo, but we mustn't talk. We could both get in trouble. I'm sorry."

"Well, thank you again for the bread."

An hour passed and the boys tired. Walking home, Tullia recalled Milo's kindness. Her eyes welled with tears of gratitude. She blinked. *What's wrong with me?*

Arriving at the villa with the sun high, the girls took the children for naps.

Faustina helped Tullia to her room. "I'll prepare a hot bath for when you awaken."

Rupinus eliminated midday meals a week earlier, but not afternoon rests or the occasional bath.

"Thank you, Faustina."

They slipped around the curtain to her bedchamber. Fed up with Rupinus' gawking, Tullia had re-hung the drape four days earlier. He never reacted.

Fading into a light sleep, she welcomed the escape from tormented emotions and unrelenting physical exhaustion.

Tullia jolted awake at loud banging from the front door. Through the blur of sleep, she thought she heard her husband's voice.

"Rupinus! Where is she?"

His vicious tone swept away her lethargy. With her heart thundering, she jumped from the bed. Intent on stopping him, an unexpected rush of energy pushed away her fear. A small, terra cotta vase sat on her dressing table. Could she shatter it and find a weapon in the pieces?

She leaped toward the table as Vitalio stormed around the curtain. Before she could react, he landed a fist to the side of her head. Falling back on the bed semiconscious, she discerned his faraway voice. "Ostia, you whore! The money's in Ostia!"

Disoriented, Tullia felt rough hands grab and turn her over. Hot air billowed over bare skin; her tunic was ripped away and a weight descended on her, crushing the air from her lungs. A rancid stench hit her nose as he put his lips to her ear, pushing her further into the bed.

"Well *lupae*, the day is here. I've found Siculus and the

money. I'll take what I want, and then you'll die." His vicious laugh became a growl.

Face down, she tried to struggle, but it was too late. Rough, calloused hands found her throat and squeezed her from behind. Air thinned. A checkered gray blackness descended. At the last moment, the pressure stopped, and she gasped, raising her head and sucking in breath as fast as she could. Strange sensations around her bottom puzzled her. Twisting, she saw his hand dip toward his tunic. *No!* A survival reflex shot through like a lightning bolt. She lurched upward, flailing with all the energy she could muster.

"Never, you filthy savage! Never! GET OFF ME!"

The weight on her body lifted as she was jerked up and slapped. The blow sharpened her senses further. She saw Vitalio's face — an ugly snarl.

Before she could move, her husband snatched her by the hair and yanked, exposing her throat. "Never?" He spat on her chest. "Listen whore, it will happen if you are dead or alive. Either way, I will gaze upon your tight little rump and take it. And once you're dead, I'll sell your children to the slavers!"

White-hot anger erupted from her heart. "Touch my children and I'll kill you myself!" she screamed, spraying spittle into his surprised face.

Flinching back for a moment, he lunged and grabbed for her neck. Tullia pitched forward, locked her arms around his head, and pulled his nose into her mouth. She slammed her jaws together, clamping like a starving wolf to a deer's throat.

She heard Vitalio scream, then felt fists pummel her head. Bright, colorful spots dotted her vision behind tightly closed lids. Hanging on with her arms, she tightened her jaws with every ounce of remaining strength, willing her teeth to dig ever deeper. She bit down harder. A metallic taste flooded her mouth. Flesh broke and bone crunched. Torquing her head with all her might, she came away, mouth full, but before she could spit, a crushing blow landed on her temple and the world went dark.

PART V

Manumission

41

Tullia felt gentle hands lifting her throbbing head off the floor. Light stung her vision. She sputtered with every ragged, half-breath. Squinting, she saw a blurry Faustina kneeling next to her. The servant said something too low to hear, and whether she was talking to her or someone else Tullia could not discern. Then, another voice — one she had not heard for weeks — rumbled above the rest.

"She alive?"

Yosef. A tear leaked out of the corner of her eye. Her mind was playing tricks on her. Yosef could not be here.

But Faustina was responding. "Looks like it. There's a lot of blood, but I don't think it's hers."

The sweet voice came again. "Tullia, it's me." A warm hand touched her cheek. "Yosef."

Tullia blinked at the kneeling figure. Trying to speak, her mouth gurgled as she choked on an object stuck in her throat. She turned on her side, heaved, coughed, and spat out a chunk of tissue the size and color of an apricot. The taste of copper lingered on her lips as she looked up at Yosef.

"Great Juno, what … what is *that*?" she croaked.

Before Yosef could answer, the memory returned. She sat up, pushing herself away from the bloody sight. "Is that his nose? Did I kill him?"

"Yes and no," Yosef said. "It's a good part of his nose, but

he's not dead. What remains of his nose is now a bloody slab."
He turned her face to his. "Are you alright? I need to finish
with him."

Tullia nodded, her heart bursting with joy at his presence.
He squeezed her shoulder and left.

Faustina reappeared, this time holding a cup of water. "To
rinse," she said, moving the younger woman's hair to one side
as she swished and spit. "Domina, you are covered in blood."
She held up a small mirror. "You look like a well-fed cannibal."

Tullia saw her face smeared with a bloody patina, the
macabre look embellished by little rivulets from tears. She
grinned at her reflection—white teeth exaggerating the grisly image. "I do look a mess, but I got him good, didn't I?"

Faustina grinned. "You did. He may stink, but he'll never
smell again."

A weak laugh broke through Tullia's lips, still coated by
the awful taste of Vitalio's flesh and blood. Pushing herself
up using one hand on the bed, she stood as Faustina draped a
robe over her shoulders.

"Where"—she paused for breath—"did Yosef come from?"

"Bath first," Faustina instructed. "He will tell you later."

Tullia was in no state to argue. She stumbled through the
atrium, and pain coursed through every limb, but she wanted to see what happened. Gritting her teeth, she lifted her
head—Vitalio's thugs knelt to the right with their hands
on their heads, guarded by the newly returned home force.
Straining her bruised neck, she scanned the room, seeing the
bodies of Rupinus and another sprawled on the floor.

"Balbus?" she asked Faustina.

"Just fine."

Tullia was glad to hear it, knowing he had risked it all to save them.

Faustina, re-asserting her role as the senior house servant, pointed at a man she knew. "Help me get her to the patio."

"Right away, mistress." He encircled Tullia's chest with a strong arm, taking most of her weight.

Once on the patio, Atia saw them, her face blanching at the sight. As she opened her mouth to speak, Faustina waved her off. "The Domina's fine. It's not her blood. We're going to bathe. Keep the children away." Atia scurried off, but not before giving Tullia an odd, knowing smile.

Faustina turned to the guard. "We're fine now. Bring more hot water from the kitchen."

The guard returned, adding more water to the steaming tub, and departed.

Tullia waited on a bench as Faustina prepared the bath. After sprinkling in a healthy amount of lavender and rose petals, she removed Tullia's robe and bloody tunic and helped ease her into the sunken tub. Tullia relaxed, enveloped by a permeating warmth and shrouded in fragrant vapors.

As the hot water soaked into her bones, she felt herself unwind, beginning to sweep away the ugliness of her confinement. As her mind jumped back to Vitalio's day of abuse, she surprised herself with the lack of emotion. No shock, no horror. *Like a day with Rupinus,* she thought bitterly. *But now it's over.* She calmed herself with a couple of deep breaths.

Faustina massaged Tullia's tight shoulders, avoiding her bruised neck. After washing, she gave her hair a final rinse. "There. You have washed away these terrible days."

Tullia turned and took her hand. "Thank you, Faustina.

We made it." She saw tears slip from the older woman's eyes, and using her thumb, gently brushed them away.

Just then, a tall, imposing figure entered. Yosef, all smiles, walked up to the tub and laid a bundle of towels, clothing, and a few of Tullia's personal effects, carefully on the bench.

"Yosef," exclaimed Tullia, sitting up as best she could. A sharp twinge flew down her neck.

"She's been waiting," said Faustina. The loyal servant stood and hugged him. "It's good to have you back."

"It's good to be back," he answered. "We're supervising a clean-up, but please get some food first. We brought enough for everyone. I'll take over here."

As Faustina left, Tullia heard her call Atia. The faint skipping of her children toward their first real meal in weeks lightened her heart.

Yosef faced her, his eyes soft. "You look better."

"I feel better." She grimaced. "I finally got the taste of his nose out of my mouth."

Chuckling, he helped her from the bath and placed her on a plush blue rug. He used soft cotton towels to dry her, then wrapped one around her body. As she leaned into him, his arms slid around her bony ribcage. She could tell he was trying not to squeeze too hard, but she pulled him in tighter. It had been so long since she had felt his loving hug, the warmth of his body, and his thumping heart against her own. The tension from the cruel abuse of the past month drained away and she hoped her legs would not give out.

Then the tears came and soon became great racking sobs. He held her until she quieted.

When the worst of it was over, Yosef placed two fingers

under her chin and looked into her eyes. "What did he do to you?"

Tullia shook her head with as much vigor as she could. "It-it's not that. I … I just can't believe it. Are we really safe?"

"Yes."

He pulled her in as she sniffled. The relief kept coming in droves, so much that she wasn't sure she could handle it.

"What happens now?" she finally asked.

"You need to join us out there with Vitalio."

"Now?"

"As soon as you can."

"Tell me what happened. How did you get here?"

"One of the working girls, Phoebe, knows a guard named Milo. He let slip of Vitalio's plan. Finding Balbus is a longer story."

"Milo," she noted. "I met him. He seemed too honest to work for Vitalio."

"The money was too good to ignore."

"It was probably the best work he could find," she shrugged, feeling nothing but pity for the young couple. "Go on."

"We were waiting nearby and rushed the villa right after he entered."

"And you took over the house while I was biting off his nose?"

"More or less. Then I heard a scream."

Tullia closed her eyes, giving silent thanks as he went on.

"Rupinus is dead, Balbus saw to that. As is the thug who molested Atia." He cleared his throat, smiling when she gave him a questioning look. "She told me about that after she slashed his throat."

Tullia waved a hand. "I'm glad they're gone." Now she understood Atia's earlier look. Victory. She swore she'd kill Linus and she did—he must have been the second body. Tullia doubted Atia would ever feel remorse.

"She knows she killed an animal," said Yosef.

Tullia pursed her lips. "And what of the worst of them? Will Vitalio die?"

"No, at least not yet. I patched his bleeding nose and delivered him to Balbus. They're waiting for you, along with Sextus. Also, the accountant will return from Ostia tonight—without the money. He hid it in Rome before he left."

Rome? Tullia wanted to ask what that was all about, but a sudden wave of exhaustion hit her. Overwhelmed, she reached for him. "Oh, Yosef. It's a miracle it all worked."

"But it did. Take a deep breath and find what's left of your strength. We need to go out and confront your husband."

She straightened, vowing to see it through.

He told her a funny story from the brothel as he helped her into a light undertunic.

"The young wife of a nobleman came in one night, heavily disguised and seeking pleasure from one of the women. She insisted I disrobe her as she fondled her companion. I left as soon as I could. Afterward, she called me back to help replace the disguise. When I arrived, she was very drunk and very naked." He gave a false moan of desire.

She snickered. "Is that where you learned how to dress a woman?"

"Of course. You know the Rule—love thy neighbor."

"Yosef!"

They laughed. Tullia twisted her damp hair into a bun, securing it with the pins he offered. He next helped her slip into a comfortable off-white tunic, securing the material with an elegant gold belt.

Yosef held up two gold earrings and a matching necklace. "From your jewelry box."

He clasped the necklace as she put on the earrings.

"Here." He held out a delicate glass bottle of rosewater perfume.

"Thank you," she said, dabbing it on her wrists and behind her ears. "It smells so good; I could have used it earlier for my lips."

"That's why I waited," he joked, taking the bottle and passing her a small hand mirror.

She glanced at herself. "Good. I want Vitalio to see I am very much alive and unscathed by his abuse. I guess I'll just tell him about the perfume since he won't be able to smell it," she giggled.

She put her arms around Yosef's neck and kissed him. She felt his heart thumping. *Is this real?* she wondered. *Have we come through it alive?* They broke the embrace, and she studied his face, his eyes, his body. He was leaner, not by much, but those rosy, red cheeks and dimples were still there. Giddiness warmed her heart, and a small laugh escaped her. Yosef's smile widened.

"What?"

"What does your Rule say about biting off the nose of evil husbands?"

He gave an impish look. "It doesn't."

42

Tullia and Yosef joined Balbus and Sextus at the table. Before she sat, Tullia went straight to Balbus who stood.

"You did it," she said with a hug.

He blushed beet-red. "Yes, Domina."

She took her seat. To the side of the table sat Vitalio, guarded by two of Balbus's men.

Munching first on a crust of bread, Tullia asked for a chance to confront the senator.

"He's all yours," said Balbus, smiling. "Try not to kill him."

She stood and considered her husband. Flanked by the two guards, he was going nowhere. A dressing circled his head and supported a huge bulge at his nose. He resembled a pig in a white bonnet.

She took a sip of wine and walked over, appraising him with her most aristocratic stare. His eyes followed her. Despite her thin frame, she knew the belted tunic emphasized her figure, and the gold jewelry reinforced her wealth — the two things he wanted.

Leaning back against the table, she crossed her arms and shifted her stance into a suggestive pose. "Hello, husband. Do you notice my "tight little rump?" She wiggled. "It's something your filthy hands will never touch again." Her smile dropped as she returned to a neutral stance. She flicked a hand. "Or maybe I'll just have Balbus cut them off, eh? That would keep your hands off my bottom but make it hard for you to scratch what's left of your nose."

Vitalio glared, unmoving.

She pointed at his face. "You could have easily been killed today, just another casualty in the heat of a battle. But, as a favor to me, you have been spared. I wanted you for my own." Her voice dropped to an icy whisper. "Let me be clear, vermin. I'll consume you one small bite at a time until you are gone. You'll die and you *will* know it was me."

He squinted. "Give it your best, *lupae*."

"Really? Only a fool does not know when he's beaten. How's your nose?" In a flash, she soft-punched the center of the dressing. Jerking back, he screamed, hands covering his face.

"Oh, sorry," Tullia mocked. "Is that tender?"

As Vitalio moaned and gulped for air, Balbus handed her a napkin. Tullia slowly wiped her hands, then resumed her seat.

"You are no longer welcome here," Balbus intoned.

"We'll see," sputtered the prisoner, his weak nasal voice a congested squeak. "I'm a senator." He paused for breath. "You have invaded my home, killed my men."

Balbus gestured to Sextus.

The lawyer pushed a small scroll across the table. "Senator, several things have changed. If you read this, you'll see there'll be no prosecutions for the killings today; your men have been declared criminals. The Senate and the Imperial House authorized this raid as a public service."

Vitalio ignored the document. "So it may say. Its legality remains to be determined."

Sextus chuckled. "Oh Senator, rest assured, it is very legal.

The Royal House has also questioned your qualifications to continue to serve in the Senate. The full body will take up the matter once today's events are sorted."

Tullia wondered how *that* was accomplished. Yosef winked at her. *Ah, he knows.*

Vitalio opened his mouth, scowled at the document, and glowered at Tullia. She returned an unwavering gaze with a cold smile.

"That's all, Senator," Balbus said as they all rose. "Take your men, both dead and alive. Don't come back."

Vitalio rose, pointing at the group. "This is *nonsense,*" he hissed, the intended impact of his words lessened by his constant wincing. "You will all be executed." His fiery glare danced between Yosef and Tullia. "And you, slave boy, will be skinned and roasted alive, a spectacle my adulterous wife will be forced to watch."

Tullia opened her mouth to fire back a retort, but Yosef got there first. He took a short step and shot a powerful fist directly into the senator's snout-like face. The dressing flashed crimson as Vitalio screamed and fell back into his chair. Tears and blood oozed through his fingers.

Yosef spit in his face. He turned to Tullia spreading his hands in a gesture of innocence. "Sorry, I'd heard enough."

"You did me one better," she said. "A man's version of my little punch."

The two guards hauled the groaning Vitalio out of the villa, followed by his men.

"Not you, Milo," called Tullia.

The young man froze as the others filed by, the last group hauling the two corpses.

Tullia waved him over, but Yosef came forward. "I know Phoebe."

Milo's face changed from confusion to fear. He looked like he wanted to run.

"Relax," said Yosef. "You and Phoebe saved the day." He pulled him away from the rest of the group, and in a low voice, explained the situation.

Balbus continued with Tullia. "Domina, starting today, we'll house men in the corral and post guards on the street. There'll be no more trouble."

She squeezed his arm. "Thank you. It's good to have you back."

* * *

That evening was one Tullia would remember forever — a decent meal for the first time in over a month, and a happy reunion with the children and the household.

But after dark, the shadows crept back through the villa, into the rooms, and into her mind. As Yosef slept next to her and the lamps burned low, Tullia felt clammy as she fell into an uneasy sleep. The horrors returned. She stood in Mama's room, nauseated from the smell of copper and vomit. Mama raised a hand, but she was dead. Tullia turned to run from the room but there was Rupinus, his hand roughly cupping her breast. With a twist, she escaped his grip and hurried to the atrium, lost. Atia cried out, moaned, and then pleaded. Tullia struggled to scream.

"Tullia." A gentle hand shook her shoulder. Her eyes fluttered open; she was gasping. "It's a nightmare, wake up."

Her whisper waivered. "Y-Yosef, it was terrible. Mama, then the men... they came back." She sobbed, burying her face in his chest. He wrapped his arms around her and rocked. Enveloped in his secure embrace, she finally fell into an unencumbered sleep.

When dawn's early light streamed through the shutters of the window, Tullia awakened, her mind still fuzzy. But she knew they had the morning before the meeting with Balbus, the lawyer, and the accountant, so she was in no hurry. With her head on Yosef's chest, she blinked and looked up to see his face smiling down at her.

"Feeling better?" he asked, kissing her forehead.

A tremor shook her before she could answer. "Yes. But the memories..."

"Give it time," he murmured. "You're safe."

"And Vitalio is not," she said as if reciting a mantra. "He will suffer."

The burning desire for revenge struck her again, her mind flitting to the deliciously satisfying moments in the study. His missing nose. Bleeding bandages. She vowed to remember it all.

Yosef shifted, and as if reading her thoughts, asked, "Feel better after telling him off yesterday?"

"Absolutely. I meant every word." She laid her head back on his chest and sighed, savoring the comfort of his closeness and the sound of Aurelia's gentle gurgles. "Once the divorce is settled, we'll find a way to destroy him."

"And the business about his hands and his life being spared?" His fingers stroked her hair.

She looked up at him. "They seemed like good bluffs at the time."

He snickered softly. "I still can't believe you bit off his nose."

"He threatened to sell the children to a slaver," she said, her voice turning grim. "He could not have reached deeper into my soul. I wanted to kill him. All I had were my teeth."

She felt the rumble of his chuckle. "You could have choked on his nose."

"I didn't care. I was ready to die."

Yosef quieted at that, and Tullia wondered if he was thinking the same as her. She pulled away and sat up at the head of the bed.

She knew she could have died at any moment—just like all slaves. Living under the constant threat of death, life no longer mattered.

"Yosef, I was a slave for a month and knew death was around every corner. But it was only for a month. I'm sure it was nothing compared to a lifetime with bad masters."

She was not bought and sold, but it was still slavery at its worst. Vitalio owned her through Rupinus and ruled by fear. The beatings, the gropings, a knife to her throat demanding favors. She could have died at any moment. Her stomach tightened. She realized her family owned Yosef. It was not really any different. Mama did not use violence for control, but the threat of it.

"Yosef, did you fear for your life when Mama threatened to have you tortured?"

"You mean after you lied to protect me?" he asked, touching her hand.

"Yes," she whispered, remembering her own terror at the possibility.

"I was scared, but also knew your Mama was a fair person. I don't think I ever feared a beating or death."

She blinked away tears. "I hope we were good masters."

He scooted up and whispered in her ear. "And you still are, Domina."

"Thank you, slave." She gave him a playful push. "But I'm serious."

He pulled away. "You and your family were good masters. Where is this going?"

"If Rome freed the slaves, or at least followed your rule, the living nightmare for thousands could be prevented."

"Free the slaves and Rome would collapse. There is nothing you can do about that."

"It still isn't right."

He faced her. "Tullia, if you want to do something, start small. How about freeing Atia and Chloe? And me, for that matter," he added in a lighter voice.

She ignored his teasing. Maybe releasing the girls could be a start. She relaxed at the idea.

"Until then," he continued, "there's not much you can do, except be a good master." He brushed her thigh. "Especially toward me."

His levity eased her mood. "Then you must behave."

43

After a pleasing "welcome back" morning in bed with Yosef, Tullia could not keep the others—Balbus, Sextus, and Siculus—waiting any longer. Hand-in-hand, they walked to the study where Faustina and the girls had laid out a plentiful breakfast.

"Good morning, Domina," Balbus said, the greeting echoed by the lawyer and accountant.

"Good morning, all," she replied. She stood alone at the head of the table, hands relaxed at her sides. "We have survived a difficult time. Each of you was instrumental in liberating the villa and protecting my family and me. For this, you will have my eternal gratitude." Moving around, she hugged each one of them, and to a man, they fidgeted.

"Now we must consider what happens next." She paused for a bite of bread and sat next to Yosef. "Once the divorce is done and Yosef is freed, we will marry." She sipped some wine, wondering if she had to even say the next part. "Treat him as an equal."

All three men dipped their heads. The looks on their faces told her the statement wasn't necessary, but that they understood why she felt she had to say it.

"Now, before Aurelia was born, we talked about my divorce. Of course, our application made no mention of Yosef—it was nothing more than a simple request to dissolve the marriage. Adultery can't be used against me."

She looked at Sextus. "Correct?"

The lawyer affirmed her statement. "That's right. But I expect your husband to introduce the affair in his counter-proposal. It will take a month or more to make it a formal part of the proceeding. Until then, you are safe from Rome's requirement to exile or kill adulterous wives. However, once the adjustment is made, you will be vulnerable."

"The divorce needs to be finalized before then," she said, feeling a little tug of panic. "Can we speed it up?"

"With the right magistrate, and I have one in mind. I am confident we can conclude the divorce based on the original filing and before his charges can be made official."

Tullia pushed down her fear. Sextus was a smart attorney. If he said it could be done, it would be done. On the other hand, she felt the pressure of time and would not relax until she was officially free of Vitalio.

Clasping her hands together, she turned her attention to the accountant. "Now, about the money. I thought it was in Ostia, but Yosef mentioned you had hidden it here in Rome. Is that true?"

Siculus twitched and spoke with clipped diction. "It was a ruse in case the senator saw the note Sextus sent you. Most of the money is invested, but not the coin. It's hidden here in the city." His Adam's apple bobbed up and down as he added, "Deceiving you was necessary for the plan to work."

Tullia forgave him with a smile. "Work with Yosef to free up needed funds to get things back to normal."

That seemed to calm the jittery accountant.

"And what did the Royal House have to do with all this?" she asked.

"It was Titus," said Sextus. "He referred me to an official from the Royal House, and also Piso, chairman of the Senate and close friend of his father, Vespasian. Piso was very angry after investigating your situation. He issued all the decrees authorizing your rescue. In the end, the Senate may expel or punish Vitalio. Until then, his every behavior will be scrutinized."

Tullia's eyes widened. "Titus?" Her eyes bounced to Yosef. "From Pompeii? How?"

"I happened to see him while I was working at the brothel," Yosef said, smiling slightly. "It's a long story, but when I informed him of our situation, he was eager to help us."

"He was in the brothel?" she repeated, incredulous. "Please explain."

The lawyer cut in. "Domina, there's more on your legal situation first. For now, please be reminded that until the divorce is final, Vitalio is the *pater familias,* and the law gives him the right to all the money. He apparently thought it would be easier to take control of the money on his own rather than get a court order, but you both," he gestured at Siculus, "hid it so well, he has yet to find it. I am now sure he'll seek relief from the court to force you to grant access. It will take several weeks, but on that claim, he will succeed. You will have no choice."

"*No!*" exclaimed Tullia, jumping to her feet. "I would sooner kill him myself!"

Yosef took her hand and pulled her back down. He addressed Sextus in a calm voice. "What are the less direct options for limiting the senator's actions?"

Sextus folded his hands on the table and looked directly

at Tullia. "There are ways, Domina. I am a war veteran as well as a lawyer. Together, they teach about winning by *whatever means.*" His eyes hardened. "And I know how to win this."

Tullia flinched at his sudden intensity. "And how's that?" she asked, feeling the spines of Yosef, Balbus, and even Siculus straighten with interest.

"Choke him off financially," the lawyer decreed. "Force the failure of his farm. Without income, he loses his seat in the Senate and the means to fight you in court."

"It'll take years to ruin his farm," she argued.

Sextus gestured at Siculus. "He discovered the man is on the brink of bankruptcy."

The accountant blushed a deep scarlet, affirming the statement with a head bob. "He's neglected his vines and olives to the point that livestock is the only source of income."

Sextus cut in. "Domina, destroy the livestock, destroy the man."

Tullia frowned. "We can't go around killing innocent sheep."

"We don't kill them. We steal them," interjected Yosef.

Sextus grinned and pointed at him. "Correct."

"Steal—?" Tullia wasn't sure, but a soft touch on her hand and a reassuring smile from Yosef told her he was certain for the both of them. *These men are smarter than I thought.* "Very well," she said with more confidence than she felt.

The chain of events Sextus outlined leading to Vitalio's financial ruin made sense, but seemed so complicated. But as she thought about it, she could see it working. Although the exact plan remained elusive, the idea helped to calm her. She let out a breath. "What else can we do to protect what's ours?"

The lawyer didn't hesitate. "Emancipate Yosef now and transfer all assets to his name. If the court forces you to turn over the money, there will be nothing there, and he still fails."

Tullia's head spun at the offered proposal but immediately recognized the logic. "I agree. Let's free him right now."

She stood and walked to the shelf behind her. Thank Juno Rupinus and the others had left it alone; the scrolls were out of order, but they were all there. Tullia flipped through several before her eyes alighted on the right one—a crinkled and worn papyrus scroll dotted with black ink confirming the sale. She offered it to Sextus.

"This is proof of my family's ownership."

The jurist glanced at the contract with skepticism. "That was before he was sold to the brothel. You'll have to buy him back."

Yosef opened his hands. "No money was involved. I was traded for the senator's free visits to the brothel."

"No matter. The two of you must deal directly with the current owner. My office can help if you like."

The younger man shook his head. "No, I'll go to Cresimus. I'm sure I can work it out."

"You mean *we*," Tullia corrected him. "I'm going with you."

"Tullia, you can't. The Subura's too dangerous, never mind the fact that no patrician woman would even think of entering a bordello."

"Yosef, I'm going." She jerked her chin at the enormous soldier across the table. "Bring Balbus if you're so scared. I'll wear a disguise so nobody will know me."

"You're stubborn." A tiny smile graced his lips. "No wonder you made a poor slave."

At that, the heads of the three older men dipped, but Tullia only snickered. "I will remind you that *you're* still a slave. Besides, what happened to your Rule? Love thy neighbor and give her what she wants."

Yosef narrowed his eyes in a playful manner. "Well, I suppose I can apply that version of the Rule, assuming you still own me."

She hugged him, oblivious to the red-faced men surrounding them. "I knew you'd understand."

After the men left, she turned to Yosef. "I want to go there now."

He shook his head. "From midday onward, the brothel stays busy. We always conducted business early in the day. We'll go tomorrow."

* * *

In the early morning, Tullia sat dressed in a shabby turtle green tunic with a black, moth-eaten head drape. Atia completed the disguise by smudging charcoal around her face. Glancing in a small mirror, Tullia saw a dirty, older version of herself.

Atia stepped back, clapping. "Oh, Domina, nobody will know you!"

Faustina snickered. "You look like a beggar woman."

"Good. Let's go." She walked out, joining Yosef and Balbus at the front door. The old soldier tipped his head at her disguise. Tullia sighed as concern wrinkled Yosef's face. "Relax, we'll be fine."

He grunted and opened the door. The pink dawn to the east reflected off the wet cobblestones as they retraced Yosef's walk nearly two months earlier. As always, the streets of the Subura were clogged with wagons and carts leaving the city for the day, allowing them to blur into the bustle.

Arriving at the brothel at sunrise, Tullia spotted the concrete Honey Pot plaque embedded in the brick wall, and the chiseled image of a copulating couple beneath it. It was no surprise—she assumed most of the customers couldn't read. Shuttered windows flanked a closed, heavy wooden door which Yosef banged with the pommel of his dagger.

The lock clicked, and Tullia saw a squat man with scarred skin peek out. "Ah, Yosef, Balbus." He beckoned them in, unable to close the door before she followed.

"Hey!" The owner waved a hand at her face, as if to sweep her away. "Old woman, get out. Whatever you're selling, I don't need, and there's nothing here you can afford." He reached for the door latch.

Tullia kept her head down. "Don't be so sure," she said in a low voice.

"What?" His close-set eyes squinted as he brandished his knife. "Get out of he—ow!"

His order turned into a squeal as Balbus grabbed his arm and twisted, releasing his hold on the knife. It clattered to the floor where Yosef picked it up. Tullia lifted her head, cocking it to one side as she studied the red-faced owner.

"I'm buying, and you're selling."

Balbus released him. Cresimus stepped back, wide-eyed. "Yosef, what's this?"

"This is Domina Tullia Flaccus, the sole holder of the Flaccus family fortune," Yosef replied. "She wants to buy me."

With eyes like saucers, Cresimus dropped to his knees

and put his head on the tile floor. "Domina. I didn't know," he babbled. "Please forgive the knife."

Tullia pushed back her drape. "Rise, sir."

The owner complied, moving slowly, eyes darting between the three before coming to rest on Tullia. Again, his head dropped. "Domina, please call me Cresimus or whatever you choose. I have never been a sir."

She shook out her hair. "Cresimus, then. You took good care of Yosef while I was occupied, and for that I thank you. I've come to take him home."

Cresimus wrung his hands, keeping his eyes on the floor. "Ah, with respect Domina, the senator sold him to me."

"Perhaps then you'd share proof of the transaction so I might buy him back. It should look something like this." She produced Yosef's bill of sale from within her tunic.

The proprietor fidgeted, sparing the scroll a quick look. "Domina, it was a gentleman's agreement. I have no paper-work."

"No?" Her lip curled and she turned. "Yosef, let's go."

"Domina!" pleaded Cresimus, bobbing up and down on his feet. "Yosef? Balbus? Say something!"

Both men shrugged, reducing the pudgy owner to quivering lips and welling eyes.

Tullia burst out laughing, a strange sound in the early morning of the brothel. "Relax, Cresimus. I was merely joking."

His lips parted, but no words came out. He stood immobile.

"May we sit?" she asked.

Yosef gestured to a stool at the wine bar when Cresimus failed to respond. "In here."

His words pushed the blustering owner to act, bowing and walking on eggshells as he led them into the room. Yosef prepared wine with honey as Tullia sat at the bar, Balbus lingering at her side.

Tullia took a sip and set her cup down. "Cresimus, I'd like to buy Yosef from you." She knew Yosef's actual market value was around two thousand sesterces but the illegal nature of the transaction between Vitalio and Cresimus allowed her to name her price. She estimated Cresimus would take three hundred.

The proprietor could barely meet her gaze. "Truly, Domina? You would pay me for him?"

She raised her brow, this time at his tentative excitement. "Yes, really. How much?"

Cresimus stood a little taller. He frowned, tapping a finger on his chin as he deliberated. "Well, Domina, and with all due respect, I could not take less than two hundred."

"Done. Yosef?"

Opening a bag of coins, Yosef extracted and stacked the sum on the bar.

Cresimus fixed on the money. "Many thanks, Domina," he stuttered.

"There is one other thing," Tullia said as he reached for the coins. The owner froze.

"Domina?"

"The girl, Phoebe. Is she here?"

He raised his brows. "Ah, well, yes, but I don't—"

"Please summon her."

"Phoebe!" he yelled, pulling his eyes away from the stacks of coins in front of him. "Get out here!"

Tullia winced and tapped her ears. "If she's anywhere in the Subura she probably heard that."

Cresimus seemed to miss the humor, apparently still thinking about the coins. After a moment, a slight girl shuffled into the room. She faced the owner, eyes lowered. "Master?"

The proprietor grabbed her by the elbow and pushed her to the front of the bar. Nodding at Tullia, he said, "This is Domina Flaccus. She owns Yosef and wishes to speak to you."

The girl dropped to the floor at Tullia's feet, her breath coming in great sobbing gulps. "Domina, forgive us," she cried. "We meant no harm."

Tullia reeled back in surprise, shooting a stunned look at Yosef, whose expression was one of utmost sympathy. He came around the bar and squatted down, bending over her. "Phoebe, you can get up. You're not in trouble."

Trembling, the girl stood, her pretty, wet face marred by islands of acne and plastered with strands of wet blond hair. Blue-gray eyes wallowed in an unending ocean of tears.

Great Juno, she's just a girl. Tullia reached for her hand, waiting for the initial flinch to pass. "You and Milo helped save my life."

The girl wiped her runny nose and sniffled. Her hand lay limp in Tullia's.

"I want you to join Milo and come work for me and Yosef."

Phoebe recoiled, her hand dropping. "But you're not my master."

"Then I'll talk to him."

Cresimus jerked his head toward the hallway and the terrified girl hurried out without a backward glance. Tullia watched her go; her heart heavy.

Her eyes found the owner again. A female slave often commanded more than males, but Phoebe's tarnished history in a brothel reduced her value to practically nothing. She suspected the oily proprietor knew that too. "Well?" she asked.

Cresimus met her gaze, now all business. "Seventy-five."

"Done," she laughed. "Oh, Cresimus, I thought you were better than that. I was prepared to pay one hundred."

His face fell. "Oh, ah, that's plus expenses of twenty-five."

"Yosef, give him the hundred." Another stack of coins settled on the counter, and the owner froze, looking intently at the huge sum of money. Tullia snapped her fingers, regaining his attention. "No more customers for Phoebe. Balbus will come by later to help her move."

"Of course, Domina. A pleasure doing business with you." He bowed, walked them to the front door, and bowed again as Tullia and her men stepped out.

44

Tullia cuddled with Yosef that night. As she rested her head on his chest, listening to his steady heartbeat, he dropped a kiss on her nose and murmured, "I'll always be there for you."

She sighed, content. After a few moments, she looked up at him by the flickering light of the wall lamps. "Yosef, tomorrow you'll be given your freedom."

"Good." He blew out an exaggerated breath. "As a freedman, I should be able to get a better job than working in a brothel."

"Yosef!"

"I'm sorry," he said, chuckling.

Her frown relaxed into a smile. "I've missed your jokes, your body next to mine, your hugs."

They exchanged a deep kiss. She moaned, wrapping her arms around his neck. He rolled her on her back, whispering, "Tullia, I prayed for you, and my prayers were answered." He pressed a kiss on her forehead. "You and the children survived." Placing little kisses on her cheek, he worked his way down her jaw. "It's so good to be home."

"Hmm," she said, tilting her neck. "You are my home and shall always be. I love you."

"As I love you." His lips captured hers again, and no more words were said.

* * *

As early morning sunshine slanted through the villa, Tullia left her bedroom, intent on updating her diary. At the sound of soft voices, she paused in the atrium.

"We usually bake our own bread," said Faustina, over the click of a metal spoon on a ceramic bowl.

"But I've never made bread," replied Phoebe in a shaky voice.

"Don't worry, child, I'll teach you." Tullia could imagine Faustina's kind face as she uttered the words. Slipping unseen to the study table and sitting, she continued to enjoy the exchange.

Phoebe's voice emerged through the murmurs. "... I see. And once the loaves are done, they go right over to those cooling racks. I don't think you'd want them flat on the counter when they are still hot."

"That's right," said Faustina. "You're a smart girl." She dropped her voice, but Tullia could just make out the words. "The Domina put her first baked batch directly on the table."

Their soft laughter made her smile. It was much worse than that. The loaves were also gooey on the bottom and burned on the top. She remembered she had argued with Faustina at every step. "You should have listened," was Faustina's terse reply. From the sound of things, she thought Phoebe made a better student. As their voices dropped, Tullia imagined they were mixing the dough, and she turned her attention to her scroll.

"Good morning, Domina. Would you like some wine?" asked Pheobe, holding a pitcher and a cup.

Looking up, Tullia hid her shocked expression. Was this the same girl from the brothel? It had only been a day, and yet... it was. Hair washed and neatly braided across her head, and with a face scrubbed of grime, Phoebe resembled any other well-bred young woman. Her missing front teeth gave her an impish smile, and her eyes, gray in the poor light of the brothel, now sparkled bright blue. Beneath a tunic that matched her eyes, her lithe body moved with a grace Tullia had not recognized the day before. Tullia's chest warmed at the transition.

"Yes, Pheobe. Thank you."

The girl poured, dipped her chin, and glided from the room.

A few moments later, Faustina brought bread, figs, cheese, and wine for the upcoming breakfast meeting.

"Phoebe seems to be doing well," said Tullia.

"She is bright and learns quickly. Milo is a lucky boy."

Yosef entered leading Sextus. They joined her at the table.

"Sextus, please eat," she offered.

But the straightforward lawyer shook his head and launched right into it. "Domina, before we get to Yosef's emancipation, there's a detail surrounding the divorce — specifically, your legal name. You're currently Tullius Flaccus Silanus."

The matter wiped all social formalities from Tullia's mind. Her lip curled in distaste. "I don't want Vitalio's name attached to mine."

"I thought not." He lifted a sheet of paper. "This declares that once the divorce is final, your name will be Tullius Flaccus. Your boys will still carry Silanus. In keeping with tradition, your daughter will be Aurelia Flaccus Josephus since Yosef is the father. As a freedman, he will represent the new Josephus line of the Flaccus family. His name will henceforth be Tullius Flaccus Josephus."

"I'll still call him Yosef."

"As you should."

She took the paper and ran her eyes over it. "Exactly what I wanted."

"Good. Now for the new business. Emancipation can be at the behest of the owner."

"So simple?" Tullia asked, rising out of her chair. Yosef stood next to her.

"Yes, for the most part. There is an old law, the *lex Aelia Sentina*, that says no slave under the age of thirty can be freed, but additional conditions were so complicated, nobody enforces it nowadays."

That was all she needed to hear. Rising to her tiptoes, she planted a kiss on Yosef's cheek. "Then you're free."

Yosef grinned and blushed. The corners of Sextus's lips flicked up, then he dipped his hand into his bag for yet another sheet of papyrus. "Let's formalize the process," he said, laying it on the table. "Please sign."

Tullia complied, pressing the wet ink onto the document with a shaky hand. As she straightened, a tear slipped down her cheek.

"Congratulations," she beamed.

"Thank you," he said in a choked whisper. Tullia resisted the urge to comfort him — she knew it was a new beginning.

The lawyer gathered his things and exited.

She pulled on Yosef's arm. "Come to the patio."

Strolling hand in hand, on the unusually warm February day, neither spoke.

Tullia broke the silence. "Yosef you are free — we are both free. You from a bad law and me from a tyrant."

"We are both free," he slowly repeated. He took her in his arms and put his lips to hers. The passionate kiss and long embrace told her he had made peace with the change. "Our future is bright," he said, his voice stronger.

After a few steps, they reached the bench and sat.

Tullia fidgeted and blew out a breath. "Yosef, I want to talk about slavery. Good slavery is wrong. Bad slavery is horrible. And somewhere in there is your Rule. How can you say you love your neighbor but still have a slave? It makes no sense."

"I don't know, but slavery is Rome."

"It is, but does slavery have to be in our villa? The house girls are slaves, and I think we're good masters. But we still own them—and we need them. If I follow the Rule, I should free them, but like Faustina asked me years ago, 'Who would do the work?' How do you follow the Rule and still have slaves?"

"I'm not sure how."

"What do Jews do?"

"I don't know, but I'm pretty sure they have slaves."

"You need to find a Jewish priest."

Late the next morning, with the weather sunny and much like the day before, Yosef and Tullia strolled to the Forum. Two guards trailed at a respectful distance. On the way, they passed the Lone Pine Tavern. Tullia shuddered.

"Are you alright?" asked Yosef.

She tugged at her light wrap. "It's nothing. But that place reminds me of the awful meeting with Balbus and the terrible days afterward."

He touched her arm.

She squinted at the building and set her jaw. *Vitalio, you vicious bastard, I have not forgotten. Vengeance burns my every memory.*

"What? Now you smile?"

"Just thinking of Vitalio and the joys of his destruction. When will we steal his sheep?"

"Not yet and that's not why we're here today."

"Then why?"

"To talk," he answered.

From a vendor, they bought a skewer of sausage, a small block of cheese, and bread. Washed down with wine, they shared the food at an outdoor table. Overhead, a wooden trellis, its vines brown and lifeless, broke up the winter brightness.

After a few bites, Yosef spoke. "After yesterday's talk, I found a Jewish priest."

She raised a brow. "How?"

"Through Cresimus. Everything can be heard in The Honey Pot."

"And?"

"There's a large Jewish quarter on the Esquiline worshiping at the synagogue Secenians. The priest is Ben-Turrina. I'm told he is very wise. I plan to go tomorrow."

She took a sip. "Cresimus is quite the resource."

"Yes." And they finished eating.

Drifting through the busy market, they found the purveyor of honey dates from seven years earlier. Thinner and still toothless, the old man seemed to have not moved.

"Five for ten," he said to Tullia, a twinkle in his eye.

"You remember?" she asked. He cackled.

"We settled on five for five," he said. "But you were younger then."

"So were you!" She exclaimed. "Same deal today?"

"That was years ago. Keep your money, I'll keep my dates. Expenses have gone up. Dates, salt, and honey cost more now."

You shifty little man, she thought. *But I like your spirit.*

"How long have you been here?" asked Yosef.

"My family's had this spot for three generations, from about when Octavian became Caesar. I was born the year they opened the Forum of Augustus." He jerked his thumb behind him at three open arches across the Forum.

"Making you, let's see, of fifty-five years," said Tullia. She remembered the dedication date from her studies with Tibulus.

"Ah, well, yes Domina," he said. He seemed impressed.

"I'll give you five and a half for five. Goes with your age."

The vendor hooted and slapped his knee. "Just for you, Domina."

He scooped up the dates and passed them to Yosef.

"Thank you, and here's six for giving in," she said with a wink.

He gave a gummy grin. "My thanks. Be well, Domina. Don't wait seven years. Come back soon."

They found a bench and sat.

"Be careful of the Rule, Tullia. You're liable to break us," said Yosef.

"Oh, shush."

* * *

Ten days after Vitalio was ousted, they met once again with Sextus and Balbus. Tullia wondered if the frequent visits made the lawyer resent taking on her case, but if they did, he showed no signs of it.

"The Senate has reprimanded Vitalio," he announced when he was hardly a step inside the villa. "He was warned to have no further contact with your family or any member of the household. His seat is in jeopardy."

Balbus spoke. "He has stayed in his apartment in the Subura where a woman brings him food." He shrugged. "Then, yesterday he went out for a meal with a magistrate known to be corrupt. I'm told the bandage is gone and his nose is a large dark scab. We'll continue to watch."

"Thank you both," said Tullia, imagining Vitalio's mangled face. *He was never much to look at anyway,* she mused, but the joy faded quickly. She knew in her heart her husband was not done with them, and even with Yosef in the house and Balbus keeping guard, she felt far from safe. She hoped this latest news would distract her husband from her and Yosef. *Let him worry about surviving, nothing more,* she prayed. *Let him worry about each day as it comes, as I did.*

45

At sunrise, Yosef followed Cresimus's directions and made the short walk to the Esquiline. East of the Subura, the neighborhood buzzed with morning commerce. Along the busy Via Tiburtina, carts trundled and creaked toward the arched Tiburtine gate, hurrying to leave the city before full morning. As long as merchants made the effort to leave, even if a little late, fines were not levied.

Squinting against the bright new day, Yosef heard the steady din of people and animals, and the clatter of wheels on cobblestones. One and two-story wooden or brick buildings crowded the street. Narrow sidewalks did little to keep pedestrians from mingling with the street traffic. His mouth watered at the sweet smell of baking bread. *Reminds me of Pompeii.*

Across the street, he recognized the square synagogue. The orange roof tiles contrasted with its red brick construction, and it appeared more solid than its wooden neighbors. For some reason, the thought of it withstanding a disaster while the adjacent structures fell apart, comforted him.

On the building's right, earthen pottery of every size and shape clogged the tight sidewalk. In the center of the burnt-orange forest squatted a little man at a wheel, spinning a wet lump of terra-cotta.

Working his way through the traffic, Yosef crossed toward him and raised a hand. "Good morning."

"Indeed it is, and all due to the glory of God," said the potter, standing. He wiped his hands on his tunic.

Skinny with sinewy arms and a full hand shorter than Yosef, the barefoot man resembled a winter shrub: no leaves, just stems. Brown hair reinforced the colorless image. Like overripe fruit ready to drop, flecks of wet clay clung tenuously to his kinky beard.

"Shopping for a pot or vase?"

"Not today. I'm looking for the priest next door."

The man's eyes narrowed. "Why?"

"My name is Yosef. I'm a freedman and a Jew. I was stolen and sold into slavery when I was young. I remember little of my faith, and I have questions."

The artisan relaxed and pointed to himself. "My name's Urbanus. My people have been potters in Rome for generations. We're also Jews. The priest is Aemilius Ben-Turrina. He's prosperous for a Jew in Rome and one of our leaders. Wait here."

The little man slipped into the shop. Yosef heard his voice followed by a woman's muffled reply.

Urbanus returned wearing sandals. "Come with me."

He scurried to the front of the temple and pounded on the door. "Aemilius! It's Urbanus!" Reaching up, he waved his hands in front of a tiny peephole, then turned back to Yosef. "He's looking through to see who it is."

The door opened to a bear of a man. White hair sprung from beneath a skullcap. Blending with a beard of the same color, it looked like he'd wrapped his face in white wool.

"Urbanus, what is it? I'm busy," he boomed.

A thumb jerked toward Yosef. "This young man, a Jew and a freedman, wants to see you."

Ben-Turrina raised his bushy eyebrows and fixed his gaze on the stranger.

Yosef took a deep breath. "Sir, my name is Yosef. I was sold into slavery as a boy and recently gained my freedom. I have many questions about our faith."

"Such as?" The priest's face remained impassive.

"When I was a boy, I memorized ten commandments and a rule."

No change. "Which rule?"

"Love your fellow as yourself."

The ghost of a smile flitted across the priest's face, but just as suddenly it disappeared. "It is a good rule," he said. "What are your questions?"

Still jumpy, Yosef pressed on. "I have two. I thought Jews had slaves. Do they, and how can a person follow the Rule and have slaves?"

Urbanus whistled.

The priest nodded and another smile emerged, lasting longer this time. "Ah, a thinker, are you? Maybe you should come in. You too, Urbanus, assuming Miriam can run the store."

"She can, she can," said the potter, pushing ahead of Yosef like a spry little dog.

Ben-Turrina closed the door and ushered Yosef into a well-lit atrium. Above the central rain pool, sunlight streamed through the roof opening. On one wall, benches faced an altar adorned with a menorah and an oil lamp.

The other side of the room resembled a busy study. A table

stood half-buried underneath scattered sheets of papyrus and an open scroll. Behind it, the wall housed hundreds of scrolls, their wooden handles poking out. Stacks of wax tablets occupied the bottom shelves.

Yosef halted, wide-eyed.

"I work as an imperial scribe," offered the priest with a knowing smile. "The Royal House and Senate bring me documents for transfer to scrolls for the historical record or other uses. The money's good and helps keep the temple running. As a Jew and a priest, they assume I do not care about what I read, which is mostly true."

"I can read and write a little," was all Yosef could manage.

"I knew he was important," exclaimed Urbanus.

The holy man gestured to a bench for his guests as he pulled up a chair before them.

"Tell us your story."

"Yes, tell us!" Urbanus echoed, squirming.

Yosef told them of his childhood in Judea. He described his kidnapping and enslavement and how his parents were probably dead. He explained how Tullia's father, General Flaccus, bought him in Antioch, transported him to Rome, and raised him as a house slave.

The priest stroked his beard. "A common story. You did well to survive."

Urbanus stared wide-eyed and said nothing.

"My last owner was his daughter, Tullia Flaccus. She married Senator Vitalio Silanus, a cruel and abusive man. When the general died, the senator imprisoned Tullia, killed her mother, and sold me to a brothel where I became a bouncer—all to get his hands on the Flaccus fortune. We were recently liberated, and Domina Flaccus gave me my freedom."

"And where is the senator now?" asked the priest.

"In trouble with the Royal House and the Senate. The Domina is litigating a divorce. We plan to wed once it comes through."

"She plans to marry you?" Urbanus gasped. "Her former slave?"

"Yes. We have loved each other for many years."

"Love or not, she'll be seen as a radical," Ben-Turrina cautioned. "It will cause trouble for the family."

"She's quite stubborn once she makes up her mind." Yosef surprised himself at his confidence. But his faith in Tullia was unshakable.

The priest seemed to understand, though the light frown did not smooth out. "Back to your questions. Jews don't have slaves. We have servants with no choice but to work for us."

Yosef's brow wrinkled. "Sounds like a slave," he ventured.

"*Sounds like* is not the same as is," said the priest. He held up two fingers and ticked them off. "Romans own slaves, meaning they own people. Jews can buy servants but can't own them. Our laws do not allow us to own people." He held out both hands, palms up, and spread them toward Yosef and Urbanus. "We're required to be compassionate and provide adequate food and shelter for our servants. Judaism says the servant was made to do work and not be abused. That means"—again he held up several fingers—"no beatings or sexual relations. We're expected to listen to complaints, and all servants rest on the Sabbath. The Jewish version of a slave is a servant required to work for you. But they're still people to be treated as such."

Yosef listened with rapt attention. As he processed the information, it still seemed the servants were slaves, after all, you bought them. But then, you treated them differently — there were actually laws to protect them. It still did not make sense.

Urbanus chimed in. "Slaves! Servants! Who has such problems?"

"I suspect young Yosef does," said the older man, smiling. "Correct? The Rule says to do to them what you would do to yourself, and since you have been a slave, you do not want others to be slaves. But you can't just emancipate them. Who would do the work?"

"Ah, yes," stammered Yosef. "How can the rule be applied? We need slaves."

"Our laws agree with that. You need people to do the work. But the rule deals with how you treat them, not if they are your servants." He held one hand palm down. "You could let them all go, but they may starve. That breaks the rule." The other hand lifted, palm up. "If you treat them with the respect deserving of all men, doesn't that satisfy the rule?"

"You have slaves?" interjected Urbanus.

Yosef ignored the potter's question. "It does," he said. "It's about how we behave toward others."

"It is," said the wise man. "Will this change things?"

It did. It filled a gap in Yosef's thinking. His heart raced at the insight. Slaves should be treated as people, a concept missing in the Roman approach to servitude. He locked eyes with the priest. "It changes everything."

"What changed?" asked Urbanus.

"Yosef's view of the world," said the priest, rising. "Now go, Yosef. Change things."

At the door, Yosef faced the great man. "Thank you, kind sir, for your time and wisdom."

The old man put his hand on Yosef's shoulder. His grasp was surprisingly strong. "The pleasure was all mine. But you must let me know how it all goes, eh?"

"I shall."

"And maybe drop by on the Sabbath sometime?"

Yosef said he would. The priest's words churned in his mind as the door closed behind him. Deeply focused on his own thoughts, he missed most of Urbanus's steady prattle. A sharp tug on his tunic brought him back; they had arrived at the shop, standing before Urbanus's multiple terra-cotta wares. The skinny man was looking at him expectantly.

"What was that?" Yosef asked.

The potter spread his arms wide. "So, you want to buy a vase or not?"

46

Tullia paced around the patio wondering if she should have gone with Yosef. What if he learns nothing, or worse yet, discovers something troubling? A deeper threat emerged. How solid was Cresimus's information? Could they trust the priest? Her stomach burned as she walked.

Finally, Yosef came out to the patio. She hurried over. He looked fine, even content, and she felt her insides relax. Maybe it was all right. "What did you find out?" she asked.

His eyes sparkled as he led her to the bench. "You should have seen it! More scrolls, tablets, and writing tools than you can imagine. He's a scribe for the emperor's court. He's very wise."

Waiting, her fingers fidgeted with her tunic. "And?"

"We can't have slaves and follow the Rule."

Her heart sank. "But what should we do?"

He seemed unbothered. "Jews have a different approach. They look at slaves as servants who work for them. Not people they own."

She frowned. "Servants who work for nothing?"

"Yes. They're people we shelter and feed."

"Yosef, why would we do that? They could just leave. Slaves can't. What did the priest say about the rule and keeping slaves, not servants?"

He took a deep breath. "The servants are the slaves. The

Jews buy slaves like Romans, but Jewish law says they cannot *own* people. Instead, they're called servants who are required to work for the buyer."

Tullia remained unconvinced. "That's just renaming a slave."

"It's more than that. In Rome, there are no laws about the treatment of slaves. Romans can do what they want. Jews are guided by laws. Jewish law says you can't mistreat slaves. And owners have to listen to complaints."

She sighed. "Yosef, we don't mistreat our slaves. And I don't think when Faustina was a slave, she had any complaints. Neither do the girls."

He shook his head. "You don't know if they have complaints because they're not allowed to speak of them. Would your mother have listened to mine? And who knows what happens on our farms? Owners don't listen to slaves because they don't have to, and that includes us."

Tullia jumped up, pointing at him. "Don't say that! We're good masters. I know Mama would've listened if you had complaints."

Yosef stiffened. His voice grew cold. "Do you remember how she ordered me to sit like a dog after she found out you learned the Rule from me? Then she spared me a beating only because she thought I told the truth, and you lied? Do you remember? And this is a house with 'good' masters."

Tullia recoiled, his sharp words cutting. Her heart galloped as guilt from seven years earlier washed over her. The long-suppressed memories roared back—Yosef scampering to squat by Mama, Mama threatening to torture him to get the truth, and her mother's final declaration, 'Lie to me again,

Tullia, and your little friend will be gone.' And all along she thought they were good masters. She shuddered at the realization that even good masters could be bad. It included her mother. *And probably me.*

As tears welled, she whispered. "Yosef, I'm sorry, especially for Mama. I'm sorry for it all."

"It was a long time ago," he murmured. "She eventually accepted me into the family. But do you see now how easy it is to be blind when you don't have to look? The Rule forces us to look."

She sniffled. "I don't like what it's made me see."

"Tullia, the Rule helps solve the problem. Jewish law basically applies the Rule. We treat slaves with dignity, as people who work for us. They can't leave since we still own them, but we can still treat them right."

She spoke slowly. "So, the Rule would say to treat slaves as we would want to be treated."

"That's it," said Yosef. "From there, the rest makes sense. There's no physical or sexual abuse. And Jews give them a day off every week."

"A day off?" she asked, brows raised.

"For their Sabbath. It's Jewish law."

Tullia stood. "Wait here."

She walked under the colonnade and pondered the information. She had been taught slaves were creatures of low birth—likened to work animals in need of guidance, training, and discipline, and most importantly, you owned them. It made it easy to get what you wanted. Always. Give any order—more bread, be quiet, get me my shoes—and it was immediately followed. Slaves are not us.

Jewish law says that is wrong. She stirred with conflict. It won't be easy. You don't just order people around—they will resist rudeness. As she sensed Yosef and the Jews were right, she felt her power slipping away. Yes, it was about power, you had to give it up to do the right thing. Feeling nervous, she would try to change her thinking but knew it would not be easy. She would start with the villa.

Tullia approached Yosef, still waiting on the bench. "We will follow the Rule in this household. We will treat our slaves as the people they are and hear their complaints. This family will be just and good, as we should have always been—especially to you."

Yosef rose and took her in his arms. She felt the warmth and comfort of his embrace, despite a pang of lingering guilt.

"I am so sorry," she murmured. "Please forgive me."

"Tullia, there is nothing to forgive. You are the love of my life. You have faced your family and society to protect me. Because of you, I stand here, a free man. I know who you are, a generous and giving person capable of great love."

He took her face in his hands and kissed her. "Together we will face the future."

Tears ran down her cheeks and she smiled. "We'll start at home. Atia, Chloe, and Phoebe will be freed and offered jobs as servants—with a day off each week."

He shook his head. "Emancipation isn't the same as treating a slave well."

"I know. We'll do that with the slaves on our farms. But first I want—no—I *need* to free the girls."

"They could leave," he warned.

"Maybe." She chewed her lip. "But this is Atia's home and

Chloe won't leave her. Phoebe needs a job other than the brothel. With a little money and a day off, I hope they'll stay. Their lives will be better. We'll make sure of it."

* * *

Tullia, Yosef, and Faustina called the house slaves together the following afternoon. The three girls stood and waited in the middle of the atrium, their expressions ranging from vacancy to subdued interest and subtle wariness.

"We have survived a terrible time together," Tullia began. "I have learned how bad it can be to be a slave, and with Yosef's freedom and guidance ..." She looked at him and he offered a look of reassurance. "I want to make some changes in this household. Starting with all of you."

Atia started shaking and began to cry. Chloe looked puzzled and took Atia's arm. Phoebe pursed her lips and squinted.

Tullia realized her bluntness had backfired. She took Atia in her arms. "Easy, it's not bad."

The girl's sobbing slowed, and Phoebe's tight expression relaxed.

Tullia held her hands out in a gesture of calm. "As of this moment, we have decided to give you your freedom. You are now free women."

Atia tilted her head, curious, and Phoebe's squint returned.

"You may stay or leave. If you stay, you'll have a job and a home in the villa. You'll be treated with respect and your complaints will be heard. Each of you will have one free day a week and be paid four sesterces a month."

Phoebe, the most worldly, took a breath. "Domina, do you mean it? We can leave?"

"Yes." Tullia bit her tongue to stop from adding, *but we'll hope you'll stay*. She could not let her personal feelings influence what they wanted.

"If we stay, would it be our own money?" pressed the young woman.

"Yes."

Her questions kept coming. "And if we leave?"

"You may still work here and be paid."

Phoebe straightened, and Tullia wondered if she was planning to leave at that moment. Liberated from the brothel ten days earlier, Phoebe showed increasing confidence by the day, now baking bread, shopping at the market, and keeping the boys in line. Tullia tried to not show her disappointment.

Faustina frowned. "Phoebe, you work and live in a nice home, and now with a little money. If you try to make it on your own, even with Milo, you'll end up back at the brothel."

Phoebe blushed. "With respect Domina, how do we know you'll keep your word?"

Atia began crying again. "Phoebe, don't leave. We're a family."

"Come with me," interjected Faustina. She herded the girls to the patio.

On their return, Phoebe came to Tullia and dropped her head. "Domina, I understand. We're a family and want to stay together. Thank you for your kindness."

Atia hugged Tullia. "Thank you, Domina."

Faustina winked at Tullia and Yosef. "Come on girls. There's work to do."

After they left, Tullia sighed. "Not quite as smooth as I had hoped."

"But smooth enough," Yosef answered, wrapping his arm around her. His eyes twinkled down at her. "I was surprised you could hold your tongue for so long."

Three days later, Tullia gave each girl two sesterces and took them to the market. Faustina and four guards accompanied them. Yosef stayed home and babysat. Atia and Phoebe each spent their money on a colorful scarf and a honey date. Chloe bought two honey dates.

"Domina, you've made a good decision," said Faustina.

Tullia listened to the girls' happy chatter. "It does look like it. How'd you bring them around?"

"Phoebe's still edgy from the brothel. I told her you'd keep your word, and even as a freedwoman she'd need work and a place to live. Staying here, she'll have both, like me. I also reminded her of all the homeless girls who end up in brothels."

47

"Did I see Chloe tending to the plants in the patio garden today?" Yosef asked as Aurelia suckled at Tullia's breast. On the bed beneath flickering wall lamps, the three lounged in their nightclothes.

"In a way. Chloe is not smart enough to tend plants, but Atia was still excited. It seems Chloe has a hobby — collecting bugs. She wants to pick out a storage box for them on her next day off," Tullia recalled with a smile.

"I hope they're dead."

"Atia said she'd make sure they were."

Yosef kissed her forehead and put a hand on Aurelia's tiny back. "I think the girls are happier. Faustina, too. She seems younger. I saw her trying to toss little Dracus's ball for him. I've never seen her play with him like that."

Tullia giggled, accidentally dislodging her baby. Before Aurelia could wail, she shifted, gently guiding her lips back. "And Phoebe?" she asked.

"She's coming around," Yosef said. "Don't worry. It's only been a few weeks. I knew her in the brothel and now she walks straighter and smiles more."

Crossing his legs, he leaned against the headboard and lifted a scroll. Tullia squinted. *Family finances.* A pit grew in her stomach, and she smoothed the tiny wisps of hair on Aurelia's head, trying not to focus on what tomorrow might bring.

Once Aurelia was done feeding, Tullia changed her and placed her in the crib. Yosef looked up.

"If we pay one hundred slaves four sesterces each month, it will cost us four hundred," he said. "We can also increase the overseer's wages from fifty to sixty. The total costs would be nothing against our monthly income of nine thousand."

Tullia slipped into bed next to him. "For the slaves, I think it will pay off. Maybe they'll work harder and be more loyal to the family, but we really can't know. But I'm certain of one thing—their lives will be better, and that's what I want."

She turned to face him, and Yosef pushed a soft finger against her lips.

"You've worried enough," he whispered, stroking her cheek. "Try and get some rest."

"I'm so nervous."

"Nerves are good," he replied, eyes closing. "So long as they don't take over."

"You don't seem nervous."

"I'm just better at hiding it than you." Yosef pulled her to him, positioning her face in his neck. "Sleep. We'll leave first thing tomorrow."

* * *

In the early dawn—it was early April—Tullia watched the rain pelt the patio and crossed her arms against the chill. She tried to ignore the squeeze in her chest that told her it was a bad omen. Awful weather on the day they were to travel to the largest Flaccus farm and inform the slaves and overseers of the new plans did not bode well.

"Domina?"

Faustina's low call could barely be heard through the pounding rain. Tullia turned to see the old servant beckoning her to the study.

"What is it?" she asked, coming back inside. They had to leave soon.

"Your first complaint."

Tullia tightened. It started with the rain and now this.

Yosef entered the room. "The other side of freedom." He had heard Faustina's remark.

Failing to see the humor, Tullia ignored him. "What? Does Phoebe want more money?" She naturally assumed it was Phoebe, the most outspoken of the girls.

"Not that. It's more of a request. Phoebe would like to see more of Milo. Maybe spend her day off with him."

Tullia froze. She had never considered what the girls would do with their free day.

Yosef raised an eyebrow. "Well, Domina?"

Her annoyance turned to anger. "This is not funny. What's next? Evenings with Milo?"

Faustina's face was impassive. "If I wanted to see a friend, would you let me go?"

The question stung; the painful answer evident. "Ah, well, yes."

Faustina opened her palms in sympathy. "Domina, it's no different for Phoebe. As a freedwoman, her time is her own, especially her day off."

Tullia had to concede the point. *Phoebe's no longer a slave, but a person. She's free to come and go.* Freedom meant independence. She felt her grip on the slaves—rather servants—loosening.

Her face became a sad smile. "Neither of you need my permission."

"That may be Domina, but respect goes both ways. Upon their emancipation, it was made clear they are still girls, and you remain their chaperon. Your approval for many activities is still required—including an unmarried woman like Phoebe spending time with a boy."

Tullia remembered. "As long as Phoebe clears her intentions with you, it's fine. And if you do have a friend you want to visit, please do."

Faustina's dark eyes twinkled. "Thank you, Domina."

After she left, Yosef hooked Tullia's arm through his and led her back through the atrium toward the entrance and their waiting carriage.

"You made a good decision," he said.

"Only after she explained it all to me," she countered. Nervousness blossomed in her belly. "Yosef, I don't know if I can do this. If I could hardly handle a simple request, what will I do in front of all the farm slaves?"

Yosef stopped in front of the carriage door and pulled her into his arms. Tullia rested her chin on his shoulder, uncaring of the rain pelting them.

"I know there's a lot to learn," he whispered. "Believe me, I'm learning too. But we'll face it together, all right?"

She hugged him closer in response. A guard gestured them in, and she entered, followed by Yosef. The door closed and the carriage took off with a wet groan. Tullia settled back against the dry cushions. She hoped the twelve miles to the farm would suffice as the time needed to calm herself.

Accompanied by Balbus and his men, they clattered and

splashed along the busy Via Nomantana, joining merchant traffic required to exit the city with the arrival of the new day. The queue edged along, finally entering the arched, northeastern gate of the Servian wall, the Porta Collina. Constructed of large blocks of beige volcanic tuff, the Porta was continuous with the protective city wall.

"It's about three more miles to the bridge over the Anio river, then we'll really be in the country," offered Yosef.

"Good, these cobblestones give me a headache."

The bumps eased at the single-arched, stone-and-concrete Nomentano bridge of the Anio. Tullia pulled back a curtain and watched the brown, churning river through the weakening drizzle. "It's usually quieter, but today all this rain has filled it up."

"No boat crossings today," added Yosef.

Like with the Via Appia to Pompeii, the driver accessed an earthen path parallel to the bumpy road.

"This is a better ride, but I hope we don't get stuck," said Tullia, rubbing her temples.

"We'll be fine. There's plenty of manpower if we do have a problem," reassured Yosef.

The dirt path proved both passable and smooth. Returning to the curtained window, Tullia saw the dwindling rain give way to a misty sunrise and the light green leaves of early spring sprouting from trees. Breathing the washed air eased her tension, as did seeing a beautiful and open landscape. It was so different compared to the packed buildings and crowded streets of Rome. *It's been a while since I got out of the city*, she thought.

"What are you thinking?" asked Yosef.

She dropped the curtain back. "I'd forgotten how nice the country could be."

"It's sure quieter and slower," he remarked. "At least for now. Things will pick up when we get to the farm."

The tightness returned to her face. She knew they were doing the right thing with the slaves, but what of the overseers? They will not be happy if their power is checked. Those who think slaves are people may be more accepting of the changes. But others will not. She could try to reason with them, but in the end, it may be up to Balbus and his men to force cooperation. She blew out a breath. Nothing to do but see it through—it was the only way forward.

Turning at a copse of three umbrella pines at milestone twelve, they made the final push to the farm. Weak sunlight fought through the thinning clouds as the carriage creaked to a stop in front of a small, white limestone villa flanked by tall cypress trees. Several outbuildings could be seen in the meadows behind.

The farm's proprietors—Rufus, bearded and spry, and his wife, Claudia, rotund with ash-gray hair streaked with a smattering of black—met them at the front door. The Greek couple, former slaves and emancipated by Tullia's father twenty years earlier, occupied and maintained the living quarters for the family, leaving farm management to Yosef. But both understood the purpose of the visit.

After a warm greeting, Claudia led them to a small bedroom for the one-night stay. "Come for lunch when you are ready."

Tullia and Yosef changed clothes and joined their hosts for a quick meal. Tullia took a few bites of bread but ate nothing else, choosing instead to sip her wine. She was jittery inside.

"We'll assemble the slaves outdoors now that the rain has stopped," said Rufus.

"And the mood?" asked Yosef.

He shrugged. "Mostly curiosity."

"A couple of the house slaves asked about the meeting. I told them I was unsure but didn't think it was anything bad," added Claudia.

"How do you think the changes will be received?" asked Tullia, taking another sip.

Claudia gave her a sympathetic smile. "For the slaves, with great enthusiasm. The overseers? Not so much. But your decision didn't surprise us. Your father treated us with great respect. Why should his daughter be any different?"

Tullia relaxed at the mention of Poppi. Yes, he would probably be proud of them today. She hoped he would still be proud at the end of the day.

She pointed to her attire. "Do you think it's too much?" In a dark green tunic with a cream-colored silk headwrap, she looked the part of an affluent noblewoman.

Claudia shook her head. "No, Domina. They will respect you as a wealthy owner. Remember, poor masters often treat slaves poorly. Your reputation begins with your appearance, although the news you bring today will affect them more than your dress."

The woman's words helped ease a little of Tullia's tension. She pushed away from the table and stood, unable to wait a moment longer. "Let's hope so."

From the back door, they followed a cobblestone path about fifty feet to an open patio. On the grassy knoll before them sat forty men, women, and children, all slaves. Quiet murmuring could be heard within their ranks while the over-seers — a group of four — lingered at the front. At a nod from Rufus, the sounds of conversation stopped, and the slaves stood. Balbus beckoned the overseers to join him a short distance away, which they did after a brief, defiant pause. Tullia watched them, her heart slamming into her chest. *That isn't a good sign.*

She faced the silent audience as her words dried up. The loud squeal of a nearby pig broke the spell and a few nervous laughs rang out.

Yosef stepped forward, recognizing several faces. He had visited often enough that many slaves knew him by sight. Every head snapped to him. "Good morning," he said in a loud, clear voice. "As many of you know, I am Tullius Flaccus Josephus, a freedman. I manage this farm for your owner, Tullia Flaccus. She'd like a word with you."

Tullia took a deep breath. She gestured for them to sit. Amidst fading whispers, they all did. "Thank you, Yosef." She expected to see forty angry, indifferent, or skeptical people, but she instead saw men and women with gentle faces and eyes wide with anticipation. Jarred by the sight, she quickly understood. *Despite it all, they still have hope.* She remembered the feeling, as she watched Balbus dragged from the tavern. Even at that desperate moment, she had clung to hope. Now, in front of the slaves, certainty brought clarity, and she knew her cause was just. She would not let their hopes go unanswered.

She opened her hands. "In accordance with the traditions of Rome, you are all slaves." Total silence. "Those traditions leave your treatment in the hands of owners and overseers — treatment that, at times, may be overly harsh. We do not agree with this, so have decided to try and improve your lives. We will apply Jewish traditions of slavery. We're not Jews but we prefer the Jewish ways. You will now be given one day off every week and paid four sesterces a month. Beatings and sexual relations between overseers and slaves will be prohibited. We'll also listen to any complaints about your treatment."

Tullia's heart raced as gasps and whispers followed the announcement. Agitated people turned to their neighbors, others looked at Tullia with furrowed brows, and still others were frozen, slack-jawed.

She felt a burden lift from her shoulders. *There, it's out.* She knew it would not be easy to make the new plan work, but the reception gave her hope. 'Love thy neighbor as yourself' dominated her thoughts.

The buzz of voices from the slaves grew louder.

After a few moments, a hunchbacked old man with a gray beard rose on rickety legs and the crowd quieted. "Permission to speak, Domina?"

Tullia dipped her chin.

"I'm a Jew." He looked around at his fellow slaves, then pointed to her. "What the Domina says is true. Jews give slaves a day off for the weekly Sabbath. The rest is law but not always followed." He returned his gaze to Tullia. "You have described the Jewish way, Domina, except for the money. Jews don't pay slaves."

His statement ended there, but she knew it was a question. "They may not," she conceded, "but it is something I would like to do. A reward for your hard work only makes sense."

The old slave blinked. "We, ah, we thank you, Domina."

Shouts of "Yes," "Thank you, Domina" and other happy cries came through. Suddenly people stood, some laughing, some talking. Several women clutched their children and cried. Ceasar's words from a hundred years earlier popped into her mind: *"Alea iacta est."* Indeed, the die is cast. They were all on a new pathway now.

Tullia quivered inside, certain they had made the right decision. Watching the happy crowd, she remembered her liberation from Vitalio, and sensed their joy.

Yosef came to her as she fought tears. "Oh Yosef, they are so wretched."

He spoke in a soft voice. "It touches you since you've experienced their lot. Feel good about this."

She wanted to hug him but needed to maintain her professional demeanor.

He read her mind. "We'll hug later. Right now, head back to the villa with Claudia and Rufus. Balbus and I will join you when we are done here."

Just then, an angry voice rose.

48

"You can't do this!"

An overseer's harsh cry split the air. Turning, Tullia saw a wiry man break from Balbus's group. Before anyone could react, he marched toward her. Balbus and a guard quickly caught him and grabbed his arms before he got too close. She watched his frenzied eyes dart between her and Yosef, then shift to the quiet audience of slaves wearing expressions of disdain.

"Settle down," growled Balbus.

"I *won't*!" yelled the man, spitting at the old soldier's feet. "This—this"—his eyes found Tullia—"this is an abomination. I quit." He turned to leave but they restrained him.

"Stop," said Tullia.

The slaves froze, watching.

She looked at the huffing man and saw the evil in his eyes. He could have been Rupinus or Vitalio. With neither fear nor hesitation, she met his gaze but addressed Balbus. "What's this about?" she asked in a calm voice, her stomach tight with anger.

"He grew excited after I introduced the new rules."

She addressed the overseer. "What's your name?"

The man glared. "Theon."

"Do you have something to say?"

Theon swung his chin at the slaves. "I won't work for a

family that pays them. They're animals and can't be trusted. There's no abuse here, we simply give their women what they want."

There were gasps from the slaves. A cold knot formed in Tullia's chest, and she took a step forward. "*You* give the women what they want?" He hawked, and she knew what was coming. "Theon, spit on me and I will cut out your tongue and feed it to you right here."

Another gasp from the slaves, but she barely heard it.

"Balbus, your dagger." She held out her hand as he offered the knife.

Theon froze and she saw fear in his eyes. Another filthy bully. She half-hoped he would spit as memories of her dying mother, the foul Rupinus, and her vicious husband flashed across her vision. She glared hard until he looked away. She shook her head and Balbus resheathed the blade. After a breath, she felt her shoulders relax.

"Thank you, Theon. There's no need for you to quit since you're fired. Get off this land. If you ever show up here again, you'll be killed."

Two guards escorted the man away.

Tullia gestured at the three remaining overseers. "Balbus, bring them here."

The men came over, heads bowed.

"Remember, you may be freedmen, but you work for me," she said. "I hope the 'we' in his remark about women referred only to him." She waited. "Any other questions about the changes?"

"No, Domina," said a gray-haired man, speaking for the group.

"Good, and you are?"

"Felix, Domina, and this is Lentulus and Donatus."

Tullia raised her chin. "The new rules go into effect today. Make sure they're followed. We'll be checking. Now give me a few more minutes with the slaves before they return to work."

Felix bowed. "As you wish, Domina. And thank you for the increased pay."

Balbus ushered them aside. Yosef touched her arm as she faced the slaves, still standing on the knoll. "One moment," she said, her heart rate now back to normal.

Yosef leaned in and whispered. "I'm proud of you. I think it's clear you mean business."

"I hope so," she said.

"Tullia, to make it work, we'll need a slave leader."

"I agree. Like Faustina at home. Somebody they can go to."

"Let them decide."

Tullia could not think of a better way to reassure them of her sincerity. "You are very clever."

She turned back to the slaves, still standing on the knoll. "We need you to pick a leader who can speak for you."

The slaves looked at her with mostly surprised faces. A man shouted, "Zadok!" followed by more yells of his name. The calls soon became a chant, "Zadok, Zadok."

Tullia slowly raised her hands, and the din faded. "Zadok, where are you?"

The crowd opened for the old man who had spoken earlier. The slaves clapped.

She beckoned him forward.

He came and stood before her; his head bowed. "Domina?"

Tullia took his elbow and led him over to Yosef and out of earshot of the slaves. "Zadok, will you be their leader?"

He gave a nervous tug of his beard. "I would be honored, Domina."

"Very well. From now on, any complaints will be brought to you. We'll check periodically about concerns. If you accept this responsibility, we'll also increase your pay to six sesterces each month. Do you agree?"

Zadok's voice trembled. "Ah, yes, Domina, as you wish. Thank you, Domina."

She left Yosef to explain how to handle complaints and returned to the slaves.

"You have chosen Zadok as your leader. Bring complaints to him, and he'll pass them along to us."

The slaves waited in silence and Zadok returned to the group.

Tullia shifted from foot to foot, unsure of what the silence meant. "You have a few moments for yourselves before you return to work," she said at last.

Yosef came to her side, but before they could leave, Zadok walked up with others following. Soon there was a line behind him. He dipped his head. "Thank you again, Domina."

His brethren followed, one after another repeating the gesture and the thanks.

A pregnant woman came last to pay her respects, speaking rustic Latin. "Women, too? Money and a day?"

"Yes, women, too," said Tullia, smiling.

The slave pointed at her belly. "Theon. I'll love baby but not him. You a gift from the gods, Domina. Bless you." She pressed Tullia's hand to her cheek.

Touched by the gesture, Tullia felt moistness in her eyes. She held onto the woman's hand, squeezing once. "Thank you and take care of yourself."

Preparing for bed, Tullia and Yosef reflected on the events of the day.

"The raise will help the overseers adapt to the changes," said Yosef.

Tullia faced a small mirror and brushed her hair. "That and Balbus."

Yosef snickered.

She sighed. "Yosef, we're fortunate to be so wealthy. These costs are nothing for us."

As she spoke, she glimpsed her reflection. Her round brown eyes danced with joy. *We did it.* She blinked. She knew there would be bumps—they still had two more farms to visit—but for now, she could relax and enjoy the moment. *We will treat our people right.* Despite her happiness, she wondered if they could just free and then rehire them. But she knew it was impossible, not to mention risky. They simply had to have a reliable workforce, never mind the costs. *It could never work.* She would be satisfied with trying to improve the lives of their workers.

Standing behind her, Yosef rubbed her shoulders. "Our wealth is nothing compared to my love for you."

Tullia stood, leading him to the bed. They lay down, and he caressed her face. His soft lips found hers. They kissed and he blew out the table lamp.

49

"It's time to start stealing sheep," said Tullia, as she strolled with Yosef and their guards through the Forum. Walking at the third hour, they beat the muggy midday heat of August and could still enjoy the sunrise. Considering the heavy crowd, it appeared most Romans agreed.

The day before, Balbus reported on the slave situation. "After four months, Domina, no complaints as yet. The slaves at all three farms are spending their money. Vendors now visit regularly. The most popular purchases are wine, sandals, and coarse linen. Being paid each week on the day off was a good idea."

Tullia had suggested a weekly rather than monthly payday. The spenders could spend. The savers could save. She felt happy for the slaves and proud of her decisions.

Meanwhile, Sextus assured her the legal matters for the divorce were moving along. At a snail's pace. No matter, she was ready to go after Vitalio.

In the Forum, Tullia listened to the gurgle of a large fountain as the crowd bustled. "So, a plan?"

Yosef's eyes danced. "We hire some of Cresimus's women to go to the overseer's shack on Vitalio's farm. They'll arrive at night, posing as an acting troupe. In exchange for lodging, they'll offer wine and entertainment, a few songs or skits, but no touching. We'll take undiluted Falernian wine for the three overseers. Once they're drunk, Balbus and his men will rustle the sheep while the women return to the brothel. We'll steal the slaves and put them on our farms."

"So, it's back to Cresimus," she said without rancor.

"Do you know anybody else with such resources? He'll do it for the right price."

Tullia lifted a shoulder, then let it drop. "He can drive the wagon with the women and join them inside. He'll want to protect his investments."

"That's a good idea. I was going to take them, but I'll ride with Balbus instead."

As she considered the plan, her mind spun back to Vitalio's cruelty, his fetid breath and rotting teeth inches from her mouth. Visceral rage burst forth from the memories that followed—Rupinus's hand under her clothes, Mama's swollen face, the whimpering Atia. She *had* to be part of every step of Vitalio's downfall.

"And I'll join Cresimus and the women."

Yosef froze. "You can't do that."

Tullia kept walking, anger making her skin tingle. "Stop with what I can't do," she flung at him. "I love you, but this is *my* decision. I need to do this. Do you understand that? I *need* it." Her fingers scratched her arms, then her neck. "Because of Vitalio, I have been imprisoned, witnessed my mother's gruesome death, and endured constant beatings and molestations. I will *not* sit by while others exact my revenge for me."

"Tullia, these are crimes," Yosef whispered. His head swung around at passersby. "If you're caught, Vitalio will ruin you, never mind that you'll end up in prison."

"I will not." Her anger evaporated. "There are no crimes

in the plan. We still own the farm, including the sheep and slaves."

Yosef recoiled, mouth agape. "How? The farm was your dowry to him."

"Dowry or not, Sextus told me Vitalio never registered the place in his name. On Poppi's instruction, Siculus simply sent the farm profits to Vitalio. Neither my father nor Vitalio checked the paperwork. Sextus made the discovery as he prepared the divorce proceedings." She winked. "We've *got* him."

"Then let's forget this plan and use the courts to repossess it." he urged, apparently unimpressed by the information.

"The legal system's too slow," she argued. "Just look at the divorce petition — it's taking forever. Besides, Sextus says it's nearly impossible for a woman to recover her dowry if she's still married — this is more direct." She paused. "I want to strike Vitalio every way I can, and I've waited long enough."

"But you going with Cresimus is dangerous," he persisted. "Drunks get violent."

"Yosef, you know very well the dangers are nothing compared to what I have endured. And Cresimus will keep me safe if he wants to get paid."

She stopped and turned to him in the middle of a plaza. Concern lit his expression, his lower lip jutted out, but then his gaze lifted, and he looked around the familiar surroundings.

"We're not here just for a nice walk, are we?"

"No," she admitted, taking his hand. "I wanted a honey date."

* * *

"Five hundred."

Tullia frowned at the squat owner.

"Yosef told me the plan. Five hundred."

"Too much."

"But this includes my expenses." The proprietor flashed an oily grin and ticked off several fingers. "Closing my business will cost me two hundred, a wagon rental and wine another hundred. And, with respect, Domina, my girls and I should also be paid."

"You're padding the fees," she said stiffly, in little mood to play his games. "Two-fifty, and you need only bring Phoebe's aunt. Phoebe and I will be the other two."

He slapped a hand over his heart. "Domina! You're expecting me to be responsible for your life for two-fifty? I refuse to do so for less than three hundred."

Annoyed her life was worth only fifty sesterces to Cresimus, she accepted his terms and made plans to go the following night.

50

Throughout the day, Tullia mulled over the evening plan, and her confidence in the mission grew. But now, as Faustina and Atia helped her dress, not so much. The fact they were not committing a crime did nothing to lessen the danger. Remembering Theon, she expected Vitalio to hire similar thugs for his farm. Just look at Rupinus. Remembering the man reminded her of those dark days and Vitalio's role. Clenching her jaw at the thought, her anger and lust for revenge replaced the nervous tension. No, dangers aside, they will succeed tonight. It was a first step in what she hoped would be his gratifying downfall.

An hour after dusk, Cresimus drove the one-horse wagon on the Via Tiburtina and out of the city. The three women, dressed in shabby black tunics and scarlet headcovers, huddled in the creaky open back. After six miles, they left the bumpy cobblestones and trundled down an earthen path for the final mile to Vitalio's farm. Moonlight threw shadows across the trail. In the warm humidity of the Anio River valley, crickets chirped.

The tightness in Tullia's stomach returned. Well, at least it wasn't raining. Her heart still pounded.

"I act most of the time, and you used to, so acting like actors will be easy," chuckled Phoebe's aunt, Maronella.

"It will be fun," chimed Phoebe.

"Master, if we are an acting troupe, we should have a song," called Maronella.

"As you wish." He coughed softly and then began:

Get to know your lady's maid,
She'll always smooth your way.
Promise her your gift of love,
She'll help you in your play.
The maid can rouse her, comb in hand,
She'll make her want to lay.
Your lady's sails, full and bright
Await your oar that day.

"Sorry, Domina," he said in a low voice. "Just trying to get into the spirit."

"I've heard worse," lied Tullia. "Is that the best you can do?" She snickered to herself, recognizing a theme from one of Ovid's poems on love. Society deemed his book inappropriate, but everybody knew about it. The text contained many stories about how men and women behave toward each other. Years earlier, she and Valeria had read several passages from a copy Valeria found in the Buteo library.

Cresimus snorted, resuming his song as Phoebe and her aunt giggled. Tullia leaned back, her head resting on the bumpy inside and, ignoring the next two verses, let his deep and surprisingly melodic voice, help calm her.

As the song came to its close, the wagon stopped. Cresimus hopped down and banged on the door of the overseer's shack with a heavy walking stick.

Light spilled from the room as an unshaven oily man

opened the door. "Eh? Who's there?" He wielded a *gladius* at Cresimus. Tullia's heart jumped into her throat as she recognized the sword. She looked to the other two women for shared concern, but they appeared unfazed.

Just another night at the brothel, she thought. It was not reassuring.

Cresimus faked a limp and hobbled back a step. "Easy, citizen. We're a small acting troupe bound for Rome. In exchange for lodging tonight, my girls"— he waved a hand, and the three women removed their headcovers — "and I can offer wine and a song."

The man flashed a nubby-toothed grin and sheathed his sword. "Boys!" he called. "Come out here and help these ladies into the cabin. We've got a show to watch."

Two more emerged from the shack's shadows, one tall, the other fat. Both barefoot, they reached stringy yet muscled arms into the wagon, lifting Phoebe and Maronella out and leading them inside. With a wolf's grin, Nubby Teeth approached Tullia, but Cresimus nudged him aside. "Allow me."

At that moment, Tullia would have handed over the five hundred if the bordello owner had asked. Instead, she took his proffered hand and stepped out of the wagon onto the soft earth. Cresimus pushed his chin in the direction of the rickety one-room shack and turned back to the wagon to grab three jugs of the Falernian.

"Go on," he whispered. "I'll be right behind you."

Tullia nearly retched at the crushing stench of sheep dung and body odor. Through waves of nausea, she saw messy sleeping pallets on the right and a fireplace to her left. A table and three chairs occupied the middle of the room, dimly lit by four wall lamps. She kept swallowing, pushing down a gag that did not want to recede.

The thump of the closed door announced Cresimus and the wine. Beckoning to the three women, he handed a jug to each. The men sat with empty mugs at the ready. Phoebe and Maronella took their jugs and poured the wine, each taking a man and leaning in but not quite touching. The men grinned, showing yellow, stained, and rotting teeth. Foul odors issued from their breath. Cresimus raised his brow at Tullia. Biting her lip, she did the same for Nubby Teeth—though her body remained more upright than that of her companions. Once they were done, they left the jugs on the table and Cresimus ushered them to the edge of the pallets. He spun on his heel and clapped loudly, overcoming the noisy guzzling of the three overseers.

"Welcome to the show! I am Roscius, and these are the Roscius Girls from Tivoli."

The three-man audience hooted and belched as they chugged more wine.

Phoebe and her aunt stepped forward. With white knuckles, Tullia gripped a tambourine, wondering how to use it.

Phoebe whispered. "Just tap and jiggle it to the beat."

Nubby Teeth's lecherous eyes never left her, and her heart thundered with thoughts of Rupinus. Fighting her fear, she looked over his head at the far wall and blew out a breath. She urged the Falernian to work quickly.

Phoebe and Maronella started a song. A child's song. Tullia knew the tune, but the lyrics were now ribald. She mouthed along anyway. The melody made it easier to use the tambourine, but her neck kinked with tension.

They sang and danced to Tullia's steady clinking. Cresimus tapped his walking stick to the beat. The men drank.

The thick, foul air frayed Tullia's nerves. Despite an upset stomach and near-paralyzing fear, she kept the rhythm.

The overseers grew boisterous. "Hey Tambourine, come up front," called Nubby Teeth.

With a thundering heart, Tullia inched forward. *Dear Juno, why did I do this?*

The other two women, seemingly unbothered by neither the dank atmosphere nor the men's salacious attention, swung their hips in time with the song. Tullia made an anemic attempt to move her shoulders to the beat. *Drink faster,* she prayed.

The song finally ended and Cresimus stepped forward. He launched into a windy joke about two whores and a soldier, allowing the women to catch their breath and regroup.

Maronella leaned into her, whispering under the pretense of fixing the curls of her hair. "You look like you might faint. Try breathing through your mouth. And relax. Cresimus is very good with his stick."

Phoebe touched Tullia's arm. "You'll be fine, Domina. It's almost over."

Tullia wanted to jump into her arms and cry. *My three most favorite people right now are a whore, a former whore, and a brothel owner.* The ridiculous insight eased the tension in her stomach. She took a decisive breath, her jangled nerves quieting into resolve. "Thank you. Let's finish this."

Cresimus called them back for another song, and the show resumed.

Phoebe and her aunt sang a marching tune. Jingle, jingle,

went Tullia's tambourine as she tried to keep up. Moving forward, now back, she stole a glance at the audience and hope flickered.

Stretched across the table, the fat man snored. The tall one's head lolled from side to side. She knew he was next. Two down. But Nubby Teeth remained awake. He shifted in his seat and fondled his crotch. A new wave of icy fear shot down her back at his hungry grin. She saw, yet again, Rupinus. Shaking the tambourine with one hand, she dropped the other toward a knife concealed in the folds of her skirt.

"Tambourine, let's dance!" He lurched for her.

Before she could react, the sharp crack of Cresimus's stick across the attacker's head reverberated through the room. The assailant went down in a silent heap, unmoving. Tullia's eyes shot toward the table, her chest squeezing with relief. The tall man had fallen off his chair and mumbled from the floor. He still clutched his empty mug. The fat man slept on.

Cresimus surveyed the scene with a grim smile. "Looks like we're done here." He capped and grabbed the jugs of wine. "Let's go. Balbus awaits our signal."

51

Once outside, Tullia wanted to gobble the clean night air. Had the world ever smelled better? Her nausea regressed each step she took away from the fetid cabin, and so focused was she on forgetting what just happened that she missed Cresimus's signal. Before she knew it, Balbus, Yosef, and five other rustlers thundered up on horseback. She tried to straighten, holding onto the back of the wagon, but she knew her face was drained of color.

Balbus pulled his horse to a stop in front of the wagon. "I assume success?"

"Complete. They're all three out with plenty of wine to spare." Cresimus held up his prizes.

Yosef reached down and touched Tullia's shoulder. "Any problems?"

Tullia kept her face turned away; if he saw it, he'd get distracted. "No, I'm fine. I'll see you back at the villa."

It worked; he nudged his horse and loped after Balbus and the rustlers. Two wagons driven by guards trailed them, heading for the slaves' quarters. Cresimus closed the door to the shack and settled the women in the open wagon.

"Great job tonight, ladies," he said. "Especially you, Domina. Very strong."

She managed a sad smile. "Thank you for your protection."

He chuckled. "All included in my fee."

A thousand wouldn't feel like enough right now, she thought, biting her lip to keep the notion to herself. She had no doubt he would take it if offered.

Cresimus opened one of the Falernians. "Domina, have some, it'll help settle your stomach."

Tullia raised the jug to her lips and took a small sip. A wonderful warmth spread across her chest, and she tipped it back again, eagerly taking in another larger gulp. "Oh my," she sighed, wiping her hand across her mouth as the sweet liquid coated her throat. "Thank you." She passed it off to Phoebe, who took three healthy gulps before giving it to her aunt. Cresimus was the last to drink, replacing the cap with flair.

"Enough fun in the country," he tooted. "Let's go home."

* * *

The wagon lumbered toward Rome, Cresimus driving at a slow and steady pace to allow the women to rest, though Tullia found none. She stayed awake, staring at nothing, saying little when Cresimus dropped her and Phoebe at the villa as the sun crept into a pink-orange sky. Faustina and Yosef met them.

Yosef hugged her, then stepped back, wrinkling his nose. "Whew, you smell worse than me."

Tullia glared at him through sleepy eyes. "I spent the night in a sheep barn with three dirty drunks."

"Domina, with respect, I must agree with Yosef," Faustina said, fanning her face. "But all three of you need to bathe. The only smell worse than sheep is pigs." She glanced at Yosef.

"Thank Juno I heated the water. We'll be quick, you can come later." Leaving him at the front door, the old servant ushered the women to the bath.

Tullia and Phoebe removed their soiled clothing and took quick sponge baths using tallow and ash soap bars. Once cleansed, they moved into the warm, rose- and lilac-scented water of the sunken tub. After a quick rinse, Phoebe stepped out.

Tullia watched the former prostitute dry herself and felt a surge of sisterly affection. *She is so young yet so strong. Neither slave nor whore, but a woman. Like me.*

The girl wriggled into a clean tunic and grinned. "Ah, that's better."

Tullia stood, fighting tears. "Phoebe, thank you for all you did tonight. Milo is a lucky man." She took the girl's hand.

Phoebe covered Tullia's hand with her own. "Thank *you*, Domina, for all you have done for me. And we were never really in any danger. My aunt had two knives just in case, and no drunk has ever bested Cresimus. Besides, you played the tambourine perfectly."

Tullia let go and slipped back into the tub. "You sing and dance well yourself."

"Why, thank you." Phoebe curtsied, then turned and helped Faustina gather the soiled clothing.

Yosef arrived as the two women left. He washed off his road grit and joined Tullia in the tub. She rested against him, listening to the sounds of their breathing and the thump of his heart. Yosef did not press her to talk, instead busying himself by running his hands through her hair, massaging her scalp, and rubbing the knots out of her neck. As he worked his magic, Tullia talked, speaking soft and slow and almost detached, as if those events happened in a dream.

"I'm proud of you," he said when she finished. "You are the strongest woman I have ever met, and I love you all the more for it."

"You were right about the danger," she admitted. "I was terrified."

"And you did it anyway."

"The others helped me." She shook her head, swishing her hand through the scented water. The ripples soothed her. "I won't do that again. And I'll never touch another tambourine."

His face feigned interest. "But I heard you play so well." His hands rubbed her shoulders, and he moved his lips to her ear. "How's that urge for vengeance?"

"Partially satisfied. I'll feel better once I hear the details of how this affects him. It's the first step in his destruction, and it was important for me to be there."

"I understand."

Tullia said nothing more. Eyes closed, she enjoyed the ensuing quiet, enveloped in fragrant rose and lilac. They snuggled, the warm wetness enhancing the pleasant contact of his body. The tightness in her chest eased and the memories of the night faded.

"Yosef," she whispered.

Under the water, he reached for her.

She sighed. They enjoyed the privacy of the bath until late morning.

* * *

Balbus arrived later in the afternoon. "Domina, we have acquired eighty-four head of sheep and sixteen slaves. The livestock have been added to the Nomentana holdings, and the slaves dispersed across all three farms. As you willed, we kept families together."

"Thank you," said Tullia.

He left and she turned to Yosef. "What do think will be the value of the take?"

He shrugged. "I'd guess something around fifteen or twenty thousand. Let's see what Siculus says later."

Lying in bed that night, she watched the ceiling dance with shadows from a dim lamp and listened to Yosef's gentle breathing. Almost at once, her thoughts turned to the slaves and their families. Each day like the last, never enough to eat, always subject to the whip, and living in constant fear. She felt foolish wondering if they were ever happy. How could they be? The dreadful pull of guilt kept her restless.

When she finally slept, she dreamed she was working in an olive grove. The sun blazed and her eyes burned from sweat. Hot and dirty, she grunted as she lifted her last basket of olives onto a waiting oxcart. An overseer leered—Vitalio. He bound her wrists, securing her to a rope trailing from the wagon where she joined other slaves for the walk back to their camp. Ahead, her son cried, and a pregnant woman moaned as they struggled to keep pace.

"Can you not slow down?" she called.

The whip snapped, searing her back in pain.

She jerked awake, body on fire.

"Tullia?" asked a groggy Yosef.

His hand felt cool on her forehead. The pain disappeared.

"Wake up. You're having a nightmare."

She sat, tremulous. "Yosef, I dreamed I was a slave. Vitalio whipped me. My son cried and I was thirsty."

He drew her to his chest. "Easy. It was just a bad dream."

"The hopelessness was worse than the whip," she whimpered.

He sighed and held her for several long moments. She felt him tense.

"Tullia, it reminds me of my weeks in the slave wagon. Your dream has given you another taste of bondage."

Raising to one elbow, she perceived his silhouette. "How did you endure it?"

He sighed. "Day by day and moment by moment. You ignore fear and think of nothing. But now, your new rules have eliminated their fear. Look past the horrors and try to remember that."

She dropped her head to his chest as a tear escaped. "I'll try."

His squeeze reassured her. Turning on her side, she molded her body with his. Her eyes stayed open and troubled, watching the flickering lamp and waiting for dawn.

* * *

Over a couple of days, Tullia resolved her emotional quandaries concerning slaves and accepted the fact that what she was doing was the best she could hope for. She looked ahead to a planned meeting with Balbus and Siculus concerning the results of the raid.

As she sat writing in her journal with Yosef, who was

checking papers about their grain shipping business, Faustina interrupted. "Here are Balbus and Siculus."

After a greeting, the men sat.

"What's the news?" asked Tullia, looking at Balbus.

"Domina, your husband suspects, but cannot prove your responsibility. The drunk overseers disappeared, the sheep have blended with your herds, and the slaves aren't talking. I'm told they're much happier now."

Tullia felt a warm glow. "That's wonderful." She turned to the accountant. "How much did we gain?"

Siculus stopped twisting his fingers long enough to check his notes. "Both sheep and slaves together are worth around twenty thousand."

"How will this affect him?"

"The next harvest will be poor without people to work the fields."

Tullia's warm glow swelled further.

The accountant continued. "More importantly, the slaves were collateral. Their loss may hamper his successful pursuit of business ventures vital to saving the farm. If he loses the farm, the value of his property holdings drops below the amount required for continued senatorial membership. He's close to ruin."

"How do you know?"

"We have people watching," answered Balbus.

As the men left, Tullia sighed. The news helped her see she had done a good thing for another group of slaves, and it eased her guilt. Better yet, she hoped they had dealt a fatal blow to Vitalio. Before she could share her thoughts with Yosef, a banging at the front door interrupted her. The sounds of Faustina's voice floated through the atrium, then the door closed with a thud.

The senior house servant entered the study looking exasperated. "An obnoxious man insists on an audience with the two of you. He calls himself Urbanus."

Yosef snickered. "He's a potter and friend of the priest. Show him in."

Disgruntled, Faustina returned with the skinny man. "The visitor." She snorted and left.

"See?" Urbanus called after her. "I told you I was important." He bowed to Yosef and Tullia. "Greetings."

Yosef stood, one hand sweeping to the side. "Good morning, Urbanus. This is Domina Tullia Flaccus."

Tullia took him in from her chair. Clad in a dark brown tunic, brown hat, and swathed in a reddish-brown beard, only his pale pink hands broke the brown monotony.

She bit back a smile. "Good morning, Urbanus. What have you for us?"

The small man straightened. "Two things. A message from the priest for Master Yosef and a special vase for the Domina."

He handed Yosef a wax tablet encased in a soft leather cover. From his brown shoulder bag, he extracted a small but exquisite royal blue vase and offered it to Tullia with both hands. "I made it just for you from a special clay. I fired it twice."

"Why, thank you," she said, taking it from him and admiring the smooth finish and gentle curves. "I have the perfect place for it."

Yosef, still standing, looked up from the tablet. "Urbanus, do you like honey dates?"

"They are my favorite," he gushed.

Yosef called for Atia, who came in wiping her hands on a rag. "Please give our guest a couple of honey dates and take him to the patio." He turned to the potter. "We will need a few moments to prepare our reply."

As Atia escorted the eager man away, refusing his request for three dates with admirable patience, Yosef pushed the wax tablet to Tullia. "You'd better read this."

52

Tullia read the tight Latin script.

> *My young friend,*
> *A matter of the utmost importance has come to my at-*
> *tention. Please visit at your earliest convenience. Perhaps*
> *tonight or early morning, and only under cover of darkness.*
> *Smudge and write over this message with your plan. The*
> *potter is both loyal and illiterate, so your response will be*
> *safe. Respectfully.*

"A matter of utmost importance?" she repeated, a tight-ness squeezing her core. The room converged on her, and she reached out a shaky hand to grip the table.

Yosef's lips formed a thin line. "He would never contact us in this cryptic way unless it was serious. The night visit means no witnesses."

No witnesses? Tullia could only think of one reason for a clandestine meeting.

"Vitalio. He's up to something."

"Has to be," Yosef said. He scratched his chin. "It could be about the sheep raid or maybe the money."

She clenched her fists. "Either way, we can't trust the bas-tard. Let's go tonight."

"Write a response. I'll inform Balbus."

As Tullia finished crafting their reply, footsteps reached her ears. Tullia placed the tablet back in its leather case and looked up to see Atia retreating and the potter taking tiny bites from his last date, a look of pure bliss on his face. Upon seeing her, he swallowed his morsel, dusted off his hands, and took back the tablet with a bow.

"Please give this message to the priest," she said. "And thank you again for the lovely vase."

He slipped it into his satchel and raised a shaggy eyebrow. "You're quite welcome, Domina. By any chance can you spare another honey date?"

* * *

At dusk, they left for the temple, and Tullia knew the rest of the household was happy to see her go. Her edginess had engulfed the villa ever since Urbanus delivered the message—she was impatient and abrupt. Only Phoebe and Faustina would talk to her.

Adding to her foul mood was her disguise—cloaked in one of Yosef's old tunics with a hooded wrap and a soot-smudged face, she resembled a beggar woman. A worn pair of Poppi's boots, stuffed with rags so they would fit, and a gnarled walking stick completed the ensemble.

Yosef's sly grin only irritated her further.

"Keep it to yourself," she growled, her anger bolstered by her grimy appearance and uncomfortable shoes. "Let's just go."

"No comment for me?" he asked, hurrying after her.

Tullia turned to appraise him, fighting back a small smile.

Dressed in scruffy workers' clothing and moth-eaten hats, Yosef and the guards looked like day laborers heading for home.

Balbus lit their way with a small pine torch. The watery flame accented the path through the swampy field to the priest's neighborhood. Once across, the quartet moved onto the cobblestone street, clogged with carts and wagons disgorging their wares. Keeping their heads down, they shuffled along, trying not to appear too urgent. Around them, light from windows flickered and distant dogs barked in conversation.

Despite the easy walk, Tullia's feet hurt. Nervousness from the nocturnal traffic added to smoldering anger. It had to be Vitalio. Again, she felt cornered by him. She gripped her walking stick until her hand hurt. This annoying walk was not helping. Her irritation peaked as they arrived at the temple.

Yosef knocked, and the door opened. Tullia blinked. Had the priest been waiting at the door?

The furry white face of Ben-Turrina came into view. "Ah, Yosef." He turned to Tullia. "And I assume the Domina, dressed to be your mother."

"Yes, sir, it's me and the Domina, Tullia Flaccus," said Yosef, one hand on Tullia's arm to stop her scowl.

Beckoning them in, the priest glanced out before closing the door. "Your men?"

"Will keep watch," said Tullia, her voice sharp. Yosef gave her a strange look.

"Indeed," said the priest, his blue eyes locked on hers. "If I recall correctly, you are a senator's daughter and a senator's wife." He gave an icy smile. "Different senators, I presume?"

Tullia felt her face flush. "What do you want?" she snapped. Yosef looked at her in horror.

"Master Ben-Turrina, please forgive the Domina," he stammered. "It has been a difficult few days."

Ben-Turrina seemed to not hear. He folded his arms. "Domina, I'm happy to assist, but your attitude makes it difficult. If you'd like to discuss the matter, please be civil. Otherwise, you can leave the way you came. I contacted you at great personal risk."

Fury welled in her chest. She prepared a biting retort, but the power of his unwavering gaze made her pause. Her mouth went dry. *He doesn't fear me.* His eyes held hers, and after a moment, she dropped her gaze. *He's a trusted member of the Imperial House. He moves in the highest circles.* The insights checked her hubris. *He may be committing treason for us.*

She took a deep breath. Yosef's rule flitted by.

Another breath came and went. Lifting a hand, she pushed back her headpiece, and her thin fingers found the priest's clothed forearm. "Master Ben-Turrina, please forgive my behavior. It's been a long night and I'm tired. I momentarily forgot my manners. We appreciate the risks you have taken on our behalf."

His eyes twinkled. "No harm done. Come this way."

"And they were different," she added as he began walking.

"Different?"

"Senators." *You old coot.*

"Ah," he said, chuckling.

Ben-Turrina brought them to a table laid with bread, olives, and watered wine. Several lamps and candles lit the room. A covered basket rested on the corner. "For your men."

Yosef started to rise, but Tullia waved him down. "Thank you. I'll take it to them."

When she returned, the two were sitting in silence. Yosef gestured at the priest. "I told him about paying the slaves and relocating sheep."

Ben-Turrina opened one hand. "It answered some questions." He pointed at a large scroll collection. "As an imperial scribe, I copy information to specific volumes, translating to Latin when necessary. Most materials consist of policies, vital statistics, or communication from the provinces—bland information without security risk—until recently. The latest included a note from your husband."

Tullia stiffened. "He wrote to you?"

"He did not. Thirteen wax tablets came two days ago. In them, I found a personal communication from who is surely your husband to a magistrate. I assumed its accidental inclusion. Yesterday, two senatorial secretaries arrived, asking to see the tablets." He pointed at the stack. "They flipped through the twelve and left without a word. Fortunately, I had removed the incriminating thirteenth item."

The priest raised his furry eyebrows. "The contents of the tablet discussed the most despicable of behaviors and a plot against you." He pushed a piece of papyrus toward them. "I copied the message and destroyed the tablet. When we're done here, we'll burn this scrap."

Tullia leaned over the table, as did Yosef.

My dear Lucius,

Can lust and mutual fulfillment ever be so delicious? Our little party was surely a success. Nobody will miss the little slave boy, but it's still a pity he died. Ah, but enough of that!

My finances have grown thinner of late. My wife has hidden her family fortune. Worse yet, she and her slave lover continue to squander my money—it is now known they pay their slaves, an imperial crime in itself. And to do so with my money! You must help me put an end to this.

Through Senate contracts, I've discovered my wife's family is vested in grain shipping. There are loopholes in the law allowing me to become the sole holder of these lucrative proxies. Official questions may arise as I tighten the noose, and I'll require your help in suppressing them. As a magistrate, I know you can do this. As my friend, I know you will. And don't concern yourself about whether your vindictive wife will ever know of your unusual sexual proclivities or our next little meeting—your secrets are safe with me.

V

Tullia winced as she sat back. "They killed a slave boy for fun?"

The horrors of seeing her broken mother take her last breath came roaring back, and just as suddenly were replaced with rage. She shot to her feet. "We have to do something!"

Both men looked at her, but it was Ben-Turrina who spoke. "We must consider certain things first. You know the depths of their cruelty. You need to find a way to move past the terrible implications of the note."

"But—"

The priest held up a hand. "We can do nothing for this boy. But there is still time to help you. Do you understand?"

Tullia wasn't sure she did, but she knew giving in to her

anger would solve nothing and the night would be a waste. Trembling, she lowered into her seat and twisted her fingers together as Yosef poured a cup of wine. The drink helped, but still her fury festered.

"You assumed the thirteenth tablet was accidental," Yosef said to the priest as she drank. "Could it have been intentional?"

"No, my young friend. The tablet's too easily traced. And why pass this information along to me? It has to be an accident. Perhaps the senator was drinking and misplaced it."

"That's very likely," Tullia spoke up from where her mouth was still covered by the cup. "Vitalio is a despicable drunk and beneath contempt."

The priest dipped his head. "True, but he's also a senator coming for you. It's no surprise he'd concoct a scheme to steal your money. More troubling was the slave issue."

She snorted. "What business is it of his?"

"None, though he may choose to make it *imperial* business." Ben-Turrina's expression grew solemn. "By paying slaves, you have wagged your finger in the face of Roman tradition. The Senate, as well as the Imperial House, value nothing more."

Her hand released the near-empty cup. "I may have given him leverage to come after us for more than money," she said faintly.

"Exactly," said the priest.

In the quiet that followed, Tullia's nervousness overcame her wrath. *Now what?*

Yosef broke the silence. "He may have many allies if he makes the slaves an issue."

"But the magistrate is probably his first and most important," noted the priest.

"Then let's cut off the head of the snake," Tullia said in a tight voice. "Who's this magistrate?"

The priest raised a brow in approval. "Good question, Domina. Lucius Porcinas. His wife, Livia, is an ambitious and cruel patrician, with access, as you say, to the head of the snake."

"She's the knife that can do the slicing," said Tullia.

Yosef covered her hand. "We inform her of Lucius's misbehaviors."

"Thereby undercutting him," she finished. The knot in her chest loosened.

"Welcome to the scheming of imperial politics," said the priest. "You learn quickly."

Tullia's spirits rose, then just as quickly fell as the implications dawned. Yosef turned and squeezed her hand. He voiced concerns he seemed to read from her mind.

"Don't worry. Tomorrow, we'll meet with Sextus and Siculus. We need to protect the family assets."

She gave him a grateful look before turning back to the priest. Ben-Turrina was folding the papyrus into a neat square, watching the wall of scrolls behind them. Every now and then he sipped his wine. His movements were precise, yet casual, the importance of his station and the weight on his shoulders in stark contrast to the menial task he was performing.

"May I ask yet another favor of you?" she ventured in a quiet voice.

The priest stopped moving and sat back, hands steepled. "Of course, Domina."

"Most of the turmoil is from our desire to apply Yosef's

rule to slaves. We believe it should be broadly employed, yet I could never use it with Vitalio. There must be a limit."

"He's ignoring the Rule as well as breaking several commandments," added Yosef.

Ben-Turrina raised a finger. "In other words, should you apply these decrees to your husband? Is he not worthy of such considerations? If not, how can you justify being selective in their application?"

Tullia opened her palms. "Rules or not, we need to stop him."

"Correct, Domina, and Jewish law says you are justified in stopping him. By doing so, you will prevent criminal harm to your family. Criminals are not protected by the Rule."

"So, we can—we can stop him and still be true to the Rule."

"Yes, Domina." The priest stood and held out a hand. "Stop him and know that God will understand. But don't forget the Romans. They may be less forgiving, and they have the swords."

53

The following day, Tullia and Yosef met with Siculus and Sextus, signing the necessary papers to protect the family assets.

They stood and Tullia spoke. "You both now know of Vitalio's plan. Please contact your informants. We need a date and location for his little tryst."

The men agreed and departed.

"Well, the money's safe," said Tullia, releasing a breath.

"Now we just need to know where and when," replied Yosef. "I may do some sniffing around."

Tullia knew what that meant. "Just be careful."

After he left, she found Dracus playing with Atia in the atrium. Sitting on the couch, Tullia watched the young freedwoman hide a walnut first in one hand, and then the other. Her son tried to pick the right one, clapping and laughing when he got it right. Despite it all, Dracus seemed like a normal little boy with a big sister. Her sense of pride at the scene eased the twist inside that always was Vitalio.

* * *

In the coming days, they heard nothing about Vitalio's plan. Tullia's rising agitation over the wait was made worse by nagging questions. Would Lucius tell others about her paying slaves? These were evil men. Soldiers might come tomorrow and haul her off. She was not sure how long she had. From what Ben-Turrina said, she suspected Livia would probably kill her husband. She hoped so, since that seemed to be the only way to stop him from talking. Her stomach ground away. The uncertainty was just like with Rupinus. The familiarity made her sad.

To ease her angst, she went shopping in the Forum. Yosef had an errand to run and would meet her there.

He soon arrived, breathless. "We found Vitalio's love nest."

Her heart jumped. "How?"

"Siculus's informant. He said the two men plan to meet in three days at a shack near the Collina gate." He offered her his arm, nodding to Balbus milling nearby with his men.

They strolled through the busy Forum, silent for a few moments.

"We pass through that gate on our way to the Nomantana farm and have probably seen the place," said Tullia. "How will we tell Livia of the meeting?"

"Cresimus. That's where I was. Maronella knows Livia's maidservant."

"Maronella?" asked Tullia, remembering her kindness that night with the overseers.

"Yes. She said she wanted to help in any way she could. She still thanks you for taking in Phoebe."

Tullia smiled inside. "How can she help?"

"She'll see the maidservant tomorrow in the market and will convey a rumor about Lucius's dalliance with a male ac-tor—an activity so egregious it could tarnish the family name for generations, never mind the embarrassment. There is no doubt the rumor will be relayed to Livia. I'm sure she'll want to catch him red-handed."

Tullia snickered. "Vitalio, the disreputable actor. That's fitting. If she catches them, it might finish my husband as well as hers. And Cresimus, again?"

Yosef shrugged. "He hears all the gossip."

They stopped under a large pine, coincidentally next to the honey date vendor.

Yosef feigned innocence. "Oh, look where we are. How about a honey date?"

"I was not fooled."

54

The day of Vitalio and Lucius's planned rendezvous, Yosef surprised Tullia. "I'm going to go watch Livia's reaction."

"Yosef, you can't. It's dangerous."

He took her hand. "I will go, and it will be fine. This is too important for us to depend on second-hand information. Besides, I can take care of myself."

She pursed her lips but knew he was right. Besides, all the attention would be on Vitalio.

"I'll be just another curious onlooker."

* * *

At dusk, Yosef blended with Lady Livia's entourage. Following a small group behind the litter bearing the mistress, he relished thoughts of Vitalio finally getting his due. Ever since he beat Tullia during her first pregnancy, Yosef harbored a deep hatred of her husband. But to take action would have been suicidal, both for him and Tullia. No... smart slaves are patient slaves, and he was patient. His optimistic nature always led him to believe that sooner or later, there would be justice. If tonight was not the end of Vitalio, he was certain Livia would be the first step in his comeuppance.

"She once had a slave beaten to death for underwatering

the wine before a dinner party," said Cresimus. "She is among the cruelest of people."

That was saying something considering Cresimus's vocation. Go ahead, Livia, unleash your fury. *I'll enjoy watching this.*

The litter stopped in front of a dead tree, a pile of bark and leaves scattered around the naked trunk. Yosef saw the silhouette of a roof in the fading light as Livia and her men approached the building.

He turned to a short man in a dirty tunic. "What's back there?"

"Used to be a cobbler. He died and the family couldn't pay the taxes. The shop's been abandoned a few years."

Yosef, taller than most Romans by at least a hand, wove through the small crowd. Stopping at the edge of a dirt path, he shuffled through overgrown foliage and found a clear view of Livia and the ramshackle cabin, a mere five feet away. His heart thumped with anticipation.

A guard knocked down the door. Light spilled out, revealing two men rutting like pigs, Vitalio on top. Livia shrieked, grabbed a burning torch, and bludgeoned Vitalio. After several blows, he escaped to the woods, screaming, his toga ablaze.

Ignoring Vitalio and surrounded by the shack's burning interior, Livia attacked her startled husband, clubbing him with the smoldering torch and unleashing vicious insults with every blow. Finally, two of her men pulled her from the pyre. Her maidservant placed a wet towel on her smoking scalp. Livia, hands on her hips, watched the shack burn to the ground, consuming her husband with it.

Silhouetted by the fading blaze, she smoothed her wet hair and turned to a guard. "Take me home."

Now that's Roman justice, thought a snickering Yosef.

Watching Vitalio race away, Yosef had resisted clapping. Livia had come through. If Vitalio made it to the nearby Anio River, he would probably survive; but oh, those burns on his back would be tender.

Yosef returned to the villa under a full moon, a pleasing spring in his step.

He entered the villa and Tullia, wide-eyed, met him at the door. "Well?"

He beamed. "A success."

She wrinkled her nose. "There was a fire?"

"Let's go sit and I'll tell you all about it."

They joined Atia, Phoebe, and Faustina for wine, as Yosef described the evening.

The women howled with laughter. "Vitalio. On fire and racing into the dark!" sputtered Tullia.

"He looked like a shooting star streaking across the night sky," said Yosef.

After more wine and jocularity at Vitalio's expense, they retired.

Once in bed, Tullia thought of a burning Vitalio and giggled. "I wish I could've seen him aflame."

"He was moving fast," said Yosef.

"A scorched bum may make sitting at long Senate meetings feel longer." She touched Yosef's arm. "Have we cut off the head of the snake?"

"Let's hope so." But he wondered inside if they had. Had Lucius discussed the slave issue with other magistrates or senators? The thought tempered his joy, but he pushed it away. They had done what they could.

Siculus arrived in the morning. All business, he fussed with his satchel. "Sextus prepared the necessary legal documents shielding the entire family enterprise from any attempt of seizure by the senator. The best approach is joint ownership with Yosef. As a freedman, Sextus assures me it's legal."

After Tullia and Yosef signed the documents, she turned to him. "Now you're rich. Does this mean I have to be nice to you?"

Yosef looked at her from under a serious, furrowed brow. "Yes. You can no longer order me to lift my tunic." He stood, and cracking a sly smile, began to loosen his belt. "My new-found wealth allows me to do it on my own."

A beet-red Siculus hurried out in the wake of their riotous laughter.

55

Several weeks after the Livia business, Tullia received a note from their lawyer. Sitting in the garden with Yosef, she summarized it for him as they watched the children flit in and out of the bushes.

"Vitalio's creditors are taking him to court," she gushed, eyes flicking up and down the papyrus. "The appointed judge, Severus Regulus, served with Poppi in Britania. Sextus says he wanted to marry Mama, but he lost her to Poppi. He thinks the judge holds Vitalio responsible for her disappearance. Let's plan to attend."

"To what end?" asked Yosef.

"Before the trial, Sextus will tell the judge of Mama's true fate and Vitalio's abuse. He also thinks we should bring money. Regulus may elect to settle the terms of the debt right there, which will allow us to buy the farm back."

On the court date, Balbus and his guards accompanied Tullia and Yosef to the Basilica Aemilia in the Forum. The white marble building held many memories for Tullia—buying a scarf for Mama from vendor booths in the front, then napping with Yosef on the knoll behind the building, and, months later, visiting a jeweler's cubicle under the portico for a necklace for her wedding. It all seemed so long ago.

"Tullia?" asked Yosef.

She blew out a breath. "Sorry."

"We are on the second floor. This way," he said, pulling her toward an arched entrance.

Leaving Balbus and the men outside, they joined a throng of people ascending the marble steps and into a large courtroom. Tullia was surprised at the number of spectators. Dressed in a dark coat, veil, and head cover, she resembled the few other women present. Murmurs floated through the air, and catching pieces here and there, she realized a bankruptcy trial for a senator represented great theater.

Yosef led her to their seats. On the left, wooden shades covered six windows facing the forum, their slates open wide to capture light and the breeze. The right wall had a similar arrangement, but the view was of the swamp and the Subura beyond. A central aisle separated two sections, each with twenty wooden benches.

Seated five rows from the front, Yosef gestured beyond the first row, where a group of somber men gathered around a table. "The creditors."

"Our allies," whispered Tullia. She spotted Vitalio at the table on the other side. He sat with his lawyer. Sextus told her it would be Menander of Sabine. "Great Juno," she exclaimed. "Vitalio looks terrible."

Yosef followed her gaze. "He does. You sure took care of his nose."

Tullia saw the inflamed nasal stump, its two nostrils gaping like black holes in the center of an unmistakable porcine face. To add to the image, the shack fire had scorched away most of the hair on his head. A black stubble of new growth sprouted through the raw, scarlet skin.

Before she could stop them, tears of joy filled her eyes. "He looks like a pig on a spit."

Snickering, Yosef pulled her close. "Try to be quiet. We're not alone on this bench."

Judge Regulus entered and the room quieted. Wearing an off-white toga with a purple border, the stout jurist resembled a well-dressed wolffish from the Tiber—close-set eyes above a row of lower teeth jutting from an oversized frowning mouth.

Jiggling with glee, Tullia cupped her hand over Yosef's ear. "Thank Juno *he's* not my Poppi. I could've looked like a turbot."

"Shh." Yosef chuckled. "Remember, he's on our side."

Despite his fishy appearance, the judge spoke in a clear voice. "Why are we here?"

The creditor representative stood, glancing at his fellow men before turning to Regulus. "The defendant owes over forty thousand sesterces."

The judge's frown intensified. "Senator, you are deep in debt, what's your stance?"

Menander rose. "My client has fallen on hard times, and through no fault of his own, cannot meet these obligations."

Regulus worked his large lower jaw as if gulping air. His eyes roved over the lawyer, then to Vitalio, who did not look up. "Counselor, it looks more like he has fallen not on hard times, but hard cobblestones. Whatever happened to his face?"

The room jittered with laughter. Regulus held up a broad, flat hand reminding Tullia of a fin.

"Never mind. Your opening statement is not persuasive. Is that all you have?" he asked.

"Your Honor," Menander pleaded. "Fate led to the loss

of his slaves and livestock. Without them, the farm is doing poorly, and he can't pay his bills. This grievous situation is due to simple misfortune, not mismanagement."

The creditors' representative sprang to his feet. "He's been falling behind ever since his father-in-law, General Cornelius Flaccus, was killed in Parthia—over a year before the loss of his *pigs*."

The judge pointed at the creditor representative. "General Flaccus, who married Fulvia Gillo, who is missing to this day?"

Before the representative could answer, Regulus turned to the senator's table. "Well?"

Menander whispered to his client. Tullia craned her neck, catching sight of Vitalio repeatedly shaking his scorched head. His lawyer's hand curled, then flattened. After a moment, he faced the judge, the words seemingly wrenched unwillingly from his mouth. "With respect, Your Honor, the case was investigated by the Senate and remains unsolved."

Tullia started to rise, but Yosef grabbed her cloak and pulled her back. "No! Wait," he murmured.

She reddened. "But he's *lying*!" she hissed through gritted teeth.

"Yes, but this isn't the time."

With his chin, he gestured to the front. Tullia followed, her eyes landing on the judge's scowl.

"Indeed." He addressed the room. "It's clear the defendant's fiscal malfeasance is not new and results from arrogance and poor character." Holding up a hand against Menander's parting lips, Regulus returned his attention to the creditors. "We'll adjudicate the case today. Will you give him more time?"

"No, Your Honor. We've waited long enough. We want coin now."

Menander shrugged. "He has two thousand."

"Five percent on the sesterce is a pittance," sputtered the creditor representative.

"It's that or nothing," countered the attorney.

"There is the farm," suggested the judge. "It can be sold."

The representative shook his head. "We can't wait for a sale—we need money now."

Vitalio's attorney opened his hands. "There is another possibility should my client's rich wife be compelled to cover the debt."

Tullia glowered at the floor, her anger returning. She pinched Yosef's hand.

"You mean the only child of the general and Fulvia?" asked the judge, echoing her furious thoughts. "The young woman and wife enslaved and abused by the senator?"

"With respect, those are unsubstantiated rumors, Your Honor," claimed Menander.

Regulus's voice turned to ice. "Two women from the same family connected to your client—one abused and the other missing. And you expect me to consider it just rumors and a case of bad luck for him?"

"Well—"

"Let me be clear, neither Fulvia nor your client's wife are a part of these proceedings. Mention either again, and like the brute Postumus, you and your client will find yourselves exiled to an island, courtesy of the imperial court."

The attorney dropped his head. "Yes, Your Honor."

Silence fell again. The judge continued to watch Menander, speaking the next words with an air of venom. "Any further questions?"

Before he could answer, Tullia stood. "Just one, Your Honor."

The audience gasped at the interruption and turned toward her. Yosef gave her hand a reassuring squeeze.

The judge blinked and raised his hand for quiet. "Yes?"

There was a commotion at Vitalio's table as Menander pushed his client back into his seat and stood. "Your Honor! This is highly irregular. Is this a street play or a courtroom?"

The judge slowly turned his head. His scarlet face looked like it might burst. He spoke in a low growl. "My friend, it is very much a courtroom — in fact, *my* courtroom. The Pretorians will escort you to the prison in the *Porticus* after this trial. You will spend one night. Your client will join you if there is another outburst."

Shaking, Menander dropped to his seat.

The judge looked at Tullia. "Please continue."

"I wonder who from the Senate signed off on my mother's disappearance," Tullia said in a loud and clear voice. "She's not missing. She's dead. I know. I was there." She punctured each word with simmering fury. Keeping her eyes on the judge's face, she raised both hands and removed her headcover. "The senator was directly responsible for her rape and death. He drank wine in the next room as I watched her take her last breath."

There was dead silence for two beats before the audience erupted in shouts of shock. Questions flew at Tullia from every direction. Vitalio glared at her but quickly slumped in his chair and tried to shrink away. Menander sat motionless, head down.

Ignoring the ruckus, Tullia remained standing and locked eyes with the judge.

After the din subsided, the judge hinted at a smile, emphasizing his underbite. "Ah, Domina Flaccus, welcome. As much as it pains me to say, investigating your mother's unfortunate death is beyond the scope of the court today."

"Very well, Your Honor," she said, feeling oddly at ease. "Let's return to the matter at hand. With your indulgence, I want my dowry back, and restoration of the good Flaccus name. Rather than wait for my divorce to be finalized, I'm happy to add six thousand to the senator's two, bringing the payout to twenty percent on the debt, with the proviso that I keep the farm."

Yosef handed her a leather purse containing the money. She jiggled it; the coins rang. Every eye turned to it. "I can pay today."

Regulus gave her a small smile before addressing the creditor representative. "Counselor?"

"Accepted!"

"Very well." The judge turned back to Tullia. "Consider it settled, Domina. The farm is yours and we'll do the paperwork at a time of your choosing."

Tullia held up a hand. "No need, Your Honor. The senator accepted my marriage gift in good faith. But he never bothered with the deed transfer. It appears I have always been the legal owner."

The gallery and the creditors erupted in laughter. Menander recoiled and Vitalio stared at the table.

Regulus stood and raised both hands, palms outward. "Court adjourned," he proclaimed.

* * *

The following afternoon, Tullia updated her diary with the courtroom victory. Vitalio was nearly finished. In her heart of hearts, she wanted him dead but knew that would be a step too far. Chuckling, she satisfied herself describing his mangled face and grilled scalp.

Faustina escorted Sextus to the study.

"Counselor, what brings you here today?" she asked, laying down her quill.

"Vitalio is out of the Senate," the lawyer said in his clipped and direct way. "The vote just came in. I hurried over as soon as I heard."

Thank Juno. "That's wonderful news."

Sextus gave her a rare smile. "The loss of the farm was the final blow. Senators ignore the most egregious of behaviors by their peers, with the exception of indigence. In Rome, poverty makes men insignificant, but it makes senators nonexistent. His civic career is over."

"And with it his power," added Yosef, joining them at the table.

Tullia's mind whirled with joy. Without power or money, Vitalio was at her mercy. She felt his grip on her all but disappear. He could not get much lower.

"And the divorce?" she asked.

"I expected the question." The lawyer rummaged through his satchel and produced a handful of papyrus sheets. "Sign these, and you're free of him. Judge Regulus also agreed to handle the divorce."

"Regulus?"

"Magistrates perform many duties," replied Sextus, his mouth twitching upward.

She signed her name with more flair than usual.

After the lawyer gathered the documents and departed, Tullia leaped into Yosef's arms. "This is the best news," she cried, wrapping her arms around his neck and pushing her cheek to his.

"I've been waiting for this day," he said softly, his lips pressed to her ear. He kissed her again and eased her down.

"I'm a freedman and you are now an unmarried woman," he said, spinning her around and catching her. They stopped, exchanging loving looks, but Tullia saw mischief in his eyes. "I hope we marry soon since the rules of Rome say the husband is in charge."

She gave a playful smirk, touching his nose with her own. "Don't be so sure. Look where marriage got my last husband."

He led her to the patio. "Let's walk."

Strolling along in the fading light of the late afternoon, Tullia felt the warm rise of contentment.

"Your vengeance is edging toward completion," Yosef said as if reading her thoughts.

"Nearly," she responded as they took a turn. She chewed her lip. "But the further down he falls, the less important it seems." With a rising warmth in her chest, she saw greater happiness in Yosef and her family.

He touched her cheek, his eyes soft and warm. "It may be time to move on."

56

To celebrate Vitalio's expulsion from the Senate, Tullia and Yosef took the household on a shopping trip to the Forum. Accompanied by Balbus and his men, the group entered the busy market. Tullia squinted as the bright autumn sun sparkled off the white marble buildings. Aurelia slept in a sling across her chest. The happy crowd fit her carefree mood. Fragrant rose cuttings from the fall bloom dominated the wares of a flower vendor selling red, yellow, and white bouquets. Chickering starlings argued over the splashing sounds of a fountain. Today, Rome seemed beautiful and for the first time in months, she allowed herself to feel the joy of contentment amidst the thrum of the city.

Yosef, the servants, and a guard took her two young boys to the honey date vendor. Tullia called after them. "I'm going to that leather shop by the basilica."

Yosef raised a hand in the air but did not turn around.

As the crowds closed in, a man pushed by, banging into Tullia's shoulder and jostling her and the baby.

"Hey," she shouted, seeing only a blur of blue as he disappeared into the crowd.

Balbus and a guard stepped to her side. "Domina?"

"It's nothing. Just rudeness."

They crossed through the heavy foot traffic. Down a side alley, they arrived at the leather vendor's tent, its walls a heavy weave and neatly tucked between a cobbler's canopy and a barber's pergola.

Tullia waited while Balbus checked the interior. "Just the proprietor," he reported. He made to follow her inside, but she asked him to wait. It would only take a minute.

The quiet shop smelled of tanned hides and featured stacks of furred pelts on a center table. Leather goods on shelves adorned two walls. Tullia drifted to a secluded display in one corner. Squatting to examine a pair of boots, she sensed a presence behind her. The proprietor, perhaps? Turning to ask about the boots, she felt a sharp pain across her head before the room went dark.

A voice cracked through the darkness of her mind.

"Tullia? Tullia." A strong hand grabbed her shoulder and gave a gentle shake. "Wake up."

Her eyes opened to a raging, pulsing headache. Wispy clouds and the brown outer wall of a tent spun across her vision, along with a spattering of colored dots. A wave of nausea crested, and she lurched to the side, spitting and groaning as foul liquid gurgled forth. Another hand, small and cool, touched her forehead, while a damp rag wiped her mouth. Blinking, Tullia twisted and recognized Yosef and the servant girls.

"Wha—where—"

"Easy," said Yosef, crouching. "Can you hear me?"

Next to him knelt Atia. It was her soft hand on Tullia's forehead. The girl also held the rag.

Tullia blinked again and tried to nod. Dizziness returned with the movement.

"They've taken her. Aurelia."

Her hands shot to the empty, flattened sling on her chest. *No, no.* Clutching at the material, she nearly shredded it with her fingers, and she wailed. "Aurelia!"

"Domina," Atia soothed, moving her hand to her cheek. "Shhh, Domina, it'll be okay."

Tullia felt the younger girl's arm move beneath her, and aided by Yosef, ease her up. The world spun, but she made it to a seated position, her back against a strut supporting the cobbler's tent. Phoebe joined them, running a hand of comfort along Tullia's arm.

"How — how did I get here?" Tullia asked, as the visual shimmers and the nausea settled.

"Whoever knocked you out dragged you through that hole," Yosef explained, pointing to a vertical slit in the tent's side.

"Where —"

"We don't know," he said with determined edginess — a growl before a fight. "We'll find her."

Tullia tried to focus, but when she thought of Aurelia she could not breathe. Another sob escaped, her heart pounding so fast she thought it might leap from her chest. "How did this happen?" she stuttered.

"Balbus wasn't with you. When you were gone too long, he went in and found the ripped tent, and you out here, unconscious. There was no sign of the proprietor."

"How long was I out?"

"Just a short spell. He sent a guard to find us in the forum and we hurried over."

The back of her head throbbed. Sliding her hand out of Yosef's, she touched a tender area the size of a radish and winced, bringing back her memory. "Except for the owner, Aurelia and I were alone in the shop. He must've taken her."

Before he could respond, Balbus arrived, escorting a man with a bloody, tear-streaked face.

"Here's the real shopkeeper," he uttered, holding the man in front of Tullia. "The cobbler said he asked him to watch the store while he went for lunch. I found him at the Lone Pine Tavern. Tell them," said the big soldier, nudging the man with his foot.

The proprietor, short and shaped like a bottle gourd, wiped his face. "A-a man offered me two hundred to leave for an early lunch." His tremulous voice raised an octave. "It's more than I make in a week, so what was the harm? My neighbor was watching the shop."

Yosef jabbed a finger at the man's chest. "Who was he?"

The proprietor held up his hands and scooted backward. "I don't know. He said he represented an emissary of the emperor who'd be coming soon. He was sent ahead to check my wares."

"What'd he look like?"

"Skinny with a blue head rag and a big earring."

"*That* was the man I saw in the shop," added Balbus.

Yosef motioned to him. "Let him go."

Balbus pulled him aside with a well-measured shove. The owner stumbled; his eyebrows raised in indignation. "Who's going to pay for my tent?" he demanded.

Yosef spun and grabbed him by the throat. "Pay for it with your two hundred," he spat. "Now get out of here." He shoved the shorter man through the new gap in his tent.

"That man, I know him," exclaimed Phoebe. "He used—"

"—to work at the brothel," finished Yosef with an approving look. He turned back to Tullia, who was still trying to shake the worst of the fog away. "He poured wine at the brothel. Cresimus fired him the day Vitalio sold me to him."

"His name's Isidorus," the servant girl offered. "He could easily have done this. He is a disgraced veteran. He'll likely be headed to the Subura."

Tullia's head throbbed with the rapid information. "We can't just go asking around there," she mumbled. "It'll look too suspicious."

"*You* can't," Phoebe corrected, smiling thinly. "But we can. I know the area. Atia and I will go. Nobody will suspect two girls walking during the day, and we both have knives."

Yosef pointed at a guard. "Join them."

Before Tullia could speak, the girls raced up the narrow road leading to the Subura, their escort struggling to keep up. *Be safe*, she prayed as Yosef and Balbus helped her stand.

"Domina—."

"No, Balbus. It's not your fault."

He dropped his head.

"We just need to find Aurelia. I know you'll help find her," she stuttered, walking on spindly legs. "Maybe somebody found her and will bring her back." She heard the desperation in her own voice, then wobbled as the darkness closed in again. Her knees buckled and one foot slipped.

"Yosef," she breathed, eyes fluttering, "I-I'm so scared."

He steadied her limp body against his. "There's nothing more you can do here," he said, his words stretching out as she fought to stay conscious. "I'll join the others—"

Tullia's head fell back, and she heard no more.

* * *

A jostling caused Tullia to open and quickly close an eye to bright light. Before she could think, she realized she was being carried. "Yosef?" she croaked.

"You passed out. We're going to the Subura."

She sighed and let herself slip away.

A sharp knock roused her and she glimpsed Cresimus opening the brothel door. Yosef set her down on wobbly legs and they helped her back to Cresimus's study. Through the mental fog, her memory returned. *Aurelia!* Tears welled as Yosef eased her onto a rough bed wedged tightly in the corner. She looked up at the two men. "Anything?" she whispered.

"Nothing yet, Domina," offered the owner. "Phoebe and Atia were here and are out looking."

Tullia moaned and tried to ignore her throbbing head. At least the nausea was better. She wished she could run out and help with the hunt.

"Rest now, I'll be right back," said Yosef, leaving with Cresimus.

She closed her eyes and silently prayed for Aurelia. She knew Vitalio was behind it but was too tired to even muster anger. It took all she had right now to battle the dread lurking in her chest.

In short order, the office door opened, and Yosef reappeared. "Willow bark tea," he said. He helped her scoot against the wall so she could sit. He placed a cup in her hands and joined her. "For the pain."

She took several swallows. Sweetened with honey, the warm drink soothed. Glancing at Yosef, she hoped he had some also. "What more can we do?" she asked when the cup was drained. "Is she alive?"

"If Vit—"

"Don't say it!" She dropped the cup and put her face in her hands, hopelessness twisting every muscle. "Please," she choked, "don't say it. I can't bear it if it's true."

Yosef looked at her, his eyes swallowed by sadness. "Her disappearance wasn't just bad luck," he said with dreaded calm. "You know it as well as I. It can only be him."

With an aching heart, she reached for him. "Oh, Yosef, he'll be merciless."

He remained silent and held her.

57

The morning brought fuzzy light through the tiny office window slats as Tullia emerged from restless dreams. She recalled unconnected images of Aurelia, Yosef, and Vitalio that left nothing but her twisted stomach. At least her headache had eased.

Shifting on the bed, she found Yosef, bare chested in his sleeping shorts, sitting frozen with a small box in his hands.

She sat up, now fully awake. "What's that?" she asked, her heart in her throat.

Yosef fixed his eyes on her, his lips a thin line.

"Yosef?" She could barely speak.

"It was delivered to the villa last night. Phoebe just brought it by."

He shook it and she heard a muffled thump. Her muscles tightened. "W-what's that?"

He turned the box to show her. An unbroken wax seal covered a small metal clasp. Tullia recognized the embossed symbol.

"That's Vitalio's senatorial ring stamp," she croaked.

"I know," he said slowly.

She touched cold fingers to his shoulder. "Go ahead," she whispered.

Yosef wedged his thumb under the latch, fracturing the brittle wax, and opened it.

Tullia saw a small, wrinkled scroll lodged into one side. In the center lay the source of the thump — a gray-brown object the size of her thumbnail. It was shaped like a little triangular mushroom. Two holes at the base gaped like tiny peppercorns.

"Oh, Juno. Yosef, what's that?"

He slammed the lid, breathing hard through his nose. "Oh, my God."

"Yosef, could that be her...?" She could not finish the question. A vision of her daughter's mutilated face suffocated her words as terror seized her heart.

"I don't... know," he whispered. He opened the lid once more, turning his eyes from the piece of flesh, and fumbling for the papyrus. "The note," he said hoarsely, passing it to her. "We-we can't be sure until we read the note."

Tullia forced herself to look at the grisly piece of tissue staring at her through little black eyes. Trembling, she pushed back a wave of nausea and opened the scroll.

> *Wife,*
> *Don't worry, I sliced that nose from a dead baby. Not yours — not yet.*

"Oh, Yosef, it's not hers!" Overcome by racking sobs, she fell against his chest. His arm pulled her in, and she heard his rapid heartbeat. He made a strangled noise, half-relief, half-panic.

"She... she's alright," he mumbled. "It's not Aurelia's."

Tullia cried with relief. How could this be? What was he doing? After several long moments, she looked up at him and wiped her eyes. "Why do I feel a little better?"

"It's an old torture ploy," he said, his voice stronger. He brushed a stray tear from her chin and moved his hand to the back of her light undertunic. "Make somebody miserable, then offer them bread and wine. Gratitude gives relief."

"He tricked us."

He gently squeezed her neck, avoiding the tender area on her head. "He knew we'd think the worst."

"And so, he did," she seethed. Anger arose from the center of her bubbling emotions as she turned back to the note.

Have I got your attention? A blade makes a cleaner cut than teeth, don't you think? Do what I say, or I'll use a knife on your little half-breed. And I'll keep her alive so I can harvest other parts as needed unless you meet my demands.

Tullia clenched her teeth but kept reading.

First, call off Balbus and the search. If I get any hint of it, I will start with your baby's nose and keep slicing until I get what I want. Second, I want you to deliver ten thousand denari. Third, once I complete some unfinished business with your tight little bottom, I'll release you both. Easy, eh? More to come.

Despite the anger, her heart nearly stopped at the thought of Aurelia suffering at his hand. *But she's alright for now. We just have to get her back.* The money was nothing, forty thousand sesterces—they had it, they'd pay it. She felt a numb composure. *I will trade myself to save her.*

"Yosef—"

His hard glare told her he knew what she was going to say. "We *will* find her."

"But he said no search. Give him the money. I'll deliver it."

"No," he growled.

"I'm not scared."

"No!"

"Yosef, we can get her back if we do what he says!"

He leaped to his feet, pacing back and forth around the tiny room. "Are you mad? What do you think will happen once he has you?"

She sat taller, feeling eerily calm. "I can survive his abuse if it means she's safe."

"This won't just be abuse, it'll be torture. Then death. What stops him from killing you both and escaping with the money?"

"He won't. His getaway will be easier without leaving two bodies behind."

Yosef slammed a fist into a palm, but Tullia slid off the bed and went to him, pressing her shoulder against his. "Yosef, please," she whispered through tears. "Stop the search. Let's get the money."

He remained motionless, his chest rising and falling like a heavy footfall. Tullia faced him, both hands on his bare chest, matching her breathing to his. After a moment, she turned her head. Her cold lips pressed against his skin.

"It's a small price to pay for our baby's life."

They held each other. Yosef's tight grip and shallow rapid breaths told her of his pain and frustration, but she did not waiver in her commitment to comply with the demands.

Yosef broke away first, his eyes sad in the dim light. "We must find her. Sending you to that savage is the last resort." His lips brushed hers. "I love you."

"I love you, too."

He sat down on the bed and stroked his chin. "Vitalio will be watching for me and Balbus. But his spies won't recognize the servant girls or Cresimus — they'll continue the hunt. We have until the next note to find her."

He looked at her as if expecting a question, but Tullia only gave him a regretful shrug. It was the best they could do.

"Will you be alright?" he asked, pulling on a tunic. "I need to tell the others."

"I'll be fine. Go."

Tullia lay down, head now throbbing. Her mind churned with fear for Aurelia. Guilt bored into her heart. "Aurelia, I'm so sorry," she said again and again, wondering endlessly why she didn't take Balbus into the shop. She sobbed, grief-stricken. Heavy fatigue pulled her down and time slipped away, disappearing like smoke in between her restless dreams.

The flicker of a wall lamp lit the room as Tullia roused in the darkness. How long had she been out? She did not know, but she felt stronger. Yosef never came back. Before she could worry, the door opened, and he appeared with more willow bark tea and bread. "It's nearly dawn. I'm glad you slept. I was out looking."

He helped her over to a chair at the office's small table. "I guess I needed the sleep. I feel better. Did you have any luck?"

"Not yet, but we should both try to eat."

Tullia managed a single nibble when their breakfast was interrupted by a thump at the back wall. Exchanging a glance,

391

Yosef crossed to the office's waist-high escape door. He released a latch, and a breathless Atia burst through the small opening. "I think we found her."

It took Tullia a few beats to speak. "Oh, thank Juno."

"You two wait here," Yosef ordered. "I need to find Cresimus."

Tullia stood, her legs stronger after resting, and took Atia's hand. "Are you sure?" she asked, trying not to let the tremble in her voice affect the younger girl.

But Atia's eyes were bright and full of energy.

"We think so."

Not for the first time, Tullia marveled at her strength and determination to look past the suffering they'd endured. She pulled Atia in for a hug, letting her chin rest on the girl's shoulder and hoping the gratitude she felt was transferring over. "Were you alone or with Phoebe?"

"We were together for a while."

Yosef, Cresimus, and Phoebe arrived, closing the office door. Once it was securely shut, Atia broke away and faced them.

"Late in the night, I found a street girl who lives behind the baths. The day before, she saw a man carry a baby into an insula. It sounded like it was Isidorus with Aurelia. She wants ten sesterces to show us where."

"It's probably Lydia," said Phoebe. "Scarred forehead?" She slashed a finger across her brow. Atia nodded.

"I know where she sleeps. We can take her the money now."

"It's still dark and dangerous. I'll trail them with the coin," said Cresimus.

Tullia buried a smile at his unexpected valor.

With no more to discuss, the servant girls and stout brothel owner wriggled through the small back door. As they moved into the alley, Tullia and Yosef heard friendly goading from Phoebe. "Remember, Master Cresimus, you're no longer my boss."

Cresimus snickered. "You weren't that good anyway."

58

Yosef fidgeted in the office chair while Tullia dozed on the bed. He estimated Cresimus and the two girls had left about half an hour earlier. He hated sitting here doing nothing, but the risk was too great. It was one thing to sneak around in the dead of night, but the daytime was a different matter. No, he'd wait.

Just after dawn, Cresimus came through the office door escorting a dirty, malnourished boy.

"Meet Darius, a known thief and rascal. He delivered a basket to a second-floor apartment in Optata's building and tried to dash away." He jerked his small prisoner. "Right?"

The lad sneered and spit on the tile floor.

Cresimus dropped to one knee, jamming the petulant child's face into the viscous splotch.

"Not today, young Darius." After several moments, the stronger man yanked him up by the hair. The boy remained motionless, a trickle of blood oozing from his filthy nose. Sighing, Cresimus fingered the dagger on his belt.

"You *will* answer questions," he warned.

Fear replaced the boy's defiant look.

Tullia handed him a rag for his nose. "What were you doing at the insula?" she asked.

"Taking food," he grunted.

"Who sent you?"

"An ugly senator. He gave me ten."

"Who's in the room?"

The boy's brow furrowed. "Why?"

Cresimus twisted his ear. Yelping, the boy gyrated but was unable to wiggle free.

"A man and a baby," he blurted, grimacing.

"Did the baby have a hat?" pressed Tullia.

"Pink."

Tullia turned to Yosef. "It's her."

Cresimus tossed the delinquent into the corner. "Sit and behave. We'll get you some food." The boy wrapped his arms around his knees and waited.

"And this Optata? Is she involved?" asked Tullia.

Yosef, backlit by weak early morning sunlight filtering through the small office window, turned to her. "I doubt it. She does the brothel laundry."

"And doused you one day with a bucket of horse piss," smirked Cresimus.

"She overcharged us."

"Enough," scolded Tullia. "What's being done?"

Cresimus held up two fingers. "Atia and Lydia are on watch. There's enough traffic to keep them unnoticed. And, for another five sesterces, that scrappy Lydia agreed to help Atia." He raised an eyebrow. "That's fifteen you owe me."

The information was worth much more than fifteen, but Yosef had heard enough small talk. He was wound tight and breathing fast. "Let's go get her."

Yosef and Cresimus met Balbus at the front door of the brothel, and together the three went up the hill toward Optata's.

"Let's pick up Atia. Aurelia will need her," said Yosef, muscles tight and walking fast.

The others grunted in agreement. The three of them were lethal. Each would kill anybody standing in their way. Isidoris, you are a dead man. *I will get my baby, and you will die.*

Optata's place, a rickety three-story building, loomed ahead. Yosef saw Atia, and a girl he assumed was Lydia, loitering across the street. A quick sweep of the surrounding area told him everything seemed normal—no spies, at least none that he could see. That didn't mean they wouldn't come or weren't already here. *We must be fast.*

An eye-watering stench enveloped them as they came to the laundry's open door where fullers, mostly children, stomped dirty laundry sloshing in vats of urine. Yosef felt his cheeks bulge as he tried to squelch the noxious fumes. Wet clothing, draped over drying racks fronting the building, contributed to the mid-morning stink. He wondered, yet again, how urine cleaned clothes. At least for the Flaccus villa, Faustina insisted all clothing from the fuller be rinsed in lavender water before drying.

Optata, a fine-boned Nubian and former prostitute, glided over. She flashed a friendly grin, her white teeth sparkling against an ebony face. She reminded Yosef of a sleek black panther. "No laundry today, Master Yosef?"

"Not today. Business with a tenant."

She glanced at Cresimus.

Her former employer shrugged. "We're both better off with you here."

"How true," she said, waving them away.

Atia led them to an open staircase snaking up one wall of

the building. As he ascended the steps, Yosef clenched his jaw, and his heart banged in his chest. He resisted running over the girl and racing to the second floor. On the verge of losing control, he blew out a breath and focused on reclaiming his daughter. He would not succeed if he was reckless. He pushed down the visceral rage he held for the kidnapper but vowed to destroy the bastard.

Once on the landing to the second floor, Atia pointed to the third doorway on the left. "There."

Yosef crept forward but there was no need. A sharp, piercing cry from the room split the air. Cresimus rolled his eyes and slapped both hands over his ears.

Wasting no time, Yosef kicked in the door. With Balbus on his heels, they rushed through, blades drawn. Cresimus and Atia followed. Through the plume of dust from the door, Yosef caught sight of Aurelia, still wearing her pink cap, sprawled in a corner, wailing. Atia hurried to her.

Unexpectedly, Yosef saw two men. Theon, the disgraced overseer jumped up from a tattered couch. He pulled a dagger and lunged for Atia, but Yosef was quicker, driving his sword into the man's chest before he could take a second step. "You should have stayed away," he growled, still looking for blood. He pulled his sword and pivoted toward the man with the blue head rag.

"Isidorus!" he roared. "You kidnapped my daughter."

The man dropped a flask of wine and teetered between the liberators. He pulled a short sword and stole a glance at the front door.

Yosef followed his gaze to Cresimus, dallying by the entrance. The brothel owner grinned. "Now you see why he was fired."

Before Yosef could respond, Isidorus attacked. Yosef dodged a woozy thrust and shoved the man aside. Before Yosef could run him through, Balbus landed a crushing knockout blow. Sounding like the crack of a whip, Isidorus's head snapped back, and he dropped like a stone.

Yosef raced to Aurelia. "How is she?" he panted, dropping to his knees.

Atia wrinkled her nose. "She needs a change and is hungry but is otherwise fine."

She handed him the baby. Aurelia gurgled, the glow of her rosy cheeks filling the dark hole in his heart. "You're safe now, little one." He turned his attention back to the room.

Cresimus looked up from the lifeless Isidorus. "Broken neck. You know about the other one. Time to go."

"The bodies?" asked Yosef, cradling Aurelia with one arm as he sheathed his sword.

"I'll handle it. I could use the fifty sesterces."

59

Tullia heard Aurelia before she saw her. Bursting from the room, she raced into the small atrium and met Yosef carrying their screaming daughter. As Yosef passed her the baby, Tullia thought her heart would burst with happiness. She clutched the wriggling bundle and cried. Aurelia continued at full wail.

"She's safe," said Tullia through happy sobs.

"Yes," Yosef agreed, almost yelling to be heard.

Cresimus cupped his hands around his mouth. "Domina, I'm glad she's safe, but a crying baby is bad for business." Maronella and another working girl watched from the wine bar, grinning and clapping silently.

Tullia could only laugh at the owner's concerns. "She's hungry." She turned from the men and bared her breast, watching her daughter latch on eagerly. "Can someone bring me some food, please?" she asked, not looking up. Several pairs of footsteps hastily receded.

Stroking Aurelia's head, Tullia murmured, "You're home now."

Between the intimacy of the moment and her deep gratitude for her daughter's safe return, she wept and laughed. *You are happy. Why are you crying?* She didn't know. Turning in a slow circle, she shielded her eyes with her free hand as the midday sun streamed through the two open windows. The morning had passed and with it her tears.

As she dried her eyes, the men returned with bread and wine. Tullia hefted Aurelia higher and covered her with a clean rag as the baby continued a quiet suckle. Taking a piece of bread, she chewed and raised a brow at Yosef.

"Was it who we expected?"

"Yes. It was Isidorus, the man with the blue head rag, but Theon from the farm also helped."

"Theon!" she exclaimed. "I never expected to see him again."

"You won't."

She squinted. "Where are they?"

"Dead."

She tried not to shudder. "Was it difficult?"

"Not at all. One room, two men against the three of us."

"Do I need to know more?"

"No."

Atia and Phoebe arrived with a pot of steaming water to bathe Aurelia. Tullia peeked under the breast cover, murmured to her gurgling baby, and passed the satiated infant to Atia. Cresimus folded his arms, tapping his foot against the floor.

"Now it's a nursery," he grumbled. "If you insist on washing her here, at least return to the office and let me get on with business."

Yosef picked up the pot and Tullia led the way to the back, holding the door open for the rest to enter. The pot on the office table, Atia spooned water onto Aurelia and Phoebe gently cleaned her with a soft cloth, as the baby kicked and gurgled.

The cooing of the young women warmed Tullia's heart. *My baby in a brothel. I never expected this.* Looking around the room she marveled at the love she felt for this scraggly group she called family. Phoebe the Christian and former prostitute,

Atia the slave turned servant, and Balbus, the loyal family soldier—all had supported her when she needed it most. She
caught Yosef's gaze. She knew he agreed with her. Sighing,
she let her mind run. *We did it. But we're not done yet.* Her
pulse quickened. The lust for vengeance flared as she tapped
her mental vault of nightmares and terror.

Balbus was the first to notice the change in her demeanor.
"Domina?"

Yosef looked up at the query.

Tullia furrowed her brow. She pointed at Darius, who had
remained sitting in his corner throughout the reunion. "This
boy is to collect his money from Vitalio today. He wants ten
more to take us there."

Darius, face expressionless, munched a crust of bread and
said nothing.

"You spoke with him?" asked Yosef.

"I reminded him Cresimus was right outside, and he
spilled it all."

"Tough to scare a street urchin."

"He knew of Cresimus—all those kids do. He's not to be
trifled with." She shifted her gaze to the boy. "Right?"

Darius gave a noncommittal shrug and kept chewing.

"How'd he find Vitalio?" Yosef pressed.

"Vitalio found him. Caught him snooping around the senator's apartment. He told him he could work for him or be
killed."

"Sounds a little fishy."

"That's what he said."

"It's true," piped Darius in a high-pitched, pre-adolescent
voice.

Yosef squinted at him. "So, for ten more, you'll take us to the senator?"

"Yeah."

Yosef pulled him up by his threadbare tunic. The crust of bread fell to the floor. "If you're lying, you'll wish the senator had killed you."

The boy seemed shaken. "I'll show you, I promise." Yosef dropped him back into his corner. "You'd better."

He turned toward Tullia and whispered, "Sorry. I'm still a little keyed up by the rescue."

She shrugged. "You're fine, I understand."

Tullia, Yosef, and Balbus moved out of earshot. "He could take us to the senator for the extraction of some vengeance," said Balbus.

Tullia tapped her chin. "Let's have lunch first. I have something I need to do."

As the men finished eating, she completed writing a note to Vitalio. Happy to close the door on her savage husband, she handed the small scroll to Yosef.

He read the document. "Tullia! You can't be serious."

"I've never been more serious. And we'll go together. I want to see the bastard's ugly face as he realizes the end is coming."

Yosef blew out a breath. "Well, this should do it. We'll need disguises."

Tullia resumed her beggar woman appearance for what she hoped was the last time. Yosef donned the dark cap of a laborer and used charcoal to make a false beard and mustache. His white teeth sparkled with a grin. There was no disguising Balbus, but Tullia knew he had little to fear.

Leaving the brothel, they ascended the hill, passing the

bath where Yosef had taken Titus. Deeper into the neighborhood, the wooden buildings grew shabbier and only a few were taller than two stories. Despite the seedy nature of the area, a bakery had a line of customers, and several vendors sold wares from storefronts. Tullia caught a whiff of Optata's fullery down a road to her left, but Darius continued walking straight ahead. After another half a block, he led them to a tiny plaza fronted by a derelict two-story building thick with urban detritus and the smell of garbage.

"Here," said Darius, standing at a street-level door. He held out his hand. Yosef gave him ten and the boy knocked.

"Who's there?" came a hoarse voice.

"Darius."

The door opened a crack. Yosef pushed into the gap as the lad dashed away. From around him, Tullia saw Vitalio clad in a filthy tunic and scruffy red turban. He glared at Yosef.

"What the—who're you? Where's the kid?"

"Never mind him. It's me, slave boy."

Recognition dawned as Vitalio tried to slam the door.

"Ah, not just yet," said Yosef, forcing his way in. Balbus and Tullia trailed.

Tullia recoiled at the apartment's squalor. Old food on dirty dishes, the pungent odor of sour wine, and the haphazard scattering of soiled clothing confirmed her impression of her husband. *He lives like the vermin he is.*

Before the ex-senator could resist, Balbus pushed him against a wall and placed a knife at his throat. Yosef closed the door. Even from a distance, Tullia smelled Vitalio's unwashed body.

"What do you want?" hissed her husband, eyes shifting between her and the men.

Ignoring the foul atmosphere of the room, Tullia offered a warm smile. "I came to say goodbye, husband. For this special occasion, I wanted you to hear my final words in person."

She pulled out her scroll and lifted it so the top met Vitalio's chin. She wanted to be able to look in his eyes as she recited.

"These are my final words to you, cruel husband." She took a breath. "Your plot failed. We have Aurelia, the kidnappers are dead, and you will soon follow. My marriage to Yosef will occur while your body is still warm."

She paused, unsure if Vitalio's wide eyes were from her message or Balbus's knife. No matter. She heard his wheezy breath amidst her deepening pleasure.

"Your death will neither be today, nor tomorrow. But rest assured it will come. On that day you'll be snatched, like what you did with my helpless daughter, and taken to the country. You'll be tied to a tree and then I will come, wielding a dull knife."

She stepped forward, staring hard into his reptilian eyes. One delicate finger extended, inches from his dirty face. "You will be *made* to pay for your unforgivable crimes against me, my mother, Yosef, and our house. And I will relish the joy of watching your reprehensible life drain away as you sputter your last miserable breath."

She stepped back, and with a tilt of her head, continued reading. "And once you're dead, I'll piss on your corpse—but don't despair. At least you'll get one last look at my 'tight little bottom.' So, thank you, husband. Thank you for the joy these words have brought me."

She turned on her heel and did not look back until Balbus

pulled the door closed on the fetid apartment with a solid click. As if the gods agreed, a cool breeze had blown away the earlier stench of the plaza. Pausing to drink in the clean air, Tullia lifted her face to the sky, savoring the petrified hopelessness she last saw on his face. It tasted sweeter than the ripest honey date.

60

"Domina, you are now a widow," announced Balbus.

Tullia, sitting with Yosef and writing in her journal, looked up. "What?"

"The senator took mushrooms. They found his body this morning."

Tullia's heart leapt. "This is wonderful news."

Two days earlier she had issued her final pledge to Vitalio. Knowing he was no longer a threat, she decided to let him worry for several more days before making good on her plan. But uncertainty gnawed at the joys of finishing him. The desire for vengeance clashed with the unease of the method. *Torture? Does this make me no better than him?* But she only had to recall the heinous crimes he perpetrated during her imprisonment: beatings, rapes, and all forms of inhuman degradation, not to mention the murder of her mother. No, he deserved it. And she knew her anger would never die until he did.

But now he *was* dead. Like dark smoke leaving her soul, the constant churn for revenge faded. She realized his suicide was the better outcome.

"Thank you, Balbus."

Vitalio is dead. Flooded with delight she suppressed a laugh. Enveloped by a sense of freedom, she felt a new beginning. Yet, thoughts of her mother tempered the joy. *Oh,*

Mama, I wish you were here. "Look ahead Tullia," came her voice, and Tullia knew she would. With her baby safe and the boys healthy, she could finally be with the man she loved. It was time to move on.

After Balbus left, she turned to Yosef. "Let's get married."

"Already?"

She nodded through happy tears.

"I'll find Sextus and a magistrate."

Sextus arrived the next afternoon with unexpected news. "I met with the magistrate. You are now a full citizen of Rome."

"How?" asked Yosef, appearing surprised.

The attorney remained all business despite the happy moment. "The *lex aelia sentia* offered a path to citizenship. The key provision is that Yosef was to be given full rights to citizenship on his manumission. I assured the magistrate this was the case. He agreed and made your full citizenship official."

"I've always preferred citizens," replied Tullia smugly.

"We're a good match since I prefer patricians," said Yosef, also smiling. He paused. "Well, we're both single now."

"And the senator's untimely death has eliminated the need for a divorce," said Sextus. He turned to Tullia. "Domina, you are officially free to marry."

It had been on her mind the moment she heard of Vitalio's demise. Yosef, from childhood friend to lover to husband. The social barriers in Rome—slave, freedman, patrician—were nothing compared to love. Her heart swelled with joy as she blinked back tears.

Turning to Yosef, she opened her hands. "Tomorrow?"

"Tomorrow."

Sextus officiated the ceremony. Balbus and the house servants attended. Afterward, the group joined the bride and groom for a meal. Interrupted by a banging at the front door, Phoebe rose to answer. She returned with a wide-eyed impish grin "Master Cresimus."

The portly bordello owner, dressed in a clean white tunic and new sandals, bowed with one arm behind his back. "Domina, Yosef, forgive the intrusion, but I wanted to offer my congratulations."

"Thank you, Cresimus," replied Tullia.

He placed a crudely wrapped bundle on the table. "For your writing."

Opening the gift, Tullia found a new wax tablet and stylus. Thank you, Cresimus. You are too generous."

He shrugged. "I know. It cost twenty sesterces."

"Am I to assume I need to pay for my own gift?"

"No, Domina. This one's on the house."

She could only laugh. "Can you stay and dine with us?"

"Where do I sit?"

Updating her journal that night, Tullia reflected on the day. The trials and tribulations of the last year finally brought her and the family to a good place. Gratitude flooded her heart, and she wondered if this was true happiness.

Yosef entered the study and snuffed the lamps. "You're done. Time for bed, wife."

Under the covers, they cuddled and exchanged tender vows of love. Tullia reached for her new husband and whispered. "I want more children."

He chuckled and blew out the bedside lamp.

Epilogue

Qumran, West Bank (AP). Today, archeologist Addison Sharp announced the discovery of new documents from the caves at Qumran.

"Several well-preserved papyrus pages from the first century were found in a previously unknown cave around the original Dead Sea Scroll site," said Sharp. "The documents appear to have been written by Yosef, the husband of Tullia Flaccus, whose journal was discovered in a Roman catacomb three years ago."

Sharp recently published the Flaccus biography using the journal. She showed Flaccus was the woman previously named by modern scholars as "The Sappho in the Fresco" from the ruins of Pompeii. She also tracked her marriage to a cruel senator and exposed her struggles with the immorality of Roman slavery.

Speaking from her archeological headquarters at Ein Feshkha, Sharp continued, "We're excited to study this contemporary account of life in the first-century Roman empire as well as follow the course taken by the Flaccus descendants. We'll release new information as it becomes available."

The Dead Sea Scrolls were originally discovered in the 1940s in caves near the West Bank and comprised many ancient Jewish religious documents. Dry conditions preserved the manuscripts, some as old as the third century BC. This discovery will add to that historical treasure trove.

Author's Note

This is a work of fiction. However, people from the imperial house came from the vast number of historical documents that have come to us from that period. I assigned those individuals fictional personalities. At times my characters quote or experience contemporary events, all accurate to the best of my abilities.

Tullia's parents were not socially engaged aristocrats but rather, well-off individuals living life as they chose it. I took liberties with Rome's strict societal rules, but then, mostly rich men in togas wrote them. With a million people living in Rome during the first century, I am certain most folks did not live strictly by the rules of old men.

In Tullia's world, there were no seconds or minutes, only hours, the sesterce was the main unit of money, and the site of the colosseum in her day was a swamp. Construction on the massive arena would not begin for another eighteen years. I used English for the names of the months since most translate easily from Latin. I also neither speak nor read Latin. I used terms from the language selectively in the text and tried to define them as they arose.

Finally, my thanks to the Aiken Chapter of the South Carolina Writers Association for their patient review of the work as it developed, Amber Schumacher for her exceptional artistic skill, and the editorial suggestions of Andrew Geyer, Felice Laverne, and Lisa Wong.

SN
April 2024

www.ingramcontent.com/pod-product-compliance
Lightning Source LLC
Chambersburg PA
CBHW060217030726
47499CB00004B/1089